3-98

	DATE DUE		

a four-sided bed

elizabeth searle

a novel

GRAYWOLF PRESS

Publication of this volume is made possible in part by a grant provided by the
Minnesota State Arts Board through an appropriation by the Minnesota State
Legislature, and by a grant from the National Endowment for the Arts.
Significant additional support has also been provided by Dayton's, Mervyn's,
and Target stores through the Dayton Hudson Foundation, the Andrew W.
Mellon Foundation, the McKnight Foundation, the General Mills Foundation,
the St. Paul Companies, and other generous contributions from foundations,
corporations, and individuals. To these organizations and individuals
we offer our heartfelt thanks.

Published by Graywolf Press
2402 University Avenue, Suite 203
Saint Paul, Minnesota 55114
All rights reserved.

www.graywolfpress.org

Published in the United States of America

ISBN 1-55597-265-9

2 4 6 8 9 7 5 3 1
First Graywolf Printing, 1998

Library of Congress Catalog Card Number: 97-70219

Cover Design: Michaela Sullivan

Cover Photograph: Steven Nilsson

F
SEA

ADB-1178

ACKNOWLEDGMENTS

"The Juggler to His Audience" by Bill Knott; used by permission of author (From: *Bill Knott Poems 1963–1988*; University of Pittsburgh Press, 1989).

Portions of this novel have appeared, in slightly different form, in the magazines *AGNI*, the *Kenyon Review* and *Ploughshares*, and in the anthologies *Lovers* (Crossing Press, 1994) and *American Fiction* (New Rivers Press, 1995).

My thanks to Elaine Markson; to Fiona McCrae, who gave this four-sided story its shape and its home; to my indispensable Girl Groups: Debra Spark, Jessica Treadway & Joan Wickersham; Gail Donovan & Ann Harleman; to Denise Kilgard; to my parents; and to all those who gave me generous glimpses of their lives and travels, especially: Karen Hellman and Robert Wilson, John Blanco and Eric Stein, Keith Smith and Eberle Umbach, my brother Bill and my sister Kate.

To John Robert Hodgkinson,
no other

First

Jo?

Alice whispered her sister's name, half waking to feel Jo's bare-limbed body curled around her own. In a twin bed, in secret. As Jo's new long arm tightened its hold, Alice plugged her ass deeper between the giant hipbones Jo had grown overnight. Of all their sleep-heated skin, she noticed, Jo's newly swollen crotch felt warmest. Then Alice gasped, the air here sweet and leafy.

"JJ?" she whispered, out loud this time.

His bristly chin nudged her shoulder. Her spine stiffened. Was she in bed with a man, her first? Dazedly, Alice stirred her legs, drifting up from deep waters. Behind her, JJ stirred too, his hold on her still as gentle and firm as Jo's.

"Jo-Joe," Allie murmured with groggy logic, remembering how the night before she'd made a shy game of inventing full names for JJ.

"No," he breathed behind her, heating her ear. "Keep guessing."

Alice opened her eyes. She confronted not the cream-painted wall of the bedroom she'd once shared with Jo, nor the cinder-block dorm wall she'd plastered with snapshots of Jo and Mom and Dad and Grandma Hart, but a slanted wood wall. Knotty pine.

" 'S OK, Alice in Wonder," JJ murmured into her hair. Twisting around, she pushed away from his bare chest.

"You're safe," he told her. As she looked into his noble bony face, she was surprised anew by her sister's eyes. Half-lidded, blue-gray.

"Hope so." Allie settled onto her heels, flushing at a new tenderness inside what Biology 101 called vaginal lips. No deeper. *No,* she had told him at the last second the night before and—miracle of miracles, Jo'd say—he had stopped.

Now, as Indian summer air wafted into his attic apartment, Allie gazed at his sheets spread round them like parachute silk. A safe landing? As wholly undeserved, she thought, as all her life's luck. The clock

3

on his orange-crate nightstand clicked. Alice turned. Acrobatically, 59 flipped to oo.

At 6 A.M. on October 11, 1984, will Alice Ann Hart begin her Last Hour as a Demi-Virgin? Allie silently intoned to Jo in their soap-opera-announcer voice, the one that audibly capitalized Those Compelling Questions.

No! Jo shouted inside Allie's head as Allie turned back to JJ Wolfe, her eyes still low. *Ya don't even know him, you dope!*

In the years to come, when Allie would replay the hour to come, Jo's imagined shout echoed above the whole scene. But it wasn't till four years later that Allie would look back on the opening hour of her life with JJ in a changed way: hard, a fledgling detective seeking clues. After all, wasn't this the first time JJ mentioned Kin? And, Allie would ask herself in '88, wasn't everything JJ hid—about himself, about the real Kin—hinted at, subtly, this first morning? Her own remembered words would seem charged with double meaning.

"I do *feel* safe here. I mean, y'know what I thought when I woke up, JJ?" Alice raised her wide eyes to him. "I thought you were my sister."

· · ·

First had come his touch between her shoulder blades in Late-Night Study. The library was closing, he told her in a softly uninflected voice. Allie blinked up at a tall wild-haired library worker, older by five years or so than the college boys. He stared down with deep-set eyes that seemed familiar. Alice had glimpsed him before: engaging in intense conversations with female students at the main desk where he stamped books like a drummer and dispensed free aspirin like a bartender, or dancing in the college disco as if his long lean body were being electrocuted in slow motion, three girls dancing not so much with as around him. A cult? Allie had wondered half-seriously. A drug dealer given to ecstatic seizures? Whatever else, he was the wildest dancer she'd ever seen.

Did she dance? he asked, his Midwest monotone breaking the silence of the deserted Study. Slowly, still sleepy, Allie shook her head. No.

Then had come his second touch between her tense shoulder blades as they'd climbed three twisting flights of wood steps to his apartment high atop an old Victorian house. It stood blocks from the college's quiet green campus: stone buildings built in the 1860s decked with a few reverently preserved spray-painted peace signs from the 1960s. His name was JJ Wolfe and he was going to show her how to dance. Allie pictured Jo rolling her eyes. But she was too stoned on loneliness to flee from him. *Going in was my first mistake,* she imagined saying gravely to Jo as she stepped through his door, sleepwalking after six nearly sleepless weeks away from home. She already felt, she imagined, a little drunk. Not that JJ let her get drunk, really. With a rising sense of gaiety and daring, Allie downed two small jelly glasses from his jug of oily dark Gallo. Oh, *this* is why people drink, she thought. Sitting cross-legged, she watched him stand and flail away to Jimi Hendrix, "You Got Me Floatin'," and Peter Gabriel, "I Have the Touch." Watch him dance was all she wanted to do and that was OK, he said, for starters. This man with her sister's eyes. So she'd rocked along on his furry black couch, sipping, steeped in the same curious calm with which she, in his arms, was to wake hours later. A virgin, still.

"Your sister?" JJ stretched his long-boned arms, fitting the slanted ceiling. A cat hopped onto the bed purring, its whiskers alight.

"Yeah." Allie hugged her bare legs, sensing she was beginning a years-long conversation. "The way you were holding me. Even the way you look."

"You shoulda seen me with my hair down below my shoulders." JJ stroked the arch of the gray cat, his mild flat voice making it easy to sit in bed, chatting.

"No, it's more your eyes—" Allie hoisted up her backpack, re-pressed her Mondale/Ferraro bumper sticker into its cloth and unzipped. "Here." She dug through Sociology 101 papers, her dad's letters to the editor.

"Well, maybe it's not so much in *looks*," Allie ammended as Jo's round face confronted her. Under Dutch Boy bangs, Jo's blue eyes stared, half-lidded like JJ's. Her short-haired head poked out behind Allie, who wore an oversized 1950s cocktail dress and waist-length brown hair, never yet cut, and a cardboard crown. O Queen of Play! Jo used to say, kneeling.

"See? We're playing *Bewitched*. I'm Samantha and she's the witch cousin Serena and we left out the husband Darrin because he was such a drag."

"*Bewitched*, yeah." JJ held the plastic-covered photo. "Back when I was schizo, I used to watch it. Summed up American marriage to me. The woman has magic powers and the dumb money-grubbing husband won't let her use them."

Allie laughed and shoved aside her backpack, wondering what he meant by "schizo." "Now that you've met Jo, we can talk."

JJ grinned. "Wha'do you want to know?"

Alice reached up and sank her fingers into JJ's hair: its warm, coarse, richly brown mass. "How long'd you say this was? Before you cut it?"

"Below my shoulders. And." JJ shook his head, his close-up face scarred by light pockmarks. "It wasn't me who cut it, kept it. Or said they'd keep it."

"Who?" Allie rested her hands on his bare shoulders, pleased by the wine taste still sweetening her mouth. Faint dawn light electrified his hair.

"The one who taught *me* to dance. My—first lover."

Her flush and their eye contact deepened by a degree. She nodded, sensing he'd said out loud what they both were deciding: he would be hers. *No!* muffled Jo shouted. *Are you abso-fuckin'-lutely nuts?*

"What was her name?" Allie lowered her hands. She folded her arms, chilly in her T-shirt and panties despite a triangle of sun warming the sheets.

"Kin." JJ leaned on the knotty pine wall. "Or so I thought," he added, his monotone sliding into a new flatness. Gently, he pulled Allie down against him. "This was back in Mass. Mental. The Massachusetts Mental Health Center."

"Oh?" A soft, respectful breath. "When was that?" She kept her head still on his chest, gauging whether this was an OK question to ask.

Ask, ask, you dope! Jo commanded, Jo always full of warnings about men and their pasts, about herpes or worse.

"Spring, 1980." JJ's chest vibrated. "Then I spent two years recovering from my recovery. Back home, here in Ohio. That's why I only graduated here last year. Mathematics B.S., no clue what to do with it. But listen." He squeezed her shoulders. "Even when I was all-the-way crazy, certified schizo, even in Mass. Mental I never hurt myself and I never hurt anyone else." He loosened his grip, adding with bemused thoughtfulness, "No wonder I'm so screwed up."

Smiling uncertainly, Alice pictured masses of mental patients giving the senile stares of the old men at the hospital where she'd volunteered as a candy striper. Stares she'd made herself meet. She sat up. "God, JJ," she murmured, frankly widening her eyes. She touched his hand. Let others do Cool, she'd decided long ago, withdrawing from that overcrowded competition.

"How about you, Allie? Your—"

"Lov-ers? Haven't had any, really." Alice sighed, relieved not to shade that truth. Already, she felt something she'd only shared with Jo: the freedom to say whatever came to her head. "Just boyfriends. You know: *boys.*"

JJ sighed sympathetically. "And you used to spoon with your sister?"

"Some nights. After acting out our soap opera. Inspired, see, by *The Young and the Restless.*" Impulsively, Allie lay on her side. "You lie down too."

The bed rocked as JJ rolled over, his long back facing her. She laughed, amazed at this man—six foot plus, tall as her dad—doing her bidding.

"Y'know in the library, JJ, you act like a bartender or something . . ."

JJ gave a low laugh. "I prefer to see myself as an Unlicensed Therapist."

"Specializing in attractive, neurotic women?" Allie inched forward.

"Unconditionally. What Isaac Asimov said about robots, I say about women. They are a 'better, kinder breed' than men."

Laughing, Alice clasped giant JJ. For once she felt bold: holding a former mental patient. Under her hands, as if by her command, his heart beat.

"What's it like?" she whispered, her cheek flattened on the cool plane of his back. Lowering her hands over his stomach, she touched the elastic of his briefs. "Does it hang light so you can't feel it, or is it heavy?"

"In between." Under her cheek, his back vibrated with his expressionless scientist voice. "Did you know every fetus starts out female?"

"Really?" Alice let her hand drift lower. Through cotton, she cupped his cock: the heat that had woken her, warmer than any other part of him or her.

"Well, that's how Freud put it. Now they say fetuses carry traits of both sexes. Then one wins out and the other. Falls back, though traces remain."

"So on a woman . . ." Allie was feeling hers more strongly than ever: the moist point of flesh with the ugly name and straining ache like a tiny erection.

"Mm hm." JJ moved her hand lower to the softer cooler curve that filled his cotton briefs. His cat at the foot of the bed purred. "And these sacs used to be or I guess they'd say now could've been. My ovaries."

"Real—?" was all she gasped. Boldly, she slipped her hand up and under his briefs. Balls, she told herself. Hairs tickled her fingers, growing from skin like pounded velvet. "Y'know what me and Jo did one time? Just once, because we scared ourselves, doing it?" The cat's purr was stalking toward them, the air abuzz. "Touched each other down there. Reaching round and down like this, like the one behind was touching her own. We wanted to see if each other's felt, y'know, the same." Allie squeezed shut her eyes. Jo'd kill me, she thought.

"Mmm," JJ answered under the cat's all-surrounding purr. Experimentally, Allie took hold of JJ's slightly thickened cock. She inched its plush skin back and forth over its stiffening center. Smashing her nose sideways, she pressed her face into the muscles of his back.

With other boys, making out felt like gym class. Hopefully, she'd position herself: her ass in gym shorts in air, her head touching the somersault mat. Hopelessly, she'd try and try to push off with her feet, let go.

Now, the cat's purr swelled. The leaves rustled like waves. Between her bent knees, Allie gripped JJ's firm muscled thigh. She was rocking against it, him. His heart was beating slow and hard, no doubt larger yet no louder than Jo's had sounded that one time. Allie held JJ's cock loosely, respectfully, feeling it rise on its own. Then—so suddenly Allie's head bumped the pillow—JJ sat.

She blinked. JJ fumbled amongst sci-fi paperbacks in his orange crate. As he pulled down his briefs, she realized what, of course, he was doing. She pushed back her mussed hair. How could she, Alice Ann Hart—Born to Be Tame, Jo joked—half forget pregnancy or herpes or AIDS, newly named? Newsmen said anyone might be at risk if they slept around and—his condom snapped—hadn't this JJ? Keeping condoms so handy; making her *want* to forget all that?

The springs screeched. He towered over her on his knees, lit by suddenly golden sunlight, his cock sticking out like Pinocchio's nose. Rubber gleamed. *What's the difference between herpes and love?* Jo had asked Allie in their last call, Jo always knowing the latest jokes. *Herpes lasts forever.*

". . . OK?" JJ's hair crackled with gold light. "This's . . . what you want?"

On her back, she hugged the sheet, missing his warmth, her nipples stiff in her softly flattened breasts. Her mouth had gone dry. Her neck nodded.

Face-to-face felt more dangerous. Up close, his eyes lost their color like water. His hot breath startled her. Shutting her eyes, she sunk her fingers back into his sun-warmed hair. Coarse, no smell or feel of shampoo. She pulled his head closer. Their tongues touched, his wine taste re-awakening hers. His strong hands ran over her so smoothly she arched her body like his cat's, his touch so different from clumsy boys' touches that he seemed another species.

Dizzily, she pulled back, amazed to be moving so fast. Who *was* this JJ?

"Did y'know," he asked in hoarse whisper. "Everything shows on your face?" Allie nodded, not even trying to deny it. "Something new for me," JJ told her, maybe recalling his previous sex partners.

Allie tightened her grip on his dense curls, as if a current were about to sweep him away. "Your hair," she whispered back, not sure why. "Your old hair, the long hair. She kept it, really? Kin?"

A name, Allie noticed even then, that startled him.

"Who?" JJ's eyes flickered, shifting to blue-green.

"Kin." Alice sensed tension in his spine. *Did she keep your hair?*

"So I hear." JJ touched her hip, his voice strained. "In letters, a few."

"Oh?" Allie tugged his hair. Absurdly, she pictured herself searching this attic apartment for love letters, herself as Mary Tyler Moore ripping open Dick Van Dyke's special-delivery package, then leaping back in panic as a gigantic automatically inflating raft bursts out, filling the whole living room.

"Not from. Kin." JJ eased Allie's panties down, his cock poking her thigh like a rubber elbow. Hot under its false skin. "Letters from. Someone else."

Who? she shaped her mouth to ask as his mouth swallowed hers. Their tongues swam together. Their teeth almost ground together. Allie shook her head as if emphatically saying *no*, as if unscrewing it, her head.

"God," she gasped, kicking her panties free. Her body, she decided as JJ fingered her, was taking over; taking its first real—deep down, she felt safe as ever—risk. Dreamily, she rode JJ's hand, watching JJ's eyes shift from blue-green to a new color that Allie felt she was floating in: blue-green-gray.

"Usually, I . . . I'm not so . . ." Impulsive, she didn't finish, swallowed up by another kiss.

The night before, JJ's rubber-skinned cock even a little ways inside her had felt impossibly swollen, too big to fit. Her vagina had tightened into a wall of flesh. Now, as her bare legs pressed his, her heart pumped with her old fear. Even now, so wet, would she turn out to be too tight inside? Too small?

"O-K . . . ?" JJ whispered in his strained, hot-breathed voice. *O* her mouth shaped as their tongues swam together again. Those women were dancing round JJ at the disco; Jo was warning about herpes or worse above the music. *You're in bed with all his previous partners too!* The cat brushed Allie's bared ass, its purr silenced. Flushing inside and out, Allie pictured those lithe faceless women and faceless Kin and the cat and JJ and herself entangled in his bed.

Her breasts flattened under his sweating weight, her nipples still hard. She braced her body. I can't. The mushroom tip of JJ's cock eased in. Her legs tensed under his. Squeezing shut her eyes: I couldn't, ever, with anyone else.

"You?" JJ sounded choked. "Want me to stop?"

"No, no—" she told him. The cat jumped from the bed, its four padded paws landing on wood. Allie winced with the pleasure of that softest sound.

"Joe," she called JJ, urging him on with her hands. Inside, as he slowly thrust, her flesh wall was beginning to give way, thick tissue beginning to tear.

"Half-right," he panted against her neck. Sliding his mouth up, he filled her ear with an explosive whisper. "James Joseph."

"Oh!" she answered, overjoyed to have it right. Her eyes opened, lashes beaded. Shimmering, his face contracted with her pain. Her tears and his sweat mixed. With his next slow thrusts, the bed rocked. She ground her crotch against his. As Allie felt JJ break through, she bucked up her hips. Tumbling all the way over, inside herself.

Between them on the sheets, a splotch of red had bloomed. They lay gasping, separated by her blood stain, their necks and limbs wobbly warm or anyhow she felt sure his were too. Like a newborn's. *What will He turn out to Be?* Alice asked herself in a slow-mo soap-announcer voice, staring into the motionless whirl of JJ's brown curls, sunlit like her own hair. His face was turned to his pillow as if he knew how much she needed to be alone, now. *And*—Alice looked at her own new body, flushed unevenly pink. *She?*

8 · 8 · 88

1

Words to Burn

JJ—

Come for Kin. I, the bride—Kin and I, the brides—want you to come witness. To have and hold, first, this crinkly crackly rice paper, fine and off-white like Kin's skin. Then, what we will wrap in this paper. What used to grow off you. Half-oily, half-dry, all alive with your kink, your burnt-brown smell and sheen. Still unwashed. Still, Kin'd say, growing.

Remember, Jimmy Joe? Kin cut it off. I watched, you on your knees between us. Dark, in that soap-smelling closet in Mass. Mental. Darker, later, in Kin's cocoon room, we three crowded closer. Infinitely. Under my pencil, this wrapping paper crackles. I make my letters light. In that darkest dark, could you tell my skin from Kin's? Goose-bumped from, for hours, you. Had to shut myself tight to stay in my own. Skin, seen through.

Have to hold tight when—if—we three re-meet. Re-Unite. On 8/8/88 at 1 P.M. in the Queens County Courthouse. NY. Please come, love. Please RSVP via Kin's phone # (printed beside his address) by midnight on 8/7/88. What d'you say, J. Joe? Will you comfort Kin? No: I mean, I hope, come for Kin. For the first time since our last night. Don't say you don't but even if you don't—

I do. Remember. I mean: I saw you first, I stole the scissors, I kept it safe for you for years. I touched it brushed it braided it sometimes, Kin too. We—Kin and me is all that means now—We will wrap it in this paper We will brush and braid it before we do We will feel you-kink you-smell you-shine. You get, Kin'd say, our drift. Got us, still. For better or worse or maybe—we'll tell on 8/8/88—worst. So, James Joe.

Give me away.

Bird

2

The E Is Silent

Alice Ann Wolfe sat awake in the dark. Shifty, flickering, rainy night dark. Stealthily, she leaned over JJ, eased open his nightstand drawer and lifted it out. A snake of a braid: cut off his head eight years before. As she resettled herself, JJ sprawled onto his back, his feet hanging off the fold-out mattress. A steamy hiss rose below from the overheated streets of New Haven. No Haven, JJ called it. His hoarse snores deepened.

As intently as Grandma Hart fingered rosary beads, Allie fingered JJ's braid, squeezing each coarse knob. Sniffing its musty funk. So bizarre. JJ's old hair: FedExed to him yesterday from New York City. Bound with two rubber bands, the rubber strained by his hairs' unkillable spring and kink.

Must be from Kin, JJ had mumbled when he'd come in holding the braid and the torn FedEx envelope. He tossed the balled-up wrapping paper into their bedroom trash. Though that fine crinkly paper looked expensive. He swung the braid at his side, pacing behind the half-closed bedroom door.

Let's just lie here and twitch, JJ had told Allie when he'd finally stopped pacing and opened that door to her. What he often told her after a tough day of classes. Meaning, she took it this time, not tonight. Ask tomorrow. Allie glanced at JJ's old clock radio, its green square-cut numbers aglow. 12:05. It was, officially, August 8th, 1988. Meaning Allie's period was one week late. Not all that late, right? Glass rattled, needles of rain straining to break in.

"JJ?" Allie whispered on impulse, touching his warm live hair.

"Mmm," he mumbled as she smoothed his curls.

"JJ—I can't sleep, thinking about it." She raised her whisper determinedly. "Why? Why would Kin FedEx that hair to you just now?"

JJ stirred and muttered, sounding genuinely confused. "Kin?"

"Of *course* I keep wondering. I mean—JJ, you awake?—back in Ohio, you told me 'someone else' sent the letters you'd got from Kin. Remember? Letters from years before you met me?" JJ rolled over. His back formed a tall wall. "And you never really explained what you meant by that. . . ."

"I'm 'sleep, Al."

"So there wasn't *any* letter with this hair? Not a word?"

He rolled toward her. "T'morrow." As his arm flopped onto her lap, she swung the braid out of his way, dropping it. JJ nuzzled her hip. *Was he too sleepy to talk?* Allie touched his forearm. Taut even in sleep with overdeveloped wrist tendons. JJ: master of guitars, computers. Of her body. She stroked his forearm as if he were one of her Severely Retarded students who might, in Special Ed–speak, Go Off. Like JJ had done when he was schizo, back when he knew Kin? Thunder rumbled, a comforting country sound.

"Hear that?" Allie whispered though he was snoring again. Rain soothed her spirits the way sun did most people's. Made her feel safe. Her hand slowed. She wished she could hear it on the roof, not just the windows.

Shush. Allie shut her eyes to conjure JJ's knotty pine slant-ceilinged attic apartment in Ohio. Sky lab, they called it when they started living together: a test ground for the marriage Allie was planning before JJ even imagined it. Shh, the leaves had advised her. In that room above the trees, she'd sat up late waiting for him to close the library. At his wobbly kitchen table, she'd typed her earnest thesis in Sociology. *America's Compassion Deficit: How We Treat the Weakest Among Us.* The next year, after they'd married in the stone campus chapel with its hundred-year-old organ, Allie had stayed up nights typing JJ's computer science grad-school applications.

She blinked hard. Here in New Haven, JJ was taking summer classes. He was about to begin his second year at Yale, to become (Alice pictured him in a pointy wizard cap) a Master of Artificial Intelligence.

She exhaled. Her hand still rested on his forearm, warmer now. Thank dumb luck, she told herself as she did every night. What her father used to say at supper in place of a prayer. Then he'd remind his girls that America was 5 percent of the world's population gobbling up 75 percent of its resources.

Allie shut her eyes. JJ would talk to her tomorrow, about Kin. Her period had been late before—later. She breathed the mist filtering through the sooty window screen. The hiss of rain softened the phone's first purr.

She squinted at the mirror on their bedroom door, ajar. Dark glass, no gleam. At the second muffled purr, Allie slid JJ's arm off her lap. "Phone," she whispered, easing her legs over the edge. JJ's snores stayed steady.

In the front room, the machine clicked. Bless it. Lifting JJ's braid from the floor like a weapon, Allie stumbled to the bedroom doorway. JJ's faint recorded voice: *We can't answer our phone now*—(because, he'd told Allie he ought to add, we're huddled beside it listening intently to hear who you are).

As Allie hurried toward the blinking light, his braid brushed her thigh. The machine gave its last throat-clearing clicks. *Record.* First, a blur of music, jazz. She set the braid on the kitchen counter, poised to answer.

"'Lo, Joe."

The speaker's sex not immediately evident. Jo, Joe? Instinctively, Allie froze her reaching hand. Slinky '40s saxophones. "It Had to Be You"?

"Jimmy Joe."

Hearing the 'e,' Alice hugged her corduroy robe, JJ's boyhood robe.

"You in, love?" A low nasal voice, shy on the *love*. A deeper-than-female pitch. ". . . you remember me, love? Sis-ter Kin, Mass. Mental. R'member, Jimmy Joe? Bird? That soldered ring? Dr. Marmal from Mars—?"

Allie's pulse beat in her throat and stomach. Dr. Marmal, the ring.

"So hurt you didn't RSVP our FedEx. Your hair and our hand-writ invitation. But if you truly won't come to us, we'll come to you. Take a shuttle flight to C-T from N-Y-C. Hop a bus to New Waven New Haven, for our honeymoon. Yep, honeymoon. Know it's been lifetimes and lifetimes but I need to—see you. Bird does too. So tomorrow, or to*day* rather, meet us at, say, five-ish? At a Korean-Japanese place: Ko No's? On a 'Whalley Avenue'? I'll be the half-breed at the—raw bar." A giggle. "Forgive me. I'm drunk, love."

Silken now, this versatile voice. Decidedly deeper than female.

". . . oh, ooh, and we still have your jacket to go with your hair, y'know? Might by then, by five, also have something important. Something I'll have to . . ." The low voice softened, a warmly confidential murmur. "Tell you, man."

"It Had to Be You" cut short. Tape halted, squealing. The red light revived. Man, Alice repeated to herself, brushing JJ's braid off the counter. The frizzy end tickled her toes. Her twin pulses beat, out of sync. Was JJ's Kin a man?

.   .   .

Tell me, Allie had urged JJ, the whole thing. And he had, he said.

They were lying on his swaybacked bachelor bed high atop the trees, deep in their first Indian-summer weekend. Ohio, 1984. He'd knelt naked by the bed, dug through a shoe box. His one snapshot from high school: eighteen-year-old JJ delivering what he described to Allie as a pre-psychotic valedictorian address on *Information Theory and its Relation to Valediction*. His bony acne-wracked face floated inside his untamed circle of hair; his urgently outstretched throat raised his head far above the jacket he wore over his robe. A cracked-leather air-force jacket, much too small for JJ. His dad's jacket. His silent cipher of a dad: a Korean War bomber pilot turned grim plumber who viewed the world, JJ claimed, through failure-colored glasses. The summer before he flew east for his aborted first semester at MIT, JJ came to believe that an alien space van rolled invisibly up his driveway every hour and replaced the robot replica who impersonated his dad with another. That summer, JJ told his dad he was attending college-prep classes when really he was driving round northern Ohio, parking, re-reading certain science-fiction novels. *The Blue World. The Faceless Man.*

Allie had nodded, resting on JJ's chest. His rib cage vibrated with each word, her head vibrating too, taking in details she would treasure. Proof that JJ had experienced suffering such as she'd never known.

JJ had entered the Massachusetts Mental Health Center with his hair uncut, unwashed, grown out into a six-inch Afro. He'd dribbled a rubber ball up and down the ward, an activity the nervous nurses encouraged, a healthy interest for a boy so tall, but really—he'd never told anyone else this, he told Allie—he dribbled the ball only to test gravity, make sure he was still on Earth. See, he believed he was the title character of a sci-fi movie starring David Bowie. *The Man Who Fell to Earth.* JJ and Allie had laughed, warm in his bed above the trees, Mass. Mental four years behind him, a fifth of Allie's lifetime.

How'd you meet Kin, your first—girl? Allie had whispered.

Kin. His one friend on the ward. A quiet—he'd hesitated and she'd thought he was mocking her choice of word—girl. Never spoke, like him. Read a lot. Poems, mostly. Inked figure-eights down her inner arms in ballpoint. She'd been brought in off the street and she'd registered, simply, as Kin.

Just "Kin"? Allie had asked, since the name itself seemed important.

An Asian-sounding name, JJ had mumbled. Yet she was as pale as him, her hair so blond it looked white. She was wispy thin, except for her breasts and she kept her mouth shut, hiding crooked teeth.

Kin cut his hair: the week JJ marked as the beginning of his recovery. The week he found himself noticing as he stared into the ward TV that *Mission Impossible* plots were better—more complex, more plausible—than *Mod Squad* ones. The first clear judgment he'd made in months.

Then, raising one hand to scratch his head, he noticed that his white-boy Afro had grown oily and matted. He wanted it gone. Kin was clean, cleaner than anyone there. Hair long and baby fine, corn silk. After his haircut, JJ wandered for the first time into one of the craft classes and made her, Kin, a metal ring, soldered it himself. Twisted, intricately connected figure-eights.

And—? Allie had to prod, for here the story stopped. Green leaf shadows fluttered on JJ's slanted wood ceiling.

Dr. Marmal, JJ had whispered back at last. Dr. Marmal comes up to me all jocular next day and says (in his whisper, JJ enunciated the words mockingly), *I hear you've been making things.*

And you said—?

Nothing.

Nothing? But what did you think?

JJ's voice had tightened with what Allie hoped was only remembered resentment; his answer had stopped her from pressing for details on Kin the way she'd do on his other loves.

I thought, JJ'd told her flatly, nothing is your own.

.   .   .

Rain seemed to resume. Had it stopped at all? Allie gazed past the machine at the black window. Thick rain swarmed over the thin glass.

"JJ?" She hugged her robe close. The boyhood robe in which, watching Captain Kirk kiss the black lady lieutenant on *Star Trek*, JJ'd gotten his first real hard-on. "JJ, you up?"

Through the rain, his intent snores rose and fell. Such concentration, even in sleep. Impulsively, Allie reached for the phone. 9 P.M. in Arizona, where her dad had retired. Stiff-fingered, she punched out the number.

He said Kin must've sent the hair, she imagined explaining to a sleepy but always clearheaded Jo. *That's all he'd say. And he seems so closed up. When usually he'd tell me, y'know, everything. Everything about anything.* Long-distance clicks of connecting wires. *Then I hear this "Kin" speak in — I'm sure—the voice of a man.* A plaintive hum in her ear; a ring in theirs.

What do you know and when did you know it?

They'd grown up watching Watergate, so this was Jo's first question for all dilemmas. Back before JJ became the one to whom Allie told all. At the second hum, Allie pressed the receiver switch. Silly to call, to overreact. She pictured Jo or Mom halfway there, Dad awakened and hacking. Sheepishly, she recradled the receiver. *OK,* Jo would've said. *What's the Worst-Case Sitcom?* Allie stepped over the braid's question-mark curl.

"JJ—" She shattered the drizzly night silence. "Wake up." And she strode forward, bumping her dad's old Losers' Lamp. A campaign button slid off the shade, a flat clack. As she swung the bedroom door, JJ mumbled. "Al?"

She knelt in the sheets, her elbow knocking the old orange-crate nightstand on her side of the bed and jarring the radio, the gun. A plastic toy, though its shape could startle. "JJ, can we talk?" Half-jokingly, Allie curled her finger into the plastic trigger. The gun shot suction darts. Jo had mailed it when Allie'd confessed that George Bush made her hit the TV's electrified screen with her fist.

"Wha—?" JJ sat upright. "What's wrong?" He stared like her pet newt come to the water's surface, sucking air. Allie lowered the toy gun. If JJ hadn't looked so alarmed, looked suddenly like someone with secrets to hide, she would've brought it out right away: the phone call, the man's voice.

"J-J?" she repeated instead. Hadn't he, she thought clearly, hidden something already: the "hand-writ invitation" Kin had mentioned? A note or card JJ hadn't even shown her? "I guess—I'm having some kinda dream." Tugging the gun off her finger, Allie lay down. Thinking: *think first*.

"Well, don't go and shoot, Al Capone." JJ rolled toward her. His forearm slid over her stomach like a Ferris-wheel bar. Allie settled her ass between his hipbones, picturing two men in this position. Trying out that picture.

"Go sleep," JJ murmured as he did after her real half-waking dreams. *OK, I will*, she had mumbled back one night, still inside the dream. Then, in a completely different voice—deep and weird, JJ'd reported the next morning; she couldn't remember it at all—she had added: *I will too*.

Remembering how she and JJ had laughed over her—sensible Alice—having a secret voice, a night-self, Alice touched JJ's wrists.

"Al?" His whisper stirred but didn't warm her hair. "You still worried?"

" 'Course I am," Allie whispered back cautiously, noticing he'd said "still." "I mean, for starters, that braid. Kin sending it. That all seems so . . . crazy."

"Well, Kin can be. Me too, remember?" He loosened his hold on her.

"But—you're sure there wasn't any sort of note? Nothing?"

"Mm hm." A neutral sound. A stray car whooshed by below.

"But why now?" Allie felt her back harden into a turtle curve. Felt JJ, behind her, stiffen too. The inch of air between them seemed to Allie subtly charged. The extra tension in JJ's long body made her think he *was* keeping secrets. How many? "And why," she continued, intending to lead up gradually to the phone message. "Why *haven't* you ever talked to me about—y'know?"

"Kin." An expressionless syllable. As Allie drew a breath to press further, JJ told her, still expressionless: "Look Al, I. Can't talk about . . ."

"Her?" Allie filled in boldly, wanting to break this tension between them.

"Look," JJ repeated in a colder tone. "Let's just forget—it. This whole Kin thing." He sighed. "Maybe it wasn't even Kin who sent that hair . . ."

"Oh?" Allie raised her head in hopeful confusion. Maybe it *wasn't* "Kin" on the phone; maybe some friend of Kin's?

"Then again." JJ twisted around, reaching into the trash basket he'd moved tonight to his side of the bed. He lifted the crumpled wrapping-paper ball. It shone in the dark, grapefruit-sized. "This's Kin's kind of paper."

Allie propped herself on one elbow, hoping JJ was opening up. "It is?"

"Yeah." JJ tossed it, catching it easily in his basketball-player hand. The paper that had wrapped his hair. "Kin used to send notes on paper like this. In Mass. Mental. Know what we used to do? Kin and I?"

He stood, switching on the bedside lamp. She blinked up at him. His surgeon green pajama bottoms slid as he turned, half exposing his lean haunches. He stepped away fast, leaving Allie in the circle of lamplight.

OK, she told herself in his wake. Was he trying to distract her? Or was he leading up to some sort of explanation? A cupboard thumped.

"Here we go." JJ reappeared, holding kitchen matches and their frying pan, the paper ball set on it. He stepped with a beat as if entering their old disco.

"What now?" Allie laughed as JJ brandished a long match like a wand.

"Except we didn't have any net, any pan. Not in Mass. Mental." Climbing over her—she ducked as the pan swung—he settled into the sheets, cross-legged. The pan balanced between his thighs. "Lights." He switched off the lamp. She took hold of his big knee, sticking out above her lap. He tore the crinkly wrapping paper. Setting half the paper ball on his nightstand, JJ bent over his work. She heard more than saw what he was doing.

Deftly, he rolled the torn paper into a tube, mashing the edges together hard. Then he set the paper tube like a rocket on the frying-pan launchpad.

"Voilà!" A click struck the pan. Flame erupted as if from JJ's fingers. "Had to steal matches outa the night nurse's purse." JJ's voice stirred the flame's liquid throb. "First I'd read the note, then light it up. Light Kin could see from the—other side of the ward. See?"

The woman's side? Allie kept hold of JJ's knee. Wouldn't women be in a separate wing? JJ lowered the flame to the paper tube. Its rim flared yellow, the lit-up paper showing faint veins like marble.

"Hey." Allie heard the tube crackle. "Hey, it's swelling." As the ring of flame descended, the durable rice-paper tube expanded, darkening to a burned golden brown. At the folded bottom, orange heat flared again.

"We have—" JJ deepened his MC voice, his hand on hers. "Lift off."

Wobbling like a hot-air balloon, the fiery puffed-out paper rose from the frying pan. As if tugged by invisible spider-web thread, it levitated. Allie watched raptly, feeling their stares alone were holding it in air.

"I don't know how it works!" JJ called out, imitating the Wizard of Oz. As the flame reached its top, the blackened puffball collapsed, disintegrated.

"Ooh!" Papery ashes floated onto Allie's upturned face. "Do it again!"

Already, she heard JJ tearing and rolling a second tube. He gave his grown-up-showing-you-the-world laugh. Which usually made her feel safe.

"Didn't it look like Rare Books, the walls?" She knew he'd know she meant their favorite library here: its marble wall panels sliced so thin sun shone through, marble veins lit up like those odd rice-paper veins.

"Mmm." JJ nodded, concentrating on the flick of his wrist. "See?" he commanded again as he lit the rim of the second paper tube.

"Oh—" And she did see, this time. She squinted; JJ's hand kept her hand in place on his knee. Words: not veins illuminated in the crumpled paper. Pencil words; spidery fine handwriting eaten up fast by the orange glow.

Up and up. This second ball rose, then burned itself out. Allie barely felt the ashes against her skin, this time.

"There you go, Allie Dare." JJ tossed the rest of the torn wrapping paper into the trash. The half without pencil print? "Hand-writ," as Kin had said, print. JJ clanked the frying pan onto the trash basket. "See, it was a flare. That's how Kin knew I'd gotten the note. Get it?" He brushed ashes off his pillow.

"I guess I—get it." Allie blinked, an ash fragment in her lashes.

"OK, so that's our bedtime story." JJ gave a brief uneasy sounding sigh and rolled over. His body tense again. "Night," he muttered as if stating a fact.

Allie lay down, moving stiffly, only her shoulder touching his curved back. But she drew a breath, determined to ask, first, about the penciled words.

"Go sleep now, Al," JJ cut in with a distinct final-sounding flatness. Allie exhaled, fingering the ash. Maybe JJ had *wanted* her to see that there were words penciled on the wrapping paper. Maybe, she thought, he wanted her to say now she'd seen them. As if he'd burned her own words, she found she couldn't speak. He stayed on his side; his eyes, if open, fixed on the wall.

"Go sleep," he repeated, this time so softly it seemed a kind of plea.

"OK, I will." She licked her dry lips, at a loss. As a shaky joke, she made her next words deep and weird, the way he'd described her own night-self speaking that one time. Wholly asleep then, wholly awake now. "I will too."

·   ·   ·

Brakes fail in rain. Mother's Valiant brakes, Mother's hands fast and frantic as the feet of Jo's gerbil, running its squeaky wheel, the steering wheel squeaking as it comes unhinged as the car skids as Jo pitches forward through the windshield glass, the vast oily puddle and Jo's face shattering.

Allie's neck jerked. Her eyes stuttered open. The rain sounded both familiar and strange, changed. She burrowed back into her head-heated pillow. Did guilty people wake each morning with minds washed clean by sleep? Mom, say, never the same after the accident. Did they feel in their first breath a forgetful sense of peace? Shush, the rain still advised.

Careful not to jar JJ's snores, Allie slid off the bed. She crouched on her hands and knees on the floor. Doggy position in recent times, on this spot. Allie shut off the still-silent radio alarm. 6:29. She sat on her heels. OK, that message. The one she ought to play for JJ this morning. What exactly had it—he, Kin—said? That he was hurt JJ hadn't RSVP'd an invitation. No doubt the note she'd seen so plainly on the wrapping paper JJ had burned. And that if JJ wouldn't come to them, they'd come to JJ. To Ko No's. Kin and his— "Bird"?

Allie stood up. Yes, she would play JJ that message, ask him her questions. Soon as she'd showered. In the front room (not a Living Room, JJ had recently decreed, but a Getting-By Room, a Surviving Room) Allie padded past their metal table. Ralph and Alice Kramden's stark apartment. She jumped at a pinprick under her heel. And she picked up the button she'd knocked off the Losers' Lamp last night. *Nixon's the One.* A joke she never understood as a kid: how this slogan meant one thing when printed, and another later.

She held the lamp steady, finding the space among the campaign buttons that covered its shade like scales. LBJ, HHH, McGovern for Peace. The lamp shade shuddered as it took the pin. Self-consciously, watched by photos on the walls, Alice headed toward the red-lit answering machine. Eyes and smiles. Dad when he could still stand; Mom before she gained so much weight; Jo showing the same sturdy face whether she was ten or twenty, unscarred or scarred; Allie holding her head high in a candy-striper uniform, pretending to be Audrey Hepburn. A few group shots included JJ, who seemed to sneak up from behind: a tall bushy-haired stranger stalking an all-American family.

Allie stepped over the braid. Through the machine's plastic window she studied the cassette tape. Wouldn't want JJ to play it while she was in the shower. Biting her lip, she twisted the dial to REWIND for one second, then back to ANSWER CALLS. The red light vanished, the message seemingly received. Not that it wasn't still there, un-erased. Kin's smooth voice: *Something I'll have to. Tell you, man.* Not wanting to contemplate those particular words, Alice dialed her usual morning number.

"Helpin'." The walnut crackle of Ms. Carmella's cigarette-smoker voice.

"Anything for Alice Wolfe?" Allie asked loudly. (How she loved being a "Wolfe," sometimes signing it *Wolf,* leaving out the genteel silent "e").

"I hear ya, Miss W. No need to shout." A Helping Hands printer clattered. "Nothin' you'd like, hon. Just New Haven New Chance Workshop."

Don't let 'em send ya there, Ms. Carmella had once warned from her receptionist throne, smoke circling her head like an obedient snake. *That's where they ship the rejects, the students th't can't hack a real workshop.*

"Wait." Allie decided—with what JJ called parallel processing?—that she could seem to do this because JJ's stipend check was late. "To*day* I'll take it."

Ms. Carmella exhaled, sending smoke signals of disapproval. As Allie scrawled the directions, her heart pumped. "—which'll put you on Manslaw—y'know what else they call that, Alice double-you? Manslaughter Street."

Allie laughed. *8:30 to 4:30,* she wrote on her pad. "Perfect," she told Ms. Carmella. And she hung up on a knowing, smoky sigh. She scribbled over the 4:30, remembering a modest sea green sign, *Ko No's,* glimpsed from bus—22? Whalley Avenue, yes. A crazy idea, but tempting. Allie Dare, showing up instead of JJ. Simply slipping inside and watching. Seeing who was who. What was what. And if JJ showed up too? If he *had* overheard the phone message? The message, Allie reminded herself, he has every right to hear.

But might it help him keep his secrets? Inspiring creative lies? She wiped her face. Why was she feeling so distrustful of JJ, on so little evidence?

"Hey JJ, I got a sub job—" she called out, turning from the unlit machine.

JJ continued his oblivious snores, unevenly spaced. Was he going to sleep late, miss his Monday class again? At MIT, before Mass. Mental, he'd said he'd lie in his dorm room, unable to shut his window, watching snow drift in over his bed. His snores sounded determined now. As a teenager, he'd told her, he'd eat supper in his bedroom while his dad ate at the table, silent whether JJ was there or not. JJ had imagined his bedroom door suction-sealed, *Star Trek*-style.

Briskly, Alice turned and strode down the entry corridor of the L-shaped front room. A shower, yes, would clear her head. She flicked the bathroom light, trying to remember when JJ had started skipping his summer classes.

The damn DOD, he'd been saying for months. Allie too had worried about reports that all the grad school's computer projects were heavily funded by the Department of Defense, aimed at making what JJ called Smart Toys. New toys for dumb old Reagan. She rubbed her eyes. At a recent party, a long-suffering Ph.D. candidate named Steinman awkwardly bragged that his program had been used in Falkland Islands war submarines, that he'd Saved the Whales, reducing the number of whales blown up instead of enemy subs. Subs, JJ had interrupted in his flattest voice, filled with Argentinean teenagers.

Allie leaned on the sink, all of it—the whales, the teenagers, the DOD—as unreal as the wondrous rows of numbers JJ conjured on his PC. His own world. She splashed her face. In the harsh light, she looked thinned down after weeks of half-conscious worry. Yes: JJ had seemed distracted for weeks, at least. Water beaded her lashes. An anxious Kitty Dukakis-glaze lit her eyes.

Snap out of it, Alice told herself. So what if JJ and the Kin man she'd heard *had* been lovers? Would that be alarming, really? Unusual, even? Shouldn't that be something she—any adult in 1988—could handle? She squeezed her toothpaste. As long as it stayed in the past, of course. As long as it wasn't—might this be why JJ kept it secret?—something he still wanted.

Allie brushed her teeth with thorough, foamy fervor. Cleaning up always cheered her. But what if she faced unwashable stains? Infected blood? She spit once, hard. Mustn't jump to conclusions. She pulled down her panties. No period yet, she noted as she sat on the toilet. Only ambiguous warmth below her stomach. Days before, she'd told JJ she was late. As the toilet water whooshed, she slipped off his old robe. What did newsmen say these days about long gestation periods? About HIV hibernating for years?

Allie tugged up her T-shirt, disgusted by her unstoppable thoughts. Her shamefully automatic assumptions. And she didn't even know if they'd been lovers, JJ and this man. If Kin was a man. So *ask* JJ, she told herself, yanking the sweaty shirt past her chin, dropping it on JJ's crumpled robe. Then she breathed, standing in her own skin. Eager to feel again, for comfort, clean.

· · ·

Tell me, JJ had whispered the last night of their first weekend, hours after he'd told her about the woman called "Kin." Now you tell me one.

Oh, *I* don't have lots of stories, she'd murmured, curled up beside him, still amazed simply by that: their skins touching all over. Not like you.

But as leaf shadows fluttered in moonlight on his slanted ceiling, she told him about Mom and Jo's car accident in the Pennsylvania rain. How the four-and-a-half-year-old boy in the VW Mom rear-ended was crippled. Paralyzed from the waist down: this boy none of them ever saw. How, weeks afterward, they'd moved to Kentucky, where Dad had been transferred. How, the first day there, a blizzard hit. Snowed in, Allie had helped Grandma Hart nurse Jo. Changing Jo's crisscrossed mass of bandages, giving her lukewarm sponge baths, feeding her graham crackers crushed in milk. Snowbound all January, saved from their new school, Allie and Jo started their soap opera: scribbling scripts under the covers, recording them on cassette tapes, broadcasting them over walkie talkies. Allie lived in the bedroom as completely as did bedridden Jo.

Mornings, spooning with Jo, she listened to the radio announcer drone off names of schools closed. *Oldham County,* he'd finally allow. Then she'd relax.

I just didn't want to leave our room, Allie told JJ in the tree shadows.

We won't, he answered, holding her. Though she should've been in class and he at work, they had stayed in his room all the next day, next night.

· · ·

Allie lathered her soft upturned breasts and narrow rib cage, her flat stomach and the smooth packets of fat in her thighs. Rubbing hard, she soaped the solid curve of her ass. And she clenched her buttocks, her own—that shut-tight word—sphincter. Ointments, she knew men sometimes used with men. Water sluiced down her back. She pictured JJ's haunches firm under a man's hands. Another way, she told herself, of making love.

Her nipples stiffened at the memory of JJ's haunches moving under her own hands, nights before. Allie rubbed the soap sliver between her palms, lather growing. How could she and JJ have what they'd always had, between them, if his Kin was a man? Then again—the soap slipped from her hands—she knew so little, really, about gay or bisexual men. JJ joked that she was like a 1950s girl, marrying her first lover. She turned to face the stream.

Weeks before, volunteering at the voter-registration table on Chapel Street, Allie had found herself defending gay rights to a well-dressed woman. But you're a nice girl, the woman had answered with the determined cheer of Allie's mom. Deep down, you think sodomy's unnatural, too; don't you, dear?

Water gushed over Allie's face. Shouldn't she make JJ talk this whole thing out? JJ, her Unlicensed Therapist. Hadn't that always been unusual in JJ, in any man? Unnatural? How he loved to listen. Allie adjusted the nozzle JJ always bumped when they showered together.

Don't, she imagined suspicious Jo advising. Don't turn to JJ now when you saw him burn that note. When you've sensed for weeks, really, JJ hiding something. What? And—Allie scrubbed herself hard, trying to stifle this unwarranted question—what *was* the maximum number of years HIV could hibernate? Jo would know. But Jo would add: *You're still writing soap plots, you dope; you're way overwrought, way overreacting.*

Alice bent. With two cranks, she halted H and C. She'd never kept a real secret from JJ. He hadn't kept secrets either, or so she'd believed. As she knotted a towel above her breasts, she pictured those penciled words, burning. Kin's "hand-writ" words. What all *was* JJ hiding? Why did she sense so strongly the only way she'd find out was by herself? She banged the bathroom door. She stepped hard, leaving five-toed prints. Newt watched from its goldfish bowl atop the fridge. Allie fitted the arch of her foot over JJ's braid. Her hair dripped onto the fake wood lid of the answering machine. Her hands—Grandma Hart's, slender but strong—gripped the dial.

Allie watched her finger press ERASE. Maybe a big mistake. Maybe, too, the first major action she'd ever taken that she'd reveal to neither Jo nor JJ.

She twisted the dial to REWIND. One, two, three: she estimated how long the message had been, tape thumping backward. STOP. It screeched with the pitch of a TV test signal. *This is only a.* Alice released ERASE and lifted her foot from JJ's braid. Guiltily, hearing something, she glanced behind her.

Test, she'd told JJ back when she'd started at Helping Hands. This job'll be a test. I want to see how strong I am. Want to know the truth about myself.

No no, Alice, JJ'd told her. You're like me. You only *want to* want to know.

Swinging his braid, she padded to the bedroom. Movement inside. Maybe JJ doing his push-ups. How long had he been up? Had he played the message while she'd showered? Half intending to confess, she opened the door.

JJ was dancing. Bare-chested in his pajama bottoms, headphoned, he was jolting his hips and flailing his arms like he used to do at the college disco. His face was contorted by music she could only hear as a tinny beat.

Shyly—she never had grown comfortable dancing—Alice stepped into the room, her movement startling JJ from his trance. How long had it been since he'd danced? He switched off his Walkman and tugged down his headphones.

"Morning. Was it this made you feel like dancing?" Allie held up his hair.

"Maybe." JJ set his Walkman on his nightstand and bent over the mattress, his long arm shooting out. "What: you snuck this from my drawer?"

"You mind?" She startled as he pulled the braid from her hand.

"It's mine." He flopped onto the bed, draping the braid over his shoulder so it looked attached. "Smells like it hasn't been washed in eight years."

"Yeah," she said cautiously. Remembering how JJ once described a Turing test. A judge asks teletyped questions to a man and a machine, trying to tell which is which. "What—what's on your mind, JJ? You got plans today?"

"D'you?" JJ asked with a slightly challenging edge. He touched her thigh, his fingertips warm. She stepped back, cutting short the line he was tracing.

"I've got a job. Till five or so. Maybe six . . ."

"Huh." Maddeningly neutral. A whiff of burned paper in the air.

"What're *you* planning to do today?" She looked down at his tall body. He was half sitting, propped by his pillow. What class was it he had on Mondays?

"Same thing I've done for weeks." JJ shrugged and caught his loose braid.

"Which is—?" Allie bent toward him, suddenly sure she had no idea. His blue-green gaze faltered. He drew a deep diver's breath.

"Drive round No Haven," he began, his voice thoroughly flattened. She stayed bent, thinking of a man who'd phoned 911 after murdering his wife with the knife they'd been using to slice zucchini bread. The man had sounded, the 911 operator reported on the news, *Very calm and very strange.*

"Just drive round in the Zephyr, then park, then hide." JJ smoothed his braid. "In the New Haven Public Library. Re-reading sci-fi paperbacks."

She straightened up shakily. Drizzle patter was filling her head like phone static. "So you haven't been—in class? At all?"

JJ shook his head, his broad nose widened. An animal smelling danger.

"For—weeks? The whole *summ*er session?" She hugged herself through her towel. Her breasts tender, nipples sharp. The mattress surrounding JJ seemed to waver, the four sides of its square.

"I've wanted to tell you," he said more gently. "But I. Can't explain if you're going to be. Scared." He set down his braid and stretched out his arm, motioning for her to curl up against his chest. "Don't be scared of me."

"I'm not." She held still as if JJ with his steady stare were photographing her. From the inside: seeing all her meanest fears. "I'm not," she repeated.

"No, Alice in Wonder." JJ met her eyes. His bluer now, clearer. "You are scared. You're looking at me like you don't know who—no, what—I am."

3

My Body to You

Above me, a boy is trying to guess my sex.

Bird scribbled in a pocket notebook, in print too fine for the boy to see. He hung from a metal bar, his body suspended at a slant. As the train jolted into motion, Bird's head almost bumped his crotch. Maybe Bird's new and bristling crew cut singed his zipper. He smelled of subway: smoke and sweat and year-old urine. The subhuman way, Kin called it. Face downcast, Bird scooted back on the plastic seat. The boy's eyes darted, lighting on three triangle points of interest. Bird's oversized brown leather jacket—Jimmy Joe's old jacket—was zipped; Bird's jeans were baggy. Nothing gave her away.

"We go-oh—" a drunk-sounding little kid called out above the whine of the rails. Bird's high-laced high-tops pressed the shuddery rubber floor, firm as a surfer's bare feet on a board. Between them, she gripped a swollen travel bag.

Metal shrieked. Loose face flesh jiggled. The train rocked and Bird rocked with it. 7 A.M. Boston time, her flight to New York due at 8:15. New York, then New Haven. The hanging boy's body swayed, loosely jointed. Under her jacket, Bird's breasts bounced. Could he see? Bird's head felt bare, no more soft curtain of white-blond hair to hide behind. She raised only her eyes, only an inch.

A zipper glinted between vertical lips of denim. As the boy shifted his weight, a diamond of white cotton flashed. Surrender flag. Did he know it was open? Boldly, sizing up Another Would-Be Assailant, Bird followed his body. Usually, she didn't raise her eyes. Girls can't; bold boys can. This one had Kin's build: all bone and muscle, lean as a whippet. No visible jiggles. His knee twitched, rhythmically. Coursing with Hormones, Kin would say. His black T-shirt sleeves were rolled up, à la James Dean.

Rebel without a Brain, Kin might murmur. Even here—underground, where it was dangerous—Bird gave a full-lipped dare of a smile. Keeping her mouth closed, as always; hiding her crooked teeth.

Rebel flicked his eyes down to her, then back up to the metal bar he gripped. A boy. Who thought Bird was another boy, coming on to him?

Her flat nipples prickled. Something to report to Kin, she decided as they all leaned left. Metal gave its plaintive subway shriek. Underneath the train's cradle motion, she felt in the fleshy parts of her body the jagged galloping rhythm of wheels clacking on track. Rebel's zipper vibrated delicately.

In Boston bars, Man Ray or Boy's Club, Kin used to sneak glances below the belt. Crotch Watching. This was back when they both lived in Boston: after Mass. Mental and before Kin signed on with Pan Am. Bird used to sit in the dark with Kin and fifty-odd men, 50 percent of them dressed as women.

They—the subhuman strangers—straightened again like blown candle flames. Rebel stood at attention as if her smile had been a soldierly salute. Was this how boy flirted with boy? Wheels clacked down the track, panting faster. *I want, you know, to know.* She wrote this line to Kin, in the new notebook he hadn't yet seen. *What better time to find out than today, our wedding day?*

"We he-ere!" the kid screeched, matching the shrill pitch of the brakes.

As a Pan Am employee—a steward among stewardesses—Kin Hwang was entitled to fly for free with his spouse. Wherever, whenever. All they had to do was get married. Officially. This is an official proposal, Kin had told her over long-distance months ago, after she told him she was giving up on men. But Birdy, Kin had exclaimed in breathless imitation of a woman's voice. So am I!

Really? She gripped her denim knees hard so her boyish knuckles stood out. The cracked collar of her air-force jacket made her neck itch. Jimmy Joe, that itch always made her think. A vaster itch, unscratchable. She tightened her fingers one by one. 8:15 flight to NY, 1 P.M. ceremony in Queens. Then a plane and bus to New Haven, if JJ didn't show. Would he, after all these years?

"He-ere!"

At the last shuddery swerve, Rebel gave an Elvis thrust. His hipbones framing her forehead, he held a limbo pose. Underground Etiquette.

"Whoa—!"

She let her body pitch forward as the train straightened. A jolt. Real Sugar and Twice the Caffeine! Bird pulled back fast, her head electrified. His cowboy cry had been harsh, his crotch shockingly soft, a springy mushroom pillow. Just barely butted. Family Jewels, Kin's mother had taught him to call his own, as if they were shiny and gem-hard and indestructible. Bird's scalp tingled. Fine hairs quivered on the bared back of her neck.

Swans, Kin had murmured one night, in high school. They were watching *To Have and Have Not* on his mother's white leather couch. They never kissed, not then and not later. *Swans,* he'd repeated, rubbing his neck against hers, slow and hard. Her neck felt long, curved, warm, then warmer. His Adam's apple filled the hollow of her throat as if she'd swallowed it whole. *This must be.* His breath had cooled her skin. *How swans neck.*

"Sorry," Bird mumbled to Rebel as the train brakes tightened their bite. She raised her eyes, her hardened lashes. Mascara. Her one mistake.

His eyes were brown, but blank as blue. His train-shaken face was city white, speckled by purple. James Dean, with acne. Young Jimmy Joe, without—maybe *he* would've been better off without—his beautifully convoluted brain. Bird bent forward, her braless breasts swaying in her jacket. Did Family Jewels hang as soft and tender as breasts? A question no one on Earth could answer.

Grabbing her overstuffed bag, she sprang up: Jill-in-a-Box. Swing your partner, do-si-do. Bird ducked under the sweat-smelling bridge of Rebel's bare arms. Free, she told herself as they bumped hips. Both bony. The AIRPORT stop skidded into the murky underground light.

"Sorry man," Rebel mumbled under the climactic screech, giving both words sarcastic emphasis. Bird pushed past a fat girl reading a sci-fi paperback. *Caves of Steel.* Sweaty flesh brushed Bird's leather arms. Metal scraped metal: a chorus of high-pitched dog whistles, each straining to hit the same note.

Round the world, Kin had promised. Puerto Rico, Cairo, Hong Kong. Hot places, she'd told him. Even now—in August, in leather—her bones felt cold.

En Caso De Emergencia, said a sign above the door. Rebel elbowed aside the oblivious *Caves of Steel* dweller. At the final jolt of the halt, he pressed against Bird. She clenched her ass muscles the way she did when, after temp service–typing jobs in nylons and high heels, she felt businessmen press her in the crush of rush hour. Her ass trembled, firm as any boy's. The scratched Plexiglas doors vibrated, trying to open. If Kin stood behind her now, would he think she was a boy? Would she feel—as she did, for once—turned on?

Bird made a fist. In the past year, she'd met a number of fairly nice men. Her first Would-Be Affair lasted three weeks, her last three months. A pattern that had begun to resemble the Morse Code's International Signal for Distress.

She rapped Plexiglas. On the other side, dumb waiting faces stared up. Would Kin make her break that pattern in New Haven? With Jimmy Joe, once again? Smoky boy's breath filled her ear. Her own breath caught. If you're ever trapped in a locked car with some maniac clawing at the windows, Mother had told her years before, give the horn three short, three long, three short. SOS.

• • •

Blood, love. Bird printed the two words, Kin's words, her pencil letters quivering. Her lips sealed over her jaggedly crooked teeth.

She blinked, her tarry lashes sticky. Early sun lit the windshield of the bus. Airport Shuffle Bus, Kin called it. Bird huddled up front, near the driver. Upholstery soaked in sound here, no subhuman clatter. Sweat smell rose from every surrounding seat. Bird felt but couldn't hear her stomach growl. One day empty. The bus rocked more gently than the train, trying to lull her, but she sat straight, on alert. Freshly chopped hair must have fresh nerve endings, like cat whiskers. Through her hair, she felt Rebel behind her, straining to see her. He'd waited for the bus, standing apart from the rest. He alone carried no bag.

"Buried," an old woman muttered, a voice from underground.

Bird turned to her window, its green-tinted sunlight, and wondered if Kin's bachelor party had ended yet. Just a few old acquaintants, Kin had told her by phone yesterday before his guests arrived. Where, she'd asked him, changing the subject. Where are we going for a honeymoon? Paris? Madrid? Kin had hesitated; a Jolt soda can had clanked his receiver. How 'bout New Haven?

Bird had sighed. Secretly, she'd been relieved JJ hadn't yet answered the invitation Kin had finally mailed along with JJ's hair, the invitation she'd painstakingly written weeks before. She remembered pressing lightly with her pencil on the fine crinkly paper in which they'd wrapped his hair.

We have to see him some-way, Kin told her in that phone call last night. Both of us, before we—what're we gonna call it? Defect?

Disappear, Bird had decided, not out loud.

Besides, Kin had gone on, following his own script. Like you said in the invitation, we might by tomorrow have something important. To tell JJ.

What? Bird had whispered, daring Kin to say it.

You know. Don't pretend you don't. What we thought we'd both have to do before they'd grant us the license. Even though we don't *have to,* not in New York state, I *told* you I was going to. And, well, I did. I have. I just don't know, yet, the—y'know—verdict.

What? Bird had asked, breathless like him. Another clank.

Blood, love, he'd mumbled.

She leaned left with the groaning curve of the bus, her eyes squeezed shut. To calm herself, she mouthed her favorite word. Whip. Her lips pursed into a kiss. Pet. *Whippet, whippet.* She wrote that down in the joggling notebook. *She disappeared, you remember. The day you appeared.* Bird slumped in her seat, not caring if Rebel saw. Weak already, so early in her fast.

Poor Panda. Mother'd named her for the black markings on her elegant white snout. The name didn't fit any more than a sleek leaping greyhound fits a fat lumbering bus. This bus bumped along in fits and starts, stuck in morning traffic. Whippets made greyhounds look slow. Whippets shared the greyhound shape, but smaller, more compact. A perfect miniature horse, disguised as a dog.

Panda loved to run and Bird loved to watch her. Mother lived then with Stepdad #2 in South Carolina, across the street from a rolling golf course. Down the street from Kin Hwang. Summer daytimes, Bird sat in the yard peeling busted golf balls and fingering the tightly wound rubber band inside. One long rubber band, the color of muddy pee. How'd it get so dirty, in there?

Behind the trash-can bin, Panda clinked her chains, pacing. Head low, like a horse. Miles down Route 2, cars would rumble. Panda's ears would prick; her ribs would stand at attention. She'd yip—a poodle sound, unworthy of her—and Bird would rush to the trash, grab her chain, yell *No no no* into the roar of approaching cars. Links bit her palms; links dug into Panda's neck, all tendon and bone. Her hindquarters quivered. The chain twisted and trembled.

Summer twilights, Stepdad #2 got home from the golf course at six. Then and only then, he'd release Panda for a run. Off like a shot: Bird sucked in her breath and watched, not even minding Stepdad's hand on her shoulder, holding her in place. Not that Bird—anyone—could run like Panda.

Whippet, Bird whispered again. Bus rumble absorbed Panda's real name.

Whippet made the golf course wild. Her hoof feet never touched the ground, like a soaring Greyhound Bus greyhound, only real. Her body became a white blur in the twilight. Bird would strain her eyes to watch Whippet fly over greens that weren't, for this space of time, meticulously manicured greens but hills, valleys. Down Bird's back Stepdad's hand would travel, slowly and lightly. Up over the swells of ground Whippet would swoop. At the golf-course border, she'd skid in the short grass, her hoof paws digging into turf. She'd turn heel, take aim, take off in the opposite direction. Pacing still, poor Panda.

Green glass vibrated. Under her half-zipped jacket, Bird's breasts bounced as they did when she tried to jog. That same pain. Across the aisle, the buried woman dozed. Her jowls jiggled as if she were shaking her head. But it was the bus that shook her head, shook all their loose flesh. Breasts, jowls, jewels.

TO AIRPORT, a giant sign said, and a ramp rose up. The bus gave a muffled bump. Above TO AIRPORT, a real plane, startlingly huge, climbed air.

How come she comes back? Bird asked Stepdad, whose hand had stopped at the small of her back. She felt herself stiffen, his touch light. His hand rested there—no, anything but "rested." A plump-fingered reddish-haired Southern boy's hand. Nails not recently trimmed. Only his fingertips touched her.

She's gotta eat, sweets.

How come? Bird wondered as Panda choked down hard nuggets of dog food. Her dark eyes bulged, too big for her skull. A bird's skull, narrowing to a point. Even as she ate, her body remained graceful, shaped like a slender yet buxom superwoman. No soft flesh: only thin efficient hips overbalanced by a rib cage spacious enough to hold her largest parts. Her heart, her lungs.

Bird stood when everybody else stood. The bus exhaled. For years now, Kin had refused to take what his friends called, simply, the test. Positive, negative. He didn't want to know, Kin said. Promised. Bird lifted her bag and drew a steadying breath. Hadn't Kin also promised to forget Jimmy Joe—a name Bird sometimes hated too much, sometimes loved too much to remember? The buried woman stayed sunk in her seat. From above, her head looked bald as any man's.

Bird held her own head high as she started down the sky-ceilinged terminal. Her crew cut bristled in air-conditioned chill. Her bag bumped her legs. Blood, love, blood. Her ankles scissored, her feet in high-tops fast and soundless, no longer hobbled by heels. Fly for free, Fly for free. Cautiously, she darted a glance over her shoulder. Not far behind, a dark head bobbed among other heads. Its oily hair gleamed. She turned back too fast to tell for sure. He had, she reminded herself, no bag. She picked up speed, wanting to run.

Whippet. That was her one clear thought the spring she turned fourteen. She'd run away with Whippet, run like her. The hot afternoon Bird first met Kin, Mother was out in a new man's car, her dirty white Mustang parked in the driveway. Bird paced beside it, on guard. Stepdad was due home anytime. They hadn't been alone in the house together, he and Bird, since the driving lesson. She'd steered Stepdad's Vega out to a red clay back road, stopped it when and where he told her to. His rusted Vega. Did she hear it already, rumbling down Route 2? Her rubber thongs flapped against her feet like wings in frantic flight. Her driveway shadow stretched out as she crouched, as she fumbled with the knotted mass of Panda's chains, Mother's forbidden keys jangling.

Halfway down the terminal, Bird spotted an arrow. She followed it, grateful for the blue-and-white picture, feeling too weak to read. She dropped her bag with a thud, bare-armed people rushing forward behind her. Phones stood bolted together in a row of three, back to back. Bird stared at the chipped push-tone dial. She tried to remember the number she knew by heart.

Somehow—how could be charted only later, by Kin, by a map of scratches and bruises—she had gathered Panda up in her arms. Panda whipped her body back and forth like a fish in a net, all muscle and bone and motion. Panda fought Bird as Bird had imagined fighting him. Her nails scraped Bird's throat and tore her T-shirt and nearly clipped the nipples of her new breasts.

Somehow, forcing her front paws together and letting her back legs churn, Bird thrust Whippet through the open Mustang door, scrambled in behind her. In the front seat of Stepdad's Vega, she'd stared and stared at the mute steering-wheel horn, trying to remember what Mother told her about the Morse Code. Two long, two short? Frantically, Panda scratched the windowpane, her ears pricking up. Did Bird hear his not-so-distant engine? Mother's key turned between her bloody fingertips; her feet found the gas.

She roared down Route 2 at a crazy tilt, wheels sinking into a red clay ditch. Late sun blinded her. Panda gave high screechy yips. Bird's grip on the wheel tightened, her hands slippery. Where were they going? She'd glimpsed Kin before, out in his yard, alone and quiet like her. Maybe that was why she swung onto the first driveway past the golf-course entrance, nearly crashing into the scrolled wrought-iron legs of his mother's carport. Her first clear look: Kin Hwang, age fourteen, rushing outside to defend his mother's house.

She fumbled for the gears, bumped the headlights. His spiky black hair exploded around his face, stiff with spray. When, frequently, his mother was away on business, he wore her robes. Before Bird, no one had seen Kin in silk.

She shoved open the door, ducked fast. With an uncharacteristically sloppy leap, her hooves skidding on vinyl, Panda vaulted over her and disappeared into the dusk. Bird smelled dog piss soaking into car carpet. She stayed ducked, the steering-wheel notches pressing her forehead.

His hands, she'd written, the first entry in her first notebook. It would take months to get up the courage to ask Kin, as if casually, Wanna read my diary? *His fingers. One, two. His fingernails, almost too light to feel, scraping my inside-most flesh.*

One of the tinier varieties of pain. She kept her head bowed as Kin bent into Mother's Mustang, slow and cautious. Her skin felt hot, holding in its sweat. Her long hair hid her face and half her body.

In Kin's mother's dark living room—it was always nighttime in that house—Bird sat on the white leather couch, hugging her bandaged knees. Her arms were bandaged too, by Kin. Her skin smelled of Witch Hazel. Her T-shirt was torn, showing a strap of her training bra. A light flickered, the softest possible.

Kin stepped toward her, so silent she felt she was watching him on a TV without sound. Peach silk shimmered over his body. His chest was smooth, hairless. With a flourish, Kin held out another weightless robe, pink and maroon. She blinked, pleased. Colors to compliment her bruises. Kin's eyes narrowed so the whites disappeared. Two clear black mirrors, glimpsed in slits. In her memory of this night, these were Kin's first words to her, ever.

Feel that. Real silk.

Her quarters clanked. Long-distance cost two dollars. Her finger stabbed out the code, all on its own. She pressed the receiver to her ear, straining for the familiar purr of Kin's phone. One, two. Her black high-tops blurred. Four feet? Across from her own, she saw his larger pair. He was standing opposite her, at the phone whose backboard pressed the backboard of hers. Five rings now. Had the bachelor party lasted all night? The VCR playing Kin's fabulously bad Karen Valentine movie, *Coffee, Tea or Me?* The sixth ring was chopped short. His machine kicked in. On tape, his voice was mock-portentous.

"There. Is. No. Beep."

Silence rolled. Bird spoke to Rebel's feet, loud enough to register above a party. "Sister Kin? I'm—I'm at Logan and—"

His receiver clattered, hundreds of miles away, cutting short the hypnotic roll of tape. Live silence, not dead. Music, too.

". . . 'low-oh?" Kin repeated, singsong. Opposite Bird, Rebel's feet stood still.

"Kin." Bird heard mens' voices muffled like TV sound.

"Berta Bird." Kin must be standing in the tiny bedroom, dressed in black, his shiny hair loose on his shoulders. "My bride-to-be." He sang a few bars of their song, their own words. "I had to be you, I had to be you-ou—"

"Sister Kin?" she interrupted. His sly eyes must be glittering so he'd seem feverishly alive yet not there, absent. "Flying Nun? Are you—too far gone?"

He gave a smoky sounding sigh, caught. Kin rarely drank just as he rarely ate red meat, protecting his Chinese/Korean/Hawaiian body. Back in 1980, he used to tell Bird and JJ that if they reached the altered states they sought via drink or drugs, it was cheating. Bird sighed back at him now, concerned.

"L-listen." She wanted to sober him up. "There's—this boy. Hanging around me here. In the Boston terminal." Rebel's toe tapped. Could he hear?

"Oh?" Kin asked, theatrically casual. But she sensed Kin straightening up, his interest always aroused when a Would-Be Lover hovered near her. Officially, from Jimmy Joe on, he'd encouraged her to find a man.

"Saw him watch me on the subway. And now he's following me around here like some kinda—bodyguard."

"Or the opposite," Kin mumbled. "Poor Berta. Don't even look at him. An' stay on the line till he gives up. Hey, now. See? You never shoulda stolen that bomber jacket. 'S too powerful." A glass clinked his receiver. "Speaking of which: you'll never guess who I called last night. Whose answering machine."

"You did?" Bird tightened her hold on the receiver. "Then we really might—go?"

"To New Waven New Haven. If Jimmy Joe doesn't surprise us and show up after all. We'll fly to Hartford, take a bus. I suggested he meet us at some bar I found in Information. We've—think 'bout it, Birdy—got something else to give him. First, that hair I cut. An' now, the jacket you stole. His hair and his jacket. That's our old Jimmy Joe: we got him right there between us."

"What? You want to give back the jacket? To Jimmy Joe?"

"Who else?" Kin asked softly enough to make Bird wonder if, for him as for her, there was anyone else, really.

"How about this boy I got right here?" Her voice rose above men's laughter rising behind Kin, drowning out strains of jazz. "Few feet away."

"Drool," Kin advised. "That'll turn the kid off. If he comes too close, scratch your ass. Pretend you can sweat. Make yourself un—"

"I *know*." She sighed. Kin would drag her into his kitchenette as soon as he saw she'd been fasting again. It was simple, really. He wanted to be her bodyguard; she wanted to be his. "But—listen. You stay safe too, Sister Kin, with your boys. And today—We'll wait for it together, y'know?"

Glass clinked. Blood, he'd told her, his voice uncharacteristically unsteady. Already, he'd said last night, done. Taken. She hadn't answered then. Someone cut off the jazz. Another quieter clink, a swallow-sized pause.

"So you'll be with me, Berta Bird? Right when I find out, for better or for worse? Hope you're not mad that I took it and all, the—"

"Test." Bird leaned on the metal shelf, her pulse stealing her energy. "Blood test."

Kin gave a nervous laugh and so did Bird. Two Southern girls. That's what Bird used to imagine when they'd giggle on the phone in high school.

"But listen, Sister Kin," Bird burst out. "You've been the *Flying Nun* for years—right? And I've told you: I bet if you'd gotten it before, it would've *shown* by now—"

"Oh, of *course*," Kin assured her. Then he hung up: a click as fumbling and abrupt as the fall of a curtain on a skit. Feeling the foolish echo of her words, Bird replaced her receiver in its cradle. For a year now, she had worried with Kin over his bouts of exhaustion. He'd feel jet-lagged when he wasn't. Slowly, Bird let go of the receiver.

Better or worst, she had written on JJ's invitation weeks ago, when she and Kin had decided to marry. Had she known Kin would take the test before *he* knew it, before he could say it? She couldn't say it either, only write it.

Bird bent for her bag, bowing under the weight of Jimmy Joe's jacket. So Kin had actually called JJ. Kin, who always did the talking, the acting. Bird straightened. In Boston, in June, Kin had taken her to be fitted for a diaphragm that she never wound up using. Outside Planned Parenthood, they were ambushed by a woman carrying a sign: *If The Womb Isn't Safe, No Place Is Safe*. She'd fixed her murderous stare on Bird. "I'm so glad *you* were never aborted!"

Standing at Bird's side, holding her diaphragm in a plain bag, Kin had stared back at the woman and replied, perfectly polite, "Pity you weren't."

Bird blinked. Tar specks swam. She blinked again. Rebel's feet still waited. Testing her ability to move, she took a few slow steps. Blood, love, blood. She halted and stared up. Two signs: painted for her. She hesitated between them, feeling Rebel hover behind her. He thought he knew what she was, by now.

Silly boy, she thought as the door swung. A metal stall was a metal stall, anyplace on Earth. Tile was tile. But MEN'S did smell stronger than WOMEN'S.

Bird lowered herself, hidden except for her feet. So simple, it should be. All she wanted was to transport, deliver, give, in a sense, her body to Kin. To guard. She looked down. Rebel's familiar black high-tops stood outside the booth. He stepped back discreetly as she peed. The odorless colorless pee of a fast beginning to work. He knows I sat, she realized, flushing the toilet.

An unnatural act, Kin had told her after Planned Parenthood, as they sat in her basement apartment contemplating the smooth rubber cup. That's what Kin imagined sex to be, with a woman. It would seem, he'd said, an . . . invasion.

Bird pulled up her jeans. Jimmy Joe's jacket creaked. In chill TV light, she and Kin used to run their hands over each other's bodies, under each other's clothes. Of all the men who'd touched her since, only Jimmy Joe had matched the tenderness of Kin's hands. Bird shut her eyes. She'd trained herself to chop short those memories. Those starring Jimmy Joe. She zipped her jeans, remembering, instead, how she'd once let fifteen-year-old Kin slip one hand under her panties, like—yet not at all like—Stepdad #2 in the Vega. His palm curved with her ass, not pressing. On TV, James Stewart snapped at Grace Kelly. *If she were mine, I'd treat her right,* Kin had whispered in a voice that matched his touch: tender and reverent. *All I'd do, all day long is . . . polish her.*

Bird lifted her bag. As she swung open the stall door, Rebel stepped forward. Taller than Kin, but not as tall as Jimmy Joe. He took hold of the metal door frame, leaning close. His breath smelled of smoke and sugar. "Where you heading, girl?"

Bird blinked. A bride, batting sticky lashes. Beyond Rebel's shoulder, she saw the odd exposed-looking row of urinals. Do-si-do. Bird ducked under his arm, feeling the floor sway like the train's rubber floor. Side by side, her leather arm and his bare arm awkwardly brushing, she and he walked down the tile aisle to the sinks. Her face in the mirror jumped out at her, no longer softened by her hair. Age twenty-five now: light lines etched around her eyes. Her fine-boned nose crooked as ever, bonier these days. Her whole face bone, nothing soft except her lips. But the fake dark lashes gave her away.

Who gives this woman?

She bent over the sink. I do, she told herself. Take her away. Bird splashed her hot face with cold water. Her fingertips trembled, as they always did when her fasts reached the serious stage. She shut off the faucet and wiped her face with a harsh brown towel, rubbing hard.

"No-ohh!" In the mirror, a towheaded kid in overalls was dragged into the door by a puffing hunched-over daddy. The daddy's glasses slid down his nose.

"Don' *god*da, Don' *god*da—" A stall door banged.

Behind her, she felt Rebel's body tense up. Ready to lunge? *Drool,* Kin'd say. Make yourself—what? Bending forward, Bird tried to scrub off her mascara with her balled-up paper towel. Waterproof, tear proof.

Protection, Jimmy Joe had answered once when she'd asked, brushing a fallen one off his cheek: what were they for? Eyelashes? The kind of science-class question JJ always knew. Black lashes stabbed the whites of her eyes now, black specks floating. A toilet-paper roll clacked.

Bird crouched by her overnight bag and dug with sudden inspiration into its side pocket. Above her, Rebel still stared. Under soft Kleenex and tampons, she rooted out a metal nail clipper. Standing shakily, her fingers shaky too, she managed to center the curved blades above her eye, forcing her tremulous eyelid to stay still. Behind her, she felt Rebel draw in his breath.

The toilet flushed, drowning the bite of the blade. Lashes fell, some sticking to her wet cheek. Her lid sprang open, prickly and stunned. Water rushed round and round and Bird had to hurry. What was more half-assed than two eyes that didn't match?

"C'mon now," the daddy was urging, his voice echoing. "All clean now!"

Her next clicks came out loud and clear. Her pulse leapt in her throat in wild applause. She brushed more lashes off her cheeks and they stuck to the sink like beard clippings. Their tips were black; their roots, blond. She turned to face Rebel. He stared as if she had shaved off a beard.

"See?" the daddy voice demanded from the back of the bathroom, overpowering the kid's shy trickle of pee. "You did have to!"

Bird blinked, wincing. Everything wavered. Rebel's eyes widened but his mouth stayed shut, shellacked by spit shiny as lip gloss. He stepped toward Bird and she bumped the sink, its wetness soaking into her jeans.

She smelled Rebel's breath again, cigarettes and sweets. I may, she told herself, kiss the bride. This morning, not this afternoon. She shut her eyes—another sharper prickle—and bent forward. Before Rebel could jump, she brushed her sealed lips against his lips. Warm and wet like Jimmy Joe's that strangest of nights. Their first night. Good-bye, she thought.

Whoa. Rebel staggered backward, then caught his balance. His wild off-center stare caromed around the tile walls.

"—not so hard, huh?" The metal door swung; the daddy's ass emerged. He was kneeling to zip the kid back into his overalls.

Bird lifted her bag, nodded. Rebel without a Brain, meet Rebel without a Body. That was how she felt, so light. Her lids burned as if from years of tears.

"'Scuse me—?" Across the tile, the crouched Daddy stared, fierce bathroom light in his glasses. The kid squirmed, struggling to unzip what his father had zipped. Slowed by the weight of her jacket, Bird started to turn away.

"Hey—" Rebel gripped her oversized sleeve. Her stuffed bag dropped. "What're ya trying t'*do*?" He tugged. The jacket strained Bird's shoulders, oppressively heavy. Cracked brown 1950s leather. With a single jagged motion—a lightning flash splitting a sky—she unzipped it all the way, jerked both arms free. Berta Bird.

"Miss?" the daddy called out, reluctantly alarmed. Invigorated by cool air, Bird turned her ass on him and Rebel, bending fast to grab her bag. Her breasts bounced under her T-shirt as she straightened. The door's thud must've echoed on tile. Bird took a great gulp of air. And she blinked hard, tearing up.

Protection, JJ had said softly. *Lashes catch all flakes of dirt, all—*
Germs? she'd whispered.
In the air. Keeping the eye—
Immune, she might've filled in now, a word not common back then.

Bird headed off down the terminal, her bag thumping her legs. Rebel's spit was evaporating on her lips. Behind her, distantly, the door whooshed. Her head felt light, her body lighter. Heads turned but Bird gave her eyes to no one.

After the ceremony, Kin might photograph them, setting his timer. Glossy black-and-white stills, stylized poses: their lips always a fraction of an inch apart. A born model, Kin had called skinny Bird in high school. *You eat like a bird, Berta,* he'd scold in what they both called—though neither of theirs sounded anything like it—a mother voice. With Kin, she ate. Feasts devoured in the blue light of late-night movies, strawberries dipped in chocolate in his mother's gleamingly unused fondue set. They lay on her leather couch, studying her slick floppy copies of *Paris Match, Vogue, Endless Vacation.* Rating bones, seeking out models who'd make the most elegant skeletons. After death, breasts and family jewels go the way of all flesh. *Bones last,* Kin would pronounce as they made up each other's faces, shadowed their high cheekbones and deep eye sockets. Kin took her picture; she took his.

Her head buzzing, Bird stepped into line at the gun-detector machine. Then darted a glance over her shoulder. Meeting her eyes determinedly, Rebel took his place too, one pregnant woman between them. The woman yawned, safely anchored. Rebel held Jimmy Joe's leather jacket balled up in his arms, a live animal he was struggling to control. *What am I trying to do?* Bird concentrated on keeping her feet connected to the floor. Her neck still itched from the decades-old dirt of that air-force-jacket collar. Her head was a helium balloon, threatening to carry off her hollowed-out bird bones.

"Next," someone said, and Bird slid her feet forward. How long would her fast last? If the worst was true, how long would she last, with Kin? Bird stepped through the electrified metal arch, turning to see Rebel slip out of line on the other side. He still held Jimmy Joe's jacket with both hands, but more loosely, a dazed hunter displaying prey. At the same time watching that prey, its spirit, escape. His eyes and mouth were open, his fly still only half closed.

White flag. As she turned, Bird imagined reaching down gently, zipping him up all the way. As she moved, she felt the notebook in the pocket of her baggy jeans. She felt Rebel's eyes on her back till she turned the corner to the gate, his marathon gaze broken at last. Goodbye, Bird thought again, remembering a book she'd once seen JJ reading. *Good-bye to All That.*

As she took her place in another longer line, she remembered how JJ had given Kin the bomber jacket, the morning after the first time. She and Kin and Jimmy Joe had been sitting so self-consciously and yet so naturally together in the cafeteria near Mass. Mental, miles away from Kin's place. The cafeteria where Kin took them after signing the two of them out for breakfast: he supposedly being the sane one. What, Kin himself would say, a laugh.

Bird shivered in her T-shirt, handing over her ticket. Some flight soon, Kin would tear her ticket, maybe flash her a stewardess smile as a joke, as if she were a prime Palm Beach Bitch. In the humid flimsy tunnel to the plane, she imagined taking his hand in an anonymous doctor's office, a waiting room.

Hazy sun misted the not-quite-sealed space between the entrance hatch and the boarding tunnel's mouth. Bird hesitated to step from the shuddering tunnel floor onto the solid-seeming floor of the plane.

Better get used to it. As her feet moved, she patted, for luck, the outer curve of the hatch door. A surface soon to be swept by upper altitude winds: unimaginably cold and strong.

When, she asked Kin once, did he first know he was gay? He answered without a blink of a pause: *Always.*

. . .

A tray unfolded. A hand, a female version of Kin's deft and slender hand, set down a sealed plastic bag. Bird drew a breath of stranger's smoke. Above her, a nozzle blew some substance thinner than air. She always sat in Smoking because the rear would be the last to crash. Not that anyplace, as Kin pointed out, is safe then. *If the womb isn't safe*—Bird unsealed the plastic lips.

You're right, lady. No place *is*. Not as long as you're you, trapped in your body like—she slipped on bulky rubber headphones—any dumb fetus.

The headphone plug brushed Bird's shoulder, unattached. As a boy, while his mother worked or slept off a migraine, Kin used to dance in his headphones. Transported, he'd told Bird in a fake DJ voice, by Music from Round the World.

"Flight attendants prepare for departure," an intercom voice commanded. Meaning, Bird knew from Kin: man your door, secure your inflatable evacuation slide. Once, Kin had slid down one. On a burning plane, in San Juan. Bird shivered now. Across the aisle, a man unfolded a *Boston Globe.* How could any flesh-and-blood being ignore the terrifying grandeur of takeoff?

Outside, runway grit began to swirl. The ground and airport buildings began to move. Bird's breasts vibrated. Beautiful breasts, or so she'd been told. By Jimmy Joe, first. The aisle man's gaze lingered, then stopped short at her shorn head and raw eyes. He bowed into his half-lowered *Globe.*

Swans, Kin had murmured, rubbing her neck with his, unhooking her bra as if untying a strand of hair. He was fifteen, like her. His fingers barely brushed her skin. She lay on her back on his mom's couch, leather cool under her body, her knees raised. Two years later, in Boston in 1980, she lay the same way on Jimmy Joe's leather jacket on Kin's futon. Jimmy Joe knelt beside her. Both separate times, bending, Kin had licked the flat nipples of her breasts. Just a taste. The touch of his tongue had been light, tentative.

The plane began to pick up speed. Bird tugged her seat-belt strap, straining not to remember Jimmy Joe on that futon. Twenty-year-old

Jimmy Joe bending over her too, following Kin's lead. The touch of his tongue gentle, but not tentative. Warm: his tongue, his whole long body. Startlingly warm under the surface cool of his skin. Leather had creaked beneath them, cool too. At first.

Eight years later now, Bird remembered the oily warmth of their sweat on leather. She tightened her seat belt to keep herself from bolting up and running back after it. Jimmy Joe's old jacket. Their magic carpet, Kin used to call that jacket in the summer of '80. Summer of Shakuhachi music and circular didgeridoo dancing and each night a new shared fondue.

Bird clenched her fist, picturing the soldered metal ring of 8s JJ had made her in Mass. Mental. An 8 lying down is the sign for Infinity, he'd told her. Forever, she'd thought he meant. What a laugh, that. She sat straighter, bracing her body. Her breasts jiggled with the plane's taxiing speed but her stomach stayed still and empty under the tight clinch of her seat belt.

When she fasted, she always reached this point beyond hunger. Like the second wind she and Kin used to find at 2 A.M., watching all-night movies. Her stomach was collapsed against itself, nourishing itself. It wasn't so much that she wasn't hungry. It was that the whole idea of hunger felt foreign.

After Kin's tongue had touched her that first time, both of them fifteen, Bird had held herself still. His model. His keen black eyes gleamed above her, matching the cool gleam on each nipple. A sculptor who's added his finishing touch. In the dark, her own knees framed his face. In the dark, the bones of his face stood out, identical to hers. Sisters under the skin.

What, she'd never asked, did Kin see as he stared down at her? What is it to you, she wondered now. My body?

Her headphone plug bounced on her shoulder. The ground moved fast and the buildings moved slowly. She squirmed to tug the notebook out of her back pocket, then the temp-service pencil. The pages curved from her ass.

Forget JJ, was all she wrote, her hands jerking. The pencil gouged the paper. She shut the notebook on its torn page. The seat belt dug into her stomach as she stuffed the book back in her pocket. She sucked her lips, hating her sour teeth. Her bad gums. She'd begun again, more seriously, to shiver.

Marry me, she'd say to Kin today. This much she knew. She hugged herself, pressing her ribs. Weeks ago, she hugged Kin good-bye, gripping his rib cage as if holding Whippet again, trying to. Marry me, for real. For better or worst. I'll be true to you, if you'll be true to me. Really? Kin might ask. Blood thumped the skin covering the hollow of her throat. If TWA detected lies, not metal, she'd prove it. If she took the test this moment, anyway, she'd pass.

Through her new rubber ears, the surrounding scream of the engine reached its highest pitch. Bird blinked, her prickly lids burning, her eyeballs burning too. Determinedly, she stared out the oval window at other planes lined up on other sunny runways. Sleek, massive machines. They quivered in place like whippets longing to run. They *want* to fly, she told herself, holding herself still. Nothing to fear. As the wheels released the ground, this—what she was about to do—seemed a perfectly natural act.

4

Another Spineless White Girl

She was as good as she was beautiful.

Silently, at 8:20 A.M., Alice recited this line in the rain. Her favorite fairy-tale opening. And what does it mean for me? she asked the unimaginable baby she hoped she wasn't carrying. Not all that good, not all the time. Splashing through the gray New Haven green, she ducked past a JJ-sized man asleep beneath a bench. His dense ruglike hair stuck out in the mud. Alice hunched low under her bubble umbrella. Good, say, depending on the light.

.   .   .

No I'm not.

Half an hour before, still hearing her own words, still hugging herself, Alice had knelt on the bed beside JJ. *No,* she was preparing to tell workshop workers. Don't drool, don't rock, don't bang your head. In the bedroom's drizzly flicker, she gazed down at JJ as if he had turned, overnight, into one of them.

"I mean I'm *trying* not to be scared, James Joseph." She tightened the knot on her towel. But you know the truth? she imagined telling him in some future talk. I *was* scared you might—as we say at Helping Hands— Go Off.

"Look, I'm scared too." JJ balanced his braid again on his bare shoulder. "Scared, y'know, of what I'm finding myself doing. Dropping out and all."

"Then— you already *are*—dropped out?"

"De facto, I assume. After missing all those classes." He gave a one-shouldered shrug. The braid flopped between them on the sheets.

"OK." Allie sighed, letting her towel knot slip. "OK, OK. I *am* scared, sure. But—not *of* you. More of . . ." She scanned the shadowy fold-out mattress, the three-legged Goodwill desk, the aluminum wardrobe closet, the orange crate filled with books. "This. Living like grad students, but—for good."

"Right," was all JJ gave as an answer. He flattened his hand over his braid.

On his nightstand, Allie noticed his Walkman was loaded with a David Bowie tape. She breathed a faint trace of burned paper. Slowly, she pulled herself up.

"Listen." She turned to the chipped maple dresser. "I gotta go."

She groped in the dark drawers. Got to keep myself together, she thought, if he's going to fall apart. Balanced on one leg, she fit her foot through a cotton hole. Got to figure out what the Hell's going on with him. Allie straightened, snapping her panties into place. First, Helping Hands. Then, Ko No's. Right?

She hooked her bra, tight today. And she opened the aluminum queen's wardrobe that their landlords, the Giovannis, had hauled up just for her. She slipped on her shirt and skirt, comforted by clean cotton against her clean skin.

"Allie?"

Startled, she turned too fast. A sign of her period or of pregnancy? she wondered as she steadied herself. JJ asked: "Still late?"

She nodded, her hair damp on her shirt. Two steps and she stood at the foot of their fold-out. "Just what we'd need, huh?" she asked, sensing it might be what he needed. Shock therapy. He stared up at her almost the way he'd stared down the breathless times they'd started to forget—ignore—her diaphragm.

"And you've got to work?" JJ lifted his hand from that damn braid. "Today?"

"Sure." Hope stiffened her spine. Maybe JJ realized how shaken she felt. "Guess it's a, our, real job now. Our one paycheck. Right?" She stood still, wanting him to say wrong. "Yesterday, I could walk out if any assignment got, y'know, dangerous. But now I'd stay. Now each job'll be a real—test."

JJ sank back against his pillow. "Look, Little Match Girl. Don't do anything that feels dangerous. And don't pretend you *want* a 'real test.' Who does?"

Allie stepped over and knelt by him again, studying his profile. Its pock-scarred hollows, its noble bones. He too looked shaken. She touched his arm.

"Christ, I'm sorry, Al," JJ murmured to the wall. "Sorry about all this."

He turned his face to hers, a slight moist gleam on his lower lip.

She gave him a hug, instead of a kiss. As she took loose hold of his shoulders, he gripped her rib cage. His strong hands tightened like he was dropping fast with her lying on top of him, dropping too. And Alice pulled herself, abruptly, upright. "Listen; listen, we'll talk—later. But, God, I've gotta go—"

Turning from him, she hurried to the bedroom door. JJ's odd parting words came out low but clear behind her. "Hope you are."

· · ·

"Scared?" The tall woman standing outside the workshop door raised her own umbrella to reveal her stern brown face. "I scare you just now?"

"No no," Allie lied, though she had crept cautiously past the sooty brick walls of Manslaw—aka Manslaughter—Street, hoping that the rain-blurred figure awaiting her at the street's end would walk away, vanish. "I just thought, from a distance, you might be a—a man or something—"

"With a big black gun?" Her unamused mouth wore purplish lipstick, frosted. Her fingers wore nails—how had Alice missed those?—of the same chilled plum. "Had us some break-ins, so we keep this locked now." She clanked her key into the peeling door. "Can't hear no knocks way down in the workshop."

"Oh." Alice lowered her bubble umbrella back over her face, wanting to burst out, as if to Jo: Pretend that didn't happen, OK? Let's start over, OK?

". . . I'm your supervisor, Ms. Sticks." She shouldered open the door, eying Allie with regal indifference. "And you're the girl from—" Through the rain, Allie caught her deliberate-sounding mispronunciation. "Helpin' Hams?"

Cardboard gray concrete sloped for wheelchairs: a bumpy ramp descending into a gym-sized workshop. Allie's feet matched Sticks's purposeful beat.

"We got it all," Supervisor Sticks told her. "Some D.D., some E.D. . . ."

"De-velopmentally, E-motionally." Alice listed the "Disableds," eager to show she knew something after months of Special Ed substitute teaching.

"Tha's what I said." Sticks halted at the bottom of the ramp. Uncovered, her hair formed stiff peaks, brushed back angrily.

"S-so they're all here under observation, pending—" Alice almost rolled her own eyes at her goody-good voice, her Helping Hands terms. "Placement?"

"You could say that." You, not me, Sticks's no-nonsense walk implied. Her boot heels clicked the concrete. "'Less you count this as a *place.*"

Struggling to keep up, Alice hurried past bins stuffed with mildewed junk mail folded so often the folds had split. The bins rested in rows on six tables; no workers filled the metal chairs yet. No windows here, no sound of rain.

"'Course . . ." Supervisor Sticks clanked her keys onto a central table. "Some stay for years. You take Eric now."

"Yeah, take Eric," a cheerful voice echoed. ". . . please." Henny Youngman as a black woman. Chewing gum at a furious rate, she waddled over from a corner, pushing a crew-cut man in a wheelchair. She parked the chair in front of Allie.

"Morning, Vi," Sticks murmured. "Let's show this sub our Eric."

"Hi Eric. Hi there." Alice touched the seated man's rigid shoulder, patted it.

"Ain't she sweet?" Sticks asked Vi. "So sen-sitive, when they do drop in."

Vi gave a cough or laugh. "Not like us, huh, Eric? Us full-time witches?"

Smiling uncertainly, Alice bent to meet Eric's eyes and found none. One eye patch, one deflated eyelid. A sliver of white showed in the slit. Allie didn't let herself look away. Eric's gray-blond head bobbed like—no, not—a nod.

"Don' let him scare you, hon'," Vi rasped, bending so close Alice breathed her tobacco gum. Gratefully, Alice gave Vi her first unforced smile of the day.

"He blind, he deaf, he crippled." Vi shook her frizzy hennaed head. "Makes you wonder what He—" Alice caught the capital "H"—"pulls such tricks for. But Eric's got the face of a baby, don't he?" Alice nodded, smiling wider. A thirty-year-old baby, his dry skin unlined. "I would too," Vi announced, "if *I* didn't have no worries left—right, Eric? Not much more this world can do to you, right?"

Shyly, Allie ran one hand over Eric's greasy crew cut. His head kept bobbing.

"Got a flyer-foldin' job today." Sticks raised her voice to supervisor volume.

A puffy-faced white woman drifted up to the center table. "Oh joy."

"And this Helping Hands girl gonna work with the Prez," Sticks announced.

The main workshop door thumped; a slow-motion army began to shuffle down the wheelchair ramp. Alice patted Eric's shoulder good-bye, bracing herself.

"Here he comes," Vi told Allie. "The Prez: James Carter. Get you a look at his hands. They found him a couple months ago tied up in a closet in some empty apartment. Don't know what all his problems be . . ."

Alice turned. Twenty or so slouched workers were filing in. A decid-edly un-slouched man walked to one side of the crowd, winking one eye shut. A video camera perched on his shoulder like a robotic hawk, sweeping the room.

The Faceless Man, Alice thought. She stiffened in the camera's light, hit by a wavelet of delayed shock. How, she wondered anew, could JJ have deceived her about attending classes the way he'd once deceived his dad—who, when Allie first met him, did seem like a robot replica of a man? JJ's dad, whose mute presence had made Allie tell herself, clearly: do not marry this man's son.

The camera light roved closer. A stooped-over worker veered from the crowd. But how, Allie asked herself, could *she* have erased JJ's phone message? Even if he did burn up the Kin letter. Didn't JJ have a right to keep his letters private?

"C'mon." Vi nudged Allie. "We gotta get Carter *away* from th' camera."

"Whose camera?" Allie blinked up at the worker who halted by Vi, wobbling.

"Channel 8's." Vi herded Alice and Carter toward a corkboard parti-tion on the front wall, camera light warm against their backs. Carter lurched along, his jaw jutting over his caved-in chest. "Told you those hands, see what I say?"

Carter's left fingers swelled like balloons knotted by a sadistic circus clown.

"Here." Vi stopped them at the partition, glancing back. The camera-man was talking to Sticks. A headphoned man balanced a long-necked light. "They're doin' some sorta in-vestigation," Vi told Allie. "For—y'know—"

"Abuse?" Alice pictured herself led to a police car in front of all America, her head under her raincoat, her name afloat beneath her, un-seen except on screen.

"For the *Monthly Magazine Show*, this comin' spring."

"And Carter—" Alice pointed her chin at him. "He's likely to—?"

"Go Off." Vi nodded like a sympathetic executioner, nudging Allie halfway behind the partition. "So Sticks wants you two back here."

"But shouldn't someone else? Someone who's used to him?"

"None of us is. ESL training, they say he need: English as a Second—but we don't know if he got a first!—Language." Vi took hold of Carter's slack elbow.

"But." Allie's eyes darted, the camera hidden now. A lurking Candid Camera? "It's just that today, this time of month, I'm—"

"Cramps?" Vi hissed companionably.

"I wish," Alice whispered. Vi gave her a steadying pat on the back. "You take it easy now. *You're* not much more'n a baby."

·   ·   ·

Behind the partition, Alice moved as slowly as Carter. Clumsy like him—a sign of pregnancy?—she held open the envelopes he sullenly stuffed, one-handed. His twisted hand rested on the table. His brown fingers puffed out from bone-thin joints ringed by dead white. Where the ropes dug in, Alice realized.

"Good work," she told him quietly. Up close, his milky brown face was heart shaped, like hers; only his heart turned upside down. Forehead low, jaw broad. His nose was too flat to support the glasses strapped on his head.

"I—" Carter told her. A sound? Alice followed his stare and saw, resting on the partition's ledge, a corncob pipe. A reward: in sight but out of reach. "I—I—"

Supervisor Sticks poked her head inside the partition. "No." She addressed Carter. His glasses gleamed as if from her eyes. "No smokes." Her nail pointed. "Not till you finish your stack." Then, to Alice: "Keep him quiet."

Carter fixed his stare on the space where Sticks's vivid face had been. With a wheeze of a sigh, he lowered his head to the crook of his arm and shut his eyes.

Allie sighed too, wanting to do the same. Shut her eyes like Carter and sink into sleep. Forget the Kin man's voice, JJ burning that note. Maybe JJ thought she couldn't handle it, a man in his past. She stuffed one of Carter's envelopes with a Whole Foods Co-op flyer. But I can handle it, she told herself. Of course I can. *Then how come*, Jo's voice asked in her head, *you erased that man's voice?*

I shouldn't have, Allie imagined telling JJ, picturing JJ alone in bed after those last fumbling minutes this morning. Usually she or JJ would phone each other before noon when they'd quarreled, clearing the air. Shouldn't she, today, call? Confess about the erased message, confront him about the burned note?

Yes, Allie decided by the time she'd illicitly helped Carter stuff enough Whole Foods envelopes to earn his pipe. As she lit it, she remembered her high school play. *The Little Match Girl*: Alice and her flames trembling wildly.

"Pie-pie—" Carter insisted, too loud. Alice stuck the pipe stem between his eagerly parted lips. The flame jumped into the bowl.

Companionably, she sat watching Carter savor his puffs. Smoke filled her mouth. She blew it back at him, stirring the cloud between them.

"Eee—" James Carter rocked in sudden glee, his pipe bobbing. He eased it from his mouth with his good hand, pointed the glistening stem at Allie's mouth.

Hepatitis, she thought automatically, leaning away. Or, she found herself thinking today, HIV. "None for me, thanks." She patted Carter's misshapen left hand, her fingertips avoiding his swollen fingers. He stuck the pipe back in his mouth. *Touched each other down there,* Allie remembered telling JJ years before. She and Jo playing around the way many kids do. The way, maybe, young JJ and the Kin man had begun their affair. Experimenting. But—Alice told JJ, already talking to him on the phone—I didn't lie about it, hide it.

"No—" Supervisor Sticks called from behind the partition. "No, Eric!"

A wooden thump sounded, startling Allie out of her seat even before Sticks commanded: "Need some help here!" Alice snatched Carter's pipe from him. Trailing smoke, she ran out into the workshop. She fell in step behind Vi, hurrying toward Eric. He banged his forehead again on his wheelchair tray.

"—get that off!" Sticks was gripping Eric's shoulders.

"Guess we know what he needs." Vi crouched to unfasten the tray. But Eric knocked it askew, a paper cup of grape juice flying off. The juice spattered Allie's skirt as she froze behind Vi, the tray falling at her feet. Eric was flailing the way JJ'd been dancing this morning. But no grace, no control.

"Watch out, Sticks, or we gonna wind up on Channel 8." Vi rolled up Eric's sleeve as Sticks held his arm. "Where that camera gone?" Vi chomped her gum.

"No i-dea," Sticks mumbled, sounding elaborately bored. The puff-ball woman drifted forward in her white dress, wielding a hypodermic needle.

"He'll look like he cryin' but he's not—" Vi's tooth winked over at Alice.

Breaking her frozen pose, Allie dropped Carter's pipe and lifted

Eric's tray. Unmistakably, blind Eric laughed. A phlegmy full-throated man's laugh.

"See?" Vi demanded. Alice watched Sticks ease the needle out of Eric's arm. He doubled over laughing, his eye patch slipping. "He likes it, see? Likes that needle, likes boilin' hot water, likes bitter black olives, the saltier th' better."

"How come, d'you think?" Alice handed Vi the tray as Sticks walked off.

"Mmm . . ." Vi knelt to re-fit the tray. Alice stepped behind Eric to prop him upright, grasping his spit-slimy wrists. Trying to hold him gently but firmly. "If something's gonna get felt by Eric," Vi told her. "It's gotta be *strong*."

• • •

After a splash of cold water and a breath of disinfected piss, Alice faced the fact. She might be pregnant. No blood yet, anyhow. And anything was possible in the world she'd woken to at midnight. She tossed her paper towel in an overstuffed barrel. It bounced off a mashed sour mound, weeks' worth of trash.

A fifteen-minute break, Sticks had decreed. Time enough to call JJ, right? Allie stepped up to the bathroom door. Nervously, as if JJ would see her over the phone, she smoothed her purple-spattered skirt. Hope you are, he'd told her. Pushing the door now, she wondered if he'd meant not "scared" but "pregnant." Wondered too if she and JJ were losing their shared second language.

" . . . that new Helping Ham," Sticks was saying on the other side of the bathroom door as Allie began to step out. "Another spineless white girl."

Allie stopped, hidden by the door as Vi gave a hoarse, considering "Mmm." A bin clomped on a table. "—when Eric had his fit, she *did* come a-runnin'."

"Nn." Sticks allowed the briefest of reprieves. "But she didn't do much."

True, Allie thought, holding the door and waiting for a third voice to break in. An impartial judge rendering a final verdict. *She was as good as—*

" 'Scuse me." Allie let the bathroom door swing shut. Facing, across the table, startled-looking Vi and unblinking Sticks. "Is there a phone somewhere?"

Alone in Sticks's office, Alice sat behind a metal desk on a stuck-in-one-position swivel chair. She dialed. JJ mumbled hello in a sleep-thickened voice.

"Woke you up," she told him, picturing ashes scattered on their sheets.

"Uh huh. Good that you did." The ever-elastic bubble of hope in Allie's chest rose, as if this were a regular call after a quarrel. "Where're you, Al?"

"New Chance Workshop."

"But isn't that the one—?" His voice was roused from its flat plain.

"Yeah. The one Ms. Carmella told me never to let them send me to."

"Christ." JJ gave a husky guilty sigh. "Sorry I didn't ask where. Before."

"Well. We had, y'know, other things to talk about. My period and all. And did you—when I left so fast—did you say you hoped I *was*— pregnant?"

"That moment, yeah. I wanted you pregnant. Anchored down, with me."

"Mmm." Alice straightened, determined to show some spine. "But listen, JJ. I—I have to tell you—well. I don't know how to start." She twisted the phone cord. "When you burned that, that wrapping paper last night, I saw—"

"Words?" She heard JJ begin to pace, a faint linoleum creak. "Christ, Al. Those words. I've been wishing all morning I'd told you. . . ."

"What?" She twisted her cord harder, studying Sticks's gunmetal gray desktop. Its galactic mass of scratches.

"It, the paper. Yeah, there was a note on it. In pencil. From Kin."

"Why'd you keep it *secret*?" Alice released the cord so it unsprung spastically. "I *saw* the words, *thought* I saw the words when it burned—"

"Ah shit, Allie. I knew you might've. And I wanted to tell you but I didn't want to get you all worked up about something that's. Long gone, for me. . . ."

"Then how come Kin sent you your hair? And wha'd it say, JJ—that note?"

He cleared his throat. A morning throat in the afternoon. "It was— an invitation. To a wedding. Today, in—" He hesitated. "Queens."

"New York?"

"New York."

"*Kin's* wedding?" Allie's voice felt loud in this small office. "Hers?"

"Kin's wedding, yeah." JJ's robotic monotone, used for strategic re- treats. "But look. It wasn't anything I was going to answer."

I'll say, Allie thought. She pressed her hand over the scratches in Sticks's desk, fine indentations. As JJ went on, his low voice speeding up, she pictured Sticks doodling away madly with a knife.

". . . that note. Just forget it, Al. It isn't anything that'll affect us, just some crazy impulse of Kin's." JJ drew an uneven breath, as if catching his balance. "I know this seems strange to you; I know we can usually talk things out, but. This is—different." He sounded almost afraid now, at least to her ears: practiced at deciphering his monotone, its shades of gray like a shifting Ohio sky. Its thundercloud undertone today. "That note, my hair. It's just—who knows? Kin wanting to get rid, maybe. Of this last piece of me—"

"Oh?" The desk's metal scratches formed an etching of JJ, spinning so fast he'd spun apart: his hair, his limbs. All those beloved pieces of him. "But listen, JJ. There's—something I have to ask you about Kin—"

"I *said*—" JJ cut in so loudly she pulled the receiver away from her ear. "Forget this; forget Kin."

And he hung up. The dial tone buzzed but Alice pressed the receiver back to her ear, not believing JJ had actually—for the first time—hung up on her. The plastic receiver vibrated with its insistent buzz.

Something I have to, she'd started to say. *Tell you, man,* she thought as she hung up herself. She blinked down at the blood-dark stains on her skirt, remembering the hesitant, softly confidential way Kin had said those words. *Something I'll have to. Tell you, man.*

"Break's up, baby doll." Vi shouldered open the office door, her arms full of brown-bag lunches. A school-cafeteria smell of peanut butter and jelly. "Sticks say you gotta come feed Eric and—" She cut herself off as Alice looked up. Vi stared as if Alice were in—but Alice blinked them back—tears.

"OK, I—I'm coming." Standing up, Allie avoided Vi's sympathetic gaze. She steadied herself against the desk, feeling sure—only now had she connected her fears to the message's specific words—what a man named Sister Kin might "have to" tell a man he'd loved. A man he might've seen secretly in recent years, Allie thought as she stepped from behind Sticks's desk. For all I know.

"Say," Vi told her in a lower voice, her tooth winking. "Want me t' feed Eric this time? It gets plenty messy. . . ."

"No, might's well be me," Alice answered with a shaky smile. "Seeing how I'm already—" She glanced again at her grape-stained skirt. "—in it."

5

I Had to Be You

"Kin?"

Bird, the bride, opened the door quietly. Her crew-cut head felt as light as her stomach. Her swollen eyelids still burned; Kin's floor seemed to burn too, black-and-white squares shimmering. In her first deep, steadying breath, she tasted a trace of the party she hoped was over. Cigarettes, chocolate fondue, sweaty cologne. A bachelor party, Kin had told her: the bachelors all old acquaintances. And were any, she wondered yet again, Kin's ex- or would-be lovers? Bird dropped her heavy travel bag.

"Sister Kin?" As she shut the door, plastic flapped. His Pan Am steward's uniform hung on the door: a lipstick sign taped to the dry cleaner's wrap. *Fly for Free*. Bird clenched the key Kin had given her years before. A grainy lipstick arrow pointed jauntily toward Kin's now-silent front room. She turned. Leftover party smoke blurred her first sight of him.

"Sister Kin," she whispered when his body solidified. He lay sprawled in black on the white leather couch he'd inherited, fallen as if from the spinning dance he and Jimmy Joe used to do. His black shoulder-length hair fanned over his face. In his arched throat, his Adam's apple—one clue to his sex—bobbed. Kin said she was but really, Bird thought now, he was the one. The beauty.

She swallowed, tasting her sour teeth. Kin's air conditioner chugged in the sunny window, the air humming like inside a plane. Bird took two steps, her knees wobbly from her flight. Party wreckage crackled. She gave the room a quick hard look. Crumpled napkins printed with a '50s movie poster: *Bachelor Party*. Plastic cups, ten or so, a few showing thick pink lip prints. A paper-towel banner sagging over the kitchenette sink: *Kin Hwang, BACHELOR BRIDE*.

A video box stood propped on the VCR beside Kin's couch: Karen Valentine in *Coffee, Tea or Me?* Solemnly, Bird faced the altarlike shelves that housed Kin's 428 cassette tapes. The most portable form of music, he maintained, always traveling with his Walkman. Bird fingered his oldest tape, unmarked. Only she knew it contained Don Ho singing "Beautiful Kauai." A secret tape Kin had listened to as a boy, just as he'd secretly avidly watched *Hawaii Five-O*, picturing a combination of Don Ho and Jack Lord as his own unknown half-Hawaiian father. Bird glanced at the dustier upper shelves holding the tapes from 1980—Ziggy Stardust, Javanese gamelan—that she never touched.

"Ber-ta," Kin murmured, sounding half asleep. "You there?"

"Not yet." She looked over her shoulder, her ears feeling cold and exposed. A photo hung above the couch: herself at fourteen in Kin's mom's velvet evening gown, too loose, dramatically black behind the clean sweep of Bird's hair, so blond it photographed white. "Gimme a minute." She stepped over Kin's vinyl Pan Am bag and pushed the bathroom door. As it shut, another hangerful of clothes flapped. Nervously, Bird met her own pink-rimmed eyes.

"Oh, man." She slid down the tile, sat with an air-jarring pop. Shifting, she lifted a broken rubber skin, cheery yellow. Condom balloons.

"Hey, Bird?" Kin sounded half awake now. "'S on the door," he called out, meaning—she stood—their outfits. They'd bought them at a shop called Unisex. White linen: elegantly simple shirts and pants. Loose fitting, freshly pressed.

Bird peeled off her T-shirt, her elbows bumping the small bathroom's walls. Bare-breasted, she bent over Kin's sink, opened his cabinet. She unscrewed the Listerine cap, shaky-fingered as a drunk. After that time with Stepdad, she'd downed half a bottle. Fasting, she lived on Listerine. It burned her sore gums. Gingivitis, Kin said she had, and he was always after her to see a dentist. He'd taken her to her first dentist years before, in Boston when they were teenagers. The first time they'd run away together. She swished and spat.

Banging shut the cabinet, she re-faced its mirror. Can't wait to *see* you, Kin had told her. When her latest Would-Be Lover said "see" like that, he meant kiss or paw. Kin meant "see," study lovingly. Especially today, maybe, with her new boyish hair? Bird squinted. Only a prickle of her lashes remained. Good. She turned to the hangers. Her nipples, always flat, tingled with chill.

Or with the nearness—Bird wondered in singsong—of Kin? Of Jimmy Joe too? She shivered. With the prospect of Kin seeing her, for once, as a boy.

"I'm chang-ing," she called to him, giddy as an actress. Her short-nailed fingers peeled away the plastic. Surely Jimmy Joe won't show, she told herself, slipping into the cool linen. The man-tailored shirt, the pants loose as a skirt.

"See?" Bird opened the door. Silently, she vowed not to be the first to mention Jimmy Joe. She drew a breath, her mouth scoured. "I, the bride."

Lazily graceful as his mom's long-dead Siamese cats, Kin rolled over, stretching his arms. His black sleeves slid down, his inner elbow hinged with a Band-Aid creased as if it'd been there for weeks. Bird stared, her chest hollowing out. How could she have pushed those words from her mind? Blood, love.

"My bride?" Kin's eyes opened: almond slits, brimming with lacquered black. "Berta Bird!" He sat up, focusing on her shorn head. "Hey now: Mia Farrow, just like I said. *Rosemary's Baby* goes punk. Perfect."

He'd always advised her to shear her hair, show off her bones. But couldn't he see what she meant to look like? She stood still, her heart suspended.

"Lord, Birdy." Kin shuffled over to her. Even sleepy, his face with its inverted-V eyebrows and sharp cheekbones looked alert, foxlike. Lightly, as if dabbing a tear, he touched the corner of her lashless left eye. "Why?"

Bird studied Kin's wideset eyes, his thickly folded eyelids barely fringed. "To match you, groom."

Kin sighed, gin on his breath. He lowered his hand to her shoulder, steadying her. His voice Carolina soft. "Didn't it—doesn't it—hurt, love?"

She took hold of Kin's elbow, her thumb pressing his Band-Aid to let him know she'd seen it. "Yep." Through the air conditioner, she began her own hum, shyly: their words, whisper-sung. "I had to be you, I had to be you-ou. . . ."

They swayed, Kin pulling her close. "Slow-dancing's too fast," he breathed. "Let's *still*-dance." As they stopped swaying, Bird rested against Kin.

"Hey." She slipped one hand into the V-neck of his black batiste shirt, onto his smooth chest. Her fingers stopped short at his nipples. "I want no hair too, like you. For our beaches. So let's—y'know, what we do for strapless?"

"Wax you." Kin tilted his head at Bird in her white shirt. "This." He fingered her shorn hair. "Has to be black. If we're gonna match." He stepped away to rummage in his bathroom. "Think I've got some quickie spray-dye—"

She faced the half-open bathroom door. Now, when she couldn't see Kin's face, she felt brave enough to ask: "So what's the—plan?"

"Welll," he began, as if they were dressing up for a night out at Crisis

Café. "Here's the scoop. County courthouse at one. Where—we see if he shows. Even if he didn't RSVP, ol' Jimmy Joe might still show." The medicine cabinet clicked. Bird shut her prickly eyes, amazed Kin could say that name so casually.

" 'Course, we tie the knot either way. Oops." Bottles clanked. "Then—how's this for high drama? *Before* we take off for New Haven or for parts unknown, we swing by the Pubic Health Center—" He laughed. Slipping the "l" from "Public" was a joke too feeble to be his own. "And get the results of my . . ."

"Test," Bird filled in, her whole mouth dry. "Blood test."

"Here." The clanking halted; Kin's voice rose. "Ebony Tresses—"

Bird braced her knees, half hoping for a faint. When they'd found out New York state didn't require blood tests for marriage, she hadn't believed Kin would go through with one anyway, alone. At long last.

"Got it done, Berta. A special rush job. Know it's kinda crazy, but I timed it for our wedding day. So Jimmy Joe could come along to hear the verdict." Kin swept out, balancing the wax box and dye bottle. "So." He arranged them on his kitchenette table, his hands never shaky. "We leave in forty minutes. 12:30 sharp." He glanced over his towel-draped shoulder. "Berta?"

Stepping up to her quickly, he gripped her arms. That's how she knew she was swaying. "Sit." She did, her pulse thick in her throat. Kin alone always discovered her fasts. "Eat." Kin shoved back the box and set down his mother's gold fondue bowl, half full of melted chocolate. "How much, today?"

"Just ginger ale, on the plane."

Kin opened the fridge, clanked a can onto the table. "You need sugar, now. Start with this." He began unpacking the wax box. Red letters on the Jolt soda can swam in front of her. *Real Sugar and Twice the Caffeine!* Too rushed for his usual grace, Kin clattered a pan onto his compact stove. Obediently, Bird sipped, bubbles exploding on her tongue. "I can't eat either, y'know." Kin knotted his towel around her neck, tight. "Not today, not last night." He began working cool goop into her hair with his deft tense fingers. "So."

"So." Bird's neck stayed stiff. "Who all was here?"

"Ohh, some steward-esses: Izzy and Steve and George T. Poor George. The late Shawn T.'s brother—?"

Bird looked at her knees, remembering that funeral: Shawn T.'s unshaven corpse in his XTC T-shirt.

"And Big Boyd from baggage. Boyd's gonna be our witness."

"What?" Bird straightened. She'd pictured only the two of them.

"Our Best Man." Abruptly, Kin released her head. "Who'd you *think* we'd get?" He shook the spray can, the ball going wildly. "Jimmy Joe Wolfe?"

"Yeah, right. Like he's gonna show."

"I'm not so sure he won't. Not sure you're so sure, either."

"Me?" She shut her eyes. Eight years before, the unspoken question she'd felt charging the air between them had been: Who was the one JJ really loved? Then, after JJ left, it had become: Who loved JJ, still? "*You're* the one who's carried round that picture JJ took of us in bed."

"C'mon, Berta Bird. You're the one who's kept and braided and who knows what-all-else his hair all these years."

In a fizzy whoosh, Kin misted her hair with dark spray. Its metallic scent mixed with the melting wax. "Not to mention his jacket. Our jacket. Where *is* it, anyhow? I asked you to carry it, not let the baggage brutes maul it. . . ."

Bird wiped her face with the towel. Kin replaced the spray cap, hard.

"Well." She took a stinging sip of Jolt. Kin lifted his double boiler. And Bird slipped off her linen pants, draping them carefully over a chair. "You know that boy? The one who was following me in the Boston airport?"

"Mmm." Kin knelt as she sat. In the pan, softened wax strips lay like lasagna noodles. He pressed one hot onto her lower leg. "Did you do what I said? To get rid of him?" Wax tightened, tugging hairs. "Belch? Scratch your ass?"

"I went a little—further." Bird balanced the cold Jolt can on her bony, square-cut knee. Her mother had often balanced shot glasses on her knees.

"You don't mean—?" He smoothed the paper backing off the moist wax, caressing her calve. "Your eyelashes? You cut 'em off in front of this boy?"

"In the Logan Airport bathroom. The MEN'S room. Wanted to see if he'd follow me in. He, the boy, thought I was—I *think* he thought—a boy too. In that big jacket with my new hair and all. I was perfect 'cept for my mascara."

"*Really?*" Kin arched his feathery V-shaped brows.

"Then, well—" Her Jolt can tipped, clattering to the floor. "Sorry." Bird's vision blurred and she reached up to rub her eyelids.

"No." Kin touched her wrist. "Lemme get something for those eyes." He stepped over the fizzing Jolt puddle. His bathroom cabinet squealed. Her nurse: ever since she'd run to him from Stepdad, the Vega. She never did learn to drive.

"Hey," she called out, bending to apply more wax strips. "Where're we flying? Tonight, after New Haven? I mean, if we even wind up going there."

"Thought you said it could be a surprise. Long as it's someplace hot." Kin emerged, holding a tube of sty ointment. "Our marriage'll be the opposite of most. Nonstop surprises. I've got weeks of vacation time and plenty of Free-Fly Points. *I* thought we'd start by hopping a late JFK flight to Puerto Rico—?"

He cupped the back of her head, starting to smear sty ointment on her eyelid. His fingers felt cold—a shock—and Bird took hold of his wrist.

"I want," she told him, lowering his hand. "To go farther."

Kin let her take the greasy tube. He sat back on his heels, watching her squeeze it. Lightly, she smeared her own lids. Slumping, Kin watched as she peeled the wax off her own legs. With each strip, she winced. Could her stubby eyelashes be peeled off? she wondered, dropping flesh-colored wax curls.

"Y'know." Kin studied that wax as if it reminded him of something. "We could—just go. Straight from the wedding to the airport . . ."

"I'm packed," Bird whispered, getting it in without breaking his flow.

"Could head straight for New Haven. Could skip the whole, y'know—"

"Maybe we should skip New Haven too." Bird stood, slipping her towel off her shoulders. Her legs were stinging. "I don't want us running after him."

"You don't mean that." Kin pulled himself up. Startling her, he reached to his highest cassette shelf. He blew dust off a tape. "You want to see him too."

Bird looked down, letting Kin think that was true. She wasn't sure if it was, but—she told herself as Kin popped the tape into his boom box—Kin wanted to think so. Didn't he? The opening note of a Shakuhachi sounded; Bird hugged her arms hard. Perfect make-out music, Kin used to say of the Shakuhachi. Because each bamboo flute note was held excruciatingly long.

Above the first pure tone, Bird heard Kin pull off his shirt and pants. She heard light cloth drop to the floor. In the first achingly extended pause between notes, she raised her eyes. Kin was naked now, hugging himself like her. His arms firm from all his swimming. He swayed to the next slowly rising note. His jaw moved with the odd chewing motion that meant he couldn't speak. Picturing naked Jimmy Joe, Bird moved her eyes over Kin's body. Lean as a whippet, free of soft flesh: except for his cock, pillowed by amber-gray balls.

Still hugging himself, Kin pivoted on his heel and padded to the bathroom. As he showered, Bird slipped her pants over her smooth sore legs. Flute notes wound around her body: a moist, intimate sound of breath on bamboo. She remembered the piece, its translated title: "Deer Calling to One Another." And she remembered too, as she could usually stop herself from doing, gentle Jimmy Joe. The one man besides Sister Kin who never seemed to her to be just—a man.

"Ta-da!" Kin filled the bathroom doorway like light. The neatly tailored white linen set off the suntan he planned to darken. Bird smiled. Kin bent, his hair brushing the floor. He lifted a strip of wax. Bird's hairs stuck out of what looked, under the kitchen lights, like waxed flesh. Another breathy pause stretched out on the Shakuhachi tape. Bird stepped closer, blinking at the hairy wax Kin studied, remembering Shawn T.'s funeral, Shawn's waxed face, one-day unshaven according to his own burial instructions.

"XTC," Kin murmured. He balled up the wax, turning from Bird, his bag bumping her hip. With his black slippered foot, he kicked aside a bachelor-party napkin. Then, before the flute could sound again, he flipped off his boom box. He shut down the air conditioner. "Let's just—" He stepped toward the door. Bird followed, finishing for him loudly above the air conditioner's dwindling hum.

"Go."

·　·　·

Big Boyd, too, wore white. His fluorescent-lit shirt and chino pants magnified his huge-bellied body and darkened his rich brown skin. He rose lightly from a wooden bench. Too fat, Bird decided with quick cruel relief, to ever have been Kin's lover. Shimmering in her gaze, Boyd stepped toward them down the courthouse hall, his body giving a slight pert sway. Besides, Bird reminded herself, taking Kin's arm: Kin always told her Jimmy Joe had been his single experience with what he called, mockingly, Love, American Style.

"Our best man!" Kin called out, his eyes darting up and down the hall.

Before 1980, Kin had met his lovers during overseas business trips with his mother. Taiwan, Seoul. Then, after Boston and JJ, Kin had signed on with Pan Am. In 1981, his first year as a steward, giddy at having found what he wanted to do—fly!—Kin had traveled from man to man. Brazil to Hong Kong to Mexico. Picking up bits of each man's food and music and language. Fooling around with fellow stewards on what he called AC/DC 10s. Freed from rainy old Boston where Bird lived, hid, mourned JJ. Or so Kin claimed. But Bird felt she heard through the staticky gaps of Kin's transcontinental phone calls how much he missed JJ, too. Or was it only, as Kin professed, that he missed her? He talked, really talked, only to Bird: saved up all his day's words for her as she did for him.

Now, Bird fixed her eyes on Kin, scared to look for herself. As his eyes stopped flickering, she knew that the hall was empty. JJ—their gentle giant, the Master of the Fast Fade—hadn't shown.

"Ah, the brides!" Boyd floated to a stop under the Deeds and Records sign. Behind the frosted-glass windows, computer printers clattered. Women giggled.

"Hi." Bird tightened her hold on Kin's arm as if entering a new bar.

"I." Boyd bent to Bird like a polite grown-up. "—am 'Big Boyd'." He inserted invisible quotation marks onto his words.

"I'm R-Roberta Olaf," she managed. Boyd's orange-brown eyes met hers, narrowing like the eyes of drag queens in bars when they realized she was real.

"So-oh, Sister Kin . . ." Boyd's tiger-eyed glance took in Kin's glossy black hair, then Bird's stiffly dyed crew cut. "You two aren't related somehow?"

"Blood sisters," Bird murmured, covering Kin's silence.

"Blood?" Boyd straightened; his T-shirt showed tiny words: *a big joke.*

"Not *really.*" Kin gave a quick dismissive laugh. "She means we took a knife, long time ago, and did the whole 'Boy Scout/blood oath' scene . . ."

"Hey." Bird turned to Kin so fast she wobbled.

Kin steadied her. "You need to sit or—?"

"Come on," she told him impatiently. Boyd floated backward. Bird and Kin lifted their bags and walked past the clattering windows to two doors. There, by the water fountain, Kin whispered: "Don't tell Boyd what we're doing. *After.*"

"You know I'd never," she answered in an equally tense whisper.

"Or about Jimmy Joe. Who's still got five minutes, by the way."

"Ha." Bird turned to the LADIES' room. Inside the stall, trembling, she dug into her overstuffed bag and slipped her notebook from her jeans pocket.

Can't you see, she scrawled, bearing down so the metal wall shuddered. *I WANT us Blood Sisters? WANT you mine for better or worst. Can't you see I left JJ's jacket behind 'cause he left us? For Good, he said or don't you remember?*

She stuffed the book back into her bag. Maybe she'd scribble out that last part. She stood with a lurch, her head light. How could she be mean to Kin today? When that looming test must be making him mock, nervously, what they were about to do? In the smeared mirror, she confronted her new black-haired self. Defiantly—Screw you, JJ; we do fine without you—she raised her chin so her slanted cheekbones matched Kin's. She thought of Boyd's dainty walk.

Kin liked people who moved beyond—Bird shouldered through the LADIES' door, cowboy style—their assigned bodies. She glanced around the hall.

"He's not out yet," Boyd told her. Not referring to JJ, Bird reminded herself. She sat on the wood bench scarred like an old-fashioned school desk.

"So." Boyd crossed one leg, brushing hers. "Sister Kin outdid himself last night. Cooking-wise." He shook his head. "Days I've been too down to shop properly, Kin's come over and whipped up feasts for me from nearly nothing."

"That's Kin." Bird shot a glance at MEN'S, searching for a word. "Resourceful. How—how long've you known him?"

"Couple years," Boyd told her. "Not that any of us 'knows' Kin all that well. Him being so . . . off to himself." Bird gave a stiffly hopeful nod. *Had* Kin been a Flying Nun? Always telling her how lonely he got nowadays, traveling.

"And how long've you known Kin?"

"Oh . . ." Bird gripped her knees. In high school, on dates, she'd made boys drop her at Kin's house. By far the most fun part: her and Kin's talk afterward, as freewheeling as she imagined postsex talk must be. As freewheeling as their transcontinental phone calls years later, Sister Kin telling her everything back then, in wild '81, '82, '83. Bird studied her knuckles. "Always."

Boyd yawned behind his hand as if politely bored. "How romantic."

A door whooshed open. Bird looked up fast, thinking it must be Jimmy Joe. But it was MEN'S. Kin's voice broke the hall's hush. "Here comes the bride . . ."

He glided toward them, his face dramatic above his plain white linen. His eyes darted around the hall. At Bird's mute answer—No JJ—he fixed on Boyd.

"Is it too much?" he asked Boyd. You know it is, Bird answered silently. Made up, Kin's face parodied a Sister face: his eyes lined, his mouth darkly lipsticked. Not at all his usual subtle bar-night style. Love That Red.

"Love-ly!" With a fat-man's laugh, Boyd rose. The Justice of Peace door burst open. Led by a boy-groom with a cowlick, a wedding party emerged. Asian girls in summer pastels. Wind-chime giggles joined Boyd's booming laugh.

"We're getting married too!" Boyd rested his hands on Kin and Bird's shoulders. The groom's glasses magnified his eyes; his mouth earnestly smiled. "Or they are, I should say. Honeymooning around the world!"

"A nonstop honeymoon," Kin chimed in. "Nothing old, nothing blue, nothing borrowed, everything new! That's all we want: nonstop new!"

The girls giggled melodiously. Kin slipped from Boyd's side and stepped up to the shortest girl, the one in the palest pink. Suddenly, clearly the bride. Bending, more serious now, Kin offered a few angular-sounding words of his dead mother's Cantonese. The bride's pink mouth shaped an apologetic smile.

Not the same dialect, Bird guessed, knowing from Kin that Chinese had more variations than Westerners imagined. Kin made a harshly consonanted syllable of regret. The bride stopped smiling; her eyes magnified like her husband's as she stared at Kin's lipstick. Luckily, another wave of mirth swept her sisters, swept them all down the hall with bright-eyed backward glances.

"Bride Time, you two." Boyd ducked Kin's swat. His laugh herded them through the doorway. "Da-dum Da-da! Here come the brides—"

From his lectern, the stocky judge watched with an impassive Edward G. Robinson face. Only a twitch of his liver brown lips betrayed annoyance. Seen it all, his sigh told a busy silver-haired woman seated behind a counter. Their second witness. Boyd and Kin were laughing loudly; Bird studied the linoleum, gray like the hall's but softened by this room's slightly less harsh light.

"Ready, y'r Honor," Kin told the judge, his voice climbing again in pitch. "Ready to get married or—as my mom used to say—'marred.'"

Stop, Bird was thinking as Kin rummaged in his bag. Stop camping this up. He presented the paperwork they'd completed weeks before. They'd set the date back in July, choosing it because of its 8s, because it'd give Jimmy Joe a chance to decide if he'd come. Or it would've, if Kin had mailed the invitation on time.

"You here and you here." Smelling of years of cigars, the judge touched their shoulders to arrange them. His subway-veteran gaze caught briefly on Bird's numb-lidded eyes. Then he stepped back behind the fake-wood lectern.

"Gathered this day in the presence of these witnesses—"

Bird's heels pressed the floor. Her head grew lighter as the judge's Edward G. Robinson voice rumbled forward, rising with a question.

A pause opened up. "Just one," Kin mumbled, reaching into his pants pocket. "See?" He drew out his hand like a magician and opened his palm.

It shone dully, still. The solder ring Jimmy Joe had made for her back in Mass. Mental. Pewter-colored metal twisted into intertwined 8s like the 8s Bird used to ink on her arms. She could barely gasp. Kin must've stolen it years before from her Boston trash basket. Rescued it.

"—the ring on her finger and repeat after me."

Bird's eyes burned as Kin slid the ring past her knuckle. It fit loosely, as always. She blinked, releasing a few hot tears. Kin looked away, his mouth tightened as if in distaste. In all their years together, she'd never seen Kin cry.

"Do you, Kin Hwang." The judge fixed his gaze on Kin's tense, made-up face. Bird watched Kin too as the judge muttered words too familiar to hear.

"—long as you both shall live?" He flatly addressed the question to the space between their heads. Bird's stomach fizzed, way beyond empty.

"I do," Kin answered in a breathy voice that brought a soft snort from Boyd.

"And do you, Roberta Olaf, take Kin Hwang—"

Bird seized Kin's arm, remembering the day he'd finally read her diary. She'd made him promise to tell no one just as Stepdad in his Vega had made her promise. Then she and Kin had sworn their blood oath. Kin had held his prized Swiss Army knife. Their smarting, freshly sliced fingers had pressed together, their open cuts joined in a kiss. A real kiss, Bird had thought.

"Berta?" Kin stiffened his arm, holding her up. Here with her, again. Wasn't he always, even when they were thousands of miles apart? Weren't the words inside her head always addressed to him?

"I . . ." Bird began. Kin's Adam's apple bobbed below his lipsticked-shut mouth. How many times had that apple filled the hollow of her throat: more satisfying—she'd come to feel, at least before JJ—than any kiss? "I do."

Kin's arm relaxed. The judge rushed the last part. "Power vested-in-me by th' state o' New York, I pronounce-you-husband-and-wife, you may—"

Big Boyd poked Kin from behind. Wan under his makeup, Kin turned to Bird. His black eyes glittered, scared and separate from his smirking mouth. His Love That Red lips puckered, ready to plant a showy lipstick kiss on her cheek. Stop, Bird thought, and she leaned in faster. Her mouth opened.

Clumsily, her teeth bit his taut flesh, aiming at his Adam's apple. His throat tasted warm and salty to her hungry tongue. Her lips sucked, her eyes shutting against the fluorescent spin of the room and the startled cough of the judge and the hole that should've held Jimmy Joe. Kin's Adam's apple bobbed between her teeth like a real apple in water. Her lips held on as she sucked harder.

"Buh—" Kin was sputtering. Red-veined black pulsed inside Bird's eyelids. Kin's fingers dug into her upper arms. With a wet suction-cup *ffwup,* she was wrenched back. Only as Kin's widened eyes met hers did she realize what she'd wanted. Only as she licked her wetly smeared lips did she realize she hadn't quite drawn it, his blood.

"Berta?" Kin touched the wet spot on his throat. A raw, bruised pink. Kin's pulse jumped there and she felt hers jump too. The only sound. Around them, the judge and Boyd and the pen-scratching woman had been struck dumb.

"C'mon." Kin re-gripped her shoulders. He hustled her to the door. The judge held it for them, his liver-lips parted. Bird leaned on Kin, wishing she'd reached the weightless rush of a faint. The secret reward for her fasts.

Once when he'd told her how it felt for him to come, Kin had described that same buoyant bodiless sensation, as if his bones and veins filled with air. Oh yes, Bird had answered so eagerly they both knew he'd put into words what JJ did for her. Maybe "coming," they'd agreed, oughta be called "going."

Together, they staggered forward. The hall stretched empty before them.

"Here come the brides," Boyd shouted, rallying to fill that space.

Over Kin's shoulder, Bird saw Boyd dig into his chino pocket and hoist out a Baggie of rice. His handfuls skittered like frozen rain behind them.

"Umph." Kin bucked open the exit door. Bird drew a breath of teeming street smells. Warm air swelled with teenage-boy voices. "Whoa, take-a look!"

Leaning on each other, Bird and Kin descended the brick steps two by two. "Whoo-whoo!" a boy catcalled as Big Boyd hailed a cab. Hurriedly, Bird and Kin piled into the rumbling backseat. "So long, Sister." Boyd shoved their bags beside them, bending over Bird's lap to shake Kin's hand. Then, with bulky grace, he backed onto the curb amidst three hopping hooting boys.

"Chill, my men." Boyd slammed the cab door. In the rearview, a white boy poked Boyd's arm. But Big Boyd floated out of view, refusing to speed his steps.

"Where for?" The driver unrolled the softened Rs of an Arabic accent.

"W-well." Bird leaned up to the scratched plastic shield, feeling Kin slump behind her. "We can't decide between Puerto Rico, New Haven—"

"Air-poor?" The driver demanded. A siren spiraled. Bird listened to it.

"Public Health Center," Kin told the driver in his real voice, low and nasal. He mumbled a number. As the cab shot from the curb, Bird sank onto their seat.

"You were right; he didn't show." Kin fingered her hickey on his neck, his sleeve vibrating with the cab's speed. "Why'd you leave behind his jacket? What're we gonna tell Jimmy Joe 'bout our bomber jacket?"

"Jimmy Joe? You don't think he'll show at Ko No's—do you?"

"Me?" Kin kept fingering his neck. "*I* think. He'll guess from my phone message I've, y'know. Had the test. And you know Jimmy Joe needs to know—"

"He doesn't! You don't either! We could turn round now: head for the airport, for Puerto Rico or where-*ever*—"

"No, Berta." Kin let his hand flop to his lap, his voice suddenly harsher. "Y'know, you wouldn't really wanna swallow my blood. Not if you knew—" He wiped his face, then stared at the pasty glisten of sweat and blush powder. "What it's like." A pothole bump, their shoulders knocking. "In me, just now."

Kin wiped his fingers on his white sleeve, leaving a pinkish brown stain. As he faced the streaming-forward street, Bird felt he alone was setting off on a journey. "But." To Bird's own ears, her voice sounded childish, tiny against the traffic clamor. "I want to—" The cab halted at a light. Know, she couldn't say.

Kin answered as solemnly as she'd wanted him to take his vow. "You don't."

His glossy head slid down. Unused to being the one to offer comfort, Bird wrapped an arm around his shoulders. Their bodies bumped as the cab jerked forward. Hectic brick walls jounced by. Kin slid lower, resting on Bird's breast. His breath felt hot through her linen. For a speeding thrumming moment, Bird cupped his head, pleased to feel him so weak.

"Peru, Bolivia," she whispered. "Brazil, Mexico, Hong *Kong*, China—"

"Uh?" The driver's dark eyes filled the rearview, fixing on them a familiar disapproving gaze. The Ameri-stare they'd soon escape. Wouldn't they? Through her shirt, Bird felt Kin's sticky makeup washing off in his sweat. He was ruining two fine linen shirts and not even noticing. This simple fact made Bird's heart begin to pound with dread. A beige concrete building stretched into view. *Public Hell*, the shimmering iron sign seemed to read as they glided by.

But he saved people, Bird found herself thinking, telling someone. Yes: Kin had herded passengers off a 727 that caught fire on the runway in San Juan, shoving them down the yellow evacuation slide that burned his own butt—from the speed, he said—when he too finally jumped ship. A dozen injuries, no deaths. The cab shuddered to a halt, blocking a traffic lane. No parking spaces.

"Four dollar fifty," the driver announced. A horn honked behind them, splitting air. Bird's ears flattened as it hit the pitch Kin's voice had inched toward all day. The keening pleading pitch of a scream.

Kin kept his face pressed to her breast. Bird felt the driver turn in his seat, felt people on the sidewalk glance at their cab. Her left hand clenched around her 8s. Once they escaped America and its prying eyes, they'd meld into—Kin'd said this about her and JJ and himself—one whole. A country all our own, she thought as the horn shifted to an even higher pitch. Kin raised his head, leaving a sweat smudge on her shirt. His eyes clear, dry. He locked his stare with hers the way he'd done years before, in the stunned moment after they'd ground their bloody fingertips together.

6

Previous Partners

In the sheltered doorway to Ko No's, Alice deflated her bubble umbrella. She bowed her head so as not to wet her hurriedly applied makeup. Rain had slowed the bus and she was late: 5:15 by now. Ko No's door, a faded salmon pink, displayed in fresher paint a vertical row of slashing black ideograms. Unreadable. Allie leaned her rubber shoulder between two. The heavy door and steady beat of rain both gave way. Ducking, she slipped into darkness. The door whooshed shut, the rain patter replaced by a sound of wild frying.

Alice squinted through yellowish smoky air. Hand-painted rice-paper banners hung over splintery wood paneling. Six high-backed booths flanked an unmanned Raw Bar. Its shelves held not bottles but cardboard photos of oysters and luridly orange fish eggs. Two women perched on bar stools, a plate of oysters between them. Both wore loose white outfits that even in this murky fried-food light gave off the glow of good cloth. Allie inched forward.

One slumped: shorter but with broader shoulders and fine straight black hair. The other—fragile looking, with delicate bony shoulders— held her head higher, her black hair chopped in a crew cut. Oils popped and spattered.

Alice's feet scraped sawdust. In the dim Old West–style mirror above the bar, she made out their faces. The long-haired one's was severely downcast, staring at the oyster plate as if about to be sick in it. A striking Asian face: wideset eyes; pointy brows; strong cheekbones; flat nose; wide sly mouth, lips oddly darkened. A man, Alice told herself, her whole-body heartbeat slowing.

Her feet slid into another sawdust step, her eyes sliding to the second face. Paler, finer-boned. Shadowy eyes fixed on the mirror, unsettling like the eyes Allie'd seen the day Helping Hands sent her to a school for the blind.

She halted. As the short-haired one glanced over her shoulder, her— clearly *her*—head turned on a slender neck, tendons standing out. Her hair bristly like fur. Alice ducked into a booth, her umbrella bumping the table. She felt those pale eyes scan the room like Channel 8's camera. From the next booth, she heard the polite click of chopsticks.

"You want—?"

Allie startled, staring up at the woman in white. No: at a black-haired short-haired waiter. "You order—?"

"Oysters," She stabbed a blurry picture on the placemat menu.

Leaving her raincoat on, she peeked over the high wood seat back. The woman in white was touching the slumped shoulder of the man in white. He looked down at a few smudges marring his sleeve. She murmured, soft halting tones. Under her loose linen shirt, a round breast curve showed.

Wispy thin, except for her breasts. Exactly how JJ had described the Mass. Mental woman who'd registered as "Kin." An Asian-sounding name, JJ had added; now here she sat with an Asian man. The woman nudged the untouched oyster plate toward him. Allie drew a breath, smelling fresh oysters. And she gave a confused glance to a plate set before her. Distractedly, she lifted a crusty shell and slurped a cool teeming mouthful, swallowed the oyster whole.

Hearing a low murmur—the man's?—she twisted back around. The man in white gave a heavy-headed nod. Abruptly, the woman lifted an oyster shell, her bone-thin wrist weighed down by its meat. She stared at the man till he hoisted his own shell. In the mirror, their faces bowed. Ceremonially, they slurped.

The man's dark lips contorted, his mouth clearly holding the oyster, whole. Beside him, the woman swallowed, wincing as if it hurt. She bent double on her stool. To spit it out? Allie craned her neck, exposing her face. The woman hoisted a travel bag from the floor. She touched the man's shoulder lightly, as if scared of toppling him. Then she stepped toward two back wall doors painted with lasso-rope script. COWGIRLS and COWBOYS.

The sizzling applause of kitchen oils surged. The COWGIRLS' door swung shut. Alice crept toward it, shooting a glance at the bar mirror. The black-haired man's face was still distorted. His mouth filled with unswallowed oyster?

Holding her oyster-cleansed breath, Alice pushed the bathroom door. It stopped halfway, bumping that travel bag. Water was running hard. The woman in white bent over the sink, splashing her face, her sleeves rolled up on startlingly thin arms. Alice poked only her head inside.

In Ohio, at college parties or at the disco, she'd met several of JJ's ex-lovers, what Jo'd call his Previous Partners, and always with the same charge of nerves. Half-frightened and half-erotic. Why are your hands trembling? one of the disco girls had asked her, distinctly flirtatious.

Alice braced her body. As if casually, she slipped behind the bent woman, her raincoat elbow brushing this woman's back. She splashed her face harder, droplets beading her chopped hair. In the mirror, Alice found her own face looking good despite bad light. Even applied on a bumpy bus, makeup made its difference. Liner held her nakedly curious eyes in place; a touch of pink brought out her lips and her cheekbone hollows, less dramatic than those of the woman in white. Allie narrowed her gaze. Her own heart-shaped face—delicate compared to most people's—suddenly looked fleshy, filled out.

Water faltered. Allie's eyes flickered to the bowed head: its black hair, dull as shoe polish. The roots white. Both faucets squealed off. *Hair so blond it looked white,* Allie remembered JJ saying as the woman straightened, her fine-boned face bare. Her swollen eyelids were open; her mouth was shut. Full lips of the kind Allie wanted, shaped like a cat's mouth.

The not-of-this-world type JJ fell for. At parties, Allie knew which girls JJ would talk to longest. Always a hush as JJ would meet their shy eyes. Now, pellucidly blue as the eyes of blind kids, the Kin woman's eyes met Allie's in the mirror. Blue surrounded by the bloodshot red of recent tears and the raw pink of her eyelids. No lashes. Their reflected gaze locked.

Girl A and Girl B, Allie thought, glancing back and forth. Girl A stood tall in her raincoat and makeup, her shoulder-length hair neatly brushed. Shorter by a head, Girl B looked stripped down, her nose crooked, her skull exposed by her crew cut. Her cat lips closed but for a triangular gap. Crooked teeth?

Alice whispered it, soft and clear. "Kin?"

Slowly, Girl B raised her left hand. Allie turned from the mirror and bent forward to see the ring. Dulled pewter gray metal twisted into interlinked 8s.

"JJ—" Allie gasped, seeing the woman's ring finger stiffen. "JJ made that!"

The Kin woman didn't move her head yet she seemed to nod. Awkwardly, like a Girl Scout, Allie thrust up her own left hand. Kin moved only her eyes to take in Allie's gold wedding band. Allie cracked a tentative smile. Kin's lips parted with her own quick startled smile: a knife flash of—yes—crooked teeth.

Eagerly, Allie turned to this woman JJ had described. Face-to-face felt more dangerous. Kin's pale intent eyes seemed pupilless. Kin formed her hushed words haltingly, like a Severely girl. "JJ—he—couldn't come. Him-self?"

Allie shook her head. Wanting to hide her husband from this woman's hungry stare. "No, no." Then, in an inspired rush, shocked by her own lie: "But he told me to come and—tell you that he just. Couldn't, Kin."

With another knife-flash of a smile, Kin elbowed Allie aside. She lifted her bag and banged into the stall. Its lock clanked. Allie heard a zipper unzip, then small pages flap. She watched the stall as if guarding it for her sister. Under her folded arms, she felt the thicker heartbeat she was getting used to, today.

Metal vibrated with sharp scratches. Kin bearing down against the locked door? A rip, a crumple, a minuscule splash: one paper ball dropped in the toilet. Alice hugged herself as it commenced again, more surely. Kin's tense pencil scratch. Tell her the truth, Alice told herself. Tell her you're here to find out who Kin is. The Asian man? She swallowed, tasting her oyster. Even if it wasn't her name, the woman in the stall fit the description of JJ's Kin, the "Kin" JJ had known in Mass. Mental. A Kin who seldom opened her lips.

Sweating in her raincoat, deciding that no, of course she wouldn't admit her own lie—wouldn't risk this woman telling JJ—Alice gripped her rubber arms. The lock clanked. The stall door swung so fast it clipped Alice's nose.

"Ow!" The door banged the tile wall; Allie pressed her hand to her stinging nose. No blood. Obliviously, Kin set down her unzipped travel bag. A plane ticket was wedged on top of her clothes. Pan Am. Kin bent, stuffing into the bag a pocket notebook. Allie's hands rose to stop the bathroom door should it swing. It could thump Kin, as kids said in Kentucky, upside tha head. But Kin straightened fast, her breasts bobbing. She creased a notebook page. This small rectangle she pressed into Allie's hand. *Jimmy Joe* was penciled on top.

Kin cleared her throat, a purr. Her words came out less halting, her voice more comfortable in whisper. "If ya tell him any-thing, tell him bye. For—be sure and say this part—for good."

"Me?" Alice blinked, her nose still stinging. Kin's blue eyes swam before her own, expanding as Kin stepped closer, looking up. Sci-fi eyes, JJ'd once said admiringly of some woman. Maybe he'd been thinking back to this woman. Her irises seemed lit by light that shone through her skin. Oyster on Kin's breath, too. Allie whispered, "You want me to give this to JJ?"

Kin rested her hands on Allie's shoulders. As if this were a perfectly natural thing to do, she leaned forward. Quickly, lightly, she brushed Allie's half-open lips with her own plush lips. A moist, shared taste of oyster.

Allie gasped; Kin bent fast for her bag. In the whoosh of the door, incredulously, Alice turned to the mirror. Mrs. Chancellor on the soap opera meeting the camera eye, as if to say, *What next?* The door was still swinging. Allie's thumb pressed JJ's note to her sweaty palm.

If she started to read it now, would Kin swoop back in? Allie stuffed the note into her raincoat pocket. As the door stopped swinging, she pushed it open again. Kin had resettled on her bar stool. Her straight back reminded Allie of certain high school girls in Kentucky, Girls Who Could Fight. Could, and would.

Allie slipped out of COWGIRLS, relieved to feel soupy darkness close back around her. She licked her own lips, the taste of Kin's oyster. Kin was touching again, gently, the shoulder of the black-haired man. Her new husband? Allie wondered, making a gritty sidestep. After all, JJ's hair had been wrapped in a wedding invitation. And these two were dressed up in white. Ready to tell JJ *something important*? Something now written in this note? The man slumped, resting his head on his folded arms like Carter. Kin twisted around on her stool. She shot Allie a burning blind-girl stare. Stay away, it said.

Groping in the smoky dark, Allie backed toward the door. She bumped one wood booth. The man in white raised his head. She heard his low nasal murmur, recognizing it. And she turned to the denser dark of the doorway. Leaving behind her bubble umbrella—leaving, for the first time in her life, without paying—Alice pushed out of Ko No's.

• • •

JJ—

See? No Kin.

Hear no

Kin

Touch no

Kin, no Bird neither.

No joke, Mr. Jim Joe. You didn't come & we won't. Come after you.

I mean: hasn't Kin always given you what you wanted? All ways?

And what that's now is: us gone. Kin kaput. Dearly departed.

Disappeared.

Round the world, we've decided to fly. For free, for real.

Departing today for parts (unlike yours) unknown.

See?
No. You don't, won't. Us again, ever.

Yours all ways
Any ways

Mrs. & Mrs. Kin

. . .

Allie's key jumped out of her hand, her whole ring clanking onto the wet sidewalk. A wiry brown man's hand picked it up, jingling it. "Thanks," Allie murmured. Courtly Tobias nodded. His rooster's crest of pommaded hair shimmered. His sunglasses were misted with drizzle.

"No prob." He took a neat sidestep, leaning on the brick wall between the glass store entrance and the tenants' door. Tobias worked for Giovanni's New & Used Furniture Emporium. Allie poked at the lock with her Zephyr key, her hands still shaky after she'd read Bird's note on the bus.

"Seen our car today?" she asked, fumbling for the right key. By special arrangement, the Giovannis let Allie and JJ, alone among their tenants, park their black Zephyr in the furniture-store lot. This shared secret made Allie feel cozy with Tobias, and bold. "I mean, seen our car go out today?"

"Uhn uh." Tobias' basso voice, a big voice for a small man, deepened.

"JJ's home sick," Allie told him, clicking in the right key.

"Uh *huh.*" A sympathetically skeptical note. He lowered his eyes to her bare toes. "Now don't you get those pretty feet wet."

He gave her a nod like a tip of a hat. Allie grinned. As she pushed open the door, she was repeating that line for JJ. What was a day without a quotable quote from Tobias? She faced the row of mailboxes. The tiny key, its minuscule click. She opened the door slowly, in case more hair or who-knew-what fell out.

A Helping Hands check; an envelope from her father addressed in Jo's round sure hand. Alice climbed the stairs fast, building momentum till, on the last landing, she nearly ran into Mrs. Giovanni.

"Goodness," Mrs. G. gasped as if it were Allie's name. "Slow down, dear. I just left tomatoes from our garden with your JJ—"

"Thanks," Allie told her, turning before Mrs. G. could initiate a motherly chat. She climbed the last flight two at a time, strode down the dark hall—bulb burned out—and halted at the door. She panted, feeling she'd navigated a series of escapes. Kin's note felt dry in her pocket. A good-bye note: intense, yes, and full of live feelings for JJ; but the *good-bye* was plain. And the plane tickets had looked real. Allie banged at the door, not bothering with her key. "JJ?"

Quicker than she expected, he opened the door, his hair brushing the top of the doorway. His deadpan face was unshaven. His pockmarks and the lines around his mouth deepened in the dim light. Nodding, he took a step back as if to let her look him over. He was barefoot but dressed in his usual neutral-colored shirt and pants. She stepped in without giving her usual hug.

"God. Feels like I've been gone for ages—"

His eyes met hers briefly: gray-blue, clear. "Your job lasted till six?"

She handed JJ the mail. "Sort of. So I'm glad we got to talk at lunch. Till you hung up on me, that is." She was pulling off her raincoat, letting it fall.

"What happened? Is that blood?" He pointed the mail at her skirt.

"Grape juice. Don't ask." Brushing past him, Allie stalked down the entry corridor, aware of Kin's note hidden behind her in the raincoat pocket. Their table was decked by Mrs. Giovanni's tomatoes. "Lemme get out of these."

She bumped through the bedroom door—the bed re-folded, a good sign—and pulled off her stained clothes, feeling JJ watch from the doorway.

"Hey," he told her quietly. "I'm sorry about that phone call. How I cut it—cut you—off. With my missed classes and everything, I'm just—on edge today."

"Me too." She cupped her hands over her bra. "I've been so worried all day. About my period and all, mainly. Do my breasts look bigger to you?"

"Hmm." JJ stepped toward her as cautiously as she'd stepped toward him. He sat on the bulky square couch, his knees poking up high since it was so low.

"Yeah. *Hmm.*" She stood before him on bare feet, cool in her underwear. Drizzle pattered outside the open window. On the couch arm, a Larry Niven sci-fi paperback lay face down beside a saucer of tomato slices. The ashes had been cleaned up, his eight-year-old hair hidden somewhere. Had he thrown it away?

"So JJ." Allie took a deep breath. "I know I shouldn't ask, but. You been thinking all day about Kin's wedding invitation? Wishing you'd gone?"

"What?" He blinked, actually seemed to have to remember. Then he touched her bare thigh. "No, Alice. Look. Like I keep telling you. That's all—" He lifted his hand, spread his long fingers. "Another life."

Alice nodded warily, suspicious of that phrase. But already she was explaining to Jo: Whatever happened was years ago; another, JJ says, life.

"What I *have* thought about all day—maybe you have too—is, y' know—"

"Dropping out?" Alice filled in, relieved to be changing the subject.

JJ nodded. He leaned back on the couch and brought his knees closer together. An invitation. Allie hesitated, then stepped forward. More awkwardly than usual, she settled herself onto his lap, his firm thighs. Her resting place at the end of many a long day. Spent-sounding drizzle-patter enclosed them. Allie held JJ's shoulders loosely, her bare feet dangling.

"Listen, Allie," he began. "Like I told you this morning, I've been feeling scared myself about missing those classes. Scared of myself, like you. But later today, reading, I started thinking." He rested his heavy hand on her thigh. "It's not *paranoia* rearing up in me again if what I'm worried about is real."

"Real?" She held his shoulders harder, as if he might suddenly stand.

"Since the DOD *is* horning in on every AI project—it is, Allie. I found out in July that even my music generation program the Pentagon rep wants a piece of. Wants to test it for voice-recognition use in battlefield management."

"Oh God," Allie whispered, relieved by this familiar topic. JJ had shifted to a Master's Degree goal to avoid doing DOD-centered Ph.D. thesis research.

"—and remember poor old Steinman and the Argentinean teenagers? How his radar-vision thesis wound up blowing up subs in the Falklands War? Well, Steinman was wandering round the lab drunk one night doing this whole Oppenheimer monologue: 'I am the destroyer of worlds.' Everyone thought it was hilarious except me. Does that make me crazy?"

"'Course not,'" she whispered against his bristly neck.

"That was the beginning of summer. All July I couldn't concentrate. Then I heard about my *music* project, how I could get decent grant money if I just . . . but I couldn't. And I couldn't decide to drop out so I started missing classes. . . ."

"You should've *told* me all this," she told him, no longer whispering.

"I'm telling you now. See, I knew how disappointed you'd be by the idea of leaving. And I haven't done anything final. I can still withdraw from summer session, officially. Make up the classes. If I don't drop all the way out . . ."

She nodded, hurt that he'd kept this secret. Why so many secrets? Shifting on his lap, she considered the prospect of JJ actually quitting.

"Guess you'd be relieved, in a way, to get out," she made herself say.

"Well, not if—" JJ moved his hand to her bare belly. She nodded, slowly.

In other pregnancy scares, they'd never seriously considered abortion. Not for them. One of the important things they agreed on: just as they agreed the possible side effects of the Pill made it too risky for Allie's healthy body.

"If you are, I'd go back," JJ told her. "For our—future. Guess I'd have to."

She let herself nod. "But maybe not. Maybe you could get a decent job with what computer training you've got so far and I'd keep working and it'd be—"

"Hell on wheels." He raised his hand from her stomach to halt a *Little Match Girl* monologue. "It'd be Hell on wheels. So don't tell me how the wheels would screw into place or how high we'd train the flames to go . . ."

She gave a real nod. "But." She looked at her own legs, her feet swinging slightly. "At least you seem like you're feeling—better?"

"I guess." JJ's legs tensed under her. Allie felt annoyed at herself, trying to steer conversations too quickly toward cheer. "Better than this morning, yeah. But I'm still not sure what's happening. In me. For weeks I've felt bad about lying to you, Allie. Then last night, burning that . . . you know."

"I know." She jiggled her foot harder. "And I do want to talk about—that." Then, at a nervous flicker in his eyes, she added, "Though not—just yet."

"But I feel it now, still, Al. That you're scared of me or something. That you're hiding something. Where *were* you after work today?"

"Nowhere." She leaned her head on his chest, picturing Kin leaning toward her. "I just had a *long* job and I'm still so worried from last night . . ."

"You mean the note, again?" He sounded like he was making himself ask this. "Are you still worrying about that note I burned?"

"Not now." Allie kissed JJ as lightly as Kin had kissed her. Silencing his warm mouth. "Later, JJ. OK?" He blinked. She blinked too, feeling disloyal for not having kissed him this morning. *Yours all ways. Any ways.*

He gave his slow half smile, obviously relieved that she wasn't pressing him about the note. Allie managed her own smile. Often after watching JJ flirt at a party, after flirting herself too, she would picture the party girl as she'd kiss JJ back at home, picture herself *her.* Now, re-living Kin's plush lips on her own, Allie kissed JJ again, hard enough to feel his un-shaven beard bristle. Their tongues swam together easily, his tasting of fresh tomatoes. But he pulled back. "Fish? They're feeding you Helping Hand girls—" He paused, tasting. "Oyster?"

"Oh, OK. I did stop someplace on the way home, for something to eat. . . ."

"Oh?" He kissed her this time, questioningly, and she kept the kiss going, determined not to lie to him anymore. Not if she could help it. Picturing Kin's cat lips, she ground her lips against JJ's. Shaking her own head. No, no.

"Yeah." She, this time, pulled back. "See, I'm starved, Mr. Bread-winner."

"So try this." JJ lifted a tomato slice. He held it as she bit, tangy juice filling her mouth. "Beefsteak," he told her. "Mrs. G. said: Sweet and meaty."

"Mmm." Allie wiped her lips with her hand, swallowing. "Yum."

"The Happy Eater," JJ mumbled, one of his first names for her. He fed her another bite, tomato seeds dripping onto their ugly unstainable couch.

She swallowed the pulp with a final hearty, "Mm-*mum.*"

"Y'know, Alice in Wonder," JJ told her as she licked her fingers. "I al-ways like the sounds you make when you eat. . . ."

"Oh?" She licked her lips. *Shouldn't* she be questioning him now, telling him right off what happened? Coming clean. That was what she intended to do.

"Sorta like the sounds you make in sex," he continued softly, easing into his scientific tone. "Except in sex, you also sound—always—surprised."

Alice laughed, rocking on his lap. JJ shifted his weight, pulling his feet up. His legs bent, almost shorter than the arms he wrapped around her waist. She felt tension release along her spine as they lay back to-gether, sinking into the cushions. She always *was* surprised with JJ: how quickly his moods shifted like the Ohio sky color of his eyes, a green-gray now, hovering above her. Your eyes are my sky, she thought, some-thing she'd be embarrassed to say. You are my weather. She shut her eyes and gave JJ a speculative horizontal kiss.

"Mrs. G. asked me about your queen's wardrobe," JJ mumbled as he pulled away, holding her loosely. He shifted to his back, almost squeezing her off the couch. "Was it big enough? she wanted to know."

Allie shifted too, resting her head on his chest. "She's so sweet to us . . ."

"You," JJ corrected, his voice vibrating in her head. "She treats me as this suspicious long-hair. She sees that hair, even though I don't have it anymore." Was this, Allie wondered, his way of saying he'd thrown the braid away? "But you," JJ went on mildly, "she treats you as if you're queen of the world. . . ."

" 'As if'?" Allie sat up straight, savoring warm air on her skin. She climbed on top of him, powered by the surge of arrogance that came unleashed when she was with JJ, undressed. Her soft yet strong thighs straddled his hipbones. From above, she stared down at him, her hair hanging against her face and her breasts straining her lacy bra. He gave a real JJ grin when she repeated, imperious as Sticks: *"As if'?"*

"Forgive me, O Queen," he murmured, planting one hand on each of her thighs. "Sweet and meaty," he told her judiciously, squeezing. She clenched him harder. Through double layers of cloth, she felt the deeply familiar stiffening in his cock, that warmest of warmths.

"Your turn," she reminded him, her voice already choked. (Meaning: to use condoms, not the diaphragm).

"Mmm hmm." He was rocking his torso, rocking her whole body. She tucked her chin to her collarbone as she zigzaggedly unzipped his pants.

"Want it down?" he mumbled. (Meaning: the fold-out).

"Yuck, no." She shook her head.

Whenever they unfolded the couch together, she remembered the first unfolding, the two of them confronted by wiry hairs—strangers' hairs, pubic hairs—embedded in the foam rubber mattress. After she'd run shrieking to the bathroom and he'd plucked out each one with hastily unpacked tweezers, they'd wound up spreading Grandma Hart's quilt on the bedroom's scratchy carpet, sleeping there and making love there for days, till it got too cold, the floor. Secretly, Alice had enjoyed walking round with rug burn on her ass.

Rocking harder now, she bent to unbutton JJ's shirt. She stayed low to swish her hair over his chest. Four years together, she thought as she moved. Long enough to earn, they'd agreed, a Ph.D. in pleasing each other.

"Me 'n top, 'K?" She halted her hair mid-swish. Then she raised her head to her longest-necked Queen of Play height. She unhooked her bra, slung it across the room with a sense of abandon that had been building since Ko No's. See? she was saying to that Kin woman, that man too. See? She was lifting one leg, then another as they wrestled off first her panties, then his pants and briefs. Still straddling him, Allie raised herself, her knees digging into the couch. JJ stretched his long arms, those endlessly useful arms, and groped in his nightstand. Below Allie, his hands hidden by her tremulously suspended pelvis, he snapped on his condom. Slowly, enjoying the rare air inside of her, she lowered herself onto him.

Straight up, she thought with a gasp as she sat. She locked her thighs around his hips. Straight up, a Kin woman might say in a bar, then later in the man's—JJ's—bed. Allie rocked on top of him, picturing Kin atop JJ moving with her abrupt grace, her face stretching with catlike yowls. Allie breathed hard, holding back her own moans. (Would she ever sound surprised again, now that he'd told her she did?) JJ thrust up deeper, jarring the rhythm of her rocking. Just as she thought she might not reach it, she bent abruptly low, smeared her mouth against his and rubbed her face on his beard bristle. She gripped his tensed shoulders to stay low as his hips bucked up.

Heat was gathering fast between her hipbones. She clenched his with her thighs. Her bent back stiffened, her body braced against his. A bump like a speeding sled hitting a rock and flying for a second. As she burst inside—surprise!—JJ rolled over under her, with her. And they *were* flying, falling, her legs wrapped tightly around him, her bump cushioned by his strong arms holding her tight too, keeping them connected even midair.

They finished on the floor: Allie on bottom with her back curved and her ankles on his shoulders, her limp feet framing his head. The rug burned her ass like the beard burned her lips and cheeks. His moan followed hers, echoing its pitch like the delayed final note of a symphony. The home note, JJ'd told her that was called. As they lay on the rug, Allie savored like sun the rough tingly burns on her skin. Inside, deeper heat began its slow-motion spread back into her limbs. That heat was seconded by a new ache of warmth below her stomach. JJ pulled himself up. He towered over her, peeling off his condom. Alice was wondering about her extra ache when JJ said, "Hey?"

In the dusky light, he squinted at his condom. Allie sat, feeling the thick wetness from inside. Clumsily, she scrambled to her feet. Wobbly headed, wobbly jointed, she half-stumbled, half-ran to the bathroom.

"Hey!" Not waiting to haul out her tampons and sanitary pads, she pounded barefoot—bare-everything—back through the front room to the open bedroom doorway. "We did it," she told naked JJ. "We're safe!"

He lifted her into a crazy hug, his hands cupping her ass. Her feet swung wildly as they stagger-spun in a shaky circle, drunk with relief.

· · ·

While Alice showered—gently lathering her skin, not thinking but watching the day's dirt spiral down the drain—JJ made a celebration supper.

Spaghetti and sauce: Mrs. G's tomatoes mixed with canned. And baked clams on the half shell, unfrozen from plastic wraps. The windows steamed inside as well as out. Allie sat at the table in a clean T-shirt and sweatshorts. She took another sloppy sip of cheap pink Gallo. Shirtless JJ stirred the sauce.

He'd always been the more precise and imaginative cook. As he sipped his own Gallo, sprinkling the sauce with orange powders, he told her not to worry. Even if he did drop out, he wouldn't turn into Eugene, Solar Carpenter.

Allie laughed as cramps tightened her abdomen. Her head felt overfull too, swarming with unprocessed sensations. "Old Eugene." She shook her head.

With his Philosophy B.A., Eugene Kerr had become a penniless Vermont carpenter who worked only on buildings powered with solar energy. He and JJ used to drink together in college, two longish-haired older students, men among boys. Androgynous men, Allie remembered them joking. The secret to picking up college girls, they'd claim. Being sensitive men, androgynous.

". . . I mean I'm not going to become an anti-Pentagon fanatic. But—" JJ set down his spoon, his brown hair damp with spaghetti steam. "It's not paranoid to see what's there. I realized today, in this book—" He headed into the bedroom, emerged with the sci-fi paperback. He *is* drunk, Allie thought, sipping to catch up. He always read her sci-fi quotes when drunk, preceding them with plot explanations she never quite followed.

A postapocalyptic world, he was telling her, in which frozen bodies from a mental institution are unfrozen for a booming black-market trade in organs. Most of the patients reacted like classic paranoids once they realized what was happening. And the real paranoids?

"They," JJ read with a swell of pride in his voice, "were hardly surprised."

Both of them laughed as he shut the book. Hardly surprised, one or the other kept saying as they sipped more Gallo and twisted forkfuls of spaghetti. They picked clam from the bready cake and real tomatoes from the tinny sauce.

"OK, OK, fuck Yale," Allie told JJ as she wiped her mouth. "The big question is: can we still call Yale Bail?"

This set them laughing again. Allie shook her head, remembering the wallet-sized card in JJ's Graduate-Student Welcome packet that listed a number to be phoned Should Student Be Detained by an Officer of the Law.

"Do we still *have* that card, even?" asked JJ, who'd refused to carry it.

"Oh sure—in the address book under the machine—" Allie looked over her shoulder at the unlit answering machine. Then back to the table. She drew a big breath. Wondering if she could, now, work up to the topic of Kin's message.

But JJ stood abruptly. "We can still catch the end of the news." Allie scooped two coffee cups full of Rocky Road while JJ unfolded the fold-out.

She settled in beside him, balancing the ice cream. Normally, when they curled on the bed together in front of the news, she felt the TV to be their own fritzy porthole on the outside world. They'd watch raptly, booing and laughing.

"Oh no," Allie called out as George Bush materialized, a flock of flags behind him. "I can do it today!" She seized her suction-dart gun. Till now, Allie hadn't been able to fire at Bush's peevish pinch-lipped face, picturing JFK's head hung above her childhood dining-room table. Solid-looking on its thick neck yet destined to explode.

"Stand back! I'm gonna shoot the preppy shit!" Allie sank her knees into the mattress. "Bang!" She pulled the plastic trigger. The suction dart bounced off Bush; the story switched to continuing conflicts in Iraq and Iran.

"Got him." JJ sat up too. Thousands of Iranian men beat their own heads with their fists in unison. Not hitting themselves all that hard, it seemed to Allie as she turned to JJ. His bare chest filled her sight. She poked her plastic gun between his wide-spaced nipples as, distantly, the phone purred.

She froze on her knees for a prayer of a second. At the next purr, she scrambled up, dropping her gun. She rushed out to the front room. At the phone's third purr, JJ took his place beside her. Side by side—so close he must feel her heart thumping—they watched the red light stop blinking. RECORD. Tape rolled, no jazz. Only muffled TV. The familiar sound of a news voice on their own TV mixed with a news voice a thousand staticky miles away.

"Allie Ann?" A live voice, loud and round.

"Jo!" The receiver felt light as Allie lifted it, switching off the machine.

"—you *are* there, Al?" Jo sounded unsurprised.

"Jo," she repeated, her own voice hoarse from shouting at Bush.

"Allie, listen up. I can't talk 'cause I got a killer quiz in anatomy in an hour. And I shouldn't be telling you this at all—"

"Then don't," Allie blurted out. She shot JJ a What Next? look.

"Oh." Jo sounded affronted, the freight train of her thoughts knocked off its track. "Oh, OK, sorry to bother you! Glad you've learned to Just Say No—"

"Sorry, sorry, Jo. I'm having a monster day. But what? Is Dad worse?"

"Dad? What could be wrong with him?" Behind Jo—was Jo pausing so Allie could hear it?—Dad started hacking. "No, Mrs. Reagan, everything's A-OK. Like Ron used to say, It's morning in America out here—"

"Oh, c'mon Jo." Allie raised her voice above Dad's distant hack. "Tell."

Jo gave the nurse's sigh she'd prematurely started to use, as if already annoyed by explaining life and death to mere laymen.

"The new meds aren't working?" Allie prompted. Her heart contracted with familiar guilt: Jo alone in the desert, taking care of Mom and Dad.

"—total backfire. It's all-night cough-a-thons and Mom doesn't want you to know but we made some calls today—oh, shoot." Above Dad's coughs and Dan Rather, wind chimes sounded. Mom pushing in from the patio?

"No, Jo," her voice protested. "That's not Alice, is it?"

"Just a sec." Jo muffled her receiver. Allie turned to JJ—he leaned now in the bedroom doorway, his bare arms folded—and mouthed, *Mom.*

"O-*K*," Jo shouted from across the country, presumably to Mom. Then she told Allie in an equally impatient voice: "Look, she wants to talk."

"OK," Allie answered weakly.

"Hey, you sick or something?" Jo demanded. "You in Match-Girl mode?"

"No, no, everything's OK, Jo."

"Bull-oney. Call me, like, late some night? Nine your time, eleven ours, when they'll all three be watching Johnny Carson?" Mom, Dad, and Grandma.

"'K." Allie braced herself as the phone changed hands. Dad still hacking.

"Alice? *Is* that you?" Mom sounded even more vague than usual; cocktail hour must've started early. "Wanted you to know that though Jo wants me to and the Homes we spoke with today—some in Sun City— all said they could take him even though he's only sixty-one, but with his emphysema and all, well . . ." Mom sighed, confused. She often loaded down her sentences with so many apologetic qualifiers that she forgot, when she reached it, the main point.

"And you—?" Alice leaned against the stove.

A giant sigh. "I can't handle this." A phrase characters used on the soap. Along with (she'd heard Mom say this too, recently) *I've got to get my head together.* "Just having made those phone calls I feel so *guilty*—"

Usually Allie would too. Instead, today, she felt fresh out of feelings.

"—no reason at all for guilt," Allie made herself say. "You and Dad don't have to make any decision alone, till we all can go over all the . . . options."

"Yes, well, I was wondering—" Mom sipped something. A martini, or had Jo gotten her back to wine, lately? Dad's hacking reached a climax. "Maybe you two could fly down here before JJ's fall classes start?"

"His fall classes?" Allie slid her eyes to JJ's.

"Alice? Everything's all right isn't it? With JJ and his classes?" Behind Mother, Allie heard a door slam: Jo leaving. Dad was quiet now; Jo must've propped him up, helped him *bring up,* as she and Mom said, his phlegm.

"Oh sure, Mom. He's almost finished summer session. . . ." Allie turned her back on JJ. Yes, she'd let Mom know JJ's schedule, when classes started; yes, she'd call later after she'd read Dad's latest letter; yes, they got it, today.

She hung up and turned, relieved to see the bedroom doorway empty. The news was off. What, Allie asked herself as she stepped up to the table, if that *had* been Kin? What was to stop Kin from phoning JJ, telling JJ what his wife had done? Standing by the table, Allie slit open Dad's latest envelope. A newspaper clipping from the *Arizona Republic*, letters to the editor. Dad's was captioned, *The Real Reagan Legacy.* Allie skimmed the words. *The true conservative stands for fiscal responsibility— The true conservative truly wants government off our backs, out of our bedrooms—*

"So." JJ stepped up behind her. His voice held no slur. "How come you didn't tell? At least tell them I won't be finishing any summer classes?"

She set the letter on the table. "Didn't want to upset them. Besides, they guessed something was up. You know. On me, everything shows."

She presented to him her wide-eyed heart-shaped face.

"Not really." JJ folded his arms again. "You seem so open, Al. But maybe that only makes you better at. Hiding things."

"Oh, come on." Uneasily, Allie plopped down on her chair. She gazed out into the humid purple dark, a horn honking below. In her reflection, her eyes looked huge. "Me?" She toyed with a clam shell. "The Little Match Girl?"

JJ sat opposite her. "The Iron Little Match Girl."

Forcing a smile, she pinched a fingerful of clam. "Didja feed Newt?"

As JJ shook his head, she stood, then stood on tiptoe by the fridge to crumple the clam into Newt's foggy water. Newt floated from its chip of brick at the bottom of the goldfish bowl, its tiny green mouth opening and its green eyes bulging in terror of the air. "Poor hungry thing!" JJ stayed silent. To him, Newt was no substitute for the cat they couldn't keep here.

"Speaking of pets—" Allie turned, annoyed by her own tense insistent cheer. "How're our mouse holes doing?"

"Rat holes," JJ corrected, but without much heart.

She opened the cabinet under the sink. Two holes—plum-sized, too small for a rat, she'd insisted—still flanked the Spic and Span and scrub bucket, filled now with hair. "Good God." Allie lifted the heavy plastic bag from the bucket. "A real rat!" She fished out JJ's thick braid. He watched her sit at the table and finger its coarse hairy knobs, slightly damp. Funkier smelling, now.

"What's up with you, Al?" JJ leaned across the table, his voice lowered as if they were still lying together on the bedroom floor. "Tell me."

"Well." Alice twisted his braid's rubber band. She longed for the freed feeling of confession. And what if Kin did phone again? Or write from *parts (unlike yours) unknown?* She wiped her sweaty face. "I do have to tell *you* something. Just like you told me about those—burned words."

"What?" JJ asked, his voice subtly strained. She sensed he sensed who it involved. Wasn't this the only way she'd ever find out more?

Twisting the rubber band, bringing out words as halting as the Kin woman's, Alice described the phone call at midnight, the message from a man's voice. "A man, I'm sure, but it said it was 'Kin.' Said it was mad that you hadn't RSVP'd some invitation and that it wanted to meet you at a restaurant here, Ko No's, down Whalley Ave . . ." The rubber band came off in her hand.

"And you didn't tell me any of this." JJ's Zucchini-Bread-Murderer voice, back again. Very calm and very strange. Allie didn't look up.

"Well, *you* didn't tell me about those words I saw burn. And that made me worried you were hiding something . . .un*tell*able. Or something you thought was untellable." She bent over his hair, unbraiding its sections.

"What the hell're you doing?"

"I'm *play*ing with this hair! That OK?" She glared at him. "Or can't I even touch something Kin touched?" Cramps were twisting her insides. "So anyway, I—I went there after work myself, just went there."

"Ko No's?" His voice stayed maddeningly flat. "You went to Ko No's?"

Allie nodded hard, combing one of the frizzy braid sections with her stiffened fingers. "And I saw her."

"Who?" JJ asked, ominously quiet. She felt his strong bare upper body lean closer. She smelled Gallo on his breath.

"Kin! Or so I thought." Allie stared at his eight-year-old hair. "I thought it was her, JJ, right off—because of the crooked teeth and her being wispy thin, except for her breasts. Like you described. Except her hair was dyed black like this Asian guy's who was with her, and I think *he* was the one who made the call." She raised her eyes. "So can't you see how con*fused* I felt? Feel?"

"A guy. An Asian guy was with her." JJ lowered his eyes back to his undone hair. "What're you—You're saying they were here—both of them?"

So he knew the man, too. Allie looked down. Of course he knew. But which was Kin? Which was JJ's Kin? She pushed aside the ponytail, its three sections still stubbornly separate. She stood unsteadily.

"What did they, you—Alice?"

She was walking down their entrance hallway, her bare feet thumping the floor. At the door, she crouched over her raincoat, fished out the note. "Here: take this. She—Kin—went into the ladies' room and I followed her and we hardly said two words but she was wearing that ring of 8s, like what you'd said you made her. And she gave me this to give you . . . ."

Blank-faced, JJ took the note. He unfolded it carefully. His eyes moved first quickly, then slowly down the lines. A poem? A crazy-woman rant? Who could tell, if JJ wouldn't? He bent over the note with such concentration that Allie held her breath. JJ was looking at the note now, not reading.

And Allie remembered Kin's blind-girl stare, sensing again what she'd sensed standing beside Kin: the energy between this woman and JJ, alive and present, an extra energy gathering now in his body.

Abruptly, JJ stuffed the note into his pants pocket. He stood, his arm knocking a plate. One clam skidded off to crack on the linoleum. JJ never shouted when he was really angry. He got dead silent. He turned now, his bare back more expressive than his face. Knobbed by spine, his shoulder blades standing out like aborted wings. As he stepped toward the bedroom, he brushed the Losers' Lamp, knocking off both McGovern for Peace and HHH.

"JJ?" Allie called after him. "You started it! Lying, I mean . . ."

She stared down at his hair, remembering the phone message she'd erased. But hadn't JJ told the original lie back in Ohio? Or was it a lie? Allie squeezed the hairs' rubber-banded end. Couldn't everything he'd said then still be true and Kin herself be, well, crazy? A woman who took the name of a man, who made that man, that "Kin," place a phone call to her ex-lover?

But wouldn't JJ tell her *that?* Tell Allie the voice she'd heard didn't belong to the Kin he'd known? And why was she still twisting her mind around, still straining to create fanciful explanations? She could hear JJ pulling on his shirt, feel him buttoning it. She turned in her chair to glimpse through the bedroom doorway JJ sitting on the mattress rolling up his socks. Melted ice cream gleamed in the coffee cups on the orange-crate.

"Sorry, Alice." His voice sounded terse, uncertain. "But if they came all the way out here . . . I have to go see." He stood and bent for his wallet and keys.

"Where're you gonna go—Ko No's?" She watched him step into the front room, his keys jangling. "Oh, JJ I'm sure they're not still there; Kin had a *plane* ticket in her bag and all—"

He stopped in front of her, bending like a father. "Someone there might know where they were heading. If they came all this way, they could be in—" He emphasized his words as if talking to a slow child. "Real trouble."

She pressed her lips together. His tone seemed to say: Real trouble's something you know nothing about, spineless white girl.

"Wait," she commanded as he started to turn. "You've got to answer me one thing. I can handle it whatever you say. I know I've been acting like I can't, but I can. Of course I can. So tell me, now. The 'Kin' who was your first lover. Was she that wispy thin woman? Or that—man?"

JJ stayed half turned, his eyes aimed down the entry corridor at the door.

"Or—" Somehow this was the hardest part to say. "Both? Were they both your—lovers?"

JJ didn't move. His jaw tightened like he was clenching his teeth. Then he said, "I can't." His bony profile looked strained, raised on his neck like his teenage face in the photo of his pre-psychotic valedictorian address. His Adam's apple bobbed. "I've told you, tried to tell you several times that I. Can't talk about that, them. I mean I won't. Sorry."

He turned all the way around, his back to Alice. Colorless cloth.

"Well, let me come *with* you—" Her hands, as if waiting for this unwatched moment, twisted off his hair's remaining rubber band.

"No," JJ told her quietly. His shoulder blades tensed.

"So *go* if you're gonna go," Allie shouted, grabbing a handful of his loose hair. "Go!" she repeated, feeling instantly foolish because he'd already started his step. She aimed the hair at his back: a sloppy half-assed hurl.

JJ looked over his shoulder as the hair fell damply to the floor between them. His eyes burned, blue now. She flushed, breathing hard.

"Sorry," he mumbled yet again, distractedly. A few strands clung to his shirt. As he headed for the door, Allie swept one arm across the table, brushing away the rest of the hair. He stepped over her raincoat and opened the door; she bumped down off her seat, crouching on the floor. As the door shut, Allie stared around at the cracked clamshell and scattered clumps of hair. She'd never be able to pick all this up.

. . .

After calling her dad (she'd thanked him for the clipping then found she could barely speak; he'd thanked her for phoning in the gruff formal manner he'd used years before on business trips when Mom let her talk to him long-distance); after sweeping the floor (she'd stuffed the hair in the mop bucket, slammed it into the cupboard); after rinsing all the dishes, Alice staggered into the bedroom. She shut the door behind her, as if she weren't alone. Everything—the floor beneath her feet, even—felt unstable.

She paced, hugging herself through her sweatshirt. And she wondered if JJ found her breasts too small, compared to that Kin woman's. Wondered, as she paced in the opposite direction, if instead he found her body too soft and feminine compared to that Kin man's. She halted at the unfolded bed where only hours before she and JJ had made love. Impulsively, Allie tugged the bed's metal handle, deciding to fold it back up. Make JJ sleep on the floor tonight while she slept on the couch.

The bed half folded, then stuck as it often did for her. Allie jerked at it. "Where *are* you?" she muttered out loud to JJ. And she pounded the upright mattress so hard it unfolded again with a clank. Clutching her hand, she fell onto the bed, the sheets half untucked. She buried her face in JJ's crushed pillow. Too worn out to cry, too wired up to sleep.

She rolled over, remembering how JJ used to tuck her into her dorm-room bed the nights they spent apart. Once they'd moved in together, she'd always felt safely bound by their double bed, its four sides. She sat up, blinking. Was he with them now? The Kin man, the Kin woman. Desperate for distraction, she turned on the TV and watched Dukakis bomb in a late news interview. Why had he vetoed the pledge of allegiance? Had he undergone treatment for depression?

As she sat cross-legged on the bed, trying to reconstruct the note from Kin, she found herself focusing on Michael Dukakis: his earnest yet evasive gaze, his thick yet wimpy up-and-down eyebrows, his habit of shaking his head as if at his own ineptitude before answering even simple questions.

Hasn't Kin always given you what you wanted? All ways? What the Hell did that mean? Alice wondered. Dukakis raised his hands, bewildered. Was JJ really not going to talk to her about it, about "them," as he'd put it? Which must mean—abso-fuckin'-lutely, Jo would say—he *had* been involved with the man. The Kin man. Allie felt her lips tighten. Thin lips, witchy unbrushed hair. Was that how JJ had seen her, when they'd fought?

She sighed, wiping her forehead. Get a grip, she told herself. So what if JJ *had* experimented that way? She finger-combed her thick, lightly tangled hair. Nothing so unusual; nothing to worry about now, years later.

Allie knelt and tugged at the mess of sheets. As long as those desires stayed in JJ's past. But would they, when she'd sensed such intense feeling coming from JJ tonight? From that Kin woman too. How did she fit in? Hadn't she treated the Asian man lovingly, protectively? Allie sank back on her heels. What *was* the "something important" he'd wanted to tell JJ? The worst possible news?

The apartment door bumped; she flicked off the TV. The bathroom door thumped shut. She listened to JJ's distant stream. Beer-heavy. The toilet flush muffled his steps as he shuffled up the entry hall. In the front room, his steps slowed further. Maybe he expected to trip over her, still crouched on the floor. *See? No Kin.* Allie lay down on her back in the untucked sheets. JJ opened the bedroom door and kicked off his heavy sneakers.

Her spine automatically relaxed, just having him home. Through slitted eyes, she watched him pull off the shirt she'd unbuttoned hours before. *Yours all ways, Any ways.* He lay beside her as if unaware that she was awake, though he knew she never slept on her back. He curved his long body, smelling of beer and sweat. Allie stayed on her back; he stayed on his side, his back to her. She fixed her eyes on the ceiling, its darkened network of cracks. Wouldn't it soon be past midnight? Couldn't she soon begin thinking of this day in blessed past tense? But then, who knew what was coming next?

JJ lay there silently. Sirens spiraled outside. Alice wiped her face again, thinking of Kin's flushed poreless skin, thinking she hadn't heard JJ bolt the door, thinking of getting up to bolt the door herself. Especially tonight.

But what, Jo asked, clear as day, *if it already is inside?*

Allie blinked hard. Her lips re-tightened. JJ was breathing unevenly beside her, not snoring. She sighed, resentful yet relieved he wasn't saying any more, at least not now. She watched his rib cage expand with each breath.

Even more acutely than the night before, she felt the extra tension in his body. The strain all this had been, for JJ. The braid of his hair arriving out of the blue. Then his wife saying she'd secretly met these people from a part of his life he might've been trying to close off. To, Allie thought, erase.

"No telling," JJ mumbled at last, his voice completely flattened. "No telling where they are." He sighed loudly. No doubt worried, Allie thought, about the two Kins. The Asian man with his head in his arms; the crew-cut woman with her stripped-down face. The two of them in, Allie remembered JJ guessing, *real trouble.* "Couldn't find any trace of them. . . ."

Resenting Kin, both Kins, Allie breathed JJ's beer and sweat.

" 'Course not." She softened her voice like Mom's old fairy-tale voice, the tone grown-ups used to say things they only wished they still believed. "I told you." Alice fixed her gaze on the cracked plaster ceiling. "They're gone."

Girl A & Girl B

1

Curaçao, August 1988

Bon Bini, Jimmy Joe—

(Or Mrs. Jimmy Joe; or both of you, if you read this together; if that's what, Kin'd say, floats your boat). Just thought you oughta know—oughta care, Jim Joe —where we are, how we are. Thought you oughta have, too, this photo of how we were. (Taken by you and only you, since only you ever saw us this way).

I know, I know; we promised we'd get gone. But for once, JJ, we aren't going to give you what you want. This is no poem, see. (Didja like the one I wrote from Ko No's? You always said I should write poems, right?) Not that you saw that poem. Not that you'll see this airmail letter or this half-naked photo, for all I know. But I'll send them to the same New Haven address where we sent your hair.

(Wha'do we got to do to get your attention, mister?)

We Know What You Want. So Kin and I were told via brochure on our first flight, not counting our shuttles to and from rainy Connecticut, your home.

We Know What You Want to Do on Your Honeymoon. The Curaçao brochure shook in Kin's hand, he was laughing so hard; he was drinking hard, too. A bottle of champagne on the plane, courtesy of Las Palmas Hotel, the Island's Finest. The cork popped before we left the ground. Honeymoons are Curaçao's specialty.

You want to kick up your heels, paint the town red and (Kin read louder as we bumped down the night-lighted JFK runway) get Romantic with a capital R. In short you want to do it all. And we've got the place you want: Romantic Curaçao. 35 miles north of Venezuela, 1710 miles south of New York. Caribbean charm with a Dutch accent. Curaçao's honeymoon packages guarantee (Kin's voice shook like his hands) a lifetime's worth of memories. (I had to take the brochure; Kin was choking on sweet cheap champagne, twenty thousand feet above the Atlantic).

Laughing too, I read him the fine print: CLIMATE (sun almost every day) LANGUAGE (English, Papiamento, Dutch, Spanish). MEDICAL FACIL—

Kin snatched the brochure before I could stop myself myself.

English-speaking doctors and one well-equipped hospital with a (Kin's voice rose, waking honeymooners in adjoining seats) Decompression Chamber!

Oh, Berta Bird, Kin told me (still so loud, JJ, it shocked me). Don't take me there! Don't decompress me! Wouldn't be a bad way to go, see? Scuba dive down, let your veins burst like bubbles. Nice and clean. No hospital, no D-C chamber!

Other sleepy brides and grooms stared; I started to cry. Expertly steady on his feet, Kin strode up the aisle, fetched me first-class Kleenex, strode back again. He locked himself in the first-class lav. Stayed there as I sobbed and twisted my ring of 8s. Your ring, Jim Joe. But it wasn't you I was crying over.

I sat alone inside the last, blackest stretch of 8/8/88. By 1 A.M. or so, I had only dry heaves left. I felt I'd been crying for two. The kind of thing I can write—even to you, even after your no-excuse no-show— but can't say out loud, not even to Kin. Not now, anyway. I felt him settle beside me again in the dark. I took his hand; he let me take it. His head was throbbing with pain so sharp I could feel it in my head. And what—not that you care—was our first sight of Curaçao?

What did we see together, holding hands at a thousand feet at 4 A.M., U.S. time, 5 A.M. here? Kin had felt the gears go down, wheels thumping and locking (he can tell when the plane's going to land right). The island had emerged enough from its lemony pink dawn haze that we made out two sailboats and many black roads winding into a dense center of green. We saw matchbox jeeps speeding round green-bordered curves. Our plane shuddered. Below us, a jeep skidded off the road, rolling into the green as if (Kin whispered) flicked off by God's fingernail.

· · ·

Listen where we've landed. Listen like you do care, JJ. In the Curaçao airport, tiny after JFK, Dutch tourists lined up to leave. Their fair skins burned so badly their noses were bloody. The airport loudspeaker played "Girl from Ipanema," over and over. I tried to meet Kin's eyes, to ask if this island he'd chosen was, to him, a big joke. But he hid behind implacable black glasses though the sun was barely out. Which drove me so crazy I'm resorting to writing to you, Jimmy Joe. Usually I can ask or tell Kin anything. Now—for a reason I don't want to get into, not all the way—I can't. At Las Palmas, in a honeymoon suite, we collapsed till sun woke me through our screenless window. In its pure unmuted light, I watched Kin sleep open mouthed, as if he were stunned.

This year, on and off, he's spent days exhausted. Like being jet-lagged when he wasn't, shouldn't be. He'd imagined feeling weak so often that when he did start feeling it, he'd—we'd both—been sure it was his imagination. You know?

In a growing square of sun, we shared a honeymooner's breakfast. A second bottle of champagne (we split it) and food that we stared down. Sticky buns, guava jelly, boiled eggs. Each item wrapped in cellophane. No plastic crackles or chewing marred our silence. My hickey on Kin's neck looked faded. Despite the sun, Kin switched on a bamboo lamp between our double beds. He squinted into the light, then—like it was growing brighter and brighter—lunged to shut it off. He shook back his hair, started pacing.

He mumbled to me that he felt like he did on flights when his mask would drop down, for real. And he knew from flight training that his Time of Useful Consciousness without Oxygen was forty seconds or so. He shook his head. Shit, he told me. I keep wondering when it's truly gonna hit. When I'm gonna Lose It.

He stopped by the window. I stepped over beside him. Didn't know what to say but I stood close. Scared of Losing It too, JJ, though I've got no right. Not compared to Kin. We blinked, getting used to it together. The sun here.

The cleeenest beeach-es, a supple brown-skinned bellboy promised Kin on our way out. Giving Kin a glance Kin cut short. Not like beaches, he added, leaning close to Kin in the elevator's sealed hum. On Autre Banda.

What's that? I asked, covering up Kin's silence. Holding Kin's hand. The bellboy muttered his answer to Kin, not me. The other side.

In front of Las Palmas, on the Topless Beach, no waves broke. Sugary white sand burned our feet. Breasts, brown and white, bounced and sagged and, on prone bodies we picked our way past, flattened out. Fried eggs. Each body vibrated with the beginnings of my champagne headache. A throb I couldn't yet feel as pain. No JJ, I didn't peel off my own T-shirt. Didn't buy sunblock or hand-woven straw hats from the women who crept along the dunes.

Why bother? Kin asked. I mean, for me. You oughta. And he lay on our Las Palmas towel in tight black swim trunks, his skin already dark-ening. His mom met Kin's dad, an Exchange Student, on a church-group retreat in Hawaii. Remember? The dad he never knew was part

Korean-American, part Hawaiian. So Kin, on beaches, cultivates naturally deep tans. A kind of disguise. Remember, JJ, how Kin described his earliest travels? How he saw himself as a true Exchange Student? Exchanging his old shy Greenville-High self for a tanner bolder boy.

Why bother, I agreed. I stretched out next to Kin in my T-shirt. Exposing my white legs, not caring if my Olaf skin burned or bled in this new, fierce sun.

Did you like him? I asked, my new lashless eyes squeezed shut. That bellboy?

In another life, Kin murmured, sounding drugged. And he told me the boy had reminded him of his first boy on his first trip to Seoul. Remember JJ: that first city where no one knew Kin, where he could—at last—do what he wanted. In a puppet-show theater, Kin had pressed the boy's knee. In the theater's bathroom stall, neither one had made a sound. I got so used to that, Kin told me on the beach. It was years, Berta, till I figured out you could make sounds, y'know?

Then, daring me to race him, he ran toward the water. His black hair flew behind him like a tail. No soft flesh, no jiggles, nothing weighing him down. Behind Kin, I laughed and stumbled. He ran along the shoreline, his heels shooting back showers of wet sand. I halted, hugging myself hard.

And, J. Joe (are you still with us?) I half remembered toddling along a lake beach in a diaper, looking for my mother. Some other mother chased me down, my body burned so badly I cried for—my mother's words—days straight. Didn't I once tell you my first home in St. Paul always felt cold? (If you didn't listen then, listen now; see us again now; try, JJ). Whenever Mother left me in my crib in that apartment, she buttoned her sweaters over my pajamas. Alone for hours, I'd pull at the cloth, never freeing myself from more than one layer. So, see, I was happy toddling down that beach. Freed from my wood cage and my suffocating clothes.

Maybe Kin felt freed like that as he swerved out to sea, his legs pumping. I splashed in waist deep. Salt stung my raw eyelids. (I've cut off my lashes, JJ; long story). Kin swam past the bobbing amateurs. I scrubbed my hair, the water darkening with my dye. Like a squid's squirt of ink. Proudly, I watched Kin, admiring the speed he's honed in years of beaches. As his splashes grew small, I panicked, splashing too, scanning the shore for the Dutch lifeguard. My husband, I'd tell him, flashing my ring. He might be, might try to—

I turned one last time in knee-deep froth. Kin had turned too, so far out. He splashed back to me. I couldn't speak, couldn't tell him how scared I'd been. But I gripped his arm hard enough to hurt. We guided each other through the sunburned bodies. Skin speckled by pink bumps, skin white with zinc. A red-faced man rubbed oil on the back of a teenage girl, her bare breasts digging into the sand. I looked away, hating this place. Kin and I stumbled through eelgrass, coarser than on American beaches. He was hungry; starved, he said. But not for the phony Caribbean dishes Las Palmas was pushing.

We lunched at the Cleanest McDonalds in South America (proclaimed by a plaque). Kin ordered in Spanish, though the workers spoke English. He gobbled down a Big Mac and my fries. We sucked one Coke with two straws, wandering past the whitewashed storefronts of Fuik Straat. Yuppie Dutch with blindingly blond hair and blood red noses passed by briskly, loaded with bags of duty-free (Kin recited from the brochure he'd memorized in the first-class lav) Swiss watches French perfumes English china Irish crystal.

I rolled my eyes with him, hearing clear contempt in his voice. So why, Jim Joe, did he chose this tourist-trap island for our—he mocks this lovely goofy word—honeymoon? Fuik Straat! Fuik Straat! Armies of *turistas* marched to its beat, but I kept stopping to wipe my gritty teary eyes. Kin fell in step behind a Group. Your eyes need to be inside, he told me, steering my elbow. So we watched a Curaçao Cane Liquor assembly line. In harmonious slow motion, old ladies hammered corks into bottles. A smell of rum and raw sugar cane. Tour groups moved in and out behind us. Was Kin, I wondered, paralyzed inside his unimaginable new life? I watched him watch tiny wood hammers hammer, corks sinking slowly deeper.

When the liquor line closed, we followed the day's final Group out into dusk. We held hands at a seaquarium. A swollen-looking balloon fish kept aggressively butting the glass, its fish lips bloodied. Delicate purple clouds.

The bulky blond guide chuckled. We call this one Herbie Jew-fish!

A Dutch joke, Kin muttered loudly, as if amazed such a thing existed.

Then, JJ: back at Las Palmas, while "Girl from Ipanema" played, I watched Kin gorge himself at a paper flower–covered buffet table. Rijstäfel: 24 Indonesian dishes. I sipped a piña colada and tried nothing; Kin tried it all: curried rice of a bright unnatural yellow, spicy pita breads, racks of raw-looking fish. Too much, too fast. Nothing tastes real, Kin told me. The spices, he claimed, were muted for tourists' tongues. The food tasted like it was still wrapped in cellophane.

Not real, Kin insisted to that now-sullen bellboy on the elevator ride up. Not real, he kept muttering, rolling in his sheets. Then how come you picked this phony place? I finally demanded of him past midnight. Or is that *why* you picked it? Kin paced between our beds. Don't know why I'm doing anything just now, he told me. But it's not, I answered fast, like we've got time for—jokes.

Kin stopped pacing. Even in the dark, I saw sweat glitter over his bare back. I held my breath, scared he might stand frozen like he'd done this afternoon. You didn't Lose It on that plane in San Juan, I told him in a second rush.

Nope, he agreed, low-voiced. I was the perfect steward. Plane in flames and I force open my exit, step aside, say: After you! He gave a short laugh. 'S easier, Berta, when danger happens the way I want things to happen. Fast. This feels more like. Shoot, my first week with Pan Am. R'member? Me too hungover to fly, serving supper to two hundred people. Kin paced faster, shaking back his hair. Felt trapped, he told me. Nowhere to go to escape this. Sickening motion . . .

Lie next to me, I told him. Imitating his old gently reassuring tone. Remember, Jim Joe, how Kin used to calm us? I'll—hold you in place.

But no. Kin couldn't stay still. He paced to the window, breathing gulps of cool unfiltered night air. Stars, he muttered as if to himself, feel closer here.

Dawn again. And I want to tell Kin, today, that we'll both feel better if we get on the move again. Start our travels, for real. Running away together was always our plan. Do you know that, JJ? How much Kin and I want to move, keep moving? Kin made me see that's what I'd always wanted, even before Stepdad #2. Whatever makeshift home Mother had scraped together for us, I felt safer outside it.

Trapped, Kin said last night. And I remembered gnawing my wood crib bars. Mother worked days, serving drinks. I chewed black nylons she left draped on my crib. She'd peel off that silky electric skin in our cold room, static crackling.

I told you some of this back in Boston. And you know you're the only person besides Kin I've ever really talked to. The only man who would listen like a girl. So—though you may never answer it—I push on with this letter. Sitting up at sunrise, watching Kin sleep and wanting to figure it out myself. Why we're here.

After I broke my nose climbing out of the crib I'd outgrown, Mother began leaving me off weekends and weekday afternoons at the ice rink. At six or seven, I skated figure-8s for hours on end. Boys caught other girls and rubbed their faces in the snow outside. But I was too fast.

Stepdad #1 panted after me on a frozen pond. Built like a hockey star, clumsy in his skates. I skimmed 8s around him; Mother laughed at him, her snow-sparkly hair platinum. Morton Giles. Mort for short, he'd say. Your Stepdad for real, Mother told me. But I wonder if she ever did marry him. The big easygoing man who shared our apartment one winter, warming it.

In Greenville, South Carolina, where we moved with Stepdad #2 when I was eleven, there was no ice. There was a house, though, our first. Across the street from a golf course where Stepdad #2—as Mother put it, as if it were something grand—kept the grounds. There was Panda, the whippet dog I'd come to love. And ballet at the Greenville Y. Mother drove me to lessons in her first bored months, before she had her job, her secret dates. In our underfurnished living room, I practiced in my tights. Quiet sullen Stepdad #2 watched from his couch. He was twenty-something, younger than Mother. Her Boy, she called him. Big like Stepdad #1, but not easygoing. His face was padded with fat that made him look like a country boy, harmless. His reddish mustache was wispy.

Turning my back, I pirouetted. Plié, point, leap. Earthbound compared to ice dancing. Behind the *Greenville Sun*, Stepdad fingered his mustache like a sore. After he gave me driving lessons in his Vega and thrust his blunt fingers inside me, his mouth sealing up mine with a taste that half a bottle of Listerine couldn't kill; after I ran to Kin and let him read my diary, let him slice my finger so we'd be Blood Sisters (we told you all that in Boston; surely you haven't forgotten) Kin and I started biking together. The first week, we shouted lost Panda's name.

The next weeks we just biked round the golf course, past dusk. Talking about our moms, about the dads neither of us knew. I, I claimed, liked not knowing. Not caring enough to try to imagine him. But Kin did try, often, grooving to Hapa-Haole Hulas through his mom's stereo headphones. He'd picture a Jack Lord/Don Ho dad swooping down to his bedside to rescue him, rescue his mom from her endlessly stressful work. Such long hours she suffered regular migraines. Kin learned to play quietly at the foot of her bed as she pressed her face between two pillows. Her head, she explained, was an egg that could crack if Kin were a noisy boy, bad boy. My mother, I bragged from my bike, let me do anything I wanted. Stay out as late as I wanted.

I never biked home, JJ, till Mother got there. She worked afternoons, a restaurant hostess. Less money, but—I told Kin—she must want to protect me from him at night. And Kin would say, his voice bumping with his bike: So you think she suspects something happened? No, no, I'd insist. No, never.

So tell her, Kin kept telling me. But Kin didn't live with him.

When I'd slip in the house late, near dark, Stepdad would crackle his *Sun*. He'd mutter to Mother that his daddy would whip him good for staying out so long. He'd lower the *Sun*. Missing supper and all, he'd say to me, so slow it might've been like flirting except that he was scared to meet my eyes, anymore.

Weekend afternoons, Kin and I watched old movies and ice skaters on his mom's white leather couch. Kin and I cut each other's hair like Dorothy Hamill's. Modified wedges. We thought our Dorothy Hamill hair was a secret no one would notice. But boys surrounded us on the bus, hooting. Sisters, sisters!

My hair grew out long so my bangs hid my face. I met no eyes but Kin's. His seemed hidden too. Black almond slits that boys at school made fun of, pulling the corners of their own eyes. Always, Kin was treated like a foreigner in Greenville, his hometown. At fifteen, I let a few boys take me on dates but I didn't let them touch me much. Waiting to tell Kin all about it. Laughing at them like they'd laughed at us. Kin at fifteen took the first of his trips to Seoul with his mom. Touching Korean boys, not talking, since they didn't speak his language. He'd felt clumsy too at first, Kin assured me. I'd start to like it, he insisted, once I met a Halfway-Decent Guy. Meanwhile, we practiced making out on his mom's couch. His mom was always gone: traveling so much it was like spotting a movie star when she'd open the door in one of the robes Kin often wore.

She called me Roberta. My mother called Kin "Ken."

Going over to Ken's? she'd ask when I was halfway out the kitchen door.

Ken Hwang's? Stepdad #2 would ask in a suspicious-sounding voice, fingering his neat mustache. He kept himself tidy except for his nails. They were the only part I remembered clearly. A minuscule scratch I could still feel, inside.

Four nights a week, I worked at a movie theater in a short skirt like Mother's old velveteen cocktail-waitress skirt. The bald manager lingered by my counter, watching me. So Kin paid to stand in the lobby and chat with me while I cleaned the Coke machine or counted candy. My bodyguard. We'd bike home so Stepdad #2 wouldn't get to pick me up in the Vega I'd refused to learn to drive.

Summer 1979. Carolina nights. Kin and I biked round the golf course in soft balmy dark, waiting for Stepdad's TV light to go off inside my house. It was then, JJ, that Kin began saying we had to stop running in circles. We had to run, he told me above the mosquitoes and the louder hum of our wheels, some*where*.

At 7 A.M. this second day, in the lemony light, Kin woke. I hid my letter to you. This letter I can't stop writing now, our second night. Because you've got to keep me company, Jimmy Joe, after this day. You're right, Kin told me at first as we dressed. We gotta get off this fucking Floating Boutique. But every place, Berta, has something worth (he drew out his favorite word) ex-per-iencing.

He led. He had a plan, like the old Kin. Our Kin, Jim Joe. The morning air was the softest I'd ever felt, filled with finely sifted pollen that soothed my burning skin and eyelids. Kin moved slowly, as if still stuffed from his feast.

We walked along closed-up Fuik Straat till sidewalk turned to sand. Goats in rope halters ambled across the road. We followed the goats past a falsely green park alive only with sprinklers into a market. The first part of this island I've liked. Wood stalls packed with fruit and raw shrimp. My mouth and eyes watered. Women in kerchiefs hummed and gutted fish. Flies buzzed, bolder than American flies. I bit my first mango, a heavy squarish pear. Smooth yet stringy like a banana. Its perfumed sweetness startled my mouth. I swished thick mango juice on my teeth as Kin in his rusty Spanish negotiated a jeep ride. Through the *cunucu,* the countryside, to Autre Banda.

The driver we hired, Rick Tapaca, promised us wild winds and wicked waves. We followed him down the sandy street to his jeep, parked behind a rank-smelling stall hung heavy with chickens, heads and feet attached. Rick told Kin in Spanish that sharks were fed on the Other Side so they wouldn't swim round to the *turista* side. But that one man swam round the whole island, both sides, once a year.

Three girls with Rick Tapaca's square face and sweet-potato skin jumped rope in our bouncing wake. The road twisted into greenery teeming with sun, a smell of hot-baked leaves. Multiple greens blurred into one. I missed my old hair, which would've whipped my face like Kin's frantic hair.

Fan palms, Kin shouted into my ear, translating Rick. Divi-divi trees!

Halfway around the island, he shouted for Rick to stop at a gravel turnoff. A wood sign in English; an ancient-looking gray stone box of a building with paneless windows. The Western Hemisphere's Oldest Synagogue. Kin walked in alone. Rick Tapaca and I sat in the jeep listening to amplified-sounding full-throated bird songs. Kin came out wearing his sunglasses, pallid under his tan. He climbed up into the jeep slowly, as if in spite of being so thin he felt heavy.

I'm converted, he whispered to me, in hoarse English. I'm Herbie, Jew-fish.

Had he, I hoped, cried at last? In its frenzy, Kin's hair blinded me. He held my arm, though the curves came no sharper than before. Was fear waking up inside him? Tell me, I wanted to say. As the road got rocky, our wheels spurted wet clay, then wet sand. The wind's roar blocked the ocean's till Rick swung round one last curve. Black volcanic rock rose before us like the hump of a whale. Beyond its topmost curve, we saw—in sunlit arches—white spray.

Un hombre, Rick shouted, maybe forgetting he'd already told this one.

One man—Kin shouted back, standing in the salt wind. His shirt blew up, his tan belly swollen as if with the smallest of babies. One man! Swims all the way round! He scrambled off the jeep, his sunglasses bouncing. And he ran up the hill of rock toward the ocean we now heard and smelled. I thudded behind him, the rock shot full of holes like coral. On the topmost mound, I grabbed Kin's shoulder, his hair swamping my face like seaweed. His sunglasses were soaked, his face slick with spume. Below us, the rough black rock sloped to a stretch of black beach. Breakers burst into geysers taller than us.

Kin gulped a mouthful of wind. He pushed me sideways. His mouth stretched; his body convulsed. His head exploded in a burst of chewed-up flesh. No: food! Moist bits of saffron yellow rice flew into my mouth, my eyes. I spat and swatted as if at a swarm of bees. When I could see again, Kin was on his knees, still vomiting.

Wet wind swept it away. Kin's chin plastered with goop then drenched, washed nearly clean. The wind hid my tears as I slumped down beside him. Pocked rock cut my knees. Bits of sour green stuck to Kin's tangled swept-back hair. I sobbed and he didn't. But he let me grip his arm, holding him in place.

Kin's hair whipped both our faces. Blue surrounded us, all wavery shades of it. Sky and ocean and the quivering line between them. Infinite, magnetic. Kin swiveled his head. All that space seemed to grow vaster and vaster around us. So we gripped each other's arms. Both of us, JJ, light enough for the wind to lift.

Or are you reading at all? Do you really not care at all? Even as you see us for the first time in years—and not just in the photo I'll enclose. (Us in '80, posing for you, wearing only your jacket between us). I want you to see us now, too, staggering back to Las Palmas. Hair and clothes sticky with puke. Told you this is no poem. I won't ever be a poet. Kin won't be a pilot or a translator. We'll be real—the "real" will make all the difference, if we can pull it off—travelers.

Back in our room, Kin took a long cold shower. He untangled his hair with a plastic comb, half its teeth snapping off. All afternoon, he lay in bed, talking on the phone. Meeting my eyes, awaiting my nods before going further.

In his Carolina bargainer's voice, in English then Spanish, Kin negotiated with far-flung Pan Am officials about the weeks of accumulated vacation time and dozens of Free-Fly Points he wants to begin using, now. He wrote down Pan Am's South American route. Long-distance to New York, Kin talked to his friend Big Boyd about subletting his apartment, shipping him more clothes. And would Boyd want to buy Kin's camera, buy Kin's 428 cassettes? The leather couch? Kin asked. I stopped my pacing. You like that? Kin toyed with his calling card. Sure, sure, he murmured. Sounded fair to him. No; he didn't need more time to think.

When he finally hung up, I was standing still, my shorts stuck against my legs. Kin kept his hand on the receiver. Maybe it felt hot, like the hood of a car after a long trip. Your music? I asked. You're selling your cassettes?

Gonna give away my headphones too. Kin sounded hoarse. Maybe to that bellboy. From now on, Berta, we're listening to music live. There's music on streets and beaches all over *America del Sur*. I nodded, my heart pumping. Kin lifted his hand off the phone. No one else *I* need to call, he announced, before we escape. Or—"disappear." I nodded again. I didn't need to phone anyone.

I've already said good-bye, Kin went on. To Big Boyd and my fellow stewardesses. Shoot: all those Red Eyes and No-Tell Layovers and Mile-High-Club fun in the lav. And my one flame-out by that stewed-shit bay in San Juan. Still, Berta. No one's been through as much with me as you.

I smiled. Remembering Big Boyd telling me Kin always seemed off to himself. I felt a rise in my chest. Though I knew, Jim Joe, Kin could've used his friends now, knew Big Boyd and his crowd might've been better able than me to comfort Kin. I sat down beside him on his bed; he scooted over to make room for me.

Guess I could call my "Grandpa," Kin told me in a drifty scratchy voice.

Yeah, right. I touched Kin's shoulder, relieved to be relaxed with him again.

Will T. Clemson, the man in Greenville who adopted Kin's mother, is a Holy Roller who mails Christmas cards addressed only to Kin. Did Kin ever tell you, JJ? I bet not. Bet I'm the only one he's told. See, Will T. cut off contact with Kin's mom after Kin was born. Conceived on that youth-group church trip to Hawaii. The first fun of my life, his mom used to say as if she meant: first and last.

I pressed Kin's shoulder only lightly. The way his mom used to touch him. Pregnant, she'd won a scholarship. She'd carried baby Kin to her classes in business administration. He'd learned early not to—her word—"fuss."

Kin shrugged off my touch. Not unkindly, just automatically. A cat shaking off water. But he told me it felt right to be running away with me again. This time, he promised, we'll *do* it right. Fly wherever we want, Bird, whenever. Do what we want. And after my vacation runs out, I can switch my flying base from New York, so we can stay away. Stay in motion. See places even I've never seen. See China. He gave the skeptical affectionate sigh he uses when thinking of his dead mom. No point trying to track down any "Hwangs" there. Mom always said she had no idea if it's her real family name. Which's, Kin finished, fine by me.

He stood as if eager to commence packing. I stood too, thrilled to be Kin's only—aren't we each other's now, legally and everything?—family.

We skipped supper. As we watched the overripe peachy sunset, I told Kin there was one more thing we needed to get rid of. I slipped it from Kin's wallet. This photo you took of us. Kin kept it since you never did let him take you. I'll ship it to JJ, I announced. So we, Kin agreed, can travel light. He grinned like he doubted I'd do it. Then he made me promise what he'd asked in singsong on the plane. That we steer clear of—New York's was his last, he swore—all MED FACILs.

See, JJ? I know you don't want to. And I won't tell much more, won't tell all. Not now. Not to you and your wife or whoever that big-eyed woman was who showed up at Ko No's. Who's reading these words, maybe. 'Cause maybe she's sneaking peeks at your mail, too. Kin hasn't phoned your machine again, you notice. Though we know where you live. But you don't know where we are now. Where we'll be living, half the time. In air. On a bumpy Pan Am 747, Kin dozing beside me. We Know What We Want to Do on Our Honeymoon.

This morning, before our noon flight, we followed the goats, bought shawls woven from brown thread that smelled of sheep. We covered our heads. We let fat flies settle on our faces, getting used to them. My peeling skin no longer burned. My eyelids burned only if I didn't squint to keep out grit. Tears kept cleaning my eyeballs. Like the rain this morning: a quick cooling shower. On, then off. Our damp shawls smelled more strongly of sheep. At the wood-and-canvas fruit stalls, only the oldest men stared. Kin's face is already so brown he might be from anywhere. I stood behind him, twisting for luck our— Kin's and my—ring of 8s.

Kin bought plum-colored melons and goat cheese and sweet hot bread, bargaining in Spanish. Throwing in phrases of island Papiamento. Showing off. I laughed, seeing firsthand how fast he picks up any new language. He crouched by a flat rock. He unfolded the Swiss Army knife he always carries, though it was sent to him by Will T. Clemson. Slowly, Kin cut our melon, studying each dripping crescent slice. Meditating. So I paced Figure-8s around him, respectfully silent. We ate in the spiky shade of a fan palm, chewing with open mouths.

Kin told me then—so calmly, JJ, it killed me—what he wants, now. To experience, Kin said, as much as he can of this world he'll be leaving.

See? We know what we want to do for the rest of his—I say: of our— life.

(And I've taken his name again, like any good wife)

Kin

8

As a Second Language

"Don't he look like he's from somewhere else?" Vi asked the way she'd been asking all September. "Guess *he'll* never tell where." She switched on Carter's Communication Computer, joggling its keyboard. "Maybe Honolulu or some such place, where the skins are nice and dark and the eyes are slanted-like. . . ."

"Who knows?" Allie eased James Carter into his seat behind the corkboard. This first week in October, his age had been estimated between fifty and sixty, his IQ possibly within normal range. Must be higher than normal, Vi had told Allie. Considering all he been through. Don'tcha think?

"Glad Channel 8's not comin' today," Vi mumbled, her tooth giving slow-motion winks. She handed Allie Carter's clipboard. "I hear they comin' just once more. Then we won't get to see the dang show till next spring."

"Plenty soon enough for me." Allie hugged the clipboard. In her new one-day-at-a-time life, next spring felt too far away to worry about.

"Good luck, baby doll." Vi bent close, emitting a whiff of tobacco gum. "Don't work the Prez too hard." She patted Allie's shoulder and, more firmly, Carter's.

His glasses still floated over his melted-chocolate eyes. This week on the bus, Allie had noticed how glasses couldn't grip the smooth flat noses of the Asian faces that reminded her of Kin. The man, Kin. Now that she alone had read the letter from Curaçao, she knew this much, at least. The Asian man's name was Kin. Sighing, Alice slumped like Carter. Relieved to be hidden back here.

The Curaçao letter had floated from the mailbox to her feet only four days before. A delayed delivery postmarked in early August. So battered-looking it might have been carried by mule train. Its envelope already half torn, which made it easier for Allie to open it herself. She had slipped out, then instantly dropped, the black-and-white snapshot folded into the letter. She had hidden both from JJ that night, intending to show him the next day. And the next.

"OK." Allie scooted closer to Carter, their knees bumping under the table. His mouth twitched, a one-sided smile. "Let's start with your alphabet."

Lifting the clipboard, she glanced at her watch. JJ was still on duty at Rare Books, a simple shelving job while he took an official one-year Academic Leave. Trying, as they'd say on *The Young and the Restless*, to get his head together.

"First, let's set up." Allie slipped out a folder marked "English as a Second Language." Carter gave his resigned wheeze of a sigh as she began arranging flash cards. A, B. Her fingers lingered on C for Curaçao. She pressed her lips together. Remembering, unwillingly, the basic facts she knew for sure: that the woman in Ko No's was "Bird." That the Asian man named Kin was Bird's husband; that he was gay. Allie tightened her lips so they felt thin. Her whole face felt tightened, pinched. JJ's jealous uptight wife. She fumbled with Carter's D flash card, hating most of all to remember that photo of Kin and Bird in bed. What the Hell did it mean? That JJ *had* been involved with them both?

Only you, Bird had written maddeningly, *ever saw us this way.*

"Look." Allie dropped the G. As far as Carter could go. "Recognize all these? Do you—" She looked again, herself. "Notice something missing?" Shakily, she lifted the flashcard stack again. Behind his glasses, Carter's eyes drifted half shut.

Before the Curaçao letter, in the hot dry weeks of August and September, Allie had tried to work up the nerve to ask JJ outright: What all happened between him and that Kin man? What did JJ feel for Kin now? If they had been lovers—and surely they had, since JJ remained so silent about it—had he seen Kin or other men in the years since? Had he wanted to? All this Allie was determined to find out, as soon as she felt sure that JJ—struggling to decide about Yale, about his future—was going to be OK, wasn't headed for some new breakdown.

Anyhow, there'd been little time to ask anything. Not with Allie working long hours at New Chance Workshop and overnight shifts at group homes, whatever Ms. Carmella at Helping Hands could scrape up. Meanwhile, JJ was withdrawing from his fall classes, applying for jobs. Alone in the evenings, they'd watch the news in a companionable shell-shocked daze. JJ cooked all their dinners. His manner was almost apologetically gentle, careful. She heard a plea in his quiet polite movements. So she was quietly polite in return, waiting. By the time she'd read the delayed-delivery Curaçao letter and studied the photo till its faces and body parts blurred together, JJ had just begun to seem OK. Each morning this week, Allie had resolved to show him what, of course, he deserved to see. But each afternoon JJ had come home from his new library job more like his old self. Each night she'd fallen asleep to JJ's comforting key clicks. He'd begun to work on his music generation program on his own, on their own computer.

"Where *is* that E?" Allie shuffled the well-worn flash cards. And she made herself consider yet again the worst implications of the Curaçao letter, trying to—JJ'd say—"process" them. Kin insisting on no more "MED FACILs." Kin saying he "would have" pursued the Curaçao bellboy in—JJ's phrase—"another life." The Bird woman plainly stating at the letter's end that Kin may not have long to live.

"Here it is." Allie slid out the E card. As she spread D and F, she resolved yet again to stop putting it off. To confront JJ today, Friday. "OK, we got it all laid out." She stared as if the letters formed some obvious word. Under the table, she fingered the wallet in her denim skirt pocket. Bird's snapshot hidden inside.

"Wake up now," Allie told Carter halfheartedly. He yawned, his big jawbone cracking, his breath smelling of stale pipe. She re-straightened his flash card row, relieved to concentrate on anything but the farfetched Worst-Case Scenario. *If* the Kin man was dying of AIDS; *if* JJ had met with him in recent years or *if* this were a case in which the HIV virus hibernated for years. ("Seven or more" was the highest estimate she'd read; this would have to be eight.) If all that, what then? What—wasn't anything too late?—could she do to protect JJ? And herself?

"Aye." Allie jerked up the A card, meeting Carter's bemused gaze. "Aye, Ah." She guided Carter's hand to the computer keyboard, the *A* key. "Good!"

"P-Pie—" he demanded after B and C. Sensing he'd get her to stop early?

"Pipe." Alice repeated the one word she knew he knew. "*Tell* me, OK?"

Sighing, Carter let her swing his hand to two oversized keys. Her grip tightened with a hope that they might communicate. But he pressed the left key, two blurred letters. Like a toddler, Vi pointed out, all Carter wanted to say was *No.*

"Your *pipe*?" Allie repeated, sure Carter understood. His finger stayed planted. Even when Vi taped reverse names on *No* and *Yes,* Carter stuck to his stubborn course. "Yes." Allie nudged his finger to that key. A cheery beep.

"I know you know that, Prez." Briskly, she stood, feeling Carter eye her ass in a way she shouldn't—didn't, now—enjoy. She filled his plastic corncob pipe. Back in August, when she and JJ still weren't touching as much as usual, she'd taken crude comfort in Carter's frank stare. His conspiratorial grins.

"Here you go." Allie struck the match. Only in the last cool Indian-summer weeks had she and JJ really started up again. She stepped carefully, sheltering the flame. One night in mid-September, they'd snuggled on the fold-out after the news. They weren't used to going without. They had gotten so worked up so fast, they hadn't stopped for a condom or diaphram. They'd pushed ahead heedlessly.

Carter bit his pipe stem. He sucked in the flame, blew it back as smoke. Allie sat close beside him. The computer hummed, a *Yes* still aglow on its screen.

Afterward, they'd agreed they hated the subtle new tension between them. But, JJ'd said, he wasn't ready to discuss Kin. Not now. Then someday? she asked, annoyed by her own timidity. Someday, he'd agreed, liking that vague word.

As Carter puffed, Alice slid from her wallet the snapshot Bird had sent. Its edges worn, its background a soft white: some sort of bed. There was—Allie studied it under the table—no mistaking them. The man and woman from Ko No's, only younger, with long hair and sly grins. Shown from the waist up: the man bare-chested in an oversized—JJ-sized?—leather jacket. The white-blond woman hugs him from behind, peeking over his shoulder, her own slim arms and shoulders and cut-off hip bare. Was she too shy to show her breasts? Kin's and Bird's pale and dark stares meet Allie's, intently. Saying to her: We dare you to look back.

Carter chuckled. Alice blinked. She met his own steady stare, aglint as if he'd caught her getting off on the photo. And, she asked herself as she slipped it back in her wallet, am I? Her skin felt hot, her pulse fluttery. Damn that Bird, she thought. Sending my husband a come-on like this. Alice pocketed the wallet, telling herself as she'd done all week: Yes, they both must have been JJ's lovers. Both at once? Outside the partition, something big fell with a wood thud.

"Alice Wolf-ee!" Supervisor Sticks materialized in the partition opening. "Go help Vi with Connie. I'll take care o' Carter here."

"Uh walla!" Connie Botts bellowed like a cavewoman as Alice ran toward the overturned table. When Connie had her period, she acted—Vi said—the way all women want to act that time of month. Kicking and writhing on the floor as Vi struggled to pin down her arms. Allie crouched at her feet, gripping her ankles.

"Wah-*lah*—" Connie strained her muscular unshaven legs against

Allie. She forced Connie's feet down, thinking of Bird in Curaçao long-ing to hold Kin in place, comfort him. *Remember, Jim Joe, how Kin used to calm us?*

Such a surprise, that line. Allie loosened her grip as Connie's leapfrog kicks subsided. Studying the photo, she had pictured the Kin man doing the opposite to JJ: stirring him up. Two men young enough to still be boys impulsively experimenting with a girl, with each other. Mutual masturbation?

But for once, JJ, we aren't going to give you what you want.

Connie Botts panted, her seizure spent. Blinking, Alice gazed past Connie's raised knees—the crotch of her shorts stained with menstrual blood—to Connie's square-jawed boyish face, marked by scabby scratches of her own making.

"Keep hold of her," Vi told Allie in a low murmur, so the words would sound soothing to Connie. "Don't want her goin' at her face again."

"Yeah, I know." Allie murmured too. "But I feel so mean holding her down. . . ." Connie tossed her stringy-haired head from side to side like a restless sleeper.

And Allie remembered Bird's description of Kin rolling over and over in his hotel bed. Remembered Bird telling JJ he was the one person be-sides Kin she'd ever been able to confide in. Only now, Alice thought, I'm not letting her.

"E," Supervisor Sticks told Carter behind Carter's partition. He whimpered, unused to being pushed so far in his lessons. Too often, Alice let him off too soon. Guiltily, she kept hold of Connie Botts's hairy ankles and listened to Sticks patiently prod Carter. "Eee, I said *Eee*. No. Do it yourself, Prez. Your*self*."

．　．　．

Released into the sunny fall air, Allie strode past the charred brick walls of Manslaughter Street. Bracing herself to show JJ Bird's letter, Bird and Kin's photo. To see him see them. If she didn't confront JJ now, she'd never get through this weekend, alone with him all day. She hurried past cannibal pigeons pecking a red-striped box of fried-chicken re-mains. And she stepped over a mass of cassette tape tangled around a plastic fork. A hobo robot's feast. She turned off Manslaw. 4:35. She'd planned to work an hour at the Dukakis booth on Chapel.

But she slowed her steps. The booth was run by a burly divinity-school student/social worker who never had time to pick food from his beard. God, that earnest bad breath. Allie veered away from Chapel

Street. No, she didn't want to hear another unregistered unemployed voter ask her, Who *was* the President now? Or another woman confide that she wouldn't vote for Michael Dukakis because his head looked too big on his body. Not today; Alice would save her strength for JJ. Show him everything as soon as she got there. Ready or not.

But she aimed toward the university. The long way home. Castles of gray stone displayed their towers, crisp against the blue sky. A New England day, Allie thought as the brick walls she passed grew cleaner. Fall was her favorite season. The invigorating air, back-to-school energy. She fell into the brisker pace of students with book-filled backpacks. Swinging her hair, Allie imagined herself a Presbyterian princess safe behind the diamond-patterned windows of these castle dorms, the lowest windows guarded by what JJ called "moats."

She gazed into one of those stone-lined pits. A letter, she rehearsed telling JJ, as a start. A letter came for you, Monday. What a relief it'd be to confess that. She wandered along the plaza of the churchlike Rare Books library. JJ had worked from seven till four inside that austere square of concrete and thinly sliced marble. Outside, the marble in full sun showed its veins. Inside, the effect was like stained-glass windows. A hush, a Gutenberg Bible under glass.

"Alice? Alice Wolfe?" Sharon somebody—wife of one of JJ's former fellow students, his "Bros"—hugged her own proud pile of books. Alice rallied a smile. She and Sharon had lunched together a few times: Sharon eager to complain about her dumb sales job and her smart husband who rarely left the computer lab. Back then, last spring, Allie had only nodded sympathetically, sure of her own husband.

"And how *is* JJ?" Sharon gave a toothsome smile.

"Oh, he's fine! Just taking some time off . . ." Allie hated her own too-smooth voice. "—on leave for a year, to sort out what he wants to do . . ."

"Really?" Sharon asked, trying not to sound pleased.

As Sharon strode off—we'll have to lunch; I'll tell you 'bout my major!—Allie stood in the cooling sunlight. She'd planned to audit classes too, JJ's second year. Scope out the master's program in psychology. Students hurried around her, laughing. A mechanical buzz startled her. She gazed up at new scaffolding: workers buffing gargoyles. Stone chips and fine powder drifted down.

No wonder townies hate this place, Allie thought as she walked on. A palace forever preening itself. Of course, she reminded herself, she was a townie too. Yet JJ had told her he sometimes wanted to show his music generation program to the Bros. Sometimes wanted to be in class again,

in spite of the DOD. Allie had given her honest opinion. If you just finish two more semesters and get your masters, you can find a non-DOD
job—maybe in education software. You can try to do enough good to
make up for any "tainted" money you might take here.

She marched past the last of Yale. The lawns, she thought, of a
British boys' school. Alice was a mild English/Irish on her mom's blue-
eyed Delaney side and a wild-eyed Scotch/Irish on her dad's. JJ was
Welsh (Think so, his dad had allowed, narrowing his eyes as if she'd
asked him a trick question). She breathed the fresh-cut grass. Weren't
British schoolboys routinely supposed to have homosexual affairs
("buggering" each other) and afterward to settle into marriages with
women? Allie sighed, annoyed by her own ignorance. Lately her life felt
too sheltered, too small. After Yale parties, she'd sometimes asked JJ if
someone was gay. He'd say *Probably* or *Probably not* in a tone of *Definitely;
Definitely not.*

Allie glanced at two passing boys. Their bookpacks bumped. Of
course she'd met openly gay men before. In college, in Late-Night Study,
she'd shared coffee breaks with wry Sid and Phillip, fellow sociology
majors who did hilarious Reagan-Bush impressions. Since Kin's phone
message, Alice had often thought back to them, trying to get used to
the idea of JJ as a man drawn to men. Since the photo had arrived,
though, Alice had found herself thinking—hoping—JJ might've been,
more, a man drawn to a male-female pair. She found this possibility easier to take. At least it didn't make her feel shut out altogether.

Lowering her eyes, Allie pictured herself naked between JJ and the
Kin man. Four hands, two cocks. What would it be like? Frightening,
exciting. JJ had taught her everything she knew. But not everything *he*
knew? She studied the clean Yale sidewalk, white as a bedsheet, and
wondered how many ways Kin and Bird had concocted to make love to
JJ. An adventure for JJ, she told herself. Back when he was so young
and—she couldn't refrain from adding—crazy. Not himself. Or: maybe
her JJ was "not himself." How could she know sex with a man or man-
and-woman wasn't something JJ still wanted? Allie bumped off the
curb. Surely it was paranoid to suspect JJ might've been meeting Kin, in
secret.

"'Scuse me." Allie brushed past a tweedy professor's-wife type.
Leaves scuttled. The New Haven green looked grayish, but it was com-
fortingly full of people. A mom pushed a bundled-up boy on a temporary Fall Festival swing set.

"Me now!" a girl behind the mom howled. Allie stopped, picturing
for further comfort herself and Jo back in Pennsylvania. Doted over by

their two grandmas and their mom. America's One Functional Family, JJ had decreed.

"Me now! *Mee!*" The girl tugged her mother's coat. Allie sat on a bench. Beside her, an old lady fed hot-dog-bun crumbs to pigeons. This time of day in Pennsylvania, she and Jo would be pumping away on their own swings, sturdy-legged like the grounded girl who soared up now. Allie glanced at the next bench. Under it lay the JJ-sized Rastafarian, only his ruglike hair showing. Where—she wondered self-consciously—were Kin and Bird sleeping these days?

She looked back at the mother, playing catch with her son. Spunky like her own mom before the accident: caring for Grandmas Delaney and Hart; driving Jo and Allie to piano lessons, Brownie-troop meetings. Her heels click-clicking.

Alice stood up, thinking of the childhood Bird had described in her letter. Her mother gone all day, leaving her in her crib. Her stepfather thrusting his fingers inside her in his car. *His mouth sealing up mine with a taste that half a bottle of Listerine couldn't kill.* Both the boy and girl were playing catch with their mom now. Alice made herself turn toward home. Not only did JJ deserve to read the letter, she told herself, but the Bird woman deserved to reach JJ.

Right? Allie speeded her steps, trying not to think of that come-on photo. Trying to be kinder and gentler; Bush's slogan. The way she'd always hoped she'd act if faced with a real test of her compassion. And surely, she reminded herself, her elaborate Worst-Case-Scenario was unlikely, unreal. Hugging her sweater, she hurried onto Chapel, too many blocks from the Dukakis booth to be spotted.

"Thirty-five cents, please?"

Allie stopped by a coin Laundromat to give thirty-five cents to the homeless lady who always demanded exactly that. Walking on, she heard her feeble phlegmy cough. You wimped out, Jo would say if Jo knew how long she'd put off talking to JJ. Yesterday, Jo had phoned again about Dad, his emphysema so bad he needed an oxygen tank by his bed. His one vice, Mom used to call his smoking. Now Jo wanted Allie's opinion on sending Dad to a Home. Don't wimp out on me, Jo had admonished. You're the expert on Homes. 'Least according to that thesis you wrote. Did ya know Mom keeps a copy of that? Your Weakness Thesis?

Oh God, Allie had answered, glad to change the subject. No.

Yeah, Jo had gone on bluntly. I looked through it. Ya know the best part? That quote on the first page. That thing about the squirrel's heartbeat?

Oh yeah, Allie had said, smiling herself. My epigraph. From *Middlemarch*.

She passed Kappy's package store, trying to remember the Eliot quote. How we are well wadded against seeing the everyday suffering around us. How if we did see it all, we'd go mad as if hearing the grass grow and the squirrel's heartbeat. "Well wadded": she remembered that phrase.

I can't start acting like Mom, Allie told herself, rounding her last corner. Unwilling to discuss things I find upsetting. Afraid what might come out. But she lingered by the New & Used Furniture in Giovanni's window, feeling a familiar last-minute weakening of resolve. She studied the new chrome, old wood.

"Whach'ya think's gonna happen?" Tobias sidled up and she fished out her key. He nodded at her Dukakis button, his rooster-crest hair shiny in the sunset.

"Oh, he'll win, he'll win." Allie shook her head the way Dukakis did on TV.

Tobias shook his head too. "Y'know Alice Wolfe, I saw a car-toon put me in mind o' you. Called: Pollyanna in Hell." Allie laughed, clicking her key. "She sayin': Nice an' warm down here! She sayin': Meet lotsa interesting people!"

Alice was still laughing, was wondering if she *did* have to confront JJ today, as she unlocked the mailbox. The mail usually arrived just after JJ got home. So she was the one to lift it up now, light as air itself. Another airmail envelope, stamped: Belém, Brasil. Addressed to JJ in the Bird woman's spidery fine pen. Another tenant was pushing the door behind Allie, following Allie—that's how it felt—as she hurried up the stairs. She half ran down their hall, alone now but still feeling pursued. OK, OK. She thumped their door open.

"Al?" JJ poked his head out of the bedroom, Walkman headphones dangling round his neck. Lately he'd been listening to music more, but only alone.

"Just a sec." Alice slipped into the bathroom, telling herself to let JJ read it first even as she locked the door. Opening JJ's mail was easier this second time. She sat on the closed toilet to slit the tissue-thin envelope. After a few lines, she stood, cranked on both sink faucets, sat down to begin again. The lightly printed words seemed ready to slide off the weightless pages that trembled in her hands.

❖   ❖   ❖

Olá, J. Joe:

Sometimes it takes years to show. What's inside, love.

We see you, even from Belém. Our Jimmy J. Your ocean eyes hold blue and green and gray. All three at once. Sure as I know that, I know what else you still hold, inside. And though I knew you wouldn't show in Queens, wouldn't show at Ko No's, I know you won't say No to what Kin needs now. Not when Kin gave us what we, back in Boston. Needed so badly—or don't you remember?

You will, groom. Our AWOL groom. I've got just enough airmail paper to make you see us. To squeeze in weeks. A Whole (as they say on the honeymoon island we left first, fastest) Lifetime Worth of Memories.

See? Curaçao to Caracas to Santiago to Rio. Kin's paid vacation days, his transferable Free-Fly Points. We flew on jets like American jets only less crowded (spices startling the airline food; Spanish and Portuguese preceding softly accented English on the loudly crackling intercoms; open-air terminals with broken escalators policed by men in khaki uniforms and surrounded by jungle) or on shuttle planes, prop planes putt-putting over delirious green stretches of Amazon. Kin whispering that we were safer, really, since a jet in trouble would fall like an aluminum stone but a small plane like this can glide.

We glided all August, see, all over South America. Kin laid low in *muito-macho* South America in the early '80s. These days, quiet as a spy, he's slipped in and out of marketplace after marketplace. Buying us fresh fruits with musical names—*pupunha, maracuja, uva*—and strong-smelling ropes of tobacco. He's cooked feasts over campfires, tempting me with his inventions: duck-egg pancakes in Brazil, fried pumpkin patties in Chile. *Churrasco* that made him sick in Venezuela. Each food so new I couldn't just swallow. I tried to taste, savor. And everywhere, JJ, on every street: live music. Talking drums and bongos and bottles and go go bells and rattles carved from gourds. We two danced like we three used to dance. Tangos in Buenos Aires, salsa-band lambadas in Caracas. For sleeping, Kin found us cheap hostels or hidden beaches. The sand untrampled, the few slow bodies ambling beside our own aglow with browns Kin's skin has begun to match.

And me? I followed Kin between wood market stalls, still pink and blond enough to draw all eyes. Men's dark eyes. Men the same everywhere on earth. *Ti quiero*, they say, seeing me. Looking for a loe-ver? one whispered in Santiago. Others asked the same thing more elaborately in Spanish, blocking my path. But if they touch me, Kin spirits me away in the wink of an eye.

And my eyes? My eyelids itched but my lashes were growing back, slowly, the way all things happen here. Slowly too, I was peeling off my old skin. Pink sunburnt strips wafted behind me as we glided along. Till Argentina, beyond the Pampas, where Kin got laid up with what seemed a simple flu mixed with the trots. It didn't go away. In a hostel room with no mirrors, Kin had me keep checking the inside of his mouth for sores. After the fever broke, Kin felt jet-lagged. Even when he'd taken too many days of rest for it to be jet-lag. But even in *muito-moderno* Buenos Aires, even when I begged, he wouldn't see any doctor. Not yet, he told me. For now, while he still can, he wants to keep moving. See?

Buenos Aires to São Paulo. Kin spinning in a circle of traveling Sufis in an all-night dance bar. Spin-dancing turns out to be religion, a Sufi dervish. Kin staggered back to the table, telling me—remember, Jim Joe, the first time you and Kin did your spin-dance, hysterical over that *Joy of Cooking* instruction for a cream fondue?—"Oh Birdy, I've been Whipped into a Mad Vortex!"

Then came our long hungover stopover in Rio de Janeiro. Its zebra-striped sidewalk, its all-day all-night music, its pickpocket street kids. They surrounded me, too fast even for Kin. They whisked *cruzeiro* notes from my shorts. Stole Fatima's money too, those quick-fingered kids. She, see, won a flight to Rio in a radio contest. She met us on our cheapo shuttle to Belém, Brazil.

Here in Belém on the Amazon, Kin needs, we need, help. To keep moving. Kin wandered the markets one day and spent the rest of the week recovering. He'd walked barefoot like the Brazilian boys too poor for the beach flip-flops of the less-poor. My feet felt hot in high-top sneakers that drew stares. I walked way too slow, Kin told me. And I lost him amidst dangling snakeskins and skimpy Brazilian bikinis and *jacara* teeth and crepey flowers and dried lizards and powdered lizards and Pepsi-Cola and tambourine-shaking monkeys and oranges in plastic net sacks and grapes in paper cups and mangos all over the ground.

The first day in Belém, I'd paid three *cruzeiros* for a mango. Fatima laughed and told Kin in Portuguese what I'd done. Needing no words, her daughter Fati pointed out to me how they fall off the trees here. Mangos, for free.

'Cept we can't live on mangos. And Pan Am can fire Sister Kin, who's run out of vacation days. AWOL. Kin's put off phoning his main office. He's been too sick to worry about anything but getting better. But this family we've met may save us. Pregnant Fatima and silent Zé and little Fati, who Kin befriended on that flight from Rio. What we need is 5000 *cruzeiros*—$50 or so—to bus all five of us back to their house near a village called Nossa Senhora Do Ó in the state of Maranhão. We can stay with them till their baby comes. Kin needs—he admits it, which scares me—rest.

And he feels at home here in Brazil. Here, JJ, everyone cross-dresses at Carnival time. One church, called Candomble, worships saints who change sex with the seasons. Most men we meet in bars joke affectionately about *Viados*. The word for gay men that means "deer." (Remember the sound of "Deer Calling One Another?") Brazil is the perfect place, Kin tells me, to get back his strength. Then get back to work—if not with Pan Am, with Trans Brasil—as soon as these symptoms pass. Soon as they hide out, he means. Again. In him. In you too maybe, James Joseph. It, like love, can take years to show.

Please don't think I want to scare you. I only want you to see from half a world away that you're in this too. In us. Even here in the sweet deep heat of Belém, the heat that's warming my Olaf bones, slowly. My blood temperature is sinking south, slow too. The way everything here, time itself included, moves.

'Cept my pen. Scratch, scratch. We won't leave another unanswered message on your machine. Not that we can afford the one phone in this hotel, where we share one bathroom with the first floor. A luxury. Outside, see, against the hotel's back wall, families in transit sleep on cardboard, guarded by chickens that flock these streets like pigeons, only cleaner. I sit alone now for the first time in weeks. Because outside, against that wall, a Snoopy cartoon movie is being screened from a truck. Kin holds Fati in his lap and Fatima leans on Zé. Cars honk, then weave through the crowd, heads hanging out windows to glimpse the square of moving light. Horns go ha-ha and kids squeal and panic-stricken chickens scramble.

Bedlam in Belém. I slipped inside, my gums bleeding from nerves. Rooster crows are all we'd hear in the hills. All night sometimes, Fatima says. You can't imagine how loud. And the rest of the time: you can't imagine how quiet.

Or how badly we now need: $50 at least, wired to Kin Hwang via Banco de Brasil, central office, Belém, PA. Kin's mother's date of death, which will be our ID for pick-up, is 10/22/80. We've spent all we had, see. A binge of food and beaches and dance bars. A lifetime's worth of memories. I know you can't have forgotten us, Jim Joe, even as you ignore us, still.

It can be in you for years without showing, love. Love, and something besides—because of—love. Don't pretend you don't know what I mean. I didn't want to tell you while Kin was still well. And I can't say it—I'm sorry—any way except: Kin is positive. HIV Positive. I didn't believe it at first either, his test.

Maybe Kin still doesn't, JJ. He hasn't, as they advised at the Health Center, tracked his T-cell count. Hasn't tracked down any AZT here, doesn't trust any drugs. Never has. He wants to trust what's natural. Wants to believe, still, that his single test might've been a mistake. So, see, I believe in it for two.

And you? You're in this too, in a way. Not physically, I hope. I feel sure. But weren't the bonds between us more than physical? Aren't they? It's a small world, JJ. Nossa Senhora Do Ó is a tiny village, inland from São Luís. Too tiny to show on most maps. Look at a map. Look at the blankest space near São Luís. Touch it with your cool fingertip. Cool outside, warm in. Our Lady of O. Join (you always were good at that) us if you want, if you dare.

Your (we are, still)
Kins

❖   ❖   ❖

"You OK in there?" JJ called through the locked bathroom door.

Alice sat inside the dry shower stall. Both sink faucets still ran, full force. She had been staring from the letter she'd read—words crowded onto the tissue pages—to the whorls of hair mixed in the drain. At first, Allie had thought of Mom the spring after her accident bursting into unexpected tears at another family's table, maybe an Easter dinner. Allie and Jo and the boys they'd avoided all afternoon had been hustled by Dad and the other dad down into the paneled carpeted basement where they heard nothing but the hollow thwock of their Ping-Pong ball. They played one game. Maybe it'd been the boys—lively, red-haired—who'd made Mom think of the boy no one ever mentioned, the one she'd crippled with her car. What Allie remembered as she stared into the drain was how she herself had wanted to believe the grown-ups' strained, reassuring smiles when supper resumed; how she had chattered about school and gobbled cold ham and joined too wholeheartedly in the act that everything was OK.

"Allie?" JJ called again, louder. He seemed to be standing in the hallway.

She blinked at the drain. Absurdly, she pictured the crazed ex-wife on *The Young and the Restless* consulting with bewildered construction workers in the living room of her mansion. The workers gaped at the plans she held and asked in horror: There? In the middle of the living room you want all that—plumbing?

"Allie! Turn off the water—"

JJ pounded the door; Allie remembered the ex-husband Brad's stunned face yesterday as his ex-wife led him at gunpoint into the finished living room. An iron cage was constructed in the room's center, complete with—the camera lingered—a shower stall and toilet, out in the open like inside a prison cell.

"Allie, *answer* me!" JJ's voice boomed. "You OK?"

"No!" Her own shout echoed on the close tile walls.

"Then lemme in!" JJ jiggled the knob, straining its lock.

"No." She pulled herself up. "I'm coming out; just back off!"

She waited for JJ's uncertain footsteps to retreat. Then she pushed aside her old red corduroy robe hanging on the door. The robe she'd worn the night she should've asked JJ what she was going to ask now. She turned the bathroom doorknob, the sink still running. She watched her feet pad up the corridor, repeating in her mind the Bird woman's bold invitation.

Join (you always were good at that) us if you want, if you dare.

Would he? Allie found herself wondering. Since suddenly anything seemed possible. JJ stood beside the kitchen table, his arms folded like a bartender's. Straight up, Allie remembered thinking as she'd straddled him on 8/8/88. He met her eyes expectantly now, sympathetically, the way he used to meet women's eyes when they'd lean on the main desk in the college library, telling their troubles.

She cleared her throat. JJ stood even taller, blocking the Losers' Lamp. He was dressed in his usual plain cotton shirt and pants. His strong-boned face opened in a question. She raised the airmail letter. His greenish blue eyes flickered to it, then back to the question on her own face.

"This came for you."

JJ nodded at the letter, his long arms folded more tightly. "Where from?" he asked quietly, as if he didn't need to ask who from.

"Brazil, this time." Alice set the letter on the table and pulled out her wallet. She kept her voice steady. "There was another letter too, JJ. Got here Monday, though it was postmarked August. I read it then I hid it in my queen's wardrobe. Didn't know what to make of it. Didn't show you, though I know I should've—"

"Goddamn right you should've. You say they're in Brazil, now?"

She blinked at his interruption, at a light in his eyes not directed

toward her. "They also sent a photo with that first letter," Alice continued at a deliberately slow pace, like a Special Ed teacher. "One of the
things that made it—makes it—so hard to bring this up. . . ." She fished
out the snapshot: JJ took a quick step.

His arm shot toward her faster than it had months before, when he
had reclaimed his hair. He grabbed the photo from her hand.

"God, JJ." She backed up a step as if he'd need room to look. He
bowed his head. A powerful silence emanated from him as he held the
photo between the fingertips of both hands, taking it in. His eyes
moved as if intently reading it. When he looked up, his face seemed hollowed out around his teeming blue-green eyes. He swallowed twice, his
Adam's apple bobbing wildly.

"Sorry you had to—see that, see them." Awkwardly, JJ re-folded his
arms, his hand half clenched as if to crush the photo. Or so Allie hoped
in the first second. But as she stepped forward again, she saw JJ's fingers
weren't all the way bent. He was cradling the snapshot in his cupped
palm. Protecting it from her eyes?

"Look." Alice gripped the table's edge. "Look, OK. I'm not gonna ask
about all the . . . details. You and him and her." JJ blinked. "But before I
give you her letters, you gotta give me the—bottom line." Slowly, he
nodded, blank-faced now. In shock, maybe. Oh no; was she going to
have to be the calm one?

"If—" She looked at JJ's Walkman headphones hanging over one of
the table's chairs, the tiny green light still on. "If I told you Kin was
positive . . ."

"Kin," JJ repeated. Out on the street, rush-hour-traffic horns were
honking.

"Kin, the man. The man in that photo. The one I saw at Ko No's. You
know."

"Yeah," JJ answered in a less flattened voice. Husky, edgy. "I know."

"That Kin, JJ. Tested positive. For HIV."

At a harsh sound from JJ's throat, Alice raised her eyes. Startled by
his staring-back eyes. Deep blue. His right hand stayed rigidly cupped
around the photo. His arms, still folded, tensed at the elbows as if he
were holding together the two halves of his rib cage. Split by his own
heart, pounding now like hers? Or, Alice guessed from his face: maybe it
was sinking under a new weight, his heart. *Weren't the bonds between us
more than physical?*

Yes, Alice told herself grimly. She cleared her thickened throat. "So.
First off, JJ, will you want to, have to—" He began to nod, stiffly, before
she'd even finished her question. "Take the—you know—test?"

9

Brazil, December 1988

Olá again, JJ—

Obrigada for the hundred dollars, *muito obrigada* from both your
Kins. I—we—wanted to answer your letter as soon as we read it. But I
had to be sure about what I'm going to say, to ask, on Kin's behalf too.
He's feeling better lately. That plus what you sent in October makes
two, as they say here, miracles. Shouldn't ask for three, our magic number. But we—I—will.

Kin is asleep now, see. Little Fati across the room and Fatima and Zé
across the wall are asleep too. I write by the light of candles and—
brighter than you know—stars. Our shutters are open; our window
holds no panes. Our new sky, its stars extravagantly massed and vastly
scattered, startles me every night. Reminds me how far we've traveled.
You say you wonder what it's like, where we are. Tonight, huge powdery
winged moths flutter above us. Slowed, like us, by the intense dreamy
heat. Since late October—hovering, hovering—we've lived in Zé's house.
Too small for us, Fatima, Fati and the *bebé* Fatima's carrying, bigger
every day.

You ask about money. Don't worry, for now. We pay only one dollar
in rent, every day. In *cruzeiros*. In mesh hammocks bought in Belém, we
lie every night in the same room as little Fati. She sleeps in a sturdy
wood bed Zé made for her. She hums her own tuneless lullabyes in her
sleep. Behind our pale green mosquito netting, Kin and I giggle, pretending she's ours. Experiencing—how's this for something new, for
us?—family life.

Fati's skin is deeply brown; her hair smells of basil. When Kin carved
Fati tiny monkeys from cashew wood, she chewed them up. One head
with an intricate scowl came off whole in her mouth. She wouldn't stop
till we'd made a glue of honey. It stayed stuck long enough for her tears
to dry, anyhow. Fatima stopped sweeping long enough to shake her
head. Bemused, as always, by us.

On the concrete floor Fatima and I sweep, Kin and Fati play jacks. Kin taught her how. Between the rubber ball's bounces, her chubby hands pounce. Kin has to work not to win, or else Fati cries, loud as the roosters. Sometimes if he's feeling impatient, feeling down, Kin leaves me with sobbing Fati and slips outside to smoke. Magazine-paper *cigarros* he rolls quickly, then smokes slowly. I watch by the paneless window, jiggling Fati since I can't talk to her.

Kin blows smoke rings, increasingly round and perfect. In between, he deep-breathes the way I've told him Dr. Marmal instructed me to breathe during panic attacks. Not that Kin admits to any panic. He simply likes, he claims, this sweet humid air. It smells of the trees that surround us. Starfruit and *jaca*. Picture low blue-green hills. A single-story house of concrete, walls one foot thick, roof of curved red tiles. A dirt yard that keeps bugs away. I sweep our floors, then our yard. I help Fatima make big rice and bean lunches. In whispers, Kin bitches to me about how Zé's hard-working brothers eye him, how they resent his weakness, his shares of food. Afternoons, Kin sifts beans in a straw dish to pick out stones. Then he hides behind *Introducing Portuguese*! Lately, he paces in the open-air back kitchen, practicing verbs and smoking.

Me, I'm growing stronger too. My stomach has adjusted to the food. My skin, after peeling, has settled into a pinkish brown. A permanent flush. My sun-bleached hair covers my ears; my stubby pale lashes are long enough to catch dust when I garden. While Kin tends Fati, I cry on and off in the garden, alone. Why am I here? I wonder some days. Here in Brazil? As I sit back on my heels, the heat seems a sort of answer. Slowing my jumpy pulse, absorbing my tears.

I dig weeds in my deep-heat trance. I picture teenage Kin sunning on his first foreign beaches; daring there to imagine a boy—not an Exchange Student dad—rescuing him. Sometimes I feel I'm exchanging myself, as Kin did, for a new bolder traveling self. Free to do, Kin tells me, what I want. So sometimes, often, I unfold the letter you sent with your money. It calms me to read the end: how you are thinking of us, of Kin. How you'd find more money for a doctor if Kin would see one. But he won't, JJ. Don't think I don't worry about that as I crouch in Fatima's Jack-and-the-Beanstalk garden. Tomato plants to my shoulders, basil to my waist. See, I can't help but feel hopeful, too, here. My arms are stonger; my back aches. My gums bleed less; my mouth tastes cleaner. From greens, not Listerine. At night, hungry after a day of work, I crave Fatima's cooking.

Steamed corn bread, thick tomato *sopa* and *Galinha piri-piri*: chiles roasted in a chicken Kin helped Fatima boil and pluck. Kids run hungry in the streets of Belém—kids small as Fati though years older—but here in the hills, this lucky rainy year, we roast corn and cashews on open fires at dusk.

At first, queasy like him, I ate to set an example for Kin. He'd gotten down to whippet-skin and bones. Night sweats and trots. Kin running back and forth to the wood single-seat outhouse with its bucket of white lime. Then weeks of dry coughs. Fatima boiled the teas she says cured him. All natural, he tells me, as if this is all the treatment he needs. No, I want to say. But he does look better each day, smoking and sipping. Bay leaf to soothe his stomach. And now, for the cough that lingers still, boiled lemongrass. His hair has grown longer, shiny black again. Five weeks now, he's spent on unpaid unofficial leave. AWOL.

Finally today, Market Day, Kin ventured to Nossa Senhora Do Ó to contact Pan Am. Families came from miles around in vans or carts to trade tools and food. Kin and I walked the cobblestone streets in hand-washed cotton that Fatima insisted on ironing. Only the poorest of the poor wear rumpled clothes, here. We sipped fruit *suca*. Swaying, we watched an impromptu samba performed to the beat of hands on a van hood. As we walked away, I felt my hips loosen, my arms swing.

Openly, people stared at Kin and me the way I used to sense people staring in the States. Because it's so open here, it's not as scary. At least not with silent watchful Zé at our sides. Kin did our talking, tracking down a phone. Fati hugged my legs—skinny, compared to Fatima's—and hid her face. The men Kin spoke with addressed no words to me. Only respectful nods. They peeled oranges quickly with the foot-long knives they carry. I watched their gestures as they chatted. Jaunty thumbs-up, emphatic slaps of open palms on fists. I tapped my foot to the rhythms of their Portuguese. Grooving to cool nasal dipthongs that blend with Kin's low nasal voice. My face relaxed into blankness.

My wife, yes, Kin told those market men in his politely tentative Portuguese. My wife, but no: not my child. Zé's *filha*; not ours. We have no child.

Ah, one man said, tapping Kin's bare arm then mine. I startled, still not used to all the casual touching here. Sympathetically, he shook his head, looking me over. God will provide, he told Kin. Do not worry; there is still time.

Behind a church, Kin phoned Pan Am from a blue-and-yellow booth called an *orelha*. An ear. Zé and Fati were outside in the crowd, sharing barbecue. In the church, light-headed with dread, I paced between the pews, hearing Kin faintly through the handmade lace drapes. At last, he stepped inside, somber as a priest. He sat by me in the front pew. He lit a *cigarro* and told me what Pan Am had told him: no more. His seven years at Pan Am had bought him weeks of time, but he'd stayed out of touch too long. His employment and the health benefits I'd begged him to use had been terminated. His remaining Free-Fly Points would be valid for three more months. A special deal, granted because of his long service.

I twisted my ring of 8s. Kin blew his own ring, of smoke.

Xiang banfa, he muttered as it dissolved. An expression of his mom's. Meaning, loosely: find a way. In a subdued version of his "What me, worry?" voice, Kin told me he'd mail Big Boyd a fake ID. Get Boyd to collect Unemployment for him. He snapped his Swiss Army knife open and closed. Maybe he'd wanted it this way, he said. Wanted to learn to live without American fat and the bullshit that justifies American fat. I gave a heat-slowed nod. Kin drew deep breaths. In, out.

Dusk comes suddenly here. A briefly beautiful sunset outlines the *jaca* trees with their football-sized fruit. Then—boom—dark. Tonight, after monotonous dominos with Zé and Fatima (they won); after jacks with sleepy surly Fati (Kin forgot to lose), Kin and I lay under our mosquito net tent in the faint candle- and bright starlight. Full, we agreed, of family life. I gazed into our window's soft infinite darkness as Kin told me what he wanted, now. I nodded again, agreeing.

And I asked him for one of his Pan Am discount certificates, still valid like his Free-Fly Points. I told him it was for you. For a cut-rate visit out here. For as long or short as you want. Kin told me I was dreaming. But he gave me the certificate I'll enclose. Still high from your letter, see, I'm bringing out my big guns.

Now: as Kin sleeps, my last Belém ballpoint scratches our last air-mail paper. Fireflies flit through the window. Frog and insect throbs surround me, the low throbs regular and steady, the high throbs quick and varied. Fati hums in her sleep; Kin coughs in his. Whole weeks, whole years I plan to squeeze on these pages. So you'll consider, when I spell it out at the end, what we want. So you'll answer this letter, a hard knock on your door. Let Kin, let us, in. Again.

Remember. Boston 1980. At first it was just Kin and me. I was sixteen about to turn seventeen; he, seventeen already. During our summer, JJ, I told you some of what had happened to us. And in my Curaçao letter. But I never told the whole story, not even to you. Now, half a world away, I will. Starting with the year of you.

January 1980. The night we went too far. We'd been talking since summer about running away. New Year's Eve, I stayed with Kin. I didn't want to watch Mother's bourbon on the rocks rock on her knee. Our house would be packed by men who groomed the golf course with Step-dad. When two or three came over for TV ball games, I'd fled to Kin's for two or three hours. So with the whole pack of them over, I decided to spend the whole night at Kin's, awaiting 1980.

We made each other up and analyzed our looks, listing what we liked (our shared bones, our insolent lips) and hated (Kin's height and skinny limbs; my crooked teeth and limp hair). We bitched about the mocking jocks who shot me leering glances and threw Kin limp-wristed waves in the Greenville High halls. Past midnight, we danced to Ziggy Stardust and to the secret Hawaiian tape Kin hid from his mom. Ray Kane and his slack-key guitar; Don Ho crooning "Beautiful Kauai." We fell asleep on the creaky leather couch.

Next morning, by eight, I slipped in our kitchen expecting Stepdad and Mother both to be conked out. But he was sitting at the sunlit table. Blindingly, it was crowded by empty glasses and bottles and jittery reflected light. I lowered my head so my bangs hid my eyes.

Yeah, I was with Kin. Yeah, all night.

Stepdad called my groggy mother in to make me say it again.

No, I said instead. And, looking straight at her through my hair: I don't got to do what he wants, right? Mother wobbled on her heels, her made-up face going blank. There it was in the air between us, in the crazy light from all the glass. Two years of me not telling what he'd done. Scared of just this: Stepdad standing to his full height over me and her. Know what my daddy'd do? If I stayed out all night? He un-buckled his belt, muttering to Mother, You step outa here now.

So's you can get her alone? Mother asked in an uneven whisper. So's you can fuck her for real?

She turned her back. That's enough, he said and began pulling his belt from its loops. I stood staring, so shocked by Mother's words that I followed her dumbly into the bedroom they shared. Stepdad stared after us, his belt halfway off. Mother shut the door. That's it, she told me in whisper. Don't try to stop him or it'll be worse. She pushed back my bangs. My dad used to whip me too, so I know.

I kept staring, not believing she was going to let anything happen. Even if she was still fumblingly drunk. She was digging through her drawer, shoving at me three pairs of her panties. We were always, almost, the same size.

Put these on under your jeans. It'll make it a little better.

Dazedly, I did. As she zipped my jeans for me, I thought of how she used to dress me in layers of clothes in our cold St. Paul apartment. My mother: who'd never so much as smacked me; who'd never done a thing to me when I skipped classes, whole days of school. Wish I'd had me as a mom, she was always telling me.

She led me out of the bedroom, both of us suddenly giggling like bad girls walking to the front of a South Carolina classroom for a paddling. I wouldn't bend, Kin had whispered once when a boy—it was usually boys—bent to take his licks.

In our living room, Stepdad's plump face looked sweaty, unsure. His mustache seemed pasted on. He toyed with his belt's buckle. I didn't move when he told me to bend. I felt Mother touch my shoulder. She bent me over the couch.

Five licks, he told her. A boy playing teacher. He gave the nervous cough he'd given that time in the Vega. A whoosh, but soft. One, two stings through my jeans and four panties. My tense giggle rose again in my throat. Then a louder whoosh. A crack like a stick snapped in half. The sound first; it took a second to feel the burn. The heels of my hands dug into the nubby couch cushion. After the next and next, my hands skidded forward, my elbows bracing me, my ass pushed higher up. I felt it all: the first licks and the ones I was getting. Then my own shuddery breaths. I ran lopsided into my room, my face all hot too.

Mother came after me, crying with me. I lay on my stomach. She knelt by my bed and stroked my hair, white-blond like hers. Hers still all stiff for that party. I smelled her hairspray as she whispered that she knew how it hurt. That she'd write notes to get me out of gym, the showers. So I wouldn't have to worry about anyone seeing any marks. He was sorry, she said. She knew he was. He'd given me more than five but he'd lost control; all men did.

When I couldn't stop sobbing, she spoke in a voice suddenly less soft, like his belt's third whoosh. C'mon, R'berta. My daddy used birch switches cut from Grandpa Olaf's farm, and I'd take my licks with all my panties on under only a skirt, no thick bluejeans. You were way padded up compared to me. I *bled*, R'berta, and when my daddy was done with me, I couldn't walk, much less run.

I had stopped crying at last, listening to her. But I kept my face in my pillow. After she finally left my room, I pulled out my diary and wrote all of it down, painstakingly slow. When their bedroom door finally shut, I snuck out my own bedroom window. I ran, cutting through two frosty acre-long yards.

It was always nighttime in Kin's house. I paced his mom's darkened living room while he read the diary. Then he looked up and said quietly, See? She knew.

He closed my diary. You were right not to tell her, Berta. She knew.

He led me to his mom's pink-and-silver bathroom. He ran a hot bath, pouring in her perfumed pearl-colored oils. Stay, I told him. I faced the steamy mirror. Slowly, I pulled down my jeans—that hurt—then peeled down my four panties. I showed Kin the marks Mother wanted no one to see.

That night, lying beside me in his own bed, Kin vowed that we would leave. The two of us. Next day, the last day of winter break, we biked defiantly together in cold dry air, round and round the artificially green winter golf course. We saw Stepdad working, driving the giant vacuum-cleaner Cushman that gathered the balls. My ass felt sore but I pedaled hard. Kin was saying we had to stop going in circles. Kin hated Greenville High, hated all of redneck Greenville, S.C. as much as I did. More: since people here made him feel more foreign than any real so-called foreigners could do. He was a traveler at heart, like his mom. She would, he predicted, understand. And he had, he revealed as our bikes bumped along, a plan.

We could go to Boston. It was cold up there, like Minnesota, my home. A guy Kin knew in Korea was studying at Boston University. Most of Kin's Korean boys had been his age. Most treated him as something precious, an exotic American. This one spoke English. He was older, into rough stuff—ties on Kin's wrists and ankles; silly stuff—and he'd written that he wanted to see Kin again. He'd buy a train ticket for Kin by phone. He'd pay for Kin to visit him in his BU dorm.

No, I told Kin at first. No, you can't. We can't. No and no as we pedaled round and round. Kin finally pedaled off mad; I wheeled my bike home. It was a January dusk, dark already at five. Mother's car was gone; Stepdad's Vega sat in the driveway. Only TV light showed in the living-room window. I looked at the dark house and thought, clearly: anyplace on earth is safer than here.

I spent the night at Kin's—his mom still away—and the next day we skipped school to get my things from Stepdad #2's empty house. One suitcase, Mother's. Kin did my packing. Kin paid for half my train ticket; my movie-theater money paid the rest. Kin was born to travel. He lit up on the train ride, pressing his face to the window while I huddled beside him. In zigzags down the jolting aisle, Kin balanced our paper trays of food with an aplomb he'd perfect years later.

Eight years later, this past September, thousands of feet above the Andes, I watched Kin zigzag up the aisle of an Aero jet in trouble. The jet was so old, the engine arrangement so primitive, the crew had to squat up front and peel back the carpet so the copilot could open a trap door and see firsthand what was wrong. Standing as the others crouched, Kin looked over his shoulder to give me, give all the frozen passengers, a perfectly convincing grin that said: What me, worry?

Our first night in downtown Boston, in a combo Hotel/Youth Hostel (Youth Hostile, Kin said it oughta be called) we shoved our metal-framed bed in front of the door. We climbed on top and pulled sheets stained with semen—Kin claimed—over our heads. In the next room, a fight or fuck progressed with rising thumps. I kept saying No: don't call him. Don't, Kin. His finger jabbed the push-tone phone that we'd paid extra for at the desk. Just enough, Kin told me as it rang in a far-off dorm. Enough to tide us over till we find real jobs. Enough to let us eat.

Before we left, Kin handed me our last ten-dollar bill. Then we trudged in stunning mind-numbing cold to a McDonald's on Tremont Street. I drank Styrofoam coffee and taught myself to smoke Kin's cigarettes. He didn't come back till past ten, clutching seventy-five dollars in cash but hardly walking right.

What? I gasped. Don't know, Kin muttered, pressing the money in my hand, his hand cold. Don't know what it was. He winced as he sat, breathing hard. Greased metal, big as a cucumber. But it's out of me, Berta; it's over. Berta, don't.

Kin wouldn't look at me while I cried. He downed my cold coffee and bitched about my smoking his cigarettes. He fidgeted. Then he had to lean on me, lurching to the T-train we had to take because he couldn't walk all the way. All I could say was: I'm calling your mom.

That subway ride and our walk against a frozen wind back to the Hotel/Hostel was like the last leg of our shuttle flight to Belém. After Kin had thrown up in the lav, after Kin and I had inched down the plane steps into crazily hot Brazilian sun, Fati playing peekaboo with Kin over her mother's shoulder; after the other passengers had filed around us, we stood on a burning macadam tarmac beside the family that would save us. Fatima told Kin how the travel money she'd won had been stolen, how they couldn't afford to go farther, go home. How they were stuck here in Belém. Kin had pieced together a reply in Portuguese. He'd tried to say that we knew how they felt. No money, a strange place.

Back in the Youth Hostel, I had to dial. Kin had to tell me the number I knew by heart. Numbers fly out of my mind when I'm scared. His mom wasn't home, of course, so we left a message on her machine at work. We lived off the seventy-five dollars, sticking together inside and outside our room. The next weekend, his mom flew up from South Carolina. She arrived at the hostel by cab. For once, she looked harried in her shell pink suit. She smoothed her bun of black hair, sitting on the very edge of the bed we'd kept in front of the door. Kin had been up and around all week, but when his mom came, he lay down. I paced.

They talked like two grown-ups. Their voices so low and the traffic sounds so loud I couldn't hear everything. I kept glancing at Kin's mom's silky blouse. Her left breast had been removed. I felt her looking at my breasts, looking me over. Then glancing back at Kin as if to say: but what do you see in her?

She smoked a single cigarette, beautifully. Kin's hand motions—the casual ballets of his own smokes—were imitations of his mom's grace. She wafted away her smoke with her hypnotic hands. Nails like pearls.

She did understand. He'd been right about that. But she insisted Kin had to finish high school or he'd never have the money to travel, she told him, in style. He nodded weakly from his pillow. She turned to give our room her sizing-up glance. Then she faced me. She told me that my mother seemed to be away somewhere but that my father was still in the house.

Stepfather, I corrected. The first thing I'd said the whole visit.

The thumps in the next room commenced. Step? his mom asked delicately. She gave her Lady-of-China look. Her brows arched as if she, who'd grown up in Greenville and spoken Cantonese only as a toddler, couldn't understand coarse English.

Step. Father. Not real, I stammered. The sexual thumps across the wall rose. My mother's second—you know—husband?

Oh yes. I had a stepfather also. She glanced at Kin, wincing, maybe beginning a headache. But you see, I never married. Not once.

She stood solemnly, as if she'd proclaimed herself a virgin. I motioned Kin off the bed, backed him into a corner. No; I wouldn't go home, not with Stepdad there. No way. Kin asked over my shoulder: can Berta stay with us, Mom?

No, I told him loudly. The thumping across the wall stopped. No, I insisted; Stepdad might come after me. Legally and all. Kin nodded, taking my hand. As we turned to his mom, helpless, she gave me an apologetic smile, saying: What can we do, then? She sighed. I have been sick, you know. I had a cancer.

Kin stepped away from me to whisper to her. She wrote me a check for two hundred dollars. I took it and Kin whispered that he'd send more. But was I sure I couldn't come back? I told him I'd be all right here. I wanted him to say no. Instead, he told me he'd only be gone three months. And Mom *has* been sick, he reminded me. Reminded himself. Then they disappeared, quietly as one person. Before they left, his mom opened the window, apologizing for smoking. Her perfume, which Kin

sometimes wore, mixed with her smoke. Cold air blew in. Alone, I shut
that window. Not to keep out the wind but to keep in the smell of it,
their house.

Alone in Boston—weeks before meeting you, JJ—I roamed bookstores.
Lingering by the slimmest books longest. Poems. Even that word was
soothing. You could read a poem whole and take it out with you. So I
told Kin over long distance. After we hung up, I paced by the bed. Why
hadn't he insisted I come back with him? Why hadn't he stayed? These
questions I wrote in the diary I'd show him only if he did come back.
And he would, I told myself. Sister Kin.

He mailed me more money. I enrolled in a typing class. MWF. I ate
candy from the class building's machines, furtively. I showered in the
shared Youth Hostel bathroom, at 4 A.M. I lay on the bed that still
blocked the door, too lightweight to stop that door should a thumping
Youth Hostile decide to shove it open. Kin phoned almost nightly. He
worried that my voice sounded faint. Lifeless, he told me. He advised me
to go to bookstore poetry readings. I could eat free cheese, Kin pointed
out. And I might even meet some halfway-decent guys.

One night after pushing this advice, Kin told me in a softly apologetic, softly excited voice that he was going on one last trip with his
mom. He'd do extra work to get his diploma early. Then he'd vacation
in Taiwan: all April and half of May. Yes, Kin agreed; he'd find his own
halfway-decent guys there. Yes, he'd have the kind of dates he liked: as
little talking and as much touching as possible. Then he'd tell me all
about it, as always. We both giggled. After I hung up, I sobbed till I vom-
ited the tears I'd swallowed. No one there to make me stop.

All slushy March, I sleepwalked through typing class, candy bars,
stomach aches. I spoke only on the phone, only to Kin. On my seven-
teenth birthday in April, with Kin half a world away, I ventured out to see
some poems, live. I liked them. Liked crunching Chee-tos with a tallish
blondish guy wearing granny glasses. He had a boy's face and a ghostly
blond goatee. I couldn't believe how hungry I was, I told him. Couldn't
believe how little I'd been living on. My voice came out shaky from lack
of use. He insisted on walking me back through the drizzly dark to the
Hostel. Then he asked, still polite, could he come in to get dry?

So we sat together on the cotlike bed—there was nowhere else to sit—
and he told me he wrote poetry himself. I nodded, shivering though it
felt warm inside. I didn't have to talk because he talked so much, about
his poetry—minimalist, he called it—and his part-time studies in com-
parative literature and his full-time job at a health-food restaurant. Did

I like tofu? Did I like French movies? Did I want to see a movie called *Story of Adele H.*? I stiffened when he touched my arm.

I'm not going to hurt you, he told me. I could hear in his voice that it turned him on: how scared I was. A waif in Kin's black T-shirt. As he wrapped his arms around me, he squeezed my breasts with trembling fingertips. I couldn't breathe, so I pulled away. Hugging myself. Why hadn't I done that with Stepdad, as soon as his hand inched under my skirt? Why had I stared dumbly at the Vega horn trying to remember SOS? I blinked hard, embarrassed by my tears. As if to comfort me, this guy with his granny glasses crooked now touched my shoulder. If Kin were here, I thought. If Kin were here to comfort me for real, I could go through with it. I turned my face to tell this boy—this man—no.

And he kissed me, his cool cheesy tongue thrust in my mouth. That had been the worst part with Stepdad #2, worse even than his fingers. His tongue-taste still alive inside my mouth, even as half a bottle of Listerine burned my throat. That taste awoke again as this boy pressed me, pushing me against the mattress.

C'mon, c'mon. He sounded pleading, and he squeezed my breasts harder as if that would make me want him more. I struggled beneath him, weak from weeks of candy bars. Gasping, I opened my mouth and he thrust his tongue inside again. That's when, unable to speak, I bit.

Bit hard: all my strength shooting up to my jawbone. To my teeth, crooked but sharp. They sank into smooth live muscle. A meaty taste of tongue. He reared back, his hairy chin butting my chin. He shook off his glasses, screamed with a big bloody mouth. Bloody murder. I screamed too, louder. Both of us spat and stumbled off the bed that blocked the door. I pulled the doorknob so hard the bed lurched back. The door made an opening big enough only for me. He was still screaming as I squeezed out. I ran, stunned by the silent hall. Even the thumping Youth Hostiles shut up to hear this boy's high-pitched yelps. Everything felt weirdly silent all around me and especially inside my head as I ran with his blood on my lips. I pounded onto wet sidewalk, ran faster when I spotted a police car. Its light sped past me, searching for me, but I couldn't run back home to hide. No!

I swayed on my feet, dizzy in a crosswalk, its lines all smeared by rain. No: he was back there, back home, his blood in my mouth. He was waiting for me, ready with his belt to give me a real whipping this time. The kind you can't walk after, the kind you can't stop. It just gets worse if you say no.

They tell me I fainted inside McDonald's. I really don't know; I wasn't there. Nowhere near the place. No address, no. I was scared he'd track me down. Who? the police woman they finally called in asked me. I shook my head hard. No, no. She noticed the blood in my mouth but didn't think to ask if it was mine. What was my name, was the main thing she wanted to know.

Kin, I kept saying, insisting. First to the police, then to the first nurse at Mass. Mental. Waiting, I traced the name on a dusty metal desk, on an office window with mesh wire on the other side of the glass. They showed me what they called my temporary room. Four beds of shadowy snoring crazy women and a door that didn't really close, didn't click. No locks here except on the elevator that led down and out. But they had a three-sink bathroom, cleaner than anything at Youth Hostile. And they had Listerine, lots of it. The night nurse didn't think it was strange that I needed so much. That I swallowed instead of just swishing. My mouth and stomach burned with Listerine as they finally let me sign Kin's name.

A Voluntary Admission. Female; white; no wallet, no ID. Age—the one number I remembered; it was my birthday, after all—seventeen. All other numbers, Kin's South Carolina phone number included, had vanished. Except for 8.

Remember, Jimmy Joe Wolfe? You were Voluntary too. You'd walked miles in hazy April sun from your dorm. You'd refused to go to MIT health services, refused to fly back home to Ohio. I didn't know any of that the first day. In what was called the Common Area, in a corner deemed Supervised Study—where we were allowed to hold the pens with which we might otherwise, elsewhere, stab out each other's eyes—you and I sat side by side on an orange vinyl couch. You hunched under the weight of your hair and your too-small leather bomber jacket. I sat stiff-legged in Kin's black T-shirt and the jeans I'd come in in and the clean underwear they'd issued me, several sizes too big. See us? Hardly adults, hardly human. Shifting, twitching, holding ourselves like we couldn't stand another second inside our skins. Or anyhow, that's how it was in me. How 'bout you?

Hunched-over JJ letting Dr. Marmal call you Jimmy Joe and broken-tongued Bird calling herself Kin. My throat was dried up from low-dose Thorazine and from not talking. We both coughed a lot that day; your throat was dry too, for the same two reasons. See? I want you now to see us then. Because it was not, of course, smarmy Dr. Marmal but the real Kin, our Kin, who was to cure us.

Or "cure" isn't right. Who was to give us—what? Our bodies, I want to say, but maybe it can't be said. What he—we three—did. With, to, for each other.

Listen. In Supervised Study, your pen scratched even harder than mine. Your Adam's apple bobbed, like Kin's. Behind your white-boy Afro, you traced old answers to advanced calculus problems. Your bony wrists showed, your jacket sleeves too short. Behind my own limp white-blond hair, I inked Figure-8s down the insides of my arms. The pen tip pressed bone through my thinnest skin. Secretly, I aimed to etch 8s into my bone. Indelible ID marks. So I traced them over and over, the blue ink blurring. My eyes caught your eyes flickering down. Apologetically, you tipped your page so I could see your own rows of ink numbers. But I shook my head quick and hard. Like: No, no; I don't speak that language.

What're you in for, was the first question you dared ink in your Calculus book margin. My first Thorazine-free week. No question mark, just words.

Bit off my tongue, I inked back on the same margin. A lie I wished was true.

Next day, Thelma—that massively obese, severely depressed woman who slept in my room—filled the couch opposite ours. Reading the *Boston Globe* in a dreamy whisper. "Infant Deaths Rise at Love Canal." Our pens scratched stealthily. You wrote your first long note, answering the *How 'bout you?* I'd inked on my palm.

Always, you printed, even before your mom died when you were too little to know, your dad made you walk around the block with him after supper. Usually silently. Sometimes you'd tell him facts you'd read about space exploration, which interested him too though he never said so. Never said much. Then, you wrote, one night last summer when you were starting to wonder what—not who, but what—your dad was, you broke your eighteen-year routine. Broke off your own unanswered monologue about gravity in space, broke into a run. You ran around the block without him, then sat panting on the front stoop, waiting for him.

Only now, a year later, did you know why no hurt showed on his face. He had plodded past you, moving no slower than usual. Because he was, see, a robot replica of a man. A different robot replaced every few hours, different robots with identical dead-eyed faces. The doctors were trying to talk you out of this truth you'd found. They were trying to weaken your brain, here.

So how'd you figure it, I asked back, in ink. *That your dad was a robot? And what are you?*

You answered (do you even remember?): *The Man Who Fell to Earth.* You told me in ink what you hadn't told Dr. Marmal: the summer before MIT, when you were driving round Ohio, a sci-fi film festival in Medina showed you the truth. First about him, then you. You were played by David Bowie. You were an alien, bone thin and pure white with feline eyes. Your ship had crashed and all you wanted was to go back where you belonged but the CIA was after your brain. You fell in love with an Earth woman and committed the mistake of sex with her. Instantly, your smooth cool alien body turned sweaty and gooey and she was grossed out, too. Slime poured off your skin; you couldn't run. After your capture, your cat eyes were surgically altered. Now you stood in a CIA mental ward. Your dulled earthling eyes watched a hundred TVs, each tuned to a different channel.

Remember? Mass. Mental, late April? When you weren't pretending to do calculus, you were reading—or staring at pictures and lists since your meds left you too zonked to really read—a book on the Voyager space capsule. In your notes, you explained to me how Carl Sagan had loaded this capsule with messages in dozens of languages and codes, photos of human beings, ninety minutes of music. You studied this book as if *you* were trying to figure it out, our planet.

Where're you from? you asked in ink. I answered, earning my first half smile from you, *Earth*. And, I confessed, *my name isn't really Kin*. My hands shook, passing you that note. You folded it tightly, slipped it in your leather jacket pocket. You begged in your next note that I tell you my real name, swearing you'd keep it secret. I refused, scared to have told you anything. You wrote, intuitively: *So who is Kin?* I shifted on the Supervised Study couch. "Friend" seemed too weak a word. "Husband" was a lie that almost felt true. "My love" felt true too, but I realized as I sat gnawing my pen that I didn't want you to think I had a love.

My sister, I finally wrote. You slipped that note too inside the bomber jacket you never took off. Not even as the ward grew warm, humid. Spring 1980. When you weren't hunched beside me in Supervised Study or closeted away with Dr. Marmal, you stood tall as any basketball player in front of the ward TV dribbling a rubber ball, watching whatever was on. I watched you watch.

Don't look at my face, my acne, you wrote. I wrote back: *Where?* You'd burned off most of your acne with your sunlamp turned up all winter in your dorm room at MIT. Your skin scarred by pockmarks. You'd gotten the idea, you admitted in ink, by writing a poem about wishing only your eyes showed on your face. Show me the poem, I wrote. Tell me your name, you wrote back.

No, I wrote. But you, after sulking for a day, passed me the poem anyway. It started: *If I could ray my face so only eyes remain—*

I liked that line, I wrote. Liked this poem too (I'd torn a page from Mass. Mental's Emily Dickinson). And, I confessed to make up for not telling my name, I didn't bite off my tongue. *I just WANT to bite it off, I'm so flabby fat.*

You're not, you wrote extra hard on the Emily Dickinson page. *I can't even look at you you're so*

You passed it to me unfinished. But I knew what you meant, I thought. I folded the poem page in half, wishing there was a pocket in the Salvation-Army dress Mass. Mental had given me. Its electric green polyester clashed with—no, matched perfectly—the orange vinyl couch. We'd both been off Thorazine for weeks by then, mid-May, but our minds were still getting back up to speed. I remembered showing Kin my diary, that first entry about Stepdad. A secret still, since I'd told Dr. Marmal almost nothing. I stared at the blank half of your note, suddenly sharply aware of Kin's absence. Of your presence beside me, awaiting some answer. Opposite us, a scrawny brown-skinned woman waited to be wheeled to ECT, Electroconvulsive therapy. Her knee jiggled as if the volts were already flowing. I kept watching her knee, inhaling your sweat, savoring its burned taste.

See, Jimmy Joe Wolfe, I couldn't look at you either: your long-boned body, taller than but as lean as Kin's. Lean as David Bowie, the first man Kin and I both had a crush on. In Kin's mom's dark living room, we'd danced to "Hunky Dory." As I remembered dancing, my heart ached with the feeling that Kin would love you too. *Kin,* I wrote impulsively on your note. *Calls me Bird.*

You held the paper close to your eyes, a spy absorbing a password. Then, as the ECT woman and I stared, you tore off the word "Bird," slipped it onto your tongue like Communion bread, sealed your lips and swallowed. Swallowed several times to get the paper scrap down, your Adam's apple bobbing. I wanted to press my throat to yours the way I'd done only with Kin. The way swans neck.

The ECT woman's knee stopped jiggling. Your knee started. Otherwise, we three sat motionless. My name was inside you, a shared secret. I looked at my green polyester lap. Though I wanted to stare and stare at you: your unwashed densely brown curls, your face of bones that showed, and especially your sealed mouth, full-lipped like mine only on you I—what other word was there?—loved it.

Late May 1980, Kin flew home from Taiwan and tracked me down, giving my description first to the Boston police. They gave him a long list of hospitals and halfway houses. Finally a Mass. Mental nurse told Kin his own name by phone. He knew it had to be me. We made that the song of our reunion. "It Had to Be You."

He visited me in the room with no lock. His shiny black hair had grown long, past his shoulders. He looked older, less skinny, and he held himself with more assurance. He held me with assurance, his arms moving easily, his body used to embracing other bodies, now. He let me cry on his shoulder, his new pongee shirt. My tears soothed my throat, still dried-up though the Thorazine had long worn off. The next weekend, Sister Kin signed me out, took me to the best Chinese restaurant he'd found in Boston and told me about his Taiwanese men. Men, this trip, not boys. I told only Kin about the tongue I'd bitten, and about you, our notes.

So happy, that first week of June, to have Kin back. Or "happy" is wrong. I felt whole again, or almost. Except there was something missing between us now because part of me, the body part, was already (how else can I say it?) yours.

I didn't tell Kin that in so many words. But I told him how you'd swallowed the "Bird," how that had thrilled me but also, I added carefully, scared me. Oh Berta, Kin pronounced in a voice both teasing and serious, You got it bad.

Even Dr. Marmal noticed a change in me. He kept me, and you, off Thorazine. We knew this from our notes. We still never talked. On our couch in Supervised Study, I sensed you sensed Kin's presence, though I'd told you nothing. Not yet, I kept thinking, wanting to keep Kin to myself. And you to myself, too. But you began spending less time in Supervised Study, more time watching the ward TV with a vengeance. The second week of June, I wrote: *What show do you like best?*

I thought it was the dumbest question. I almost didn't ask. You folded the note, stood, returned to the TV on the far side of the Common Area. The next morning, in front of the TV, you stopped dribbling your ball and thought—your first clear thought in months, you told me later—that *Mission Impossible* was better than *Mod Squad*. The plots more complicated, the characters more plausible. You tried to scratch your head but your dirty dense hair, longer than an Afro by then, stopped you. You wanted it gone. You told only me, in ink. In indelible blue letters, I told you that I knew someone who could cut your hair.

Your Kin? you scrawled back. I only nodded. It had to be secret. You insisted on that. Having a secret made my own blood thump too. Sister Kin planned it. How he'd hide in the big Common Area cleaning closet after visiting hours. How I'd steal scissors from the central desk while the night nurse counted out her cuplets of pills. How you and I would linger late in Supervised Study near the closet—we'd seen janitors shuffle up to it—then, when the nurse commenced her rounds, doling out meds, how we'd meet Kin in there.

The closet was dark. It smelled of strong soap and ammonia. Its air made all our eyes water. We'd never been so close before: you and me. You stood on your knees between Kin and me, facing me, your long tensed back facing Kin. I felt safe with Sister Kin so close, too. Even on your knees, you were tall, your eyes level with my breasts. I was wearing a new silk shirt Kin had given me. I felt my breasts—no other words for this—meet your stare. My flat nipples prickled, almost stiffening. Kin's scissors bit through your thick hair, a satisfying *schnap* sound. Schnap, schnap. Kin's hands moved gently and steadily. Your head stayed still between us, your breath startlingly warm against my silk. There in the dark, I wanted Kin to take hold of your head—gently, slowly—and inch it forward, ease it down. I wanted to lean back against the door, spread open my thighs and feel, really feel, your full warm-looking lips, your hidden tongue.

After the last *schnap*, all of us breathed hard like it'd been hard work. You stood. Hair fell from your shoulders; I bent to gather it up. You faced Kin, looking down at him in the soap-smelling dark. Maybe that's when you first knew he wasn't my sister, was a man. Kin whispered: You wanna be alone, now? You two?

No, no—I whispered from the floor. My whole body shaking. I sensed you shaking too though it didn't, on you, show. You've gotta stay, I told Kin through your legs. We heard footsteps, outside. We held our breaths, dizzy with ammonia and burned sweat. When the steps passed, I reached between your feet to sweep your last long hairs into a trash bag. In breathless whisper, I asked: Can I keep it, your hair? My first spoken words to you. You answered yes, breathless too.

That mean we can get outa here? Kin asked, not breathless at all. I stood, shouldering open the closet door. We burst out together, knocking over a mop and gasping, then laughing. We huddled on the orange couch in Supervised Study, unsupervised now in the dark. Kin made it easy, sitting between us. He held my shaky hand. I held the bag of your hair on my lap. Kin turned first to you. As if it were the most natural question, he asked: You're a virgin, aren't you?

You nodded so hard I sensed you'd been waiting years to be asked just that. Your new short hair made a halo around your bony pale face.

She, Kin began, and I didn't squeeze his hand to stop him. Berta, that's her real name. Berta is, too.

Then Kin turned to me. The planes of his deeply familiar face shone, his hair and eyes darker than the surrounding darkness. 'Cept, I added to Kin. And I whispered into his ear what he alone already knew. What I hadn't surrendered to pushy falsely patient Dr. Marmal; what I suddenly wanted you to know, too. Kin winced as he always did when, rarely, I mentioned Stepdad #2.

He turned to you. You bowed your head. It looked like you two were sharing a prayer as Kin whispered. I heard only: Her stepdad, his fingers.

My translator, I thought. I took hold of Kin's hand again with both of mine. Your large hand closed over my grip. I stared down at our triple clasp, a solid knuckly shape in the dark. Your hand cool, then not. Kin whispered to me: I can sign the two of you out this weekend, Berta. I can take you two to my place.

I caught my breath. And you'd be there?

If you want, he told me, South Carolina soft. Down the hall in a temporary room, someone moaned. Possibly pleasure, probably pain.

I nodded. You on the other side of Kin nodded too. The moan rose, echoing. Our triple-hand clasp tightened, locking mine between yours and Kin's. I couldn't move my hands anymore than I could stop my head, nodding still. Did I already sense what we—we three—would wind up doing? All summer, all ways?

Under our green mosquito net, a world away from that night, I asked Kin what he most wanted to do, now. He had two clear and immediate answers. See China. And see Jimmy Joe again.

That's when I asked him for the Pan Am certificate, for you. In the candles between us, I could almost hear the crackle of Kin's rice paper those last weeks at Mass. Mental. Our July notes burned and rose in little rockets each time we set up a date with Kin. You or I would sneak into the Common Area to watch.

See my flare tonight, Jimmy Joe? If you fly here, meet us any weekday at the Nossa Senhora Do Ó postal station. But if—as we guess is likely, given your wife—you won't join us here, join our travels, then after China we'll come to you. We have to fly back to the States sooner or later, with Kin's Free-Fly Points expiring. In our mosquito tent, hours ago, we made tentative plans like any husband and wife. Fatima's *bebé* is due in late January. We can stay here till then. You can join us here till then. Kin will ask Boyd to collect his Unemployment; Kin will find us a flight to Hong Kong, only a boat ride from Guangzhou, his mother's real home.

Our whispers stopped. Frogs took over, louder than American frogs. My stomach growled. Too much meat, I mumbled. In Nossa Senhora

Do Ó, I'd eaten the Brazilian barbeque. Pork and beef and chicken, roasted together on steel swords.

But no water, right? Kin whispered, sounding sleepy yet alert.

'Course not, I told him. Then I asked: How can *they* eat so much meat? Everyone 'round here. When they're all so thin . . .

Most of them drink the water, Kin muttered back, sadly matter-of-fact. So most of them have worms.

I couldn't answer. Fati wasn't humming in her sleep in her corner. We'd been keeping her awake. Kin began to hum, tunelessly, an imitation of Fati's meandering sleep hum. She giggled, humming too. Gradually, as my pen began to scratch these pages, Kin slipped into sleep breaths, rough and deep. Now, the purple night sky has melted, dissolved. Despite the danger of thieves, I've kept our shutters open all night. The fireflies have left our room. Or maybe they just aren't showing anymore. In the half-light, I see the exposed wiring on the walls of this house. The first house I've understood. Each beam shows. Each wire leads to its switch. This, Jim Joe, is the longest letter I've ever written. But I had to finish it tonight. I have to send it this first week of December, giving you time to contact us before January. To fly in on your discount certificate, if you want. Whether you fly or write or not, you'll be seeing us next year. Ready or not.

Between these lines, as a predawn breakfast, I eat—no, they say here *succão,* suck—slices of orange. Savoring juice so tangy my nose stings. My stomach stirs, wanting more. Something's happening to my body in Brazil, JJ. Something to do with this heat. Moist, all-surrounding. Savage—mildewing clothes overnight, smearing my ink words—yet gentle. Soothes and stirs me up, both at once.

Makes me feel, as I haven't since our summer, alive in my skin. If Kin's mission is to experience the Earth he'll be leaving, maybe mine is to experience—learn to experience—the Earth I've barely visited, before. Not for years: my senses blocked somehow back home. My memory blocked too. Here, as this heat sinks into my bones, I keep re-living our summer. My first, in a way, on Earth. Remember the man and woman etched on meteor-proof steel on the Voyager spaceship? How you told me they were designed to look nonthreatening, raising weaponless hands? Saying: we mean no harm. Saying: we're here.

We wish you a good new year, a clean blood test. We lie side by side in our separate mesh hammocks. We two plus you made—briefly, but what on this Earth doesn't happen that way?—one. A miracle of sorts. A once-in-a-lifetime experience. One Kin may long for but would never ask for, again. Kin wants only to see you. To visit. Not much to ask, is it? Considering what we got, from Kin? Considering that you want to see him too, again. There is still time, the men of Brazil tell us when they find we have no children. God may not, as these men say, but I hope you will. Provide. Comfort for Kin. While there is still

your
Kin

10

One Functional Family

To help her wait for JJ—who'd gone out to buy the test—Allie turned on *The Young and the Restless*. Her drug of choice. Outside, this last day of February, cars whooshed on slushy streets. She sat Indian style on the fold-out bed. As the familiar *Young and Restless* theme swelled up, she felt her stomach tighten. With cramps or morning sickness? She blinked at Mrs. Chancellor sipping tea with Phillip Chancellor III. Beneath their low urgent TV voices, the new couple downstairs was shouting, live. Only their curse words carried through the floor.

"Fuggin'—Fuggin' Bitch—"

Allie rocked to their monotonous rhythm, glad she wasn't hearing Connie's cavewoman shouts in the New Chance Workshop. Would she keep working there if the test said she was—really, this time—pregnant? Would JJ resist sliding back into his winter depression? What Allie called to herself his Kin depression.

Married? Mrs. Chancellor gasped to shy drug-addicted Philip III, who'd grown from a ten-year-old to an adolescent within months. *But you're so young—*

And Restless, Alice thought distractedly, lifting her hot chocolate. Don't forget Restless. She slurped. A typical No Haven day: sooty, slushy. Something falling from the sky that wasn't quite snow or rain. She shifted, pressing her abdomen. Its ache seemed not quite menstrual, not quite not.

I've been throwing up all morning, she'd told Sticks by phone. A lie that felt true. But, she'd added—because if the home pregnancy test said Yes, they'd need the cash—maybe I could come in for the afternoon? A door slammed below.

Mrs. Chancellor's evil maid poured more tea. Allie checked the clock. JJ had been gone twenty minutes. They'd know in hours—not weeks, as with the HIV test. The October day that JJ's results came in negative, she remembered, they had walked home holding hands through gloves.

After they'd solemnly toasted the test with Gallo, JJ had given the one-word answer she'd already guessed. *Both.*

That was all, really all, he wanted to say. He'd taken her hand again, his hand cold too because their heater had begun shutting off, mysteriously.

Both Kins had been his Kin. He'd loved—he said this quite flatly—both.

What do you mean, "loved"? Allie asked, flushed from wine and cold and the dizzying picture of JJ lying on the soft white mattress between the Bird woman and the Kin man. Do you mean both in bed at once?

Lowering his eyes, JJ nodded. Yeah. Something like that, Allie.

But what? she asked after another strengthening sip of Gallo. What exactly did you do with Kin?

Enough, JJ answered, releasing her hand. Enough so I needed the test.

His voice sounded strained; everything felt so strained again between them that Allie only nodded. As snowy weeks passed and JJ stayed low spirited, distracted, she wanted to talk more: about how much it plainly hurt him, knowing the Kin man he'd loved was dying. But she sensed such questioning would somehow—she hadn't felt this before with JJ, with any subject—intrude.

Allie munched a saltless saltine. A Scrubbing Bubbles commercial dissolved into Brad still locked in the cage in his ex-wife's mansion. Would she join him behind bars for a candlelight meal, he was asking the ex-wife, eying the keys on her belt. Allie rolled her eyes but kept watching. Lately, her soap seemed more silly yet more comforting than ever. Sometimes JJ watched too. Since Bush's election, she had boycotted the news. Not that she and JJ could watch it together anyway, with him working overtime. Then working at home on his Music project.

He'd gathered catalogs from other grad programs—Indiana U. and Case Western; less prestigious than Yale but maybe, therefore, less pressured by Pentagon representatives—and he'd also brought home the Yale catalog for next fall. Sometimes, he still ventured down to the computer science building to pick up his paper mail. Since nothing came but conference flyers, Allie assumed he really went there to hang out. Check up on his Bros.

She chewed another cracker, hopeful whenever she imagined him going back. Imagined them, somehow, going back to the way they were before this tense summer and fall. Weren't the worst scenarios behind them, at least?

If, Allie added to herself, Kin and Bird stayed gone. But *would* they show up here? Those ex-lovers who had such a hold on JJ's feelings. Who therefore must have shared more with him than the sexual experiments she'd imagined at first. She glanced from the TV to JJ's nightstand, its lower shelf cluttered with cassettes, including one—Japanese Shakuhachi music—he'd never unsealed, though he'd bought it in November. She faced Phillip III sobbing on TV and remembered the quiet depression JJ had fallen into after learning of Kin's HIV test. All winter: JJ eating and talking little; JJ sitting blankly at his computer, making few key clicks. How would it effect him if he did see them? The sickly Kin man. The bold Bird woman. If she'd mailed JJ that sexy photo, what might she try to pull in person?

As Phillip III stormed off the screen, Allie dug into the saltine box for the last cracker. Strangely, the long letter from Brazil that arrived mid-December had helped set things right between her and JJ. She had presented it to JJ, sealed.

Is this Glasnost? he'd joked. The New Openness. Or should I say New Closedness? He'd kissed her before, side by side on the couch, they'd read it. Then they talked more frankly than they'd done after JJ's test. First, JJ told Allie he'd send back the Pan Am discount certificate. He'd write Bird that he couldn't fly to them. But he'd send more money. He'd sell his old electric guitar, his books. And if Kin and Bird ever showed up here, JJ finished, we'll—you know—handle it together.

Allie had nodded, sensing he'd forced himself to say this last. Good, she told him carefully. Because Bird's still in love with you. I mean: What was she thinking? Sending you this Pan Am thing. Reacting, I guess, to you telling her that you've been thinking of them, that you'd pay for Kin to see a doctor. . . .

I want, JJ answered evenly. To help Kin however I can.

I understand that, she assured him. Given what you three went through, what Bird describes, I can see better now why you'd still have feelings for . . .

Them, JJ filled in. Then he took hold of Allie's hand.

And they sure do for you, Alice told him, wondering—and deciding to say it out loud: Do you think they've had any other men, other threesomes, after you?

JJ lowered his eyes and shrugged, his hold on her hand loosening. Before he could pull away, she asked, Would that bother you?

He hesitated, then—maybe not wanting to break the spell of truth between them—nodded. Alice squeezed his hand. She thanked him for being honest, told him she wanted to do the same. Then she admitted that Bird's description of her and JJ's first encounters at Mass. Mental, their mutual attraction, had been a relief to read. Because her worst fear, she confessed in a nervous rush, was that JJ secretly yearned to be with a man. Still. That their own lovemaking—the most real experience of her life—was, for him, less than real.

No, no, JJ whispered right away. No, Allie. Christ. Don't think that. He pulled her close to his warm solid chest, her old favorite resting spot.

I don't want to—think it. But I do, sometimes. But—I suppose this shouldn't matter, but—*was* it Bird first? That you fell in love with? Bird mostly?

JJ shook his head at the "mostly," looking confused. Bird first, yeah.

And have you—Allie raised her head to look him in the eye. Have you met Kin, the man Kin, since that summer, ever?

No.

Have you met with other men, since Kin?

No, not in that way.

Have you wanted to?

Here JJ shook his head more slowly, his eyes still steady. Not really.

Not *really*?

Not in any way that made me do anything. But Jesus, Al. I find my-self *think*ing about sleeping with. All sorts of people. Imagining it, in passing. Don't you?

I guess. Alice had managed a half smile, remembering the Bird woman kissing her in the bathroom, pleased to have kept that from JJ. Her small secret.

Listen, Al. JJ had lifted Bird's letter, waving it as if to demonstrate its lightness, its transparency. All of that was, really was. Another life, y'know?

No, she had answered, less shaky. I've only had one. Life, I mean.

I know. JJ had eased her head back down against his chest.

Alice slumped now, pushing aside her empty cracker box. No doubt in months or years, she'd make JJ describe how it had been with Kin. Sexually, emotionally. How it felt different than with a woman. How much he missed that undeniable difference. Things she both wanted and didn't want to know.

The actress who'd played Mrs. C. for a decade sipped her poison tea. Looking back on years of real trouble. Allie licked her chocolate lips, sticky as a kid's.

We'll be OK, JJ had murmured behind her only last night, cupping her breasts. They did, he agreed, feel bigger. But we'll be OK, even if you are.

Curled together against the cold, they had agreed that if she was pregnant, they shared the blame. They had both let birth control slide in frozen December. They'd made love with a new roughness and reck- lessness. They'd wanted—must've wanted, JJ had murmured last night— to seal it, their marriage.

The phone purred. So faint Allie thought it was the TV phone but Mrs. C. went on sipping. At the third purr, Allie jumped up, skidding on the linoleum. Jo!

She ran into the front room and seized the receiver. Jo had promised she'd phone before "cadaver class" at nine, Arizona time; eleven, Allie's time.

"Have ya taken it yet?" Jo demanded right off, loud and clear.

"Shush." Allie smoothed her already-faded Dukakis sweatshirt. "Mom might overhear. No, JJ's not back from the drugstore. He said maybe he'd stop by the Computer Department on the way. He does that sometimes but I think he said it today because he knows how much I like him to . . ."

"Oh yeah?" Obligingly, Jo asked this in a stage whisper. "So it looks like JJ might go back, for real? Wouldn't he have to if you *are* knocked up?"

Allie leaned against the counter. In the gray light—outside, fitful snow swirled—this room looked especially stark. "May-be. But don't tell Mom that."

"I *won't.*" Jo sighed, no doubt rolling her eyes. Lately, Jo had given Allie all the gory details of her search for Mr. Right, Mr. OK, Mr. (Jo's latest joke) He'll Do. Allie had told Jo her own troubles, not going into the ones most on her mind. "And if there *is* a baby, it's simple. What- ever's best for the baby is best, period."

"Right." Allie hugged herself, grateful for Jo's certainty.

"And, Allie? I've been thinking." Jo shifted to her old bossy tomboy tone. "If Dad *does* get in this Home, maybe this summer you and JJ could come stay with us. You could help us move Dad and you wouldn't have to work summer jobs."

"Hey, yeah." Allie straightened up at the prospect of getting away from New Haven. Hiding out where they couldn't be found? "Maybe JJ would *want* to just study and all. And we spent Thanksgiving *and* Christmas in Ohio with his Dad. . . ."

"Right. Mr. Personality."

"You said it." Allie shivered, remembering JJ's dad's dank mobile home, wheelless, set in concrete. "Oh Jo. That trailer thing *is* like a motel inside—nothing personal, no photos . . ." The door lock rattled. "Hey, I hear JJ."

"So lemme know," Jo stage-whispered.

"Stay tuned." Allie cradled the receiver as the door swung.

"Got it, Al." JJ stomped his feet. His hair, kinkier in winter, sparkled with snow. His eyes too seemed brightened today. "So how's the guy in the cage?"

Allie laughed. "Brad? Still locked up—they always drag out the dumbest plots longest." She padded to the bedroom. "Show's still on. Jo called and—oh, no."

She stopped in the doorway. JJ came up behind her, his down jacket cool and damp against her sweatshirt back. His skin smelled pleasantly of snow. Together, they watched the evil maid sneak up behind passed-out Mrs. Chancellor.

"Old Brad basically told the crazy ex-wife he'd sleep with her if she'd come *in* the cage with him. So, y'know, he can grab the keys or whatever—"

The camera zoomed in on the teacup—in case anyone still didn't get it.

"Maybe he doesn't want the keys," JJ mumbled over the swell of music, close to her hair. "Maybe old Brad's just getting horny in that cage."

"Yeah." Allie faced him as the credits rolled. "Answer These Compelling Questions," she intoned in her old soap-announcer voice, taking JJ's drugstore bag. "Is Alice Ann Wolfe Knocked Up? For Real, this time? For Good?"

"Know what I think, Allie? What my sixth sense says?" JJ blinked.

"Don't tell me, Master of Artificial Intelligence. You're always right." She set the bag on the table and pulled out the Comet that was weighing it down.

"I'll do that," JJ said, but Allie was already bending to the cabinet below the sink. Her eyes flickered to the mop bucket, JJ's dark loose hair still there. Secretly, she kept hoping he'd throw it away. She clanked the Comet into place.

"By the way," JJ told her mildly. "Tobias agrees with me about the rat holes."

"Oh?" Allie opened the fridge, glad to hear JJ's old light tone. She lifted the cellophane-covered cup she'd filled today with her morning piss.

"I was telling him about those holes, how they were this big—"

As the fridge door swung shut, JJ made an OK sign, approximating the plum-size of the holes gnawed in their cabinet wood. "I told him, Al, how you thought that was too small for a rat to get through. And

Tobias said—" JJ imitated Tobias's wise-sounding basso voice. "'Them rats. They *big*, but they *soft*.'"

·   ·   ·

"Let Ms. Wolf-ee change Eric," Sticks told Vi. "Seein' how she's made such a mira-culous recov'ry." Alice stood in the corkboard partition opening. Sticks and Vi knelt by Eric on the changing mat in the corner opposite Carter's.

"Uhn huh." Vi grunted as she rose. Her chin moved slowly, chewing her tobacco gum. Her tooth sent scant glints. Sticks rose more quickly, facing Allie.

"Hi, Vi." Allie tried to catch Vi's eye. Walking through the new snow—JJ'd offered to drive her but Allie wanted to walk—she had imagined telling Vi her news: Vi, who'd given birth to two boys in her teens and who knew Allie was late again. JJ hadn't wanted Allie to go to work at all, but she'd insisted, wanting mainly to tell Vi. "What's up?" she asked as Vi brushed off her knees.

"Nothin you need t' hear, babe." Vi gave a That's-the-Way-It-Is sigh.

Surprisingly, Sticks rested one red-nailed hand on Vi's slumped shoulder. "You go sit with Carter till we're finished here. Jus' let him smoke."

Sighing, Vi waddled out. Allie sank down by Eric, lying on his back still dressed. His eye patch in place and his deflated eyelid closed. Allie touched his sweater arm. "What's wrong with Vi? Something with her son—?" That Vi's son was in trouble Allie had gleaned from conversations between Sticks and Vi.

"Who told you that?"

"No one." She'd wished Vi *would* confide in her. "I don't know anything—"

"I'll say." Behind the corkboard, someone pounded a table. "Izat Carter?" Sticks took a step, then glanced back. "You do know how to change a diaper?"

"Well, I—"

But Sticks was clicking away. Awkwardly—she'd never changed an adult diaper, only baby diapers on day-care jobs—Allie rolled Eric on his side. The plastic torso mold that encased his body stuck up through his blue sweater. His mother knit all his sweaters, mailing them in. She never visited Eric. His drool dripped onto the mat; Allie fumbled with the tissue box beside him.

She had expected to cry. To hug JJ, feeling the wonder of what they'd done. The terror of it too, but also the wonder. Big breathless emotions. So far, though, the main thing they both seemed to feel—to think—was *No.*

Yes, the red stick had told them after soaking in her first morning urine.

Yes? JJ had examined the stick, re-read the directions and examined the stick again. He'd done all this in the detached scientific manner Allie tried to adopt now, peeling on rubber gloves. She unfolded the unwieldy adult diaper.

She had held JJ hard, whispering, We oughta take a second one. But as she'd pressed against JJ, she'd felt more surely than ever the swollen tenderness of her breasts, the sense she'd had for weeks of talking through a filmy fleshy haze.

"Stay still for me," she murmured. Eric was propped on his side by his plastic body suit. His arms, stronger than his stunted legs, made flipperlike motions. Allie heard table bangs start up again, louder. What had possessed Carter?

"OK now . . ." Inching the fabric first past flesh-colored plastic, then past the flesh of Eric's legs, Allie eased down his pants. She untaped his soaked diaper. Only piss, she was relieved to see as she unfolded it. The ammonia smell—adult piss mixed with baby powder—stung her eyes. For a second she thought she'd cry.

"Control it, Carter—" Sticks commanded distantly. Allie blinked back her tears and set aside the wet diaper. "Control. Your hands. You hear me, Carter?"

The table bangs stopped; Sticks and Vi must be holding Carter's wrists.

"Good boy," Allie murmured to deaf Eric, and she plucked a Handi Wipe. Three dispensers sat in a row: tissues, rubber gloves, soapy pads. Gingerly, she wiped Eric's bony ass. Averting her eyes from his cock, she maneuvered the fresh diaper into place. Another bubble of drool slid off his lips. Eric's face stayed rigid like his body, as if for this procedure he too distanced himself.

"There we go." Allie pressed the diaper tape into place. In relief, she stood on her knees to stuff the sour-smelling used diaper inside a plastic bin.

"*Carter*—" Sticks shouted. "What's got into you?" Calmly, Allie pulled up Eric's pants and rolled him onto his back again. As she peeled off her gloves, she noted that his slack mouth curved. He knew it was over, this small shared ordeal.

"Good boy." She patted his arm firmly. Eric could've thrown one of his fits. Maybe her baby, like Eric, would sense from her hands that she needed help.

"Glad I'm working with you today." Allie whistled, close to Eric's face so he'd feel the air. He gurgled. "And we'll do your Sensory Stim thing, OK?"

Sensory Stimulation: letting Eric splash his hands in a pan of warm water.

"Miss Wolf-ee." Sticks was clicking toward Eric's partition.

Alice stood and turned. "Can I do Eric's Stim program today?"

"No time." Sticks blocked the partition opening.

"We oughta make time," Alice answered so quickly she startled herself.

Sticks nodded, seeming startled too. "We oughta," she surprised Allie by agreeing. "But not today. Can't. I need you with Carter, like usual."

Allie heard him bang his table. Picturing the flesh curl inside her, she told Sticks. "Please. Today—I'd rather not work with Carter. Not if he's Going Off—"

"Look." Sticks lowered her voice. "Vi's not up to Carter today. So it's gotta be you." Pivoting, she clicked back toward Carter's partition. "An' we need the Prez working. We got a contract job, a deadline." Sticks stopped at Puffball's table, lifting a box. "Don't forget: make 'em wear those rubber gloves."

"But they won't," Puffball muttered. As Allie hurried to follow Sticks, Vi brushed by, heading for the office, holding a shiny pack of cigarettes. Behind his partition, Carter sat slumped. No smoke smell. His pipe must have been denied him after his table banging. His pit-bull jaw jutted out. Uneasily, Allie watched Sticks set down a box of tongue depressors and a pair of rubber gloves.

"Now I *know* how hard it is to keep gloves on these workers. But the front office in all its wiz-dom sent us this job and we're gonna do it right." Sticks lifted a handful of oblong paper packets, fanning them out. "You make Carter wrap those tongue sticks inside these packs. And yes, they're for real doctors."

"Look," Allie began to object again, but Sticks was clicking away again.

"Listen up," Sticks announced from outside the partition. "The Channel 8 van just pulled in." Someone groaned. "This gonna be our last time, they say . . ."

"OK." Allie said out loud, firmly. Carter blinked behind the glasses that never quite gripped his flat nose. "No funny business now, Prez." Beyond the partition, steps thudded. The camera and light men. Here to film final footage for their exposé, weeks from its rumored spring-time airing. Got no room to worry about that, Allie thought. Picturing again a curl of flesh afloat inside her like the hamburger curls Newt ate. No: like Newt itself, wide-mouthed and wide-eyed.

"Closer." The cameraman sounded far away. Tongue depressors clicked.

"You gotta put this on." Alice rolled up the glove, stretching it open. Carter reached with his good hand into the box of untouched tongue depressors. "No—"

Looking bemused, he stuck one in his mouth, sucking it. "I said no." Allie dropped the glove and tugged the stick from Carter's tobacco-stained teeth. Surprisingly quick, he scooped up a handful of tongue depressors. He crammed them into his mouth. They bristled out like catfish whiskers.

"Stop this." She kept her voice low, mad that she'd let him get away with so much for so long. Carter chuckled, several contaminated tongue depressors dropping from his mouth. He clenched the remaining one between his teeth like Popeye's pipe. And he pulled himself unsteadily to his feet.

"No!" Allie stood so fast she bumped the table against Carter. Swaying, he reached out and gripped her shoulders. His whole stooped-over weight leaned on her. She half staggered, picturing her fetus jarred in its fluid.

"*Stop* it—" With both hands, Alice shoved Carter away. All too easily, he lurched backward into his seat. A thump: tailbone against plastic.

She gasped, feeling hot brightness hit her back. Carter's glasses hung diagonally, still strapped on his head. "Sorry, sorry—" Alice spun around. Light hit her face: blinding white. Carter groaned. Spinning again, blinking through blobs of light, she faced him. He'd sprung back up, towering over her.

"I—I—" Carter lurched forward, his eyes dangerously dazed. And Allie stumbled back a step, losing her own balance. She fell onto the floor, sitting hard on her padded tailbone. My baby, she thought.

"Wha's wrong?" Sticks and the cameramen crowded round. Behind her tensed stomach muscles, Alice felt her insides to be safely unshaken.

"Not me," she gasped into the hot light. "Him—" She pointed toward Carter, meaning he was the one who needed help. But the cameraman bent to her, his video's snout focused on her face like a dental X-ray machine.

"Who, Carter?" Briskly, Sticks stepped over Allie's outstretched legs. Twisting around, Allie saw Carter grip Sticks's strong arm. Steadying himself. All he'd wanted, maybe. "See?" Supervisor Sticks trained her narrowed gaze on Allie on the floor. "*He's* not gonna hurt *you.*"

. . .

Outside in bracing cold, Allie's feet packed down sidewalk snow. She veered onto the longer campus route. Playing it safe, she told herself, now that she was walking for two. Protecting two. Was that what she'd been trying to do, pushing poor old Carter? She shivered as she remembered Carter's dead-level stare when she'd left work minutes ago. His eyes had seemed melted down, brown staining his eyeballs. He'd watched her leave, staring like a hurt, resentful child.

But he's a grown man, Allie reminded herself. A big man who *could* have pushed her, hit her. Accidentally, on purpose. Either way, he could have hurt her, maybe even hurt her fetus. She hurried past a tall Yale tower, one from which flunking students were rumored to hurl themselves. No, Allie decided with a shudder. She wouldn't fight this instinct to guard her baby against all dangers, however improbable. Her baby and herself. One and the same, as yet.

Panting cold visible air in the vestibule, Allie squeaked open the mailbox. Only bills. She gripped them as she climbed the stairs. Could she afford to quit Helping Hands? At shift's end, she had told Vi she was thinking of looking for a safer job. Safer? Vi had answered gruffly. Oh sweetie, *this* place is nothin'.

"JJ?" Allie let herself in and marched up the corridor, unbuttoning her coat.

"Al." At the table, he blinked up from *The Mind of a New Machine.* Torn official-looking envelopes lay spread around him. He really had stopped by the department for mail. Good. She halted. Their Crock-Pot was simmering with beef and spicy vegetables that JJ must've chopped.

"We've got to talk." Sighing, she sat opposite him.

"Christ." He set down his book. "Guess I'm still in shock. You too?"

"Not anymore. I got—jarred outa shock. See, I had this tussle with Carter—"

"What?" JJ leaned over the tabletop, his blue eyes instantly greener and clearer.

"No, no; nothing *hap*pened. But I sort of fell on my ass and it scared me, made me want to quit. Maybe I'll get fired anyway by Helping Hands. It was all captured by Channel 8, but I don't even want to think about that. . . ."

He nodded. "Sure, you should quit," he told her. "I never did want you working in that kind of place. We can get by on what I make."

"No, no. I'll find another job, JJ—just something safer. I know we can't get by on your library money alone. But . . ." She looked at the envelopes from other colleges. At his dad's air-force strongbox, full of bills. "I feel like now with the baby coming you need to decide. What you're going to do about school."

Her eyes rested on *The Mind of a New Machine*. All JJ's books seemed to share the same cover: a stylized human head. Circuits instead of brains.

"I told you, Al. Long time ago. If you were pregnant, I'd go back to school. So I'd get my degree just after the baby came. And you know I've found out my credits *could* transfer to other programs. Places too small to attract the DOD . . ."

"JJ?" she interrupted, bold today. "Can I say something? This is Yale. You're already halfway to being a Master of AI. You already have taken DOD money, in stipend checks. It's inevitable; it's everywhere in some form, I bet. And if you want a job at a cool good-deed-doing company like Kurzweil—I *know* you'd love making software for synthesizers or for reading machines to help the blind—you need Yale. That name. Two more semesters wouldn't be so bad. . . ."

JJ lowered his eyes. "We'll talk about this later."

"OK, sure." She drew a big breath. "But JJ, another thing. One I want to talk about now, since it's been on my mind today. Kin and Bird. You know how she said in the long Brazil letter that they wanted to see you? That if you wouldn't fly to them they'd come back here and 'see' you somehow? Well. You seeing *any* ex-lover would bother me right now, because of our baby. But Kin and Bird. Well . . ."

" 'Well' what?" JJ raised his eyes challengingly.

Allie lowered hers. "Look. It's not just that Kin's a man and the whole threeway thing. That upset me, sure, but I'm handling it fine now. As long as it stays in your past. But you've gotta admit: Bird sending you the photo, the airline certificate. All that crossed the line, JJ. And if Kin and Bird do come after you *here* . . ." She looked up. "C'mon, JJ: her actions, the whole tone of her letters. God, it's so clear Bird's still in love with you. And she and Kin *do* seem—well, unbalanced. Who knows what they're like now? What they really want from you? You haven't seen them since the days when *you* were, well—"

"Alice, stop." JJ stood abruptly. "You don't know what the Hell you're talking about." He turned to the Crock-Pot, sticking in the wood spoon. "What I had with them. It wasn't some kind of 'crazy-man' behavior, if that's what you've been telling yourself. They more than anyone helped me *out* of that—craziness. Kin and Bird helped me more than I can. Say." His voice lowered to its flattest plane, way beyond Ohio. "And if they come here, I—have to see them. And, given how you're saying you feel about them. Yes: alone."

"Alone?" Allie echoed. JJ kept his back turned. "Wait a minute now." She stayed seated, but felt she was standing. "After Bird's Brazil letter, you *said* we'd handle it to*get*her if they showed up. And now you're saying we *can't* see them together? Because of how I 'feel' about them? How'm I *supposed* to feel about ex-lovers who try to lure my husband into flying across the world to them? Look, I don't care how this sounds. How jealous or small-minded. I've gotta follow my *instincts*. And I want you to agree you won't see them alone."

JJ clanked the wet glass lid in place. He glanced over his shoulder at her, narrowing his eyes. Like Sticks sizing her up that first day, or Carter this last.

"You 'look'." JJ turned back to the stove, gripping it, his elbows sticking out. "I never went searching for them. Though, in a way, I—wanted to. Wanted to fly out to Brazil and find them and—I don't know. Take them someplace safe. And now if they show up here in who knows what state, I can't and won't say I'd—" He faced her at last, folding his arms as if to control his hands. "Slam the door."

Behind his dense curly hair, beef steam rose as if from his head.

"I didn't *say* 'slam the door,'" she told him, her mind in full spin. "But, God, maybe I *oughta* with you standing here telling me you wanted—and d'ya still *want?*—to fly off and goddamn rescue them and. God. *Did* you ever send back that airline thing?" Reaching impulsively into his strongbox, she fished out a packet bound by one giant paperclip: three red-and-white-edged airmail envelopes.

"Al, for Chrissakes—"

"You didn't!" Shakily, she pulled the folded Pan Am discount certificate from the torn Brazil envelope. "You kept this; you told me you'd send it back but you kept it! Would you even've warned me before taking off for South America?"

"Calm down." JJ stepped closer, half raising his hands as if she were catching on fire. "Christ, I'm not taking off *anywhere*—"

"Not now, huh?" she found herself asking, her voice choking. "Not when you're stuck here with this bitchy pregnant wife and all—" She began to cry, crumpling the certificate. "Shit JJ, I'm so sick of all your *secrets.*"

"Al, c'mon." JJ knelt, taking hold of her shoulders.

"Why'd you *keep* this thing?" She raised the certificate between them.

He averted his eyes from it. "You keep it," he told her abruptly, releasing her shoulders. "Keep all the letters. I don't want them. Take them." He pushed them toward her, the three envelopes she'd dropped on the table. She blinked at them, her eyes still blurred. "*Take* them," JJ insisted, shoving the whole pile into her lap. Like, Alice thought dazedly, an addict handing over his stash.

"God, JJ." She set the crumpled Pan Am pass on top, bowing her head over the unclipped envelopes. You, she wanted to say, are still in love with them. She screwed up her mouth to hold back more tears. Her face felt ugly, contorted, her lips stretched thin. Her teary eyes darted again to his strongbox. Amidst his disrupted papers, she caught the dull shine of that black-and-white snapshot.

"C'mon now, Al." JJ reached across the table and banged shut the metal box. He drew a slow breath. "C'mon, let's calm down. We're both—on edge. Today . . ."

The edge, Allie thought. She didn't nod. But she muttered, "This baby's going to my head, JJ. Like I'm feeling for two." She lifted the paper pile from her lap and set it on the table, her side. "Can't *we* fly away?" She stared up at him boldly. "Jo says we oughta come out to Arizona this summer. Since they'll need help moving Dad to that Home. Then, see, you could just study all summer and . . ."

"No, Al." JJ sat back on his heels. "I don't want to live off your parents. I'll work double time so you don't have to work. But I want to stay here." He met her eyes. "You could go there alone for a while, though, if that's what you need. . . ."

"What? You *want* us to be apart?" JJ started to shake his head but Alice couldn't stop her own voice, rising again. "Why? Are you hoping they'll come here? Show up at our—" She shot a teary-eyed glance over her shoulder. "Door?" She started sobbing, letting her face crumble. God: was her whole pregnancy going to be like PMS? Her nerves snapping in a second. Could she handle a baby at all? She bent with her sobs, feeling ugly inside and out. What if JJ *did* run off with them? He started to pull himself up, bumping the table. A *"table" has four legs*, Alice thought as she gasped for breath. JJ had programmed such basic facts into a computer once. A *"tabletop" may be square or round*.

"Sorry about all this, Al." He was standing, reassuringly tall. She felt small, taking hold of his thigh. "And no, I'm not hoping they'll come here. Not at all." But you wanted to fly to them, she thought. "I doubt they will. They're halfway round the world." He stroked her snow-dampened hair. "C'mon. You're acting as paranoid as me. We're both in shock, is all. About the baby. But we'll be OK. . . ."

"I don't know 'bout that. Oh JJ, I don't know what's gotten hold of me, of us." Allie looked up at him, her neck craning. "I pictured it today. Pictured it to look like Newt. You think that's sort of how it'll look in a few weeks?" She snuffled.

"Hope not." He kept stroking her hair.

"Why not? It'd be green. An alien. Like its dad. *The Man Who Fell to—Earth*." She rushed on, asking in whisper: "Can't you feel it? That it's here?"

"Not yet." JJ's hand cupped her head. "Doesn't seem possible . . ."

Following the pressure of his hand, Allie pressed her face again to his solid thigh, his pants still damp from her tears. "Try to feel it, JJ," she told him, gripping his leg harder. "That we're three, now."

11

Manila, April 1989

Jim Joe—

Don't know how to say Hello from here. Don't know—if I didn't have your last letter, that breakthrough of a letter—how I'd stand it here. Manila: sunk in muggy yellow gray smog. Kin sleeps now, coated with sweat like the spume on Outre Banda. Manila is the real Autre Banda. In the dark outside our bed-sized room, Filipino kids chant words neither of us knows. Yet we're grateful to be here, any here, grateful and glad to write you "care of" what Kin calls the Big Y.

So with no Filipino Hello, I say in plain English: Thank you Jimmy Joe, for the money you wired us in Brazil in the last days of 1988. Thank you much more for the Yale Computer Science Department address you sent with that second gift. So: only you will read this? Your worried little Big-W Wife won't get hold of it first? Though you didn't say in your letter that she'd been reading my letters, I bet that's why you want them sent, from now on, care of Big-Y Yale. Are you there now, surrounded by humming computers, hidden from your Wife? Is she what's making you feel, as you put it, "trapped" in "many ways" just now? Mrs. Jimmy Joe with her sweet face and humming, all-seeing eyes.

What I want to say here—to propose—she doesn't want to see.

Your letter and money arrived via Nossa Senhora Do Ó before Christmas. How happy we were to read that you'd been tempted to fly to us! That you often find yourself looking at our photo. That it "unhinges" something in you, every time. Then all the questions you asked—I'll answer each of them, saving one for my letter's end—all that made me feel as if you were coming back to us, at last. Turning in that direction, anyhow. I didn't dare say so to Kin. But secretly, I celebrated that fact as Fatima and Zé roasted us swordfuls of pork and beef for a farewell barbecue. Fireworks crackled in Our Lady of O on Christmas night. The Virgin Mary (no, her statue) floated (no, lurched) through the streets on a flatbed truck decked with lace and winking lights. Blue, yellow, green.

You ask where we'd go, from Brazil. Well, in the first days of 1989, we flew with the last of our Free-Fly Points to Hong Kong via Egypt, then crossed Pearl River on a Xinghu ferry. Here's where things start to blur; where Kin started to weaken again. In February, in Guangzhou. Its streets packed full as a Boston subway car amid a rush hour that never ends. The Unemployment money Boyd sent us bought a room at Guangzhou Youth Hostel. We heard Cantonese Rap on the street corner below, Kin mouthing from his bed the kids' barking rhythmic words. We rubbed Tiger Balm salve into each other's backs, for warmth. In our shared hostel bathroom, one boy always squatted on the toilet seat, leaving toe marks like the footprint we found on our sooty windowsill. While we were out rounding up English students, see, a thief stole my baggy jeans and Kin's batiste shirt.

I made Kin mad—stonily silent as a wet cat—by speculating that maybe Li, a whispery voiced boy-faced student who was earnestly attempting to convert Kin to Buddhism, had been the thief. Wanting to wrap himself in Kin's clothes.

You ask me, JJ, how he is: Kin. Worse, lately. Mid-March, a fever trapped him in our room, his neck swelling (he wore his black scarf when students came) and his limbs thinning out. Still, he refused to see a doctor. Remember, Jimmy Joe, how Kin never took aspirin, saying it'd muffle his body's messages? How he wouldn't try pot with us? Only wine, cigarettes. All March, we lived on Double Happiness cigarettes and steamed Mantou buns.

Some nights, we let families rent our room. Like little Fati multiplied, giggling on our bed while we slept on the floor mat. Once, a trio of horny brothers surrounded Kin. He opened his mouth, showing them the sores. Bowing, they backed away. Maybe we'd still be huddled in the Guangzhou Youth Hostel if not for Carlos. Kin's on-and-off lover years ago. On a plane on fire in San Juan, Carlos and Kin had herded passengers onto evacuation slides. Carlos tracked us down in April, hearing through the Pan Am grapevine Kin was sick.

In his spotless AeroMexico steward's uniform, he knelt beside Kin's bed like an old-fashioned suitor. He reminded me, Jim Joe, of my mother's favorite man, Morton Giles. Mort's stocky hockey-player body, his persistent grin.

Carlos had a deal to propose. In Spanish Kin translated for me. Free tickets on a puddle-jumper to the Philippines. And, if we can hang out for two months in Manila, a June-special flight to Mexico. When Carlos and his lover aren't flying, they live near the border town of Agua Prieta. Kin and I can stay in their little house there, tending their garden and marijuana patch through August 15. Almost our anniversary, I didn't say. Carlos accepted a handshake from Kin to seal the deal. Letting his white-toothed grin fade, he kept hold of Kin's hand. He had tested negative. In San Diego, in Mexico City. He told this to Kin, not me.

As if Kin had tested positive for him, in place of him, Carlos pressed Kin's hands between his. I stayed planted on my side of Kin's bed. Carlos in his shiny uniform and St. Christopher's medal rose from his knees. I watched Kin meet his eyes. A black rich as blood. I looked at my feet on the scratchy mat, knowing I should've left them alone. Knowing, JJ, that in another life, an ex-lover like Carlos or a friend like Boyd would've gathered Kin into a circle of men. Caring for Kin, as Kin's New York friends cared for a man named Shawn T.

After Carlos rushed off to his flight, our room felt colder than ever. I climbed on the bed beside Kin, trying to remember what he'd told me about Carlos in Mexico, in '81. Weekends on a hotel balcony in Puerto Ángel, sunning and swimming; cooking shrimp Carlos caught. Saying little, in broken Spanish. Back then, see, Kin always claimed he wanted touching, not talking. Though he'd do plenty of talking afterward, with me. That setup, he used to say, suited him. Didn't—his voice always mocked this '70s phrase—tie him down.

In our cold hostel room, I took Kin's hand, imagining it still warm from Carlos's grip. I asked him if he and Carlos had ever gotten—serious?

Coulda, Kin told me slowly. If my Spanish'd been better. If I'd made it better. But, I don't know. He squeezed my hand more loosely than Carlos had squeezed his. Guess I wasn't inclined to *wholly* join with anyone when I'd already. In a way, y'know. Joined with—He hesitated but said it. You, Berta.

Me and—for one summer, the summer that sealed Kin and me even more tightly together—you, Jimmy Joe. This morning, as we lurched into Manila on the airport bus (bumper-to-bumper drivers using brakes more than gas and horns most of all) I wondered if Kin too keeps thinking of you. Not, I want to tell him, thinking of you in my old stalled way. In a new way. With a new purpose. Our old purpose—experiencing this world—may have to wind down now.

In our low-ceilinged ground-level HOTOL room, Kin and I did talk about you, eventually. First we collapsed on a mildewed mattress. Above our room, an air conditioner chugged, dripping water like plentiful sweat onto the alley below.

Kin muttered that an ex of his used to say there were three temperatures in Manila. Fucking hot. Too fucking hot. And too hot to fuck.

I inched open our net curtains. In the building opposite ours, a TV faced out into the alley. Below our window, kids mumbled at the screen. Filipino lilts.

Did you want to, with Li? I asked, my eyes on the window. The kind of question I'd have written down if I hadn't filled my last notebook in Hong Kong.

Fuck? Kin sighed. 'Course I wanted to. And 'course we didn't. We did kiss, close-mouthed, after Li gave me a good-bye present. A book. *Meditations on Not-Being*. Funny, 'cause that's what I tried to do, round Li. Not be. Not feel.

Hey, I interrupted, pointing out at the TV. Isn't that, like, Calgary?

Picture this, Jimmy Joe. Through irregular streams of air-conditioner drip, Kin and I watched flickering clips from the Winter Olympics. Figure skating! Midori Ito of Japan twirled and leapt faster and higher than seemed possible for any human. Only as she froze her final spin did we see her face so full of joy some spilled into us. We spun on our bed like you and Kin, only slow, holding each other's elbows, tottering. We fell on the squashy mattress, Kin panting as if we'd done more than dance. He squinted at the lithe men gliding on screen.

What, I asked hesitantly. If I—found you a man here who was sick too . . .

Oh per-fect, Kin muttered. We'd have us a Night of the Living Dead. No, no. If I did anything now it couldn't be with a stranger. It'd have to be. With someone I truly. You know. He coughed, shaking his head. 'S crazy, Berta. But y'know what I find myself thinking about, lately? Ever since his last letter . . . ?

I nodded and said it for both of us. You, me, Jimmy Joe.

I climbed off the bed, not ready to reveal the plan that was forming in my mind. We fought about me going out for food, alone. Kin stood too, wobbling as if we'd just stopped spinning. You'd slow me up, I blurted out. He scared me by nodding. By handing me, JJ, his Swiss Army knife. As Kin sank into sleep—his one drug, he brags—I dug into his bag for our money. My hand found a folded square, a *Time*-magazine page. "Suicide Made Simple?" I skimmed the review of a Hemlock Society book that gives directions for foolproof pain-free suicide.

Does that answer your questions about Kin's mood, his future plans? Outside, under the hand-printed HOTOL sign, words from *Time* spun inside me. Lethal doses of nonprescription drugs, videotaped good-byes. My head stuck up above parasols. Below me, a hand seized my ankle. A crouched boy with scabs covering his face like premature acne. Nimbly, he began unlacing my high-tops. But I kicked my foot free. Clutching the Swiss Army knife, faster because of it, I swerved into a propped door. Hairy coconuts swung above me. The store goods hung in detachable bundles, no room for shelves. I bought oranges and beef sticks and cigarettes. A muscular jockey-sized man stuffed it in a filmy bag like a produce bag in a Boston supermarket. Is such plastic thick enough to suffocate a suicide?

Outside, I breathed burning rubber, chicken-and-rice suppers. I walked slow, composing this letter in my head. Deciding to ask you yet again, JJ, to join us. As you alone can. To visit, this summer, our temporary home in Mexico. I can tell from your last letter you want to. So look at a map. I did, on the prop plane. Agua Prieta borders Douglas, Arizona. Sister Cities, I chanted to myself as I swung my bag, hoping to break it. But its plastic was stronger than it looked. I'd poke holes in it after we ate, I vowed. And I walked faster, heading for you.

Now, Jimmy Joe. As you contemplate this invitation, complete with place and time, I'll tell you what Kin and I remembered—re-lived, in a way—tonight. So you can re-live it with us. The present-day Kin and me. In 1989, in Manila. Of all your questions, the last two surprised me most. First: that you'd ask what we two remember, of we three. Almost like you can't do it yourself: remember us. When I got back with our food, the light in our HOTOL room had grown orange gray. Kin woke crossly, telling me I should've let him sleep. He coughed, exaggerating his cough maybe. I unfolded his knife and peeled our oranges. As kids' voices in the alley grew festive, I told Kin how I'd escaped the sneaker thief. I didn't ask about "Suicide Made Simple." Instead, I drew our net curtains and asked: R'member your mom's fancy bedsheets, draped over your windows?

Remember, JJ? Boston, summer 1980. Kin nodded. Silk, he murmured.

A cocoon of a room, I remembered, sitting beside Kin on our mildew-smelling mattress. Orange peels sweetened the air. We sighed together, then laughed at our lush sighs. Hazy orange-tinged light bathed the room, dimmer than the June afternoon light that had filled Kin's Commonwealth Avenue studio apartment. Walking distance to Fenway Park, to Kenmore Square and the BU bookstore where Kin with his high school diploma and passable grasp of Chinese worked—remember?—in foreign books. For fun and extra money, he tutored transfer students in English. You remember that apartment. Cars and buses and drunk BU students and T-trains were muffled so far up in the old-fashioned brick building. Remember the wood wainscoting and bare hardwood floors Kin had proudly waxed? And his new futon, un-folded that first afternoon, mid-June?

To sign us out of Mass. Mental for a Twenty-four-Hour Leave, to look old enough, Kin wore a beige linen jacket and pants his mom gave him for graduation. The linen set off the mahogany tan he'd cultivated swimming at the beach and sunning on the roof of his new building. As he led us into his apartment, Kin chatted about his 200-some cassette tapes, music from round the world. He slipped off his jacket. In his white ribbed tank top, he stretched his brown swimmer's arms. Cooler in this heat, he told you. You were sweating away in your same old bomber jacket.

We stood still, Jimmy Joe, as Kin bustled around us. His movements carried the new assurance he'd brought back from Taiwan. He pre-sented me with a pre-poured glass of what looked like the wine he poured for you from a chilled bottle. You and I had been off Thorazine for weeks, so we could drink. But Kin knew I wanted my head clear. He knew too I worried about my bad gums. I sipped my cool glass. Ginger ale spiked with—I met Kin's bright narrowed eyes—Listerine!

R'member the cocktail you mixed me? I asked Kin, peeling a last orange.

Sister Kin's Brew for Nervous Virgins. He smiled, nodding to the chants in the alley. The kids were inventing a game as they went along.

I swished the orange's juice the way I remembered swishing the Lis-terine. Not that I clearly imagined kissing anyone, not since I'd bitten that tongue.

No clue, I told Kin, wiping juice from my lips. What you had in mind.

Me? Kin shook his head in his new slow way. No, it was you. You two . . .

Us? I sucked my orange pulp.

Us? I ask you too, Jim Joe. Picture us. You in your newly chopped hair and your too-small jacket; me in Kin's black T-shirt and my too-big jeans. We sat stiff as our chairs, Kin's café-style table between us. Your wineglass untouched. Kin sipped his, sitting cross-legged on the futon in his linen pants. I showed him the ring of 8s you'd made me the day before, the day after your haircut.

You two knew what was gonna happen before I did, Kin claimed in Manila. Outside the kids chanted numbers from quickly changing points in the alley. Kin and I watched the shaded window as if the TV were on, showing the scene we were both seeing. R'member, Kin asked like this was proof. The mirror?

I didn't laugh. I shivered in Manila's heat to think of you asking Kin to cover his mirror. Kin fetched his long black scarf. Polite too, he asked why.

In your flattest Mass. Mental voice, you explained that Kin's wall mirror reminded you of the oddly placed mirror in Dr. Marmal's Therapy Room. A two-way mirror, you claimed. As you spoke, I realized I'd sensed that too.

Once, I told you and Kin shyly, When I'd had therapy with an intern, we came out of that room and Dr. Marmal was stepping from the door next to ours. He stopped like he'd been caught at something and asked in his ultranormal way, How *was* your session? The young intern looked surprised, I said.

You asked, Wha'd Marmal do?

Dr. Marmal, I told you, glared at the intern like: You flunk, Bub.

At that, you cracked a half smile. I looked away from your full lips, wanting to stare. Kin laughed. You're right, he told you. The mirror's gotta go.

Laughing too, we watched Kin drape and knot the black scarf over the mirror. With a magician's flourish, he pulled from his dresser drawer a second scarf and tied it over the lamp beside his futon. The room turned golden brown, the light projecting faint flowery patterns onto the walls.

Sipping your wine—you remember, JJ—you offered your own mirror story. Once Dr. Marmal had asked why you weren't drinking the medication for your Thorazine-parched throat. You said, Because it tastes like warm spit. And someone behind the two-way mirror laughed; you heard it. A live laugh!

As I giggled with Kin, you turned to me. Your eyes averted.

Schizophrenics, you informed me, have unusually acute hearing. All our senses are stronger—Marmal says so. We *need* stronger senses to survive with our ideational filters shot to hell; all sortsa thoughts getting let in. It's true. I don't need Marmal to tell me my senses are sharper. I can hear music miles away and smell when women are having their periods—oh, sorry.

Your scared blue eyes lowered to your basketball-player-sized sneakers. Casually, Kin asked you what else Dr. Marmal had told you in the mirrored room. You mumbled more examples and Kin nodded. Then you told us how Dr. Marmal once left you alone there so you could phone your dad to discuss the round-the-block walk in which you'd broken away from him. You described that walk to Kin the way you'd described it to me. But, you concluded, Marmal's mirror was watching you. So, though you'd wanted to, you hadn't picked up the phone.

Kin pointed to his scarf-covered mirror and to the phone by his futon. Call now, he told you. Bird and I'll watch, he said, but we'll be right here in the open.

We both giggled; you didn't. You walked up to the phone and said, I can't.

Kin stood too. Want me to dial? he asked, as if this were the logical next question. Kin glanced over his shoulder at me, like: Is this all right? Then both your backs were turned to me. I swished more spiked ginger ale on my numbed gums. With the robotic lack of expression that I admired, you recited your father's Ohio number. Kin dialed, his fingers as deft as a receptionist's. He held the receiver out to you. All of us heard the rings beep.

You stiffened at the sound of your dad's abrupt: Yes? Hello?

Even with him so tiny in the receiver, I heard his instant suspicion. Yes—?

Kin drew the receiver to his own mouth. His voice came out South Carolina smooth. Yes, hello. I'm calling from the Massachusetts Mental Health Center.

You and I exchanged amazed glances. You backed up a few steps. Outside, horns sounded. Kin cupped the receiver. Mmm. Yes, with your son.

You sat again at the table, leaned forward to watch Kin. Kin hammed it up, knitting his brows. Yes, he told your dad. I am his doctor. Yes, well, your son—Jimmy Joe—he's disturbed by a certain memory. A walk you two were taking one evening, Mr. Wolfe. Jimmy Joe ran away—? You remember that too, Mr. Wolfe? What's that? You think—that's when JJ's troubles began?

Kin rolled his eyes. You cracked another half smile. You didn't feel me stare because you were staring so hard at Kin, spellbound. Across the table from you, I twisted my ring of 8s. Across the ocean in Manila, I twisted the same 8s. Nodding as Kin asked if I remembered that phone call. Who could forget?

Well, your son has something to say to you, Mr. Wolfe. Kin arched his articulate inverted-V brows with a question: you want to talk? You, Jimmy Joe, shot back a pleading look: No, you!

I mean, Kin continued into the waiting phone. Jimmy Joe wants me to say that he's sorry if he hurt you by running away during that walk. But in my opinion, sir, Jimmy Joe would've been better off if he'd kept right *on* running.

An extended pause. In his suspicious tone, your father asked an abrupt question. Kin deepened his voice. Yes, he repeated. I *am* Jimmy Joe's doctor.

He asserted this with such conviction that you and I both believed it. Anyhow, we both sat silent after Kin hung up. Then Kin turned to you, doctor-faced. He asked you what you'd told us Dr. Marmal had asked you one session, out of the blue. The question hadn't struck us as hilarious until Kin intoned it in a perfect smarmy Dr. Marmal voice: You want to *pierce* your father, don't you?

Our laughs mixed easily. Remember? You almost fell off your chair. When we'd settled back down, you told Kin about *The Man Who Fell to Earth*, borrowing from Kin his self-mocking tone. You were still serious, but not all the way.

Nodding, Kin flipped through his vast collection of cassette tapes. Got some Bowie here, he told you. You came up beside him. Hey, you told him, pointing to a tape. Carl Sagan put this didgeridoo music on the Voyager.

So Kin played it for you on his portable boom box. The winding, vibrating, circular notes of a wooden aborigine drone trumpet. You nodded along, fiercely jiggling your foot. Then: a ch'in piece; also, you said, included in the ninety minutes of music aboard the spaceship Voyager. Kin described a ch'in to us, its lacquered box body and seven silk strings. Sounds meant to portray fish in water, fallen blossoms. Then, for me as well as you: David Bowie.

Oh good, I breathed. Emboldened by a few sips of Kin's wine, I said to you and Kin something I'd never said out loud. I love to dance!

Kin cranked up *Ziggy Stardust and the Spiders from Mars*. Our high school favorite. It was growing dark outside; Kin's scarf-covered lamp glowed.

First, JJ, you watched Kin and me dance to "Soul Love." I kept my eyes half closed, pretending in the golden brown light that Kin and I were alone. Though I liked the feeling of you watching us. Then it was us watching you dance to "Lady Stardust." Your animal grace, David Bowie sang. The words repeated inside me. Your long forearms slashed angular shapes in the air. You danced so wildly we jumped up halfway through and danced around you. Then I fell back on the futon. I watched you and Kin dance super-fast to "Star Man." At the end, you both fell down, Kin beside me. Soon we were swaying side by side, singing along with "Suffragette City," shouting together at the climax. Then laughing together as a neighbor below Kin angrily thumped her ceiling, "C'mon up," Kin shouted down to her. "Wham 'n bam us, Ma'am!"

We swayed together languidly to her furious broombeat, the three of us sitting Indian style on Kin's futon. David Bowie was singing to us, telling us we weren't alone.

In the silence after "Rock 'n' Roll Suicide," Kin and I giggled as if we had something planned. We didn't, exactly. We were making it up as we went along. Kin rose from between us, lightly. He slipped a new tape into the boom box.

Our new song: "It Had to Be You." No words, just sleepy-sounding clarinets and snare drums. You stayed on the futon, sweating in your jacket. Kin and I slow-danced in front of you. This time I shut my eyes. This time Kin spoke to you softly over my shoulder, telling you how we'd danced in his mom's living room; how we used to watch old movies, lying together on her white leather couch. As the song ended, Kin asked in his softest voice if you'd mind taking off your leather jacket and spreading it on the futon.

So that Berta, Kin murmured, squeezing my shoulders. Can lie on it. She likes, Kin told you, the feel of leather on her skin.

I nodded. I did like that, I realized. And I opened my eyes to watch you, Jimmy Joe, as you stood and pulled off your cracked brown jacket. Your father's Korean War bomber jacket. You spread it carefully over the futon like Sir Walter what's-his-name spreading his cape over a muddy puddle.

Don't look, Kin told you. He stepped up to his boom box, slipped in his Shakuhachi tape. Slow bamboo flutes. You faced the silk-sheet-covered windows. Your back was bare looking without your tight jacket, your shoulders bony but broad, your stance soldier straight. Listen, Kin told us in a measured teacher's voice. Each note is held. So long you almost can't stand it. As are. The silences.

The sheet curtains undulated in the June evening breeze. A flute note strained, a sound of moist breath on bamboo. The room was going dark.

Ready? Kin asked me under the dwindling note. I nodded, longing to feel leather again against my bare skin. Trying not to think further ahead than that, I undressed myself. I pulled off the T-shirt and jeans. I peeled down my panties. Then I faced your soldier-boy back. I let Kin unhook my bra, his fingertips barely brushing me. My breasts bounced free. My skin breathed the balmy air.

Don't look yet, Kin reminded you though you hadn't moved. You faced the curtains as if hypnotized by their undulations. I sat on, then lay on your jacket, my skin savoring the cool leather. The bamboo flute sighed down to nothing. Kin knelt beside me. With his black mica eyes, he looked me over. He touched my loose hair, spreading it out, white-blond in the dark.

Perfect, he breathed to me. Meeting my eyes so I could stop him if I wanted, he spoke to you. Jimmy Joe? You can see her now.

See her? you asked expressionlessly, still facing the bedsheet curtains.

I mean, Kin told you in the gently teasing tone he'd taken with you from the start. That's why we're here, love.

Remember? As if you couldn't believe Kin or anyone would call you "love," you turned. Instantly, I shut my eyes. I heard and felt you cross Kin's wood floor. When I opened my eyes, you were kneeling beside the futon, tall on your knees. Kin, shorter than you, stood on his knees on my other side. Your eyes moved over my body as if over the pages of the books you were always feverishly reading in Mass. Mental. Your own body stood ramrod straight, tensed up with the tautly strung nerves of a twenty-year-old virgin.

I lay before you, tensed up too, seventeen years old. And—despite Stepdad's fingers and his tongue and the other tongue I'd bitten—a virgin, too. I stared hard at your face, Jimmy Joe. Your bones stood out under the scarred skin you'd burned clean with your sun lamp. A layer of skin burned off, I imagined. So your nerves felt exposed, like my own. Your soft-looking firm-looking lips stayed sealed. Your eyes kept moving over my body, trying to read it.

Quietly, Kin pulled himself up from his knees. Barefoot, he crept behind you and covered with his hands your prayerfully intent eyes. I started too, my shoulders tightening along with yours. Guess who? I expected Kin to say. Instead, only to you, Sister Kin whispered: Now look.

You bent forward haltingly, blinded by Kin. As you touched me, I remembered Kin's words about the Shakuhachi. Each note held so long you almost can't stand it. Your fingertips felt cool on my skin. Was your sense of touch somehow heightened too? I wondered. You touched me lightly, tenderly, like Kin. I halfway thought those *were* Kin's hands. I blinked. But he had bent forward with you. Kin's hands still covered your eyes.

Y'know, he whispered into your ear. Back on my mom's leather couch, Berta and I used to—He hesitated, then spoke the word I was thinking.—play.

Kin released your eyes. You lifted your stiff-fingered hand from my thigh. Kin padded back to the other side of the futon and knelt again.

Like this, he whispered over me to you. He met my eyes, asking permission. I nodded, wanting to feel again, for the first time in years, his wet tentative tongue. Kin bent over my right breast. My nipple tingled but stayed flat.

Jimmy Joe? Kin raised his head, leaving behind one cool gleam. His lips gleamed too, thinner than yours. I nodded again—a slight movement of my chin—and Kin whispered again, straight to you: Jimmy Joe?

I squeezed shut my eyes, suddenly scared you might turn rough, impatient with this delicate game. But you bent over me slowly, careful not to startle me. Your tongue was warmly wet, its touch gentle, not tentative.

I should go, Kin whispered. Before he could stand, I hooked my hand around his neck and pulled him down. We rubbed our necks together like in high school, like swans, while you, Jimmy Joe, kissed and kissed my breasts. A hidden network of nerves under my skin began to flicker into life.

Oh, I told Kin. I arched my neck searchingly, rubbing harder till I found Kin's Adam's apple. I made it fill the hollow of my throat. Kin pressed back so hard I gave a gasp. Your kisses stopped; you pulled away along with Kin.

You stared down, asking: Are you—did I hurt you? I shook my head. Even as you towered above me, JJ, your tense stillness calmed me. As did Kin's familiar face. Both of you respectfully awaited my cue. No music now. All I heard was your breath. I whispered to Kin and he, as if translating, to you: Keep going.

Your mouth, I meant. My eyes were open. My chin touched my collarbone as I watched the top of your head. You inched down my body, half hidden by my breasts. Kin started to rise, but I gripped his hand like the hand of a midwife. I was a girl about to give birth as I raised my knees and opened my thighs to you.

R'member? I whispered to Kin in our cramped HOTOL bed. Outside our window, Filipino children shrieked with laughter at the game they'd made from nothing. Remember how you got us going, Sister Kin?

My hips were rocking. The kids resumed counting: a chant of slow steps.

No, Kin breathed in his old teasing tone. Tell me. He took my hand. Tell me how it felt, what I was doing. What *was* I doing there, Berta Bird?

Holding my hand. Holding me down, Sister Kin, so I wouldn't float off the futon. Off Jimmy Joe's jacket. You *do* remember that jacket: our fucking Magic Carpet . . .

I raised my knees as I'd done years before. I rocked my hips harder on the mildewed mattress, wanting Kin to feel my slow motion. Of course it was nothing like years before: my legs taut and trembling; your thick-chopped hair brushing my inner thighs. At the first probes of your tongue, I arched my spine and dug my fingers into Kin's palm. I ground my head against the futon that felt hard and soft at the same time. I squeezed Kin's hand so tight it must've hurt.

Hours ago, I squeezed his hand only lightly. His free hand slipped under our sheets, beginning to move. I kept moving my hips. But here in Manila, the slight sweat I generated felt grimy. Not fresh and miraculous like the sweat that broke out all over my body in the high silence of Kin's room when you raised your head from between my thighs. Too soon, that first time. But still.

Oh, I remember telling Kin, breathless. Circuits of new nerves vibrated in my skin. My moist innermost flesh felt soothed and stirred up. My face was wet. The leather felt damp beneath me. Wetness shone on your sated-looking lips. I whispered, still to Kin: Thank you, thank you. Kin told me softly, ever the polite South Carolina boy: Thank him, Berta.

I blinked through the humming darkness. You stood on your knees at the foot of the futon, so tall. Your face intently deadpan; your mouth sealed. At the crotch of your pants, an unmistakable bump had risen. I sat up fast, scooting back, leather squeaking under my ass. Now, I felt sure, you'd demand what I wasn't ready for. *He lost control,* I remembered Mom saying. *All men do.* I pulled my knees together. Kin rested a hand on my stiff bare shoulder.

Don't go—I blurted out, facing Kin. My bodyguard.

He stroked my arm. Then he told me and you both: No one has to do anything they don't want to do.

The single rule of our game. Kin rose like a flustered hostess. I stood too, flushed under my thrilling new skin of sweat. Wanting to calm you down yet wanting to help you feel what I'd felt. So I motioned you to lie on your own jacket. You were too long for that futon: your feet on the floor, your knees poking up. Your erection tried to poke up too, under your pants.

To give it some air—the warm air felt so good on my own skin—I knelt and unzipped your fly. Brave because of Kin, I pulled down your briefs, your pants halfway on, halfway binding your legs together. I stared over your tensely expectant body at Kin, his fox face, seeking further instructions.

Your mouth, Kin mouthed to me. Or maybe he only touched his own lips.

Giggling nervously, I stared down. Your penis looked darker and thicker than Kin's. Not that I'd ever seen Kin's, anyone's, like this. Alive, was all I could think. It's alive. I whispered to Kin, like a kid on a double dare: No, you.

Or maybe I only—on impulse—climbed on top of you, Jimmy Joe, straddling your rib cage. You told me in a choked whisper that I didn't have to do anything. But you sounded painfully strained by how much you wanted something done. *You*, I told Kin over my shoulder. And he answered, his voice all shaky: No, no, Jimmy Joe doesn't want—

I turned from Kin to you. Do you? I whispered. Want him, *his* mouth—?

You jerked your chin the way I had jerked mine. A nod. Your eyes burned with blue. You gazed at Kin the way you'd done as he'd phoned your father. The way you'd done as he'd played his tapes, as if the music were unfolding from him. I stayed on top of you, my thighs gripping your rib cage.

And were *you* holding *him* down? Kin asked me years later on our HOTOL mattress. His hidden hand was still pumping under the sheets, but weakly.

No, I told Kin, my voice strong like the kids' voices in the alley outside.

No. I remember how still you lay, JJ, as Kin knelt at the foot of the futon. Your eyes were closed but I knew under your lids the blue was still burning. As Kin bent to your crotch, I bent too, curving my back sharply so I could kiss you. Your lips tasted of me. Your body beneath me relaxed and stiffened with the same rises and falls I had, at last, experienced.

And behind me, I told Kin in Manila as I stilled my hips. Behind me while I kissed Jimmy Joe, I felt against my ass a few bumps from the top of your head. Just by the way your head was moving, so slow and sure; just by the way Jimmy Joe was rocking, I knew. How *good* you were, Sister Kin.

Beside me on the mattress, Kin nodded. His wide mouth curved. I tried not to remember the little flare of jealousy inside me, that first night. For a moment, Kin's lips looked as full as yours. Then his eyes closed.

One man in Taiwan, he managed to whisper, his hand under the sheets pumping slowly. This man in Taiwan told me. That I gave. Heavenly head.

Kin's hand tightened around mine. But he let out only a faint sigh. His hidden hand stopped moving. His head sank into his pillow, his eyes still shut. He gave a second sigh, defeated-sounding. Nothing like our huge, happy, collective sigh after your head had arched back and Kin's head had risen. I collapsed on top of you, Jimmy Joe, breathless from all our kissing. I panted with you and Kin, rubbing my neck against yours to feel our shared sweat. Then you and I looked up, seeing the hard-on Kin tried to hide. You now, I told him boldly. I took

Kin's hand. More than anything, JJ, I wanted him to experience what I'd never imagined I could; experience it—as I'd never imagined he could—with me.

I know you remember. Our pleasures and yours intersecting, eventually, into three-pointed stars. We laughed that first night, giddy with the possibilities of our new powers as we switched positions again. Round-robin. Fumblingly, our bodies flushed, you and I arranged Kin on the sweaty leather.

We looked at each other over Kin's prone body with eyes washed clear for the first time in ages. Your new relaxed face told me, Jimmy Joe, you too had needed to play this step-by-step. Slowly, gently; the way nothing before in my life had ever happened. Our shared gaze that night was infinitely brighter than the weary sleepy gaze Kin and I exchanged in our HOTOL room tonight, Kin's eyes as bloodshot as mine felt. Kin kept his limp hand hidden under the sheets. His face so lifeless I knew he hadn't been able to come.

Heavenly head, huh? I whispered to him. Then, more shyly: Wish *I* could give you that, Kin. Now . . .

He shook his head. Not you, Berta. Not even if I wasn't . . . deadly. He shut his eyes again. Not between sisters . . .

I sighed, agreeing. See, Jimmy Joe: Kin and I never could go very far, except when you were there. He pulled his hand out from under the sheet.

Good thing I got nowhere, he muttered. We'd of had to wash our sheet. I mean I'd of had to. He rolled over, his ribs forming striped shadows in his skin. Don't know if I woulda had the strength, just now . . .

I nodded, slumping on my pillow. No pillowcase. Wish we could at least make, I mumbled, a Jimmy Joe fondue. Kin gave a scratchy laugh. Chocolate-dipped bananas, I reminded him, or cheese with white wine. He drifted off as I went on. I used to watch the cubes of cheese, y'know, soften and melt and—expand. Felt like that was happening to my own flesh. Slowly, all summer.

As Kin's breaths deepened, I pictured you and me and him lying together in luxuriantly shared sweat. Our limbs angled out like the sides of one star. Kin is sound asleep now, JJ, with the harsh ceiling light on. How much longer before he considers it? Suicide Made Simple. My pen is slowing, but not because I'm sleepy too. Far from it. Here in Manila, on the other side of the world, I feel something, as you might say, unhinging in me. A door not only opening but falling off, flying off. I told you I'd wait till my letter's end to answer your last question. Has there ever been another man we loved, together?

Arizona. He had agreed to spend the summer there, helping Mom and Jo move Dad into his new Home. Maybe by April, Allie reasoned, the baby had begun to feel real to JJ. Or maybe he'd sensed how much she needed this summer away, resting. She released his slightly stiffened arm, balancing herself on her slightly swollen ankles.

In September, they'd drive back across the country to a bigger apartment, nearer campus. They could barely afford it, even with JJ's teaching assistantship, his DOD grant money. His Bros had teased him about taking that money as they'd loaded the U-Haul. Saint JJ, they joked. Next, they claimed, he'd work for Killing Machines, their name for the Pentagon-funded AI company, Thinking Machines.

"That was fun today," Allie told JJ. "Packing up, then you and Steinman dancing around me. I haven't seen you dance in so long. Sorry *I'm* in no shape . . ."

"I like the shape you're in." JJ glanced at her ever-fuller breasts.

"Listen, JJ." She sped her steps to keep pace. "This summer won't be so awful out there with Jo and free rent and even a pool." She tossed back her shiny hair.

Why wouldn't JJ meet her eyes today? He said he felt OK about going back to Yale, even relieved to have been forced into the decision by the baby. Yes, he'd take DOD money so they'd survive this year. Then he'd work wherever he wanted.

"I've only got a few more things to pack for the car," Allie went on in a carefully light voice. "My shoe box of letters and all . . ." She studied his profile for any flicker of remembrance. Had he, she'd been wondering since last night, gone through her own shoebox and moved Bird's Curaçao and Brazil letters back to his dad's strongbox? In which she thought she'd glimpsed, as JJ packed last night, the red-and-white piping of an airmail envelope. Could it be—surely not—a new one?

"Fine." JJ barely nodded.

"Fine," Allie echoed. Telling herself: no, he must have reclaimed those old letters. His letters, after all. Yes: she'd find them gone if she checked her shoe box tonight. Why, though? She took JJ's hand, not wanting to worry about Kin and Bird. All that felt so distant, really, like everything from before her pregnancy.

"Look, JJ," she began again. "I know it's crazy for me to be happy about all this. I know the first year'll be hard. But these past weeks in day care, I've started feeling sure I *will* be able to handle the mother part. Hugging and diapers and all."

She touched her stomach. She'd quit New Haven New Chance Workshop for a job in regular day care. No Special Ed, no agression, however mild. "Maybe next year I can work at the Yale Child-Care Center." Allie swept her eyes over the lawns and tall stone walls and workmens' empty scaffolding. "You *know* I've been thinking Early Childhood Ed is more my thing than Special Ed. Everyone eventually gets burned out in Special Ed. But Child Ed is, y'know . . ."

"Kinder and Gentler?" JJ asked, imitating George Bush's whine.

Allie laughed. "Yeah, it is!" JJ gave her an absentmindedly affectionate smile.

She was through with Special Ed, she'd decided back in May after Channel 8 had broadcast the long-dreaded *Monthly Magazine* exposé. JJ had tensed up along with Allie when the camera finally briefly showed her sitting on the floor, looking dazed as the announcer's voice informed viewers that all Special Ed workers faced occasional danger. Behind Allie, only Carter's legs had been visible. No names.

"I'm gonna miss my kids this summer." For the pleasure of the sounds, Allie recited her favorite names from the downtown day-care center where she'd worked since March. "Tawanda and Yolanda and Joselito . . ."

Distantly, beyond the shimmering lawns rolled for one hundred years, beyond the castle dorms, a siren spiraled. "God." Allie squeezed JJ's hand. "We used to hear nonstop sirens down there, downtown. When they whirled by, I looked out the windows—through the tissue-paper flowers we taped up—and the glass seemed so flimsy . . ."

She squinted toward Yale's tallest tower. "Ever since you told me students jump outa that top window at finals time, I go past this stretch fast. Hey, what's that?"

They stopped in the tower's shade. It was drawn in the gritty concrete in red chalk, its shape blurred but unmistakable. Allie gasped. "I don't believe it!"

JJ made a hard-edged sound like a laugh. "I do."

Bull's-eye. Someone had chalked a big bull's eye target under the tower, a last sight for any plunging flunking suicide. The circles held grades. *A* in the center, then *B, C, D* in the outer rings. *F* was left unstated. *F* was the rest of the sidewalk.

"Let's go," Allie told JJ. But he was releasing her hand and stepping onto the central *A*. "*J-J*—" Allie turned and started down the sidewalk alone.

"Hey, c'mon." JJ's steps scraped cement. "Want to stop by Rare Books?"

"You won't miss that place, I bet," she murmured as they resumed walking.

"In a way I will. It was quiet. No one. Wanted much from me." JJ gazed across the cement plaza at the square building, its marble panels dulled in the sun. "In a fire," he told her almost cheerfully, "all oxygen would be sucked out of the glassed-in shelf area. So the rare books'd be saved and workers like me would die."

Allie shifted her weight, her ankles aching. "Let's go home, OK?" She started walking again. Then she turned to see JJ still standing there. "JJ?"

Together, they walked silently down the last green Yale blocks. "What're you thinking?" she asked as they crossed the New Haven green. "I know, I know. You don't want to spend three months with my parents, right?"

"No. I like Jo. I'll like talking politics with your dad. If he can still talk that talk." They passed the Rastafarian's park bench but no one was under it.

"I'll make sure everyone leaves you alone a lot, JJ. Mom'll be watching her soap half the time. Y'know what Mom calls it, and now I'm starting to understand what she means?" Allie hurried to keep up. "The Young and the Rest of Us."

JJ grinned, his eyes on the trampled-down grayish green grass.

"Don't forget: we're taking our Mac. You can work on your music genera—"

"Voice recognition. That's what it's got to be, now. Voice recognition for real-time battlefield management." JJ stepped from the grayed green onto sidewalk. "Jesus, Al. Sometimes I feel the Pentagon *is* seizing control of my brain. Like in *The Man Who Fell to Earth*." He stopped walking so she could catch up.

"Oh, come on." Before Bird's second Brazil letter, Allie hadn't known how important that movie had been to JJ. But then, Allie reminded herself, Bird hadn't seemed to know the secret reason why the Mass. Mental JJ had dribbled his rubber ball. Testing gravity. Maybe he'd told different women different secrets.

"*You're* in control of your brain." Allie turned onto crowded Chapel Street. "You'll work at Kurzweil or anyplace you want, once you're a Master of AI."

"Artificial Intelligence, right." JJ kicked aside trash. "Master of Artificial Emotions, Artificial Compassion . . ." They passed the thirty-five-cent lady, silent today, sunning herself in linty haze outside the Laundromat. "Anyhow, I can't go much further with my music program on our little Mac. I need a heavy-duty machine. . . ."

"Then what *have* you been doing on our Mac? Lately?" Inside, Allie braced herself for some new revelation as they passed Kappy's Liquor.

"Fun stuff." JJ leaned down so she could hear above the traffic. "Fooling around with an algorithm that composes lyrics. Remember I used to say all lyrics are going the way of the Talking Heads? You know: 'Stop Making Sense.'"

"Oh, right." She rallied a cheerier tone too.

"Now I feed our computer random samples of words, separated into nouns and verbs. And it arranges them into, you know, 'sentences.'"

"Oh yeah? Has there been anything that halfway *did* make sense?"

"One line," JJ told her above the rumble of a bus. "A question."

"What?" Behind the plastic bus stop shelter, Allie stood still.

JJ pronounced the computer-generated words clearly, as if each one were capitalized. "'Can We Commit the Unusual?'"

"Wow." Allie widened her eyes. "Really? Our little Mac wrote that?" She laughed. "'Can We Commit the Unusual?'"

A man hefting a Kappy's bag side-glanced at her. JJ laughed too, taking her elbow. "Think I oughta make it 'may'?" he asked as they aimed for the last corner. "'May we commit the unusual? Mother, may we?'" They stopped together at the curb. "By the way." JJ touched her shoulder. "Y'know what else I've made our Mac do? Catalog our cassette-tape songs according to the emotions they evoke. Using that system, I've put together some Mood Tapes for our ride to Arizona."

"Mood Tapes?" As they crossed the street, Allie gamely widened her smile.

"Right." JJ shifted to a mock-scientific tone. "So you can actually program my moods. Slip in different tapes to produce different effects. I mean: affects."

"Really? What kinds of moods are, like, included in this package?"

"You'll see. I'll lay it all out for you tonight."

"OK." Allie kept smiling as they passed the sunny windowcases of Giovanni's New & Used Furniture Emporium. Queen-Size-Sofa-Bed Special.

"They're at it again," JJ warned, stopping at the tenants' entrance.

"Oh, boy. *The Newlywed Game.*" Allie heard shrill voices through the screen window on the second floor. The newlyweds' springtime fights encouraged audience participation: comments shouted from other windows. Once, Allie'd had to stop herself from hollering back, Have you no shame?

"Yeah, yeah—" the man was screaming. "I *am* fucked up—"

"A rare moment of tenderness," JJ mumbled to Allie, easing open the door.

"—but you're *fucked up too!*"

Furniture thumped from above. As JJ and Allie climbed the stairs, the newlywed woman's theatrical sobs echoed in the stairwell.

Allie sighed as JJ unlocked their door. What a relief it would be to head for a safe haven, however temporary. He swung the door shut behind them.

"I'm so glad we're moving closer to campus." She stopped at the end of the entry hall, facing the dark, almost empty room they'd packed up this morning.

JJ addressed her back. "Are you wishing I'd wanted that student housing?"

"No." She turned to him, conscious of her breasts' important weight.

When in her new pregnant boldness she'd insisted that they find another apartment for next fall, JJ had told her he didn't want to live in the grad-student housing tower on campus. Not even if they allowed babies. At twenty-nine, JJ felt too old for dorms. Allie pretended to be disappointed, but secretly she didn't want student housing either. JJ would be easy to track down there.

"No; that's OK . . ." She let her voice trail, let JJ think he'd had his way on something. Because really, she'd gotten her way on everything, hadn't she? But then, she wondered as he stepped toward her, why did he look like the one who was feeling guilty? *Was* he hiding some new letter in that strongbox he'd packed in their car trunk last night? Below them, a chair or table crashed.

"God." Allie leaned against JJ as his arms wrapped around her. "Can't you see?" she whispered. "We're getting outa here just in time."

. . .

Alone in their darkening bedroom, Alice knelt by her nearly emptied queen's wardrobe. JJ had gone out to buy them one last Sallie's Pizza. With effort, Allie lifted her paper-heavy shoe box. And she pulled herself up, unsteadily.

All morning, no one had let her lift a thing. She'd wrapped dishes in newspaper. JJ and the Bros hauled boxes. As at Yale parties, she and JJ both flirted: JJ with one of the Bros' wives, a fragile-looking theater major who spilled out to JJ the woes of life at the Yale Rep; Allie with a bare-chested Bro who kept trying to explain to her the Chinese Room Paradox. Toward the end of the packing, the radio played "Computer World" by Kraftwerk and JJ began, mock-robotically, to dance.

Steinman, who'd let his hair grow long, tapped Allie's shoulder. So she swayed her hips with his and JJ's, resting one hand on her belly.

Then Steinman spun around them both, his black hair blurring his face. JJ laughed loudly, seizing Steinman's hand. Suddenly Steinman and JJ were dancing around Allie, her gaze darting between them as she laughed too: Steinman's hair wild; JJ's eyes lit up, unnaturally bright. The three of them moved in one syncopated rhythm.

Remembering how JJ on their walk had closed off the subject of their shared dance, Allie felt sure all over again now that Steinman with his new long hair had reminded JJ of Kin, that dancing in a threesome had reminded him of Kin and Bird. With a tense tired sigh, Allie sank onto the fold-out couch. She balanced the shoe box on her lap, its cardboard pressing her belly. A solid curve of flesh now, though she still pictured her baby to look like her newt. Steinman, the last to leave, had carried off their sloshing goldfish bowl today. He'd agreed to keep Newt for the summer. Tender-hearted Steinman: destroyer of Argentinean teenagers.

Could JJ be attracted to him? Though, Allie remembered, he only talked computer-talk with Steinman, as with all his Bros. Keeping his distance. Because JJ preferred talking to women? That "kinder better" breed. Or might JJ keep his distance so he wouldn't find himself attracted to a man, again? Allie opened her box, bowing into the whir of the fan. She riffled through her neatly folded letters and editorial clippings from Dad—"George Bush Sees No Evil"; "The Dangers of Do-Nothing Government"—till she felt the paper change texture. It crackled, thin as tissue. One, two, three letters: each still stored in its red-and-white-edged airmail envelope. The initial thick one from Curaçao; the thin one from Belém informing JJ of Kin's HIV test result; and the thickest of all from Nossa Senhora Do Ó in Brazil, complete with its unused Pan Am certificate. She didn't have to re-read that last letter to remember how Bird had told JJ they'd come see him here. *Ready or not.*

Allie slipped out the green Pan Am certificate she'd kept so that JJ—if he did look through her box—would know she trusted him. Now, on impulse, she tore it in half. She crumpled each half. Then she tossed both stiff balls into the makeshift moving-day trash bag. And she stuffed all three letters back in her box, re-fitting its lid: the cardboard softened in the heat, her hands sweaty. She shoved the box aside.

OK, then. She was breathing hard. If the old letters were still here, what new airmail missive had she glimpsed in JJ's strongbox last night? Or had she only imagined that flash of red-and-white stripes? She pushed back her hair, sick of her own circular worries. *So tell JJ what you saw*, Jo advised, a clear voice in Allie's overloaded mind. But Allie sank down on the fold-out. Overheated too and—despite or because of her worries—sleepy. She cupped her breasts, feeling through cloth her thickened nipples. But, she told Jo, I don't want to bring that—them— up again. Not yet, anyhow. Not now, when all I can deal with, all I have room to deal with, is what's happening inside me. Making this baby, making myself into a mother.

And that's just who you're acting like, Jo decreed. *Mother.*

Oh please, Allie thought. Shutting her eyes; longing to nap. Remembering, for comfort, Mom back in Pennsylvania. *Swallow*, she'd say before trips, offering a spoonful of jelly speckled with crushed pill. Uneasily, Allie remembered their first moving day. The drive to Kentucky a week after Mom's accident. Mom had been the one to insist they proceed as if the accident hadn't happened. Mom, who served all suppers at six sharp. Allie's stomach gave a queasy stir. Hadn't that car trip to Kentucky been the first time she felt what she'd felt so often these past months? Unprotected, unsafe. Sensing—as she'd sensed then, years ago—there were dangerous secrets at large. She hugged herself, pinning down her fluttering skirt.

Stop, Mother had told Dad strangely early on that first day of driving, halfway through Pennsylvania. *Ee ave tuh sto-op,* she'd insisted, her words distorted by her blistered lip. Though it was only noon, anxious Dad pulled into a Howard Johnson's motel. Eleven-year-old Alice kept wondering: What next? What next?

You know your mother will never get over it. . . . Grandma whispered behind Allie that night in the Howard Johnson's room. They were lying on one double bed, Jo on the other. Dad had led Mom off to their own room.

What? Allie was almost too scared to ask. Her tongue toyed with her braces.

A boy, Grandma whispered. A little boy, four and a half.

Hawf, Grandma pronounced it, Rhode Island style. Her whisper lowered so doped-up bandaged-up Jo wouldn't hear, through her sleep.

A little boy in the Volkswagen your mother crashed into. He's paralyzed, the doctors say. For life. So you, Alice Ann. You must be a good girl now, for her.

Allie managed to nod. Her tongue loosened a tiny rubber band on her braces. She thought, don't swallow. As Grandma's Chiclet gum-scented breaths rasped into delicate snores, Allie sucked her rubber band, envying Jo's Darvon-deep sleep. Jo had been knocked unconscious instantly in the crash. Grandma Hart's words settled over Allie's chest like the lead apron the dentist covered her with for X rays. She wanted to run down the hall and climb in bed with Mom, comfort her. But then Mom would know she knew. Shutting her eyes, she wished she didn't know about the boy. Mom hadn't wanted her to know.

. . .

It was dark when her eyes fluttered open. At first Allie thought the body curled close to hers must be Grandma Hart's. Then she squinted at the rectangular shape of her queen's wardrobe. Squeezed behind her on the folded-up couch, JJ was sawing his way through his snores. With difficulty, she turned to him.

"Ya OK?" JJ sounded more than half asleep. She nodded. He mumbled that there was pizza in the fridge. Clam, her favorite. He hadn't wanted to wake her to unfold the bed, he added, his legs awkwardly bent. His feet hung off the couch arm.

"Want some?" Allie pictured them eating together. Talking, really talking.

"Sorry, but I gotta sleep. Gotta make Ohio by t'morrow . . ."

"Right." She pulled herself up, her breasts aching. They planned to stop over at JJ's dad's in Ohio, his cemented-in-place mobile home. Though JJ's dad had retired as a plumber, Allie always sniffed lingering dampness as they sat in front of his flickery TV, the science shows JJ and his dad watched in a silence they'd shared for years. Heavily, she padded to the bedroom door. Calmer now, after her sleep. Telling herself to stop inventing soap-opera plots. Imagining intrigue.

She stepped into the front room, its walls stark with her photos packed in the U-Haul. Late one night during their Christmas visit, she'd glimpsed from the bathroom window JJ's dad in his small frosty yard with his telescope. Guiltily now, groping toward the fridge, she remembered stepping into that cold Ohio night. JJ's dad had turned with his narrowed, perpetually suspicious gaze. Hadn't she played on his paranoia? Hadn't she given her words an exaggerated implication of danger as she'd quietly informed him that some people JJ'd known at Mass. Mental might be trying to track JJ down. That they might phone, looking for information about JJ. For his new address, if she and JJ were to move. That these people were—her breath had formed an extravagant plume—*crazy*.

JJ's Dad nodded: once, hard. His lips, full like JJ's, sealed so tightly Allie felt sure he wouldn't tell JJ, wouldn't give out JJ's number or address. That had been how Kin and Bird tracked down JJ before. Yes, JJ's dad confirmed curtly. Someone had phoned, last summer, July maybe.

Someone who'd said they were friends of JJ's, someone who'd phoned years before too. Someone who'd sounded. Odd.

Allie steadied herself against the table. Remembering how she'd re-coiled from the intolerant sound of that *Odd*. Recoiling again now, more deeply. Wondering this last night in New Haven if she was any dif-ferent inside, the way she was acting. But, she told herself, I'd fight *any* ex-lover trying to insert themselves back into my husband's life. Espe-cially now, since he's the father of my baby.

She inched forward—no Losers' Lamp to bump. They were taking that lamp back to her dad for his Nursing-Home room. She drew a shuddery breath, picturing Dad's dark level gaze. Blinking back tears— of sudden happiness this time; she was so glad she'd be seeing her par-ents—Allie opened the fridge. No newt water sloshed when the door unsucked. She lifted the Sallie's Pizza box, set it on the table edge, and padded to the bathroom to pee. Every hour or so lately. Then she flipped on the front room's light and confronted, in the middle of the rented table, JJ's new cassettes. They were arrayed around the Rand McNally road atlas. His Mood Tapes. Munching pizza, Allie read the titles and content lists that he'd printed in ink. Would these give her some clue to JJ's true mood, whatever he might be hiding?

The tape titled *Lugubriosity* included "Telephone Line" by the Electric Light Orchestra (Allie shook her head, thinking of the choked-up male singer begging the phone operator to let it ring forever more!). *Maudlin* featured Cyndi Lauper singing "True Colors." *Night of the Living Id* was wall-to-wall Heavy Metal.

Allie chewed her pizza crust. Your father, she told her baby, is a man of unreadable moods. All fathers, maybe. She recalled a line from one of the Heavy Metal songs. He comes to us a veteran of a thousand psychic wars. She swallowed.

Maybe JJ would focus on the baby more once it showed more. Allie set down *Night of the Living Id*. Maybe JJ already focused on it; maybe that's what was distracting him as it distracted her. Making her feel she was the one enclosed in a filmy bubble of flesh. Making her impatient with anything outside herself. Outside us, she told the baby. Letting plastic clatter, she pushed aside all of JJ's tapes.

She wiped her greasy mouth with her fingers. With the cleaner back of her hand, she wiped her forehead. Languidly, cars whooshed by on the dark, humid street below. Thank goodness for Mom and Dad's cen-tral air-conditioning. We'll stay inside all summer, Alice told the baby, pressing her stomach.

We'll be OK, once you come. She eased the Rand McNally atlas forward. JJ's snores sawed on steadily. Alice flipped past Ohio, opening the atlas pages to the less cramped-looking western states. Missouri, Colorado, Nevada.

Outside in the hallway, footsteps sounded. She listened. Imagining, stupidly, Kin and Bird showing up here, as they'd promised. A muffled key jangled. Another apartment's door opened. Allie slumped in her seat, feeling foolish. Knowing, of course, she wouldn't worry about an ordinary ex-lover this way. Trying, now, to reason with herself. So what if Bird *had* written JJ again? Maybe JJ had simply been reluctant to bring it up, given the way Allie had reacted before. Overreacted, he'd say. What if those two *did* see JJ again? Kin and Bird. Those ex-lovers he'd claimed had "helped" him so much. As if—this was what Allie had taken to telling herself lately—the three of them had engaged in a form of therapy. So naturally JJ still felt for them gratitude, affection. Would it be so awful, Allie thought wearily, if they visited him, talked to him? What else, realistically, would happen between him and them, with Kin sick? With JJ married, awaiting a baby? Get real, Allie told herself for the hundredth time as the hallway door thudded. She sighed, wondering if the baby had felt her speeding pulse. Half hoping it had; she wanted company.

A lock rattled; a bolt slid into place. Got to focus, Allie thought, on the future. She flipped past Nevada, flipped farther west to the wide-open states bordering wild wide-open Mexico. Texas, New Mexico, Arizona. If they *were* somehow pursuing JJ, Kin and Bird wouldn't know where to begin to look. Allie lingered over those uncluttered yellow states, wanting to believe that. Vast spaces, desert spaces. No, she told her baby. They'll never find us out there.

8 · 8 · 89

13

Mexico, August 1989

Hola, JJ—

Come for Kin. I, the wife—Kin and I, *Señor y Señora*—want you to come and celebrate 8/8/89. One week from today. *El aniversario de boda.* Now that it's almost here, I wonder if you really will. Your last letter was so short. Please don't say no now, J. Joe, when you've given every sign of saying yes.

When we got that letter at the Agua Prieta American Express office in July and learned you were in Arizona—*Muy cerca de aqui!*—Kin ate a full meal. Following recipes I'd learned from Estella without words, I made Kin corn roasted with chiles and lime from the garden and fruit *batidos*: papaya. We toasted you and your Phoenix PO Box number in Kin's befringed bedroom. For Kin to lift his glass takes more strength than he has. So don't let him down. *¿Entiendes?*

We have a date. On 8/8/89, as early as you can make it. Drive or hitch to Douglas, Arizona, then step through the border turnstyle to its Sister City. Walk one block straight ahead—*todo recto*—to *La Farmacía de Rosita.*

Don't not show. The thing about Mexico is (we hope, anyhow) no one says no. Get married in ten minutes; get divorced in ten minutes. When Kin could still walk on his own—before his pneumonia and his two weeks at the hospital in Ciudad Juarez—we hitched out near Bahia Kino, to *la playa.* Kin told me the water was the warmest he'd ever swum in. Though he, always such a serious swimmer, was able only to wade. Leaning on each other, we climbed the jagged slippery rocks. On American beaches there would've been signs: No Diving, No Climbing. Here in Mexico: *nada.* Kin and I mounted a rockface slicked by ripe-smelling *algas.* Below us, waves pounded rocks with a ferocity that set our bony bodies vibrating. Above us, sky stretched out high as the sky in Brazil.

No one can hide under such a sky. No one tries to. Here in Mexico, the people remind me of you, Jimmy Joe, back in our shared summer. Senses heightened, filters open. Here, salsa burns not only your throat but your stomach and guts too. In Agua Prieta, in a *billares* where Kin on good days hears the live music he craves, mariachi dancers flail even more wildly than you. Here, afternoon heat rises so fiercely we do nothing at its peak but sleep.

Here on the roads where—slowly, from Estella—I am learning to drive, there are no two-car accidents. It's always three or four cars piled up, crashed together with unstoppable force. Race cars, all. Here, there are no speed limits.

Flocks of crosses mark the number of drivers who died on certain curves. Roadside shrines memorialize them: miniature stone chapels with tin flower-wreathed roofs and, flickeringly visible through the sway of drapes, candles.

Back in sunny early June, on our way home from *la playa*, Kin and I visited a shrine of a different sort. Wish I had my camera, Kin murmured for the first time in all our travels. *El Monumento* for a Mexican general, circa 1910. His enemies or his friends—it wasn't clear which— pickled his chopped-off fist.

Inside a stone tower, embedded in curved dark wood walls, encased behind glass, afloat in amber fluid: a hand clenched in rigor mortis. We stared from a wrought-iron spiral staircase. The hand circled slowly, withered but human. A pickled fist. Small for a man's, fingernails intact, skin waxy yellow like a lima bean, tentacle nerves trailing from a severed wrist. A hand preserved by friends or enemies or both, like your severed hair. For hate and for love. *El odio y el amor.* Isn't there any word in any language that means both at once?

Though our hate—from those first years, after you left the way you left—is long gone. Will you even know us when—I won't say "if"— you see us?

Sister Kin lies in his small cool room, surrounded by cheap extravagantly fringed rugs and lamp shades. He reads the Buddhist book that Li, the student who loved him, gave him in Guangzhou. *Progressive Stages of Meditation on Not-Being.* He lingers over chapters on "Accepting the Not-Self" and "Achieving the Clear Pure Nature of Mind." With a new bemusement, he listens to Spanish versions of American '70s songs on Carlos's radio. Music he cares about, though, he wants to hear live. So he picks through chords on Carlos's guitar, teaching himself to play. Then he puffs his forbidden cigarettes, relaxing his V-brows and turning his gaze inward like old men we saw in Guangzhou. Smoking their long clay pipes. Sometimes, Kin's told me, he remembers how he helped care for his friend Shawn T. in New York. How Shawn's flesh, what was left of it, came to resist all needles. How Shawn's body, Kin felt, wanted no further treatment. Juarez, Kin says often, was his own last hospital.

Afternoons, I weed and water the garden where Carlos grows chiles and tomatillos and squash and cilantro and, hidden among the shaggy fragrant mint, marijuana. From his window, Kin watches my dusty dirt clouds rise and settle. Late afternoons, hoarsely, he tutors me. Together, we decipher Carlos's paperback mysteries or poems from a used leather-bound book I bought. I'm the one who goes out now. So I'm learning a Second Language, at last. *Lo Necesito.*

These days, Kin and I talk in both Spanish and English, talk so freely I don't feel the need to write in a diary. Kin tells me he admires the road-side crosses. He likes the skeletons that Carlos collects; he laughs at the springy-necked *turista* dolls and fingers respectfully a more detailed skeleton carved from wood bleached like bone. Seed-corn teeth, hollow eyes. Kin rearranges the dolls, switches their clothes. Gaily dressed skeletons line our bookcase, our windows. One dangles above the bath-tub—*bañera*—that only Kin uses, lately. Lingering warm baths. In honor, he says, of his blissful first swims: pearly pink bubble baths his mother gave him when he was a toddler. He and she quiet together after a day of bouncing—he in a backpacklike sling—from class to class.

Weak as he is now, Kin scours the tile after his baths. He reminds me never to use his towel. One night he asked me, blinking as if waking from a yearlong daze, if I've been protecting myself from his blood (his mouth sores used to bleed and now, after his pneumonia, he coughs up bloody phlegm into tissues that litter his bed) and from his piss (he's so worried about wetting the bed that we sleep separately, me on the couch in what you'd call the living room).

Not exactly, I told him. Not, I added fast when Kin looked stricken, that I put myself deliberately at risk. He nodded, shifting his worried stare to his wall. To a mouse-sized cockroach. We both watched it scut-tle away.

Most nights, back from Estella's, I describe what happened—not much, so far—and Kin predicts where it might lead. All I know is that Estella Hinojosa, My Lady of the Dog Track, is paying me to bathe and teaching me to drive.

Si. I am learning to drive. We use Estella's Bonneville and, when she pays to watch me bathe, her *bañera*. Estella is a gambler, a lady of mod-est means. I'll tell you all about Sister Estella, all about Sister Kin, when we meet on 8/8/89.

Kin's lately distracted eyes brightened like mica when I told him what I wrote you in Manila, what I—what other word is there?—proposed. I asked if he had any message for this letter. And Kin wondered if you remembered how, when you were schizo, your senses intensified: stronger hearing and smelling, a charged-up sense of touch. 'Cause that, Kin says to tell you, is what he's felt lately, in waves. In this desert where everything is stripped down, clear.

Come by 7 A.M. or so. Your time zone is ours, here on the border. And we need to beat the heat. The thing about Mexico is: It deepens even Arizona's heat, sharing but re-frying Arizona's air. That's how close you are. If *you* have no car, find a bus, a passing truck. Find any way to come. For Kin. *Por favor.*

This is a test, Jimmy Joe. We know it's not an easy one. We know, too, you set up your own PO Box for our letters. Actions speak loudest. We hope only you will read this invitation. We hope your wife—she must be, though you won't say, one of the "ways" you feel "trapped"—won't even have to know. This is a test between you and us. You didn't show in Queens, at Ko No's, at Our Lady of O. You have to show this time, James Joseph, because we're running out of that. *Tiempo.*

You have to come to us. I am learning to drive, but I have no car.

(And I no longer have his first name; I no longer use it.) *Si?*

Bird

14

Just Say No

Alice Ann Wolfe half woke, sensing light through her eyelids. Groggily, she reached out to touch JJ's long warm body. Then she blinked to see JJ gone. She stayed curled around her belly, facing his rumpled stretch of sheet, his half of the twin beds they'd pushed together. They'd covered the crack between with a double-bed fitted sheet, strained all summer. Corners kept popping up.

She heard JJ open a drawer. The baby gave its fish-gill flutter. Allie slitted her eyes as he stepped to the window, shirtless in his surgeon green pajama bottoms. As he lifted the drape and studied the starless sky, she thought he was contemplating another midnight swim with her. She waited for him to turn.

This first week of August, the end of her sixth month, Allie had exulted in how strong she felt when she'd expected to grow weak. One July midnight, she and JJ had crept from the ranch house in only their robes. The yard was surrounded by a tall stucco fence. Night heat warmed their air-conditioned skins. JJ dimmed the pool lights. He slipped in without a splash. Then he helped her down the low-end steps. She floated easily, her shiny breasts buoyant, her belly supported by soft chlorinated water. And by JJ's hands, underwater, sculpting her full flesh curves. Wet, they climbed out under a luminous yet hard-edged desert moon. JJ, who never lay in the sun, settled into a lawn chair. Together, their skins goose-bumped and gleaming, they had soaked in moonlight.

JJ turned. His deeply shadowed eyes didn't seek hers. Balled up in one hand, he held cotton briefs. The cream-colored drapes swayed shut. Allie stayed motionless, the baby too, both of them—she felt—holding their breaths. Another drawer opened: so slowly she knew he was trying not to wake her. She squinted at his clock. 12:10. Allie exhaled with the drawer he eased shut. 8/8/89. Of course, she'd eyed that date on Mom's kitchen calander. Maybe JJ needed, now, a late walk down the cul de sac. Time to think. The baby gave a flutter Allie pictured as its fingers, wiggling. She wanted to press her belly but didn't move.

Hadn't JJ been more quiet than usual, this week? Listening to his *Night of the Living Id* tape through headphones, hunching over his computer in Dad's old study, typing a syllabus for the Operating Systems class he'd teach as a TA in the fall. All July, he and Allie had kept busy with the twin tasks of moving Dad into Desert View Nursing Home and moving Jo into a Tempe apartment near ASU that she'd share with another nursing student.

Couldn'ta done it without you two, Jo had told them, meaning more than that JJ had hauled her thick nursing textbooks up her new stairs. She couldn't have left Mom without Allie there to ease the transition.

JJ edged the room door shut behind him—or not quite. No click. Allie sat up in the half circle of his lamplight, startling the baby into a hard-heeled little kick. Through the all-surrounding hum of central air, through the walls—soundproof after the hear-through walls in New Haven—Allie strained to make out JJ's steps. She pictured each closed door JJ must be passing.

First, in the next room: Mother, dozing fitfully on her side of the king-sized posturpedic mattress. In June, she'd confided to Allie that she'd never gotten used to having Dad home. A weak, hacking, retired Dad. Now, in August, Mom told Allie she couldn't get used to having Dad gone. After only two weeks, Mom had arranged for her own Trial Visit at Desert View. Though she at fifty-six was healthy despite her weight. Though, if she moved in too, Grandma Hart would pitch a fit. Grandma insisted she could care for her son here, in his real home.

Allie hugged her belly, her tanned arms dark against its whiteness. Did canny Grandma Hart hear JJ outside her room? Allie heard the bathroom door thump. The shower cranked on. A distant hiss. She shivered, pulling up the sheet. Across the wall, faint bedsprings squeaked. Mom, wakened from her light glass-of-wine-before-bed sleep? *Oh, he's fine; he's just got a lot on his mind. The baby and all.* Allie let the sheet slip, her body bare beneath it. Throughout July, she'd kept reassuring Mom about JJ. He treated his mother-in-law in a polite yet distant manner Mom seemed to distrust. Grandma Hart—polite yet distant herself—liked JJ more, cracking thin-lipped smiles at his wry remarks.

Last week, Allie had confided to Grandma that she worried JJ might be feeling trapped here, what with the baby and her family all around him.

'Course he feels trapped, Grandma Hart had rasped in her no-nonsense Rhode Island accent. He is, now. Or he'd better be, Alice Ann.

The shower cranked off. Uneasily, Alice looked away from the not-quite-closed door. On her nightstand, the paperback *Middlemarch* she was re-reading lay beside a bound copy of her senior thesis that Mom had set out. Allie hadn't touched it, not even to move it. Waiting for JJ to finish his dressing, she skimmed the ever-more-embarrassing title—*America's Compassion Deficit: How We Treat the Weakest Among Us*—and tried to remember without actually opening the thing her epigraph. Her Eliot quote about walking around "well-wadded" with stupidity. The bathroom door clicked. Allie waited, his steps muffled by carpet and walls, barely detectable until the bedroom door opened.

JJ stood fully dressed in its dark rectangle, staring at Allie naked on their makeshift double bed. She pulled the sheet back over her tender breasts.

"What?" she asked him. As he met her gaze, she felt her eyes widen.

"Alice." He closed the door, stepped toward her. He sat on the mattress edge.

"What?" she demanded, holding the sheet bunched at her throat.

JJ took her free hand, his hand damp from the shower. She breathed aloe shaving cream as he leaned close, his eyes blue. "I have to go out today."

"Where?" Allie squeezed his hand, fighting the urge to say, Don't tell.

"To Mexico. Just down to Agua Prieta, a border town."

"*Mexico?*" Her wrist tensed. "What's in Mexico? Are my parents driving you crazy? Cause you know Mom's Trial Visit starts tomorrow and then we'll have two whole weeks. Just us and Grandma Hart here, almost alone . . ."

JJ shook his head so slowly Allie's whole arm stiffened. "It's not a trip."

She swallowed. "It doesn't have anything to do with—it couldn't be . . . ?" JJ nodded, letting her pull back her hand. "Kin. Kin and Bird."

JJ looked at his own large hands. He told her in his flattest voice that Bird had written him via Yale months before, asking that he meet her and Kin in Mexico, that he visit Kin today, the anniversary of their marriage. Kin had been very sick; Kin wanted to see him. It would only be one day. A few hours over the border, then he'd drive, he told her, raising his eyes at last, right back.

Allie let her stare sink into his. "She wrote you—months ago?"

He nodded. "In April."

"A-pril?" She squeezed her handful of sheet, picturing his locked strongbox. "You mean all the while I was—thinking that we'd be getting away from them out here, you knew we'd be moving *toward* them?"

JJ started to nod again. "Well, sort of." Then he shook his head. "Not really. No. See, Allie, I didn't know what they'd actually do till Bird wrote me here."

"Here?"

"I rented a post office box, Alice. For Yale to forward any letters. Bird had given me a Mexico address and I wanted to know if they were really there or—"

"A *post* office box?" Allie straightened. "God, and what *else*?" She scooted her heavy body back over his twin bed. Awkwardly, she heaved herself to her feet. She felt not gloriously rounded now but unnaturally swollen. She groped in the half dark for Mom's old flowered robe. Hugging it around herself, she tied the belt. Only then did she step back to JJ in the lamplight. 12:40 A.M.

"That Bird woman." Alice breathed hard, standing above him. "Is after you. She sent you that photo taken in bed, that Pan Am thing. Don't forget. *I've* read her letters too, or the ones you didn't hide." She met JJ's blue gaze. "Look, I couldn't stand you running off to *any* ex-lover just now. But them. God. She's crazy, JJ; Kin's dying and together they might even be dangerous—"

"No." JJ touched her hip as if to halt a step. His voice came out low, tightly controlled. "I've told you. They aren't crazy any more than I am, anymore. Kin wasn't in Mass. Mental at all. He helped us, Bird and me, more than any doctor." Allie sealed her lips, hating that *Bird and me*. "Kin's the one, I've *told* you, who got us—Bird and me—*out* of all that. Craziness. Understand? Can you try to?"

Numbly, she started to shake her head no. And JJ added in a second rush, his voice still strained, " 'Course not. I can't expect you—especially just now—to understand this, handle this. I know that. *I* couldn't handle remembering it myself, what happened between me and them, till Bird wrote me from Manila—"

"The letter you hid?"

"Yeah." JJ held her hips with both hands, as if she might fall. "And now, Allie, with Kin so sick, with him asking to see me, I—can't not go."

"No." Allie felt herself stiffening against his touch. "I won't let you—"

" 'Let' me?" JJ met Allie's eyes, a flash in his own. But his tensely strained voice stayed low. "Christ, Al. Everytime we try to talk about them it brings out this side to you that—" He shook his head, stopping himself.

"That what?" She felt her own eyes flashing. "*Finish* it, JJ—"

Abruptly, he lowered his hands from her hips. "You talk about letting me go to Mexico? Christ, if you'd 'let' me hear Kin's phone message, 'let' me travel a few blocks to Ko No's, things might never've gotten to this point—"

"Oh really?" She stepped back fast, wobbling. "So this's all my fault, me and my dark side? Well, *I'm* seeing sides in you *I* hate. How deceptive you can be, how disloyal to me. God, I shoulda known you'd run to them eventually when you saved that Pan Am thing—your little ticket to escape, right?"

JJ had stopped shaking his head. She began to shake hers.

"Then that day we were moving when you and Steinman were dancing with me and I could see your eyes light up, see you feeling it was like—"

"Nothing was ever like—"

Allie stopped her next breath, her head stilled. She blinked at him. "Right," she managed. "That's exactly it, for you." JJ stood, starting to protest, but she turned away, repeating his words slowly: " 'Nothing was ever like—' "

"No." He stepped up close behind her. She stayed turned, furiously blinking back tears. "No, Alice." He lowered his voice again, seeming to stretch it tight over the loud harsh voice that had blurted those words. "I—I'm sorry I said that. Sorry to put you through all this. It's just—" He waited till she looked at him to finish. "Kin is dying and needs to see me. And given all that he and Bird and I've been through—been to—each other, I. Can't not go."

"*No.*" Allie took hard hold of his arm. "Don't go a-*lone*. Let me come too—"

"You?" JJ stared down at her belly as if she'd said something incomprehensible. "You with me—and them?"

"*Yes*—" She tugged his arm, letting herself shout. "Why the Hell *not?*"

"Calm down." JJ gripped her shoulders, his eyes lit like Bird's. "Look," he told her. "I don't know what the Hell I'll find out there. So I need to go alone."

"*No!* You can't go and *leave* me here like this—"

"Alice?" Outside the door, her mother's voice quavered. Her knock seemed to quaver too. "Is something wrong in there, Alice? Are you OK in there?"

Allie pulled back from JJ, her voice almost breaking. "Mom?"

The door inched open. Mom's round face filled the crack, flushed above her own pink robe. "What's wrong, dear? Is it—are you feeling cramps or—"

"No, no." Allie cupped her belly. Not wanting Mom to fade politely away.

"Then what . . . ?" Mom took an uncertain step, her quilted robe brushing their doorway. Her face without her tasteful makeup looked bare and startlingly older, her round Mary Tyler Moore cheeks fallen.

Her short layered hair was mussed, no longer tinted auburn brown. This summer, she'd let Loving Care slide and her gray roots show. Against her tan, her blue eyes seemed pale.

"Nothing, really." Allie didn't try to steady her voice. "JJ's just, he's—"

"I." JJ stepped forward. His voice came out so calm Allie almost felt reassured. "I have to drive down to the border. To Mexico, today."

"*Mexico?*" Mom gaped up at JJ. "Why on Earth—?"

And Allie thought—feeling her mom think it too—Don't. Don't tell.

"Well, it's complicated." JJ shifted to his Zucchini-Bread-Murderer monotone. "I made an appointment down there, and I have to—"

"See an old friend," Allie filled in like a shaky sitcom wife, hating her own foolish words. "JJ has an old friend there from—college. Sick, see."

"Sick?" Mom asked her as if prompting her. "Do *you* feel sick?"

JJ looked at Allie too, maybe afraid she'd say yes. What would he do? She shifted her pregnant weight. Kin wanted to "see" JJ. Was that so threatening? Could she deny a dying man this simple request? Slowly, Allie shook her head.

JJ exhaled. Then he stepped over to her, taking hold of her shoulders. "Looks to be a four- or five-hour drive. Maybe more. And I'll get gas, get breakfast. So." He squeezed her shoulders, his fingers cool and strong. "I have to go." He kissed her lightly on the mouth, his cushiony lips cool too. His eyes still held their blue Bird light. "I'm sorry. Really. I'll be back before dark." He released his hold on her. "Sorry to wake you, Jo Ann." He nodded at Allie's mother. "'Scuse me." He ducked through the doorway, too short for him with his longer summer hair. Mom took Allie's hand as his muffled steps disappeared. Far across the house, Allie heard the garage door rattle, picturing their U-Haul boxes shuddering. Central air hummed, nighttime silence reclaiming the house.

"Well, good Lord," Mom began in a dazed nighttime voice. "He seemed . . ." And when Alice didn't fill in the blank, "not himself." Allie nodded, letting go of Mom's plump hand. "I don't suppose," Mom ventured in the softly apologetic tone she used to talk about food, "—you're hungry?"

While Allie peed in the slightly steamy bathroom, Mother toasted English muffins. They slathered them with margarine and grape jelly. Allie's greasy fingers dropped the butter knife. Bending with a Mom-like grunt of effort, she set it in the sink, then looked at the muffin she'd buttered. "Can't eat this now . . ."

"Why?" Her mom lifted her own muffin on an Irish china saucer.

"Dropped the knife." Allie pushed back her unbrushed hair. "It's dirty . . ."

Mom stared. "The knife is dirty *now*, Alice," she said slowly. "But you buttered the muffin *before* you dropped the knife."

Alice blinked in the kitchen light. Too bright, for this hour. 1:15 A.M., according to the sun-shaped clock hung above the butcher-block counter.

"Nothing's wrong, is there, Alice?" Mom asked carefully after they'd settled at the table. "Nothing serious, I mean. Between you and JJ . . ."

"No, no," Allie told her—shakily, she felt.

But Mom was nodding, chewing. Without her hair flipped up, her cheeks plainly sagged. "I'm sure it's just a mood. Being locked in here all summer with us old folks. And if there *is* something bothering him, it'll do him good to talk with a friend. *You* shouldn't have to handle all that right now. . . ."

Allie chewed her muffin and sweet jelly. She couldn't mention Kin and Bird any more than she'd mention the four-and-a-half-year-old boy Mom still didn't know Allie knew had been crippled in the long-ago car crash that had left Mom so skittish and homebound. Mom sighed. "This's been such a stressful summer for all of us. I know *I* can't handle extra stress these days, now that . . ." She jerked her soft chin toward the renovated rec room where Dad's expensive hospital bed and oxygen tank still resided. "Well, you know." Mom fingered her crumb-speckled saucer. "Guess I should cancel our Blind-Library session. . . ."

"No, no. JJ said he'd be back by dark, Mom. So we can still go. . . ."

Mom cleared her throat as if seeking a tactful reply. Tuesday evenings, Allie drove her to the Library for the Blind. In separate booths, Allie and Mom read into tape machines, recording Romances and *Dog Fancier* magazines and textbooks. Doing good without, Allie felt, getting their Helping Hands dirty.

"We'll see." Mom patted her mouth with her napkin. "By the way, Alice. While you were visiting Dad yesterday, I taped the soap for you. . . ."

"You didn't have to do that," Allie murmured. JJ had taught Mom how to videotape *The Young and the Restless*, inordinately pleasing her.

"But Monday shows are always so good. Oh Alice, you and Grandma Hart oughta watch the tape while Jo and I are with Dad today. It had Mrs. Chancellor and Nikki and that awful Brad—they never should've let him out of that cage!"

Allie sighed. "Yeah, well. Guess I *could* use an extra dose of soap. . . ."

"Oh, I feel guilty. Hooking you on that show when you were just a girl." Mom heaved herself up and lifted the plates. "Now you're an addict, like me."

· · ·

Propped by both pillows on the pushed-together bed, Allie fingered her own smooth cheeks. Not slack and soft yet, like Mom's. In the already dissipating dark, she pictured round-cheeked Mary Tyler Moore furtively opening the package addressed to Dick Van Dyke, the gigantic automatically inflating raft bursting from the box. Yes: that was what marriage had turned out to be like. Ripping open a sealed package, no idea what was inside.

Allie touched the strongbox. It rested on her outstretched thighs, hidden by her belly. JJ's dad's air-force strongbox. Retrieved from JJ's side of their closet; unopened as yet. How had he kept so many secrets? Her fingers drummed the metal lid. Since spring, she'd sensed he was hiding things but—like Mom—she'd been so stupidly reluctant to press him on what. She sighed, tasting jelly. Wondering, first, how often and how intensely he'd been thinking of them.

Nothing, he had said, his worst words, *was ever like—*

She fingered the strongbox's unlocked lock. Left open, maybe, on purpose. Nothing was like the sex they'd had, or the love. Or—she felt wearily certain—both. His first love, after all. Didn't JJ always say that he'd been "imprinted" on her, since he was her first? That Allie was a freshly hatched duckling, following round the first creature it saw. She stopped fiddling with the lock, remembering her first sex with JJ, how she couldn't imagine doing that with anyone else, ever. But how she'd always insist, later, it wasn't JJ being her first that made her feelings so strong. She yawned, stretching her mouth as wide as it would go. Tired of inventing explanations. Of trying to dismiss Kin and Bird, erase them.

You're in bed with his previous partners too, Jo used to warn. It's true, Allie thought as her yawn subsided. As if Kin and Bird and JJ surrounded her on three sides, she shifted closer to her own side of the bed. *A side to you that*—JJ had begun to say tonight. How would he have finished it, if he'd let himself? A side that seems narrow-minded, mean-spirited. Slowly, she opened his strongbox.

Near the top, hidden by receipts, lay the black-and-white snapshot of Kin and Bird. JJ must have studied it often, recently. Their smooth bare skin, their intent inviting stares. Allie stared back now. Resenting that Bird woman. Yet remembering—Allie licked her own sticky lips—how she'd half enjoyed being kissed by her. How she'd enjoyed touching Jo, years before. In one of these twin beds, in secret. Hardly anyone is totally gay or totally straight, a bearded grad student had told Allie at some Yale party. Everyone exists on a continuum, he'd claimed, with "1" being straight and "5" being gay. But Alice, he'd decreed, seemed a rare "1," an old-fashioned totally straight *femme*. Oh, I wouldn't be so sure 'bout that, Allie had replied. Just because it seemed the sexier side to be on.

No, she told JJ in her mind, fingering Kin and Bird's sly photo. I *can* understand you having more than one side in that way. As long as you're on, as you stay on, my side now. And she dug through his bills, remembering his soft underwater touch. Then, after their midnight swim: his tongue warm on her wet skin. She had always known from JJ's touch how much he enjoyed her body. She knew it still, inside her skin. The real question, she felt as she dug deeper, wasn't was JJ "bi" but was he—an old-fashioned term—"true"?

True to his wife, even as he was drawn back toward his first loves? As an ex—truly ex—lover? Allie uncovered, at bottom, two airmail envelopes. Did JJ even *know* how he felt about Kin and Bird now? Probably not, she told herself, lifting, first, the thin one postmarked Mexico. Not till he gets there, in person.

Allie pushed aside JJ's strongbox, letting its lid clank shut. She fumbled with the envelope, her hands tremulous like Dad's hands, yesterday, at Desert View. As she slid the letter out, she pictured Grandma Delaney's closed casket, years before. Dad's large hand holding Allie's small hand. The avuncular funeral director distributing thorny long-stemmed roses to drop on the casket lid, saying softly to each family member: Watch your fingers, watch your fingers.

She unfolded Bird's letter with care. Dangerous, she told herself. Dangerous, in both big and small ways, to stand near death.

At the sight of Bird's spidery print, Alice gathered all her breath. Speaking, silently, to her baby. I don't know what this'll say. What's going to happen to us, she told it. Him or her. She pictured Jo rolling her eyes as she did when Allie referred to "our" due date. You're the only one who's pregnant, Jo had reminded her jokingly. The man can walk out on the whole show at any second. Allie flattened Bird's letter, finishing what she wanted to tell her baby. But I'm here no matter what happens out there. She bowed over the letter, sensing outside her circle of lamplight a starless sweep of dark. Picturing as she began to read JJ in the black Zephyr driving into that desert sky, racing to get there in time.

· · ·

Jo? Allie thought, her throat too tight to speak.

Taking a deep toothpaste-flavored breath, she stepped into the kitchen. She held the archway edge, facing her sister's back. Jo was bent over by the sink, twisting the seal on a trash bag. Allie stared, remembering

Bird's Manila-letter description. *Mrs. Jimmy Joe and her humming all-seeing eyes.*

Allie took a shaky step forward. She'd been awakened minutes before, at 6:35 A.M., by the familiar sound of Jo telling Grandma not to do the trash. *No Grandma; let me!* Allie blinked, her eyes blurred from her restless sleep. Jo had come over early to pack up Dad's books and to drive Mom to Desert View.

Potato-solid Jo: dressed in an ASU T-shirt and khaki shorts. Her hands twisted away briskly. Jo had inherited Mom's round, grounded body. She hefted the bag, her bouncy short-cut hair lightened by Arizona sun, a blonder brown than Allie's. To keep her from sweeping outside, Allie spoke, hoarsely. "Jo?"

Jo turned. Round-faced, round-eyed. The faint scar from the car crash made her seem to be knitting her brows. Jo's gaze was bright, never overbright. Jo's eyes were always the same shade of blue, light as a summer sky.

"What?" Jo stepped up and took hold of her shoulders. "Allie, what?" Alice burst into tears. Jo hugged her hard, her old spine-crusher hug. "What, what—tell." Jo shook her, black coffee on her breath. And she shot a glance over Allie's shoulder. "Tell quick, before Grandma or Mom comes in."

Alice blinked, seeing her own face afloat in Jo's eyes. "JJ's—gone."

"Gone?" Outside the kitchen window, a ceramic bell *thong*ed. Over Jo's shoulder, Allie saw the pinkish dawn sky, the softly lit patio, the blue-green water rippling as the automatic pool cleaner chugged on its rounds. Beyond the pool stood the hundred-year-old saguara cactus with, Jo'd decreed, its W.C. Fields nose.

"Gone where? *Look* at me—"

Allie submerged herself in Jo's clear blue gaze. "A day trip. To Mexico."

"*Mexico?*" Jo released Allie's arms. "What the Hell for?"

Allie covered her mouth, sobbing again, remembering more lines. *We hope your wife—she must be, though you won't say, one of the "ways" you feel "trapped"—won't even have to know.* With an impatient tongue click, as when Allie'd shrink back from a childhood dare, Jo led Allie over to the table.

Waiting for Allie pull herself together, Jo poured a coffee and a milk. She cupped an orange in the sure-handed way she used to hold the oranges Dad gave her for practice on Grandma's diabetic injections. Expertly, Jo had sunk needles into the thick orange skin. She gave her no-nonsense nurse's frown now.

"OK, OK." Allie sipped her milk. "JJ's in Mexico to visit—an ex-lover. One of his 'previous partners.' I mean—God; I've gotta stop hiding things—two."

"Huh?" Jo pushed aside her peels and one sticky crumb-covered saucer. So Mom had already eaten her cinnamon-roll breakfast.

"Two. Ex-lovers." Outside, the pool-cleaning machine was stuck, churning up turquoise water. "A woman and a—man."

Distantly, Grandma's shower hissed. Allie felt Jo stare. All the years Allie had been in college and in New Haven, Jo had been home dating boyish boys.

"A man?" Jo asked in a frankly bewildered tone.

"A man." Allie met her stare. Years before Jo had leapt out of their Kentucky backyard bushes and startled Allie from a honeysuckle-scented trance. *Are you a friend of the Indians?* Jo had demanded, her face fiercely distorted. Allie had stared back, not sure what game this was, if this was a game. She had answered with a quaver of real, not play, fear: *Are you an Indian?*

"JJ was—lovers with a man?"

When Allie nodded, Jo slurped her coffee. "OK." She managed a shaky version of her let's-get-real tone. "OK Allie, so tell me. Fast. What do you know 'bout this—man thing—and when did you know it?" Jo's *when* had wavered.

"I've sorta known it for a year. But I didn't want to tell you, Jo. I'm sorry. See, I only found out for sure a couple of months ago when JJ told me how he and this woman and this man had some kind of—of three-way thing going—"

"Three?" Jo struggled for control of her face. "Jeez, I always thought JJ was too wild for you." She shook her head. "I mean I got to *like* JJ and all, thought he was smart and funny and all. Even thought he was kinda sexy. Always thought if you two had one thing, it was—y'know—"

"I know." Allie glanced out at the pool where she and JJ had swum under the moon. "And we do. I mean, he *is*—God, if nothing else—sexy."

Jo kept shaking her head. "So maybe it, his affair, was *mostly* with the woman and not so much with the man—?" Allie shook her own head but Jo pushed on. "Listen, are you sure JJ and the man ever even fucked?"

The bathroom door thumped, then Grandma's bedroom door.

"Yes," Allie told Jo. "Absolutely sure."

"But maybe," Jo seized on Allie's own initial explanation. "It was just some sort of kinky—experiment-type thing? Trying it out once or twice or—?"

"No." Allie shook her head. "I used to tell myself that. But, God Jo.

Reading the last of this woman's letters last night and hearing JJ say—he's always saying—how back when he was messed up they *helped* him so much—"

"*Oh,*" Jo burst out. "JJ did all this when he was *crazy*? Because he *was*—"

"No," Allie found herself protesting. "No, JJ's made a big point of saying *they* were the ones who pulled him *out* of his craziness. And, God, in this goddamn letter from Manila everything sounds so. I don't know: *tender* between them. Which's why, see, part of me wants to kill them, but a-*nother* part feels like, given all they went through, I oughta try to be more, more—"

"More of a *doormat*?" Jo cut in. "Sitting here so pregnant *letting* your husband cheat on you with both sexes at once? As some cheap-thrill thing?"

"Wait now." Allie held up one shaky hand. "—I didn't say JJ was down there today jumping in *bed* with them . . ." But even as she spoke, she felt obvious words from Bird's letters beating with her own heart. *There are ways that are safe.* And: *Yours (all ways, just once more?)* "All I'm saying," she stumbled on, "and this is what scares me. Is I think this was, this is. More of a—*love* thing."

"Oh, please. 'Love'?" Jo leaned forward, her matter-of-fact bossiness reviving itself. "Three people rolling around in bed together? That *is* a sex thing, honey; a *sick*-sex thing. You gotta wake up and smell the coffee." Jo gestured broadly toward Allie's cup though it held milk. "You gotta wonder if these two Mexico Ex-es ever really *were* 'ex,' if ol' JJ's got some double-life thing going here. Face it, Allie. A leopard can't change its stripes—"

"Spots," Alice corrected. But she met Jo's stare, feeling she was eyeball-to-eyeball with some clear blue truth.

"Jo dear?" From the back of the house, Mom sent up a thin-voiced shout. "I'm starting on Dad's books—"

"I'll be back in a few minutes, Mom! Soon as I finish the *trash*—" Jo turned again to Allie like a mother mid-scold. But Allie cut in, eager to steer this out-of-control conversation away from JJ himself.

"What about *us*, Jo?" Allie asked as Grandma's bedroom door thumped again. Grandma's walker creaked toward the den; Allie leaned forward so her belly pressed the table. "What about what *we* did that time when *we* were kids?"

She fluttered her own fingers. Jo averted her eyes the way they'd both done years before, vowing to tell no one what had just—as Jo put it—happened.

"That," Jo whispered to the table. "Was playing. And it scared us, remember?" Her brows knit around her faint scar. Allie shook her head.

"But something *in* us made us *want* to play like that. And who's to know what's 'playing' and what's—God—deadly serious?" She blinked, regretting her choice of words. Grandma's walker creaked onto the thicker carpet of the den.

"Hey." Jo shook her head as if waking herself. "You're not saying JJ—that this man in JJ's past has, like, AIDS or—"

"No," Allie told Jo, hating her own foolish lie as she shook her head. "No, no." Grandma's walker closed in; Jo took hold of Allie's hand.

"Look," Jo whispered, sounding shaken herself. "You gotta get a grip. You got a *baby* to think of, here." Grandma clanked into the kitchen archway. Jo used her last seconds to whisper, "Don't forget: you need JJ more than ever—"

"Girls?" Grandma asked sharply.

Allie froze the way she'd done a long-ago night in Kentucky. A witch had appeared in their bedroom doorway: Grandma Hart hunched in her thin old-fashioned nightdress with her unbound breasts sagging to her waist. Her face looked haggard without her glasses. Creases around her nose stood out as vividly pink as (Allie remembered now the shock of thinking this then) the pink openings between her own and Jo's legs, openings that didn't yet have a name.

"Morning." Alice twisted around in her seat like she'd twisted in her bed, Jo behind her. Grandma had fixed her witchy stare on Alice as Jo had scrambled back to her own bed. They'd only been sleeping, that night.

"Morning, Grandma," Jo said so matter-of-factly Allie's shoulders relaxed. It was not the nighttime Grandma but the daytime Grandma who creaked forward on her walker, her pewter hair curled under its invisible net, her sharp-edged glasses glinting. She wore a lightweight pantsuit, a style she'd worn since the '70s. Grandma Hart, who'd been the first girl in East Providence to bob her hair.

"What on Earth are you girls whispering about?"

"Oh—" Jo raised her always-loud voice to Grandma amplitude. "JJ's gone off on a trip today. A little day trip to Mexico."

"Mexico?" She halted her walker.

Jo stood, positioning her body between Grandma's faded yet sharp green eyes and Allie. "JJ's seeing some old friends there."

"Mexican friends?" Grandma asked in her Rhode Island rasp.

"Friends from college." Allie let her own automatic lie sound lame.

"Well." Canny Grandma clicked her tongue like Jo. Thinking: a woman?

"Jo-oh—" Mother's faint singsong voice called from Dad's old study.

"Hold your horses, Mom!" Jo glanced at Allie: is it OK if I go? Are you OK? She gave a weak nod. Jo sidestepped into the kitchen archway, hesitating.

"You know," Grandma told Jo as if they were two nurses consulting about Allie. "Your mother left a—" She gestured toward the darkened den.

"A videotape?" Jo clapped her hands. "Good idea. You two can have a little soap with breakfast. Doesn't seem like morning here without Dad's CNN on. . . ."

Normally, Allie knew, Grandma would've been appalled at such a suggestion. Today, she creaked her walker back into the den. Allie followed, grateful the way she used to be on sick days when Grandma'd let her watch nonstop TV, bringing her iced orange juice she called "orangeade." Allie sank into Dad's tweedy recliner. The TV lit the den with its harsh artificial light.

Alice braced her jaw against thoughts of Mexico. Victor told the eternally on-the-verge-of-tears Nikki, *We have loved as few have loved.* The scene shifted to Mrs. Chancellor. Since Brad had escaped from his ex-wife's cage, this had become the dumb plot: Mrs. Chancellor kidnapped by her maid and replaced in her mansion by an impostor look-alike played by the same actress. Today, the impostor phoned the real now-bedraggled Mrs. C., bragging about how she'd made love to Mrs. C's implausibly dense husband. *And he told me,* the fake Mrs. C. told the real Mrs. C, *that our sex was better than ever!*

Allie let out a bark of a laugh. Grandma muttered, "Now this is *too* much."

Split screen: two Mrs. Chancellors. One laughing sadistically; the other sobbing in cruel close-up. "Oh *please.*" Allie uncranked the recliner. Hating that Bird woman suddenly for making her feel so ridiculous, so helpless.

Grandma's rocker stopped rocking. "Dis*gust*ing."

As Grandma struggled up, Allie stood too, turning from the soap. A childhood game she was trying to outgrow. She followed Grandma's clanking walker back into the kitchen. *Yes, Brad was saying on TV. I love my wife with all my heart. But I have a very. Big. Heart.* Allie helped Grandma clear the table. Unable to stop this soap-opera image she pictured JJ and Bird in a border bar, sharing a salty-rimmed Tequila Sunrise. JJ and Bird and Kin.

"Someone has to clean up this mess." Grandma squeezed lemon soap into a stream of water that drowned the TV voices. "But you ought to rest. How that husband of yours could run off to Mexico just now is beyond me. . . ."

"Me too." Allie set aside Grandma's abandoned walker. "Grandma," she said above the splash. "You shouldn't work like this, with your *heart* and all. . . ."

Grandma scraped the saucer that held Mom's cinnamon-roll breakfast. Under her mint green pantsuit top, her dowager's hump stood out, solid as granite.

Heart attack's the fastest way, she had told Allie once. *Believe me, Alice Ann, that can be a mercy. I've seen, as a nurse, all the slow ways to go.*

Allie had nodded, young and scared and thrilled to have Grandma confide in her. She'd nodded harder as Grandma made her promise, *when I go,* to notify the Rhode Island School of Nursing's alumni newletter. Grandma always read its obituaries, then asked Allie to fetch her solemn graduation-day portrait. She'd let Allie mark the careful pencil *X* over the heads of the girls who had died.

"Your poor father," Grandma murmured. Allie lifted a dish towel, thinking of Bird and Kin's photo, of JJ writing Bird that the photo "unhinged" something in him. "*I could care for my son the way I once cared for my father-in-law.*" As Grandma plunged a knife underwater, Allie answered her loudly.

"But Dad's told me you *hated* taking care of Great Grandpa. Dad even said *you* said Great Grandpa Hart treated you like a *Shanty*-Irish servant girl—"

Grandma turned. Through her fogged glasses, her alert green eyes sparked. "True. But I *did* take care of him. All the while working nights as head nurse."

"I know, I know." Allie took the hot wet knife. "I used to think that meant you were head of all nurses, everywhere . . ."

Grandma chuckled, a dovelike sound. "Did you."

Allie set the knife in the drainer, her fingertips burned. Inside, she felt the baby roll over as if sensing the water's steamy heat. What did JJ mean "unhinged"? She drew a breath of steam, imagining dry heat hundreds of miles away, across the border. "Oh, Grandma. How can you *stand* this water so hot?"

Grandma raised one dripping hand, its usually white blue-veined skin as red as a newborn infant's skin. "A nurse has to be able to stand anything."

15

We Know What We Want

Inside *la Farmacía de Rosita*, at 7:30 A.M., Roberta Olaf Hwang paced between carpeted-over holes in the floor. Inside her mouth, her tongue probed new sore holes in her gums. After half an hour, her feet knew how to miss the mini-canyons that carpet sagged down into, strained on the thready verge of tearing. *By 7 A.M. or so*, she had said in her note to JJ. The ceiling fan stirred Bird's hair, bluntly cut below her ears and bleached by the world's hottest sun.

Behind the counter, Rosita's quiet daughter watched the leather jacket Bird held draped over one arm. Its coconut-oiled animal smell mixed with store smells of *cigarillo* smoke and rubbing alcohol. Bird glanced from the bumpily carpeted floor to the ceiling—holes covered by tacked-up plastic—to the old-fashioned brass clock above the *Farmacía* counter, then down to Rosita's daughter and finally, following her gaze, back to her own richly brown jacket.

New: bought the night before by Estella. Bird's legs slowed in her loose jeans. She slipped a sugar-crusted lemon drop from the *Dulce el Limon* pack she'd just bought. And she sucked intently, swallowing sour-sweet juice. What had happened hours before in the cramped dog-smelling front seat of Estella's *coche* still felt dreamily unreal because Bird hadn't yet told Kin.

He'd been asleep when she'd gotten home, past midnight. He needed his strength for today. Bird turned to the door, its growing square of dusty sun. Maybe she'd tell Kin and Jimmy Joe together. If Jimmy Joe showed. She stepped past the mysteriously well-stocked shelf of hair dyes, Autumn Auburn and Platinum Blond. Models on the faded cardboard boxes wore outdated black eyeliner and '60s flips. Other shelves, always almost empty, held equally outdated bottles of Alka-Seltzer and dried herbs in stapled plastic bags with handwritten labels and the chalky Mexican *aspirina* Bird bought for Kin's headaches.

At the door, she hugged her jacket—a deeply familiar creak—and cracked her lemon chip. Her remaining bad tooth loosened. Sweetness pooled in the gum holes left by Estella's *dentista*. He'd pulled two teeth, her new sore gums a relief after the jaw aches that plagued her in humid grimy Manila. Would JJ's presence, the jolt of it—Bird shut her eyes hard in the sun—make Kin consider seeing a doctor?

"*Hasta luégo,*" she told Rosita's daughter as she stepped off the wood stoop.

Sick of simply waiting. With languor left over from last night, Bird headed toward the border. Step-by-slow step, her pulse beat up into her tensed throat. The sidewalk varied: cracked and brown between shops, then patterned or painted blue. Stores on this main street were widely spaced, separated by boarded-up windows. Passing *Idealea* barber shop, Bird glanced in at the gold and green two-headed snake painted around the walls. Her eyes skimmed past schizophrenic border-town signs, some hand-lettered—*Closed/Cerrado* and *Coronet Bar/Billares*—then froze at a mustached man's flirtatious black eyes. He pointed to Bird's eyes, spread his fingers as if to imitate daisy petals.

"*Las floras,*" he told her. She gave a brief smile, brushing past him. Her lashes had stopped growing: half their old length. White lashes that startled Bird too in mirrors. She stepped over a crushed lizard. Back when he could take walks, Kin admired how neatly sun here dried corpses, down to bleached skin and bone.

"*Perdóneme,*" a squat woman murmured, a chubby baby in gold-stud earrings gazing over her shoulder. Her braid bounced below her boxy ass.

"*Perdóneme,*" Bird echoed. And she paused under the scant red-striped awning of the grocers where she bought bags of ice chips. Extra careful these days about local water. One fucking bacterium could do me in, Kin told her in his new matter-of-fact Mexican tone. An' who wants to die of diarrhea?

The grocer's modest window display buzzed with fat flies. Eying the yellow melons, Bird remembered Estella's bare plentiful skin last night. And JJ's skin years before, its distinctive surface cool and deep warmth, its smell of burned sweat. She stepped back into sunlight. Fierce already but she didn't squint. Aging American cars rattled by, spewing the sweetish smell of unburned gas. Bird made out the flash of the border's turnstile as she stepped toward the modern beige building that housed *Customs/Inmigración* and quickie Auto Insurance offices.

She climbed off the curb—all curbs so high here—and picked her way across a gravel parking lot. Then she slipped behind the lone phone booth, hugging her sun-heated jacket, staring toward the gate's concrete arches and giant turnstile. Quarter till eight by now. JJ late. She peered in at the phone's rotary dial. Her heart knotted—still, always—at the thought of JJ's call, that last night. Bird leaned her forehead on scratched Plexiglas. Despite her pulse, she felt almost drowsy after her few hours of fitful sleep. Back in Mass. Mental, in June of 1980, she moved through whole days in just such a sexy, tired-but-wired daze.

No matter what they'd done with Kin in Kin's silk-draped room the night before, Bird and JJ would sit together silently on the orange vinyl couch in Supervised Study. Deadpan twins. They'd slip each other the rice-paper notes that they'd later, at night—for the thrill of communicating from separate wings—burn. One of them would wait in the Common Area, watching for the flare.

Bird squeezed shut her eyes. She pressed leather to her stomach, feeling its heat through her tank top. Always—especially now, nearly 8 A.M.—the creak of leather reminded her of JJ's jacket under her bare ass, wet with their mixed sweat.

· · ·

In those first June weeks of 1980, she and JJ and Kin made love mostly with their hands and mouths, like kids. Gentle, clumsy, hungry kids. At first, she and Kin would kneel on either side of JJ and Kin would guide Bird's hands, showing her how to touch and rub JJ's cock, sometimes moist from Kin's mouth. Bird's mouth too, eventually. Even mid-July, even after they'd started doing or trying almost everything (Around the World in 80 Ways, Kin used to say), what Bird wanted most, still, was JJ's mouth.

JJ eating her, Kin called it, though it felt to Bird like the opposite. Being fed and fed. Her body, for once, lovingly tended. Aglow with strokes. In Mass. Mental's dictionary, Bird had looked up *ménage à trois* and found it meant "household of three." She liked better the nearby word "ménagerie": "a collection of wild or strange animals." That was more how she saw them.

We're a ménagerie à trois, she told JJ in her last Mass. Mental note, in early July before they were released: JJ to a Cambridge Halfway House, fee paid by his dad, and Bird to Kin's apartment. They never did form a "household of three."

But all through June and July, Bird wore JJ's ring of 8s like a real wife. Sometimes, in his too-small apartment on Commonwealth Avenue, Bird would catch Kin catching its glint. Kin had found her a job with him at the BU bookstore. They'd spot each other at work, daydreaming. They'd quarrel over Bird's sloppiness at home. Kin's snapping black eyes would snag on her ring.

Even in absence, Jimmy Joe charged the hot air of their apartment.

The main thing they did there that summer was wait for him. Kin would heat cheese or chocolate in his mom's gold fondue bowl. When JJ arrived, they'd all slice french bread or bananas or the "bite-sized young vegetables" they dipped into their favorite fondue: Classic Cheese, melted with olive oil and wine. The first time they made it, Kin read aloud a gourmet cookbook line that set them laughing, its words alive with the extra meaning everything suddenly held. *For so simple an affair, the controversy that surrounds the making of this dish is vast indeed.*

Armed with shish kebab skewers, they'd eat their finished fondue in a circle round the gold bowl, dipping into rich cheese or satiny chocolate or real cream. They'd drink wine but not—since Kin decreed that reaching ecstasy through drink or drug was cheating—enough to get drunk. Laughing, they'd discuss what they agreed mattered most, what lifted ordinary lives into the realm of the spiritual, what Kin deemed to be the true paths to ecstasy, what had been utterly absent in Jimmy Joe's prior life: music and poetry and sex. Bird read aloud from poets she chose at the bookstore. Adrienne Rich or Sylvia Plath or Garcia Lorca or Bill Knott, who'd written their favorite poem: "The Juggler to His Audience."

Bird loved to recite that entire three-line poem with tremulous intensity.

> *One in my hand*
> *One in the air*
> *And one in you.*

Playing off whatever tone Bird set, Kin and JJ would chose from tapes they bought in obscure cavelike Cambridge shops. Dueling music. JJ danced fiercely—Kin and Bird ducked his slashing forearms—to hard rock: Jimi Hendrix or Peter Gabriel or King Crimson. Kin sat in his own cross-legged trance while Bird and JJ slow-danced to music from places Kin longed to visit. Music Kin said aspired to a state of *Tè*, meaning "that by which things are what they are." Gyütö monks from Tibet chanting hypnotic variations on the same note or the pure bells and bronze gongs of a Javanese gamelan (What time is it? Bird had asked after that tape ended and JJ had answered, Two years later) or Ya-Rab-Toba, an aggressively repetitive Egyptian musical prayer with mizmars and tabla baladi and JJ shouting that his brain was going to explode and Kin shouting, Don't fight the power of *Tè* and Bird drowning them both out by switching the tape to one they all loved.

David Bowie or the circular-breathing aborgine didgeridoos that never ended—Bird danced 8s and 8s around Kin and JJ as they spun their Sufi circle—or their favorite make-out music, the Shakuhachi.

Then sinuous Swedish violins to accompany snake-mate writhing on the futon. And, for postsex celebration, South American party-band music Kin joked was named after them. *Trio Electrico.*

One night in heated mid-July, after they'd collapsed together, JJ startled them from their sated daze with what he called the world's first technological weapon. Bagpipes. A march: "The Battle of Killie Krankie." JJ pulled on only his dad's leather jacket, still sweaty from their sex. It's in my blood, he claimed above the tape's harsh piercing bagpipe skirl. I am, he shouted in his flattest Ohio voice, a bomber pilot's son. He stood at attention in front of the booming boom box, his jaw locked as if invisible bombs were bursting all around him.

Kin jumped up next. Imitating his mother's extravagant hand motions, he lit a cigarette. Her One Pleasure, he pronounced. Lynn Mae Hwang and the Eternal Cigarette Dance! As bagpipes skirled and screeched, Kin drifted naked round the room as if to silk-stringed Ch'in music, his hands wafting his own smoke. Blessing the room with—Bird thought dazedly, sitting up—holy smoke.

As if blinded, JJ stayed stiff in his bomber-pilot stance. The bagpipes sounded to Bird like a giant version of the childhood kazoos she'd made folding wax paper over a comb. Giggling, naked too, she jumped off the futon last. She dug through Kin's dress-up drawer, pulled out a pair of black nylons. Above the rising battle march of bagpipes joined by drums, she announced: Here's *my* mom! And—on an impulse that felt instantly right—she tied the nylons over her eyes. A blindfold. As Kin laughed loudly, appreciatively, as the bagpipes skirled even higher, Bird groped toward Kin's table, calling out in her mom's exaggeratedly vivacious party voice: Why, I can't see a damn *thing*! What *are* you two do-ing?

She bumped a chair, sat down hard. And she shouted toward the blurry black dancing figure of Kin: Fetch me my Jack D. an' watch me balance him on my knee! In nylon-grainy shadow, Kin sashayed to the fridge, dumped ice in a glass, glided over to Bird and set the pretend bourbon on her knee, square-boned like her mom's. Bird felt JJ in his stubborn soldier stance and Kin posing above her with his suspended cigarette watch as the glass wobbled, then steadied. She tensed both her bare legs. Bagpipes surged together. Blindfolded Bird pictured hundreds of men blowing and pumping the bags as hard as they could, marching forward in defiantly bright plaid skirts, flashing their proudly bared knees.

Kill 'em, Bird shouted to those bagpipers. As the march climaxed—attack of the men in skirts!—she jolted up, her glass cracking on the hardwood floor. To the martial beat of bagpipes that were no longer playing, Bird stomped on jagged shards of glass, cutting her foot. She started crying as JJ broke his endless salute, sobbing as he gathered her in his leather arms and carried her back to the futon. He untied her nylon blindfold; Kin hovered above her with Band-Aids and Bactine. No, she told them, still crying because it felt good. She stuck up her bleeding foot. First, she told Kin in a bold childish voice. Make it all better.

Gravely, like a real mother, Kin bent and kissed her bloodiest cuts. He straightened, wearing her blood on his lips. As if, as always, reading her mind, Kin faced JJ. Lowering her bloody foot, Bird watched the two men give each other a long hard kiss. A warrior kiss, she thought, sitting up. Then JJ kissed her: a taste of her own blood mixed with his and Kin's spit. They grinned at each other with their red-smeared mouths. Comrades in arms, blood siblings. Kin and JJ bandaged Bird's cuts. That night, for once, they slept together.

Most often, no matter how jubilantly they had danced and made love and collapsed on top of each other, JJ didn't stay the whole night. He'd loll and chat but before falling asleep, he'd slip out. After he left, Bird and Kin would talk for hours more. They'd analyze his shifting blue-green-gray moods, his abrupt departures. JJ, Kin would say admiringly, was a Master of the Fast Fade.

Toward the end of July, JJ began showing up late after sessions with the Halfway-House's woman shrink, Dr. Lovenski. Unlike Dr. Marmal, Dr. Lovenski actually seemed, JJ claimed, halfway rational. He quoted her to Kin and Bird as they ate their lingering fondue suppers. She'd told him Episodic Schizophrenia was common in young men, triggered by explosions of hormones. She told him his father—who sounded to her like a hardened case of clinical depression—had left JJ unequipped to deal with any emotion, much less the rush of emotions unleashed inside a twenty-year-old body, far from home for the first time. Peaks and plunges Dr. Lovenski warned JJ against, urging him toward more level moods.

Dr. Love, Kin called Dr. Lovenski, mockingly, claiming *he* was the real Dr. Love. JJ wouldn't laugh the way he laughed at most of Kin's jokes, his own and Kin's humor mixing easily. In August, joking at first, Kin and Bird and JJ began talking about traveling together. Kin and Bird began scraping together money for the trips the three of them planned fancifully, over fondue. Hawaii for starters. JJ seemed startled when Kin mentioned saving actual money. He said he wasn't sure when Bird asked: *Was* he going back to MIT next fall?

One night, mid-August, JJ muttered something about maybe applying *somewhere else*. This same night, for the first time, Kin brought out his Nikon camera. JJ snapped them, once. But when Kin tried to photograph JJ dancing, JJ stopped abruptly. He said he was sorry, said he had to leave. Fast Fade.

What would happen when summer ended? Late into that night, Kin and Bird worried together. It was Bird who suggested Kin take the larger apartment on the top floor of his building, near the roof where he sunned. They could live there together, Bird told him. The three of them. JJ was scheduled to leave the Halfway House. He agreed, vaguely, to move in with them through September, maybe longer. He implied without exactly saying so that he was enrolling again at MIT.

The last night of August, 1980, their last night in Kin's original apartment—their last night ever? Bird was to wonder for years—everything felt different.

Before that night, when JJ had fucked Bird—the way grown-ups do, she always thought, preferring to rub or lick like kids—Kin would rub his neck against hers or hold her hand or even ride JJ's heaving back as it happened. When JJ and Kin had experimented with what they all called going all the way, the experiments tended to break down: Bird in JJ's leather jacket straddling JJ on his hands and knees; Kin naked on his knees trying to enter JJ from behind. Often as not, JJ would balk and they'd wind up collapsing together, gasping and laughing. Before either Kin or JJ lost their hard-ons, Kin and JJ and Bird would go at each other with their hands and mouths. Roughly, playfully. Sometimes the three of them would lie in a row on their sides, curled close together, pressing between each other's thighs, trading places.

Bird liked it best in the middle, warm and protected: JJ behind her and Kin in front, their skins and limbs touching her so many ways she'd lose track of whose was whose. When a cock slipped or thrust inside her, though, it was always JJ's. When she kissed a mouth, it was JJ's too. She and Kin, even in the deepest heat of that summer, never kissed on the lips.

That last night in Kin's small silk-shaded apartment, JJ made love to each of them separately. He shut off Kin's serene Ch'in tape. He spread out his leather jacket on the futon like always but then quietly pushed back Bird, first. Dazed, she stood at the foot of the futon sipping her wine and watching as Kin sucked JJ's cock, Kin's head moving slowly, surely. Then Bird turned her back and stared at the undulating bedsheet curtains as, for the first time, JJ took Kin from behind. Bird only listened, watching the silk swell. JJ barely made a sound. But Kin's heavy breaths and final joyful shout startled Bird.

She kept her back turned till JJ touched her between her shoulder blades. She let JJ in his new intent decisiveness take her hand. They waited for Kin to roll off the futon and—he didn't need to be told what JJ wanted—step back too. Bird met Kin's black satisfied stare, giving him permission to watch. Though permission hadn't been needed between them for anything they'd done before.

Unlike Bird, Kin watched all the way through. He sat at the table, loose-limbed and naked, watching raptly—Bird felt him watch; she needed to feel him still there—as JJ had gone down on her, licking her till she came. Then, not bothering with a condom as he'd always done before, he climbed on top of her. *In Kin*, Bird thought as JJ slid inside her easily, lubricated by her wetness. JJ's cock had been in Kin. She kept thinking that, rocking under JJ as he thrust in and out so fervently leather creaked and creaked. *In Kin, in Kin*. She clenched her own fists in place of Kin's hand. She left half-moon cuts in her palms, red marks that she'd stare at the next day, upstairs in the new apartment, waiting for JJ.

1 September 1980. For hours, she and Kin waited in that new nearly empty apartment. Too big, too expensive. Kin's futon was unfolded, his boom box set up, both dwarfed on the hardwood floor. The bay window proved too big for the silk-sheet drapes to cover, letting in afternoon light. Premature fall chill filtered through the high panes. Kin bustled by the stove, melting a special bittersweet chocolate fondue. Bird perched on the uncushioned bay-window seat, flipping through Adrienne Rich and watching for JJ to cross Commonwealth Avenue between rush-hour traffic. She kept examining those crescent cuts on her palms, shifting to feel the moist tenderness between her legs. She kept listening to Kin hum and wondering if Kin hadn't liked it a bit too much: what JJ had done the night before. Bird had liked it and she hadn't, both at once. She shut Adrienne Rich.

She'd loved the part with his mouth, as always. And the all-the-way part too, more than ever before. She'd loved having JJ to herself; yet she'd hated being separated from Kin, his always-comforting touch. Or maybe what she'd hated was the knot of suspicion that tightened now inside her chest as she watched Commonwealth Avenue darken, smelling Kin's scorched chocolate. Finally, long past five, the phone Kin had plugged in hours before rang. Its ring dwarfed too by the new apartment.

Kin, always the brave one, answered. Bird crept over beside him, the receiver between their heads so she heard JJ's faint voice. He was calling from Logan Airport. He was about to board a plane to Ohio. No, he answered Kin's low-voiced question. No, he couldn't come over first and talk, couldn't keep on with this at all. What do you mean? Kin managed to ask. Both Bird and Kin held their breaths as JJ answered in his flattest Midwest monotone.

He had enrolled at a small private college out in Ohio, a late acceptance. Dr. Lovenski had suggested it for its slower pace, its proximity to his father, to home.

What? Kin breathed, incredulous.

JJ started mumbling. I can't say, he told them haltingly. Can't put in words what I've—you know. Felt for you. Both of you, he added so Bird knew he knew she was listening. She broke in, tugging the receiver away from Kin.

You told Dr. Love about us? she asked, imagining somehow police, arrests. Being committed again to Mass. Mental, against her will.

No no, JJ mumbled. Then he added more in his real voice: Never.

That last had been for her; JJ understood as always her fears. And he told her, almost in whisper: I'd never tell anyone.

So, Kin cut in, wresting the receiver away. So you're ashamed?

No, JJ insisted. But it—was something between us. Us three.

Bird on the other side of the receiver nodded, clenching her hands. She hadn't begun to believe what was happening. A flight was announced behind JJ.

Listen, listen: I only told Dr. Lovenski I was in an affair with two people and that it . . . scared me. That I was doing things, feeling things that scared me. That I sometimes felt like I was being pulled between these two people, like I was this *body* they were using to get at each other. Like that's what they really wanted. . . .

No, Kin interrupted. Bird took hold of his arm, breathing the smell of scorched chocolate. That Dr. Love, Kin was saying in a tensely level voice. She's twisted everything around in your head, Jimmy Joe—

She hasn't, JJ cut in. All too clearly, Bird heard him through the wrong side of the receiver. Look Kin, it's not Dr. Lovenski who's making me do this. It's me. I—just can't.

More silence; a voice asked a muffled question. Then JJ again, close in, the receiver maybe pressed to his lips. Look, I can't talk. It's just. Too much for me and I. Need to be where it's quiet, where I can be alone. Where I can *think* . . .

Kin said nothing, his wide lips sealed in a line. Bird couldn't stop herself. She gripped the receiver and burst out: But you might come back then, later?

JJ's answer, explosively close to his receiver, vibrated between Kin and Bird.

No, Kin.

He meant both of them, Bird knew. Kin pressed his head right up next to hers, so they took in the last words together.

I have t'go, JJ mumbled. For good.

A dial tone burned Bird's ear. All through bleak September of 1980, she half hoped she might be pregnant from the last unprotected sex with JJ. But it turned out when she finally went to a clinic that she'd stopped menstruating only because she'd all but stopped eating. Kin had all but stopped cooking. Though he'd regularly forced Bird to break her fasts, to share with him nights of wine and crackers and mournful mbira music. They waited for JJ to phone or write but shared a sullen conviction that he wouldn't. They had no idea of JJ's address. But JJ had their address. He knew they worked at the BU bookstore. As it turned out, Bird and Kin didn't live long together in the too-big too-light apartment.

After his mother's funeral in South Carolina that fall, Kin flew back to Boston changed, depressed but restless too. With money from his mother's house, he traveled. He flew alone to Taiwan. By 1981, he was taking Pan Am steward training in Boston, living in an apartment near Logan. He kept telling Bird to get out of her new basement apartment in that same old JJ building. Get out, go out. Sporadically, she dated, beginning her string of Would-Be Affairs. A BU English major and fellow Bill Knott fan who gave poetry readings around Kenmore Square; a friendly temp-service administrator who moved into the top-floor apartment and agreed to forward any letters the post office missed to Bird in the basement. She wrote JJ after tracking down his address through a phone call to a Mr. Wolfe in Elyria. Meanwhile, she described her Would-Be Lovers to Kin just as he described his real lovers to her in crackling transatlantic calls. Men in Puerto Rico, in Greece, in Spain. Men who spoke little or no English.

Sometimes, when Bird could scrape up the fare, she and Kin flew together: week-long trips to New Orleans or Florida. When AIDS began striking Kin's friends, Kin became—or so he claimed; Bird was never sure—Sister Kin, a celibate Flying Nun. From one extreme to the other, he said proudly. He sought extremes: in music, weather, love. He transferred to New York in '86, urging Bird to follow. But she didn't want to leave the building they'd shared with JJ. She liked flying to Kin for frequent New York City weekends, though. And she left the BU bookstore to become a temp worker. She liked the change, the constant changes of scene.

You're a traveler too at heart, Kin kept insisting from New York.

Come fly with Sister Kin, he'd say. We can get married, he began urging in '87, a joke at first. In late '87, as Kin started feeling jet-lagged when he wasn't, really, he pushed the idea in earnest. Bird had worried with him over his days of exhaustion. Unlike everyone else he knew, she never urged him to take the HIV test. He'd held out, he bragged, longer than anyone. He'd gotten his passport blood tests way back in '81 and, with his connections, didn't need more to keep flying. Marry me, he kept telling Bird. In the summer of '88, Bird heard a new urgency in his voice.

In the summer of '89, in Mexico, in what Kin called one of his dark nights of the soul—when his moans woke both himself and Bird in the next room, when Bird gripped his shoulders as he shuddered—Kin confessed that he hadn't pushed the idea of marriage till he'd suspected he'd test positive. And, though he hadn't consciously thought it at the time, he worried now that he had trapped her into promising to care for him, for better or worst. Bird kept hold of his hopelessly bony shoulders, trying not to breathe his sour night breath.

No, she'd told him. I knew you were positive too, I think. Deep down. And I *wanted* us to get married. Really married. Kin had managed a nod, silently agreeing. That was what they were, now.

· · ·

"*Señora, señora,*" a trio of girls called out.

Bird blinked her heated eyelids, her gritty lashes. She raised her face from the Plexiglas, hugging her leather jacket, hot like her skin. Three girls in red-embroidered dresses pounded past Bird's phone booth. "Señora Fer*n*andez!"

Bird steadied herself in their wake. Squinting, she gazed toward the concrete archway several hundred feet away. The turnstile stood empty, much bigger and thicker-barred than Boston subway turnstiles. In front of the border booth, an old lady sat in a lawn chair guarding her stuffed American Safeway bags. The girls crowded round her and bounced on their heels. A sleepy-faced customs guard paced by the booth in his black uniform, smoking a *cigarrillo*.

Shopping carts waited by the turnstile for border-crossers. Who, Bird wondered, officially owned the carts? Their bars gleamed in the sun, zoo cages.

As if checking a watch, she glanced at her ring of 8s. Must be, now. 8 A.M. at least, when she'd told him 7. The girls in their red dresses tried to push through the turnstile together, then laughingly realized they couldn't. One by one, they crossed over. As their bouncing black heads disappeared down the asphalt road that led into Douglas, Arizona, the old lady dozed in her lawn chair.

Bird sealed her mouth, her lips still pleasantly swollen from last night. Her tongue probed her loose tooth. A salty trace of blood. Swallowing, she watched the flat horizon. She was beginning to feel like the phone booth—empty, open—when she spotted, first, his hair.

His head: taller by many heads than the dark-skinned teenage boys walking in front of him. Inside the States, still. Was it him? JJ in sunglasses striding slowly toward the border booth, the turnstile? His tall distant body wavered in sunlight. Bird stiffened, her heart jolting up to her throat. Not even beating. This man might've parked his car in Douglas but he was walking so slowly she wondered stupidly, incredulously, if he had walked all the way from Phoenix.

The paralyzed pulse in her throat fluttered as the man's walk took on a long-armed swing. Jimmy Joe. The Mexican boys surrounded him, shoving each other to be first through the turnstile, shouting as if with Bird's own excitement. Shading her eyes, she made him out. Unmistakable. His body still lean but more solid looking; not so bony under his colorless shirt and pants. His shorter hair still formed a thick curly halo, reddish brown in the sun. His face looked more deeply shadowed, his eyes hidden by dark glasses that made Bird feel he was blind.

Jimmy Joe Wolfe. Automatically, he ducked his head as he entered the turnstile, all doorways too low for him. He revolved in slow motion, gripping the bar. The border guard gave JJ no glance. In Mexico, Bird dazedly remembered writing a week before, No one says no. The turnstile halted.

JJ stepped into Mexico and stood between gleaming cages on wheels. He stared as if he too wasn't sure what they were. Shopping carts, Bird had to remind herself as she stepped from behind the booth. Hurriedly, she shrugged her jacket on like armor. JJ could see her if he'd turn his head. But he stood planted in place too, between the carts. The boys filed around him, chattering in Spanish.

JJ's eyes must be moving, Bird sensed, behind his sunglasses. He used to case new rooms that way. Not moving his head, only his ocean-colored eyes. She braced her body, thrusting her hands into her pockets. Her light head hummed.

Because of his sunglasses, she couldn't tell when JJ spotted her. Maybe he privately absorbed her presence before making his abrupt quarter turn. Now, his long shadow pointed at her. The sandy crunch of his steps rose as he strode forward. Bird un-thrust her hands from her jacket and—to give them something to do—inched up its still-stiff zipper. Her eyes swam with brightness. If she blinked, his approaching body might not only waver but vanish.

Gravel crunched loudly under JJ's feet like the small stones were breaking. His body blurred. Bird had to blink, feeling hotly released tears melt on her overheated skin. What the Hell could she say to him? She saw white strands in his sun-brightened hair. She saw his lean face, decidedly older, still scarred by pockmarks. New lines creased his forehead above his sunglasses. Only when he stopped with a final gravel crunch, so close she smelled his distinctively burned sweat, only then did Bird look at his mouth.

His lips had lost their ripe color, but their full shape was so much the same Bird sucked in both her lips. She bit to keep from speaking first. She locked her knees so as not to lurch forward. What she wanted to say into the roar of sunlight between them was: We traveled all the way around the world to see you here, today.

Silently, she fixed her intent gaze on JJ's dark green-tinted lenses. Shaded by his body, she didn't have to narrow her eyes. He spoke in his old Midwest monotone, his voice deeper now or maybe his throat felt thick too.

"Bird."

She sensed his eyes moving up and down behind the glasses. Like young Jimmy Joe on his knees, straining to read it, her body. She cracked a smile so wide she showed JJ the crooked teeth she used to hide. Her teeth with their new gaps.

He didn't smile back but swallowed hard. His squarish Adam's apple bobbed. And he pulled off his sunglasses, his wedding ring glinting. Bird's quick pulse began to slow. New lines bracketed his deepset eyes. Their blue seemed lost.

"It is you," JJ told her, sounding unsure. Was he noticing changes in her too? She gave a chin-jerk. Squinting, JJ looked at her jacket. Sun gleamed in its grainy sheen. He pointed, his finger touching her leather sleeve. "That's not—?"

"Yours?" She shaped the word with care, her throat parched despite the lemon drop. "Your old jacket?" She pulled her arm from his touch, not ready for it yet. "Nope." She hugged the leather, grateful for its weight. "It's mine."

Last night, it had passed Estella's leather test: water sprinkled on the sleeve Bird clutched now. If the water beaded, the leather was fake. If it sank in, real.

JJ nodded as if dazed too by the heat and the tension, his face all sweaty. On impulse Bird reached up, wiping one fingertip on his warm faintly bristled cheek. She rubbed her finger against her thumb to feel the wetness. Real.

"You still don't sweat." He shifted in the crunchy gravel as if that hadn't been at all what he'd wanted to say. Bird glanced at her side, half expecting to see Kin there. She'd barely ever, she realized, spoken to JJ alone. Only at Mass. Mental surrounded by patients or at Kin's apartment, eased into conversation by Kin. "You never did sweat," JJ added, then stopped like shy Jimmy Joe.

'Cept in bed, Bird thought. A car with no muffler rolled through the border arch behind JJ. She leaned closer. "I *have* started, y'know. Sweating again."

"You have?" he asked blankly, no trace of his old full-lipped half smile.

"Last night." She pushed back her hair and felt JJ spot her ring.

His voice rose from its monotone. "That ring—that's—"

"Yours, yeah." She touched his bony forearm. His skin cool as ever under the sweat. "So, Jimmy Joe. Kin's *en casa*, resting up. Waiting for you."

"Almost turned back," he answered in an abruptly matter-of-fact tone. "Spent an hour or more driving around Tombstone, deciding."

"Driving?"

He nodded. Looking down, her hair hot against her flushed cheeks, Bird unzipped her jacket. Everything felt much more awkward than she'd imagined it could feel, with him. JJ's voice startled her from above. "How is he—Kin?"

She raised only her eyes. "You coulda found out for yourself, Jimmy Joe. Anytime this past year, if you cared so much." Shocked by her own words, she shrugged off her jacket, exposing her thin strong arms. JJ swallowed again and Bird watched his firmly sealed lips with annoyance. Remembering now how hard it had always been to get him to talk, open up.

"What's that?" He jerked his chin toward her darkly spotted shoulder. *Grano del sol*, Estella called those spots. What came from using no *loción*, no protection.

"Too much sun." Bird shrugged again, her movements as jerky as his. Had it been a good idea at all, bringing him here? This new grownup Jimmy Joe?

He folded his arms, his cotton sleeves rolled to his elbows. He'd always covered his body, even in summer. His gaze took in her tank top, her breasts.

To break that steady half-lidded gaze—she didn't want it on her now, out here—she inched forward, hugging her leather. Up close, JJ's blue irises showed the greens and grays that had reminded her of him in oceans all over the world.

She licked her swollen lips. What *was* going to happen today, with him? Matching the masterful flatness of his voice, she asked only: "Where's your car?"

. . .

Inside, the house still held the cool air of early morning. JJ ducked his head as always, stepping in behind Bird. A cockroach whose size no longer startled her scuttled along the tile floor. The small front room was shaded by fringed red curtains. Dangling skeleton dolls and beach photos of Carlos and his cheerful muscle-bound lover decorated the walls. Gardenias scented the air. Bird had set a second bouquet in the bedroom, masking the odor that came from Kin, his body.

"Kin's back there." She nodded toward the closed bedroom door across the room. "Maybe still sleeping. He—he needs more and more sleep, lately. . . ."

JJ nodded too, still wearing his sunglasses. Awkwardly tall in this low-ceilinged room, he stood by the half-size fridge and gazed toward Kin's door.

In the Zephyr—JJ drove it over the border though he couldn't afford quickie Auto Insurance; $50, cash only—Bird had haltingly described Kin's condition. How he'd woken on July nights choked, breathless. How he was diagnosed with Pneumocystis carinii pneumonia; how he didn't let the Tex-Mex–border hospital test him for cancer of the esophagus. Driving and nodding, JJ had studied the winding road, the dirty pink or turquoise houses, the Joshua trees and TV antennae poking over tin roofs. The vacant rocky slope leading to Carlos's small stucco *ranchero.*

"What scares Kin most," Bird told JJ now, wanting to say something more to prepare him, "is these spells of confusion he gets lately. Sometimes he wakes up not knowing where he is. He'll talk like he's on a plane preparing passengers for takeoff. Or he'll piss in his bedroom corner, thinking it's the bathroom."

"Jesus." JJ touched Bird's leather shoulder, so lightly she couldn't feel it. She'd slipped her jacket back on in his chillingly air-conditioned car. She looked down at her feet in scuffed sandals. In Manila, she'd sold her high-tops for food.

"I wish," she added in a low voice. "You coulda seen Kin, y'know, sooner . . ." She stopped, not wanting to sound mean again. But JJ nodded, agreeing. "Why didn't you go to Ko No's, Jimmy Joe? How come you sent your wife? *Did* you?"

"Look." He shifted on his feet. "I got your wedding invitation and my hair. But not the phone message. She—my wife, Allie—went there on her own."

"Al-lie." Bird repeated speculatively, her throat tightened. Allie of the heart-shaped face, the lustrous brown hair, the big dark eyes.

JJ stared over Bird's shoulder again at Kin's waiting door. His jaw tensed. Distantly, through the window, chickens squawked. "Like I tried to tell you in my letters, though. I want to—I know this's coming late, but—help you two."

She took a step back, wondering if Kin was listening. "We're not counting on anything from you, or anyone." She began backing around the brown couch she slept on. "We've gotten by on our own. Kin was collecting Unemployment for a while. But in Manila, he started worrying the friend picking up his checks might get hassled. So he told him to stop." She halted by Kin's door, still facing JJ as he stepped over to her. She blinked up into her own face distorted in his sunglasses. "You remember how Kin always—takes care of his friends?"

JJ touched her shoulder again, pressing so she felt it. "I remember."

As if these were the words she'd been waiting to hear, Bird opened Kin's door. The blatantly seductive murmur of a Mexican disc jockey greeted them. Kin lay dozing, but Bird knew he'd been up. He'd managed to change into the white cotton traveling clothes Estella had helped her clean and press. Red-tinged light bathed Kin's sunken face. No tissues littered his sheets. It must've worked, Bird thought, stepping onto the worn wood floor. The day before, on and off all afternoon, she'd beaten Kin's back with her fists. He'd coughed up phlegm. Yes: his breaths sounded less congested today, rasping in his open mouth.

La música del amor, the Mexican DJ drawled. Not daring to look at JJ, Bird switched off the radio. Then wished she'd left it on. A fly buzzed. Red fringe shimmered on the window shades and on the lamp hanging by the double bed. JJ cleared his dry-sounding throat. He stepped into the bedroom as if into a gardenia-scented viewing room. Mexican funeral flowers, Bird remembered now. She took JJ's hand the way she used to when they'd step into Kin's silk-shaded apartment, giddy with a shared sense that anything might happen.

JJ gave her hand a brief squeeze then released it. He took off his sunglasses. Stiffly, he knelt beside Kin's low bed. He stared down so intently Bird stared, too.

Kin lay on the red-striped sheets. His long dried-out black hair, trimmed yesterday by Bird, spread over the pillow, framing his starkly sallow face. Kin's bones stuck up. His skin looked thin as cloth, draped over an elegant skeleton.

"God," JJ whispered, as if that's what Kin had become.

Kin's high cheekbones, his pride, slanted above darkly pronounced hollows. Narrowing her eyes, Bird saw that Kin had dusted on light powder—so far, he'd been spared purple lesions on his face—and, surprisingly, that he'd darkened his wide half-open mouth with red lipstick. She blinked above JJ's motionless head. She hadn't seen Kin in lipstick since New York, their wedding day. Then as now, she wanted to wipe it off. She edged around the bed and knelt by the woven trash basket holding a relatively small supply of balled-up tissues.

"Sister Kin," she murmured. His mouth closed. His eyes flickered open: glittery black. Bird tightened up, scared that he was waking scared. He blinked. His lipstick made sense now, its red answering the dark brightness of his eyes. Three bold slashes of color.

"Berta." Kin's wideset eyes, bigger these days in his new face, flickered to JJ then—as if from a too-bright light—back to Bird. He fingered her leather sleeve.

"Estella bought this last night," she mumbled, flushing. "Real leather . . ."

Kin barely nodded. Bird bent close enough to smell that his breath was sweetened by lemon drops and his skin doused in Carlos's spicy aftershave.

"He's real too," she whispered.

Kin's face remained motionless, masklike. But his eyes began moving as busily as JJ's brightened eyes. He and JJ staring each other up and down.

"Long time, no—" Bird gave her old nervous giggle.

"Love," Kin breathed, barely moving his lipsticked lips. "You're here, love."

Bird pulled herself up. Feeling tall for once, she stood over the two of them. In self-conscious Spanish, she asked Kin if he wanted a *batido*. He nodded. JJ relaxed slightly, maybe relieved to see Kin move. A fly was buzzing, closer.

"Want one too?" Bird asked JJ shyly, as if he were a visiting stranger. "I mixed some at dawn: strawberries and sugar and bagged ice . . ."

"Bagged?" He raised his shadowy eyes. Bluer now, distracted.

"Ice from 'cross the border." She hooked her thumbs in her jacket pockets. "I buy it at the grocers here. So the water's, y'know, good."

"Sure." JJ too gave a minimal nod. A fly was buzzing over his head.

Bird turned like a waitress. Relieved to edge out around the bed, the room air heavy with gardenia and aftershave and sweat and—under it all; could JJ tell?—that sour whiff of sickness. Rotted fish. *Was* JJ close enough to smell Kin yet? Bird stepped from the bedroom. The Juarez doctor, who'd wanted to test Kin for cancer, had explained Kin's smell to Bird bluntly as *decaimiento*. Decay.

"Can't believe," Jimmy Joe was telling Kin. "I'm seeing you."

With shaky steps, Bird crossed the front room. A cockroach skittered under the half-fridge that she opened. She hefted Carlos's ceramic pitcher and poured two glasses of bubbly pink liquid. Kin was murmuring a few words. She set the glasses on a metal tray. Breathing the *batido*'s chilled strawberry scent, she lifted the tray along with the oversized ice bag that held leftover chips. For Kin's dry mouth. Cautiously, Bird carried the tray into the silence that Kin didn't mind these days. But JJ, still kneeling, must've been taken aback by a quiet Sister Kin.

"I—don't want one myself; I'm just not—" Bird settled the tray by the radio and handed JJ his foamy glass. "I couldn't eat a thing." Kneeling on the other side of the bed, she rested the ice bag beside Kin's stack of books. The Buddhist book was covered by a paperback murder mystery. *Besar y Matar.*

"Here." Bird lifted Kin's glass. He raised his head from his pillow. Together, they tilted the glass forward. Kin swallowed, painfully slow.

"*Gracias.*" He sank onto his pillow and wiped his mouth with his fingertips.

"*De nada.*" Bird set the glass over the mystery, feeling more relaxed with this formal tone. She nodded at the butterfly-style canvas and metal chair by the shaded window. "*Siéntate,*" she told JJ. "*Por favor . . . ?*"

He stood. His animal grace, Bird remembered David Bowie singing as JJ settled his long body into the chair. His knees poked up high. He sipped his *batido* and set it on the floor, widening his broad nose. Taking in the smells of this room? Window light electrified his hair. His forearms rested on his knees, his large beautifully shaped hands clasped. *I can't even look at you*, Bird remembered JJ writing to her in Mass. Mental. *You're so—*

She bit her lips. "First let's just—talk." And her face re-heated. Suggesting talk first seemed also to suggest she expected something more, later. But now she wondered how she could have proposed that in her Manila letter to JJ. "What—" Bird began. "What've you—wha'd you do after Boston, Jimmy Joe?"

Like a man interviewing for a job, JJ looked at his hands. "In college, in Ohio. I, y'know. Majored in math, hung out with musicians. Got into computers . . ."

Kin roused himself, obviously not wanting to waste time on small talk. "Any men, Jimmy Joe?" He struggled to clear his throat. "Af-ter me?"

JJ stiffened further but—Bird's hopes rose that they'd be able to talk again, somehow—answered. "Lots of what you might call flirtations. Nothing that went very far." He shook his head. "Nothing much at all, since I got married."

Bird narrowed her eyes to gauge if he was lying. And JJ shifted in his seat as if about to stand. To flee? A cough erupted in Kin's throat but he swallowed it down. He addressed JJ softly, determinedly, like the old Sister Kin drawing out his guests round the fondue bowl. "An' now you don't even—want to, with men?"

JJ spoke straight to Kin. "Sometimes." He shifted again. Awkward, still, but less like a job applicant and more like, Bird thought, a Mass. Mental patient with a therapist. "Sometimes if a man reminds me of— you. What we, we three, had. But then there isn't ever any Bird . . ." JJ cut himself short like twenty-year-old Jimmy Joe. And—Bird's back straightened—he did stand up.

"Hmm." Kin seemed not to notice JJ on his feet. "Never any other Bird." He gave his scratchy cough. "Never any-one other than Bird," he rephrased with effort, "Who *I* really wanted to. Talk to, after." She touched his arm, saving his words for later contemplation. "Not that I didn't meet men I coulda talked to. 'Course I," he added to JJ, Southern style. "*Have* had other beaux. All over the world . . ."

"Uh huh." Tall JJ shifted on his feet. Then, in a Jimmy Joe burst: "Look. Look, I'm sorry but I feel. Pretty strange talking like this." He paced to the open bedroom door, Bird following him with her eyes. Was he headed for a Fast Fade? "Think I oughta," he told her at the doorway. "Call my wife. Tell her I'm here. . . ."

Bird shook her head, trying to sound as calm as Kin. "No phone."

"Oh." JJ looked from Bird to Kin. "Sorry, but I. Feel strange just—" He raised his long-fingered hands as if poised to shoot a basket. "Being here."

"On Earth, y'mean?" Speculatively, from his pillow, Kin gazed up at JJ. "Jimmy Joe, Jimmy Joe. When've you ever *not* felt strange, just being here?" He gave a throatier cough. Bird helped him slurp more *batido*. "Any-how, where were we? Oh yeah, my beaux." Kin focused on Bird like they were alone together as usual. "Coulda stayed with some of 'em, yeah. If I'd stayed still long enough . . ."

"Like, with Carlos?" Bird set down his drink clumsily, a twist in her heart as Kin nodded. For all his openness, he still hadn't told her much about Carlos, though she'd caught him studying the sunny beach photos of Carlos and his lover. Standing still by the bedroom door, JJ—Bird noticed—studied Kin.

"Sure, Carlos." Kin blinked up at JJ as if freshly surprised by him. "Carlos Cruz was, is. The saint who's letting us stay in this house." He sighed, his voice whispery hoarse. "Met him in a plane on fire on a runway in San Juan. . . ."

"Think I told you in my letters," Bird added to JJ. "How Kin *saved* people—?"

"I know he did," JJ answered softly. And Kin went on, maybe not hearing.

". . . 19—82, '83. We'd meet at this hotel in Puerto Ángel, near Acapulco. Balcony bigger than the room. We'd tan so brown we looked like brothers." Kin lifted his own glass, his wrist trembling. "We'd cook shrimp in my hibachi grill. Carlos'd make up dirty, pretty songs on his guitar." He swallowed more *batido*, a slow process. "I was. Oh." He squinted up at JJ. "How old were you, when we—?"

JJ stepped back to the foot of the bed, facing Kin. "Twenty."

"Twenty or so." Kin raised his V-shaped brows, slipping an ice chip into his mouth. "So I was. Too young to ap-preciate Carlos. Not that we had—the kind of thing *we* had. You and me and Bird." Kin met JJ's stare across the mattress, pointedly. "But still. Good cooking, good music, good company. Kindness."

JJ leaned forward like the old intent Jimmy Joe interrupting Kin, waving a drippy fondue stick. "Look Kin, I. Never should've left you two—" He glanced at Bird too. "The *way* I did." He swallowed. "I had to leave, but I didn't have to leave so. Suddenly. But, like I tried to tell you. Both of you. I needed to go where I could think. That's what I—not wanted but needed." JJ's eyes flickered between them. "And in college, see, after Boston, I found computers. This world I could sink into where everyone left me alone and everything connected, made *sense*."

He looked from Kin to Bird as if he'd just spoken a foreign word they couldn't possibly understand. Then—Bird half relaxed—JJ settled back into his chair.

"Mmm." Kin cracked his ice chip, his voice taking on his old semi-mocking tone. "Guess Dr. Love'd say we both got what we. 'Needed.' Felt like I did, for years. Touching, not talking. 'Course, I already, always, got plenty of talking with Bird. An' sometimes now I worry that Bird didn't—" Another cough rumbled up.

"Get anything else." She steadied Kin's shoulder as his cough died down. "But," she added in a rush. "I worry that *I* didn't *want* you to have, y'know. Much more than sex with those men." Kin gave her one wobbly nod. "And me. Well, you know better than anyone, Sister Kin. I didn't want anything *but* talking, back then. Not for the longest time . . ."

"And now-ow?" Kin coaxed in a hoarser version of his old Sister Kin voice. "What all *did* happen with you and Estella last night?" Bird drew a shuddery breath; Kin added, still a polite Carolina boy, "Estella. *Explica a Jimmy Joe.*"

"Oh, right." Bird felt her skin's heat deepen, remembering how Kin had told her long ago in that same softly chiding tone to *Thank Jimmy Joe.* Was JJ remembering too? As she glanced up at JJ—his eyes fixed on her now like he'd been waiting for a chance to stare—she sensed that something more than talk might yet happen among the three of them, the new three of them.

· · ·

Staying on her knees, Bird told JJ how one June evening she'd hitched with the kids down the hill to a small racetrack outside of town. She'd wanted to see dogs shaped like whippets run. To try her luck at betting, raise some *pesos.*

"And I did. Won my first-ever bet. So I was grinning, feeling good, wishing Kin could've come. Then at the cash-in booth, a guy tried to pick me up. Bragged that he spoke English, that he worked at the track, that he had to 'take care of' this white-speckled greyhound that'd snapped its leg in the race I'd won. I said, What do you mean, 'take care of'? He said, 'The opposite of what it usually means.' I was so high on winning that I followed him under the stands to these cages. This stink of raw meat and dogshit and dog. One greyhound was lying outside a cage. So thin, his organs showed through his skin. I swear: round shapes of his liver and intestines. Like meat through butcher paper. The guy told me, 'That dog won't even make it into your *tacos*'—"

As if he hadn't heard this before, Kin winced. Bird pulled herself up. Weighted by her jacket, she paced on the side of the bed where JJ had knelt.

"You were getting scared—?" Kin prompted from his pillow.

"Scared to be alone with this guy—he *smelled* like dog meat—when I spotted a-*nother* guy stepping from behind the cages, holding another starved-looking dog. I backed away, *real* scared till the other guy stepped into light. And it wasn't a guy but a tall, wide—a *big* woman. Estella."

Bird stopped at the doorway, her back to JJ as she remembered Estella holding out the limp whimpering dog. Slowly, Bird slipped off her leather jacket and draped it over her arm. Her skin tingled with relief. She breathed in, feeling her breasts strain her tank top. Exhaling, she met JJ's eyes.

"Right from the start, Estella was staring at me like—" Bird grinned at JJ, showing her teeth with all their gaps. "You, right now."

Kin choked, laughing. JJ—looking startled, as if he hadn't known he was staring—joined in with his low dry laugh. Their laughs mixed as easily as ever.

"Anyhow." Bird paced more slowly, wondering where she was leading. *Was* she leading? "I wound up helping Estella Hinojosa load the dog into her old Bonneville convertible. She'd bought the dog, see. And she gave me a cigarette. Like this." Bird shook one from a pack lying on the radio. Lighting it, she sucked a mouthful of smoke. As gently as Estella had done in the hot starry dark of the parking lot, she knelt on the bed and slipped the cigarette between Kin's lips.

"*Muchas gracias,*" he murmured. These days, though he barely inhaled, he savored his forbidden cigarettes.

"Then she asked if I was hungry." Bird resettled the jacket on her arm, watching JJ watch Kin. "I rode with the dog's head in my lap. Her house was off by itself—lotsa roses climbing the walls and a yard full of dogs." She breathed Kin's smoke, remembering the rich smells of Estella's kitchen. "She fed the dog first, then me. Hauled out a pot to make *sopa*. She had—has—big hands and a long horsey face. A ponytail—black hair but not like Kin's. Coarser, like a real horse's tail. Like—" Bird glanced at JJ. He was still watching Kin smoke. "Yours." She stood, surprised and ashamed by a little flare of jealousy inside her.

"So anyhow, I ate. The kitchen was steamy, and we both smelled of dog. Estella asked, real polite, in Spanish, if I wanted a bath."

Kin cleared his throat loudly. Bird looked down. "And I asked myself: Do I want a bath?" She drew a breath of smoke, feeling JJ's eyes shift to her. "I did. So she ran me a bath in her old-fashioned boat tub and I—don't know why; I just knew it was what she wanted—I said, in Spanish, You wanna watch?" Bird met JJ's gaze. Wanting him to understand what had happened to her this summer.

"That's how it started, our routine. Couple of nights a week. We'd meet at the track and bet. Then pick up any dogs worth saving. I'd help feed the dogs and we'd eat and if I felt like it, I'd take a bath. She'd lean on the sink, smoking and watching. Then," Bird turned from JJ, "she'd pay me. For feeding the dogs, she said. But it was for the bath. I *wanted* to bathe for her, so it seemed . . ." She silently asked Kin to find a word. The Spanish she'd learned escaped her now.

"Cool," he muttered through his smoke.

Bird nodded. " 'Round July," she hurried on, watching JJ half smile at Kin. "I managed to tell her I wanted to, needed to learn to drive."

"You still weren't driving?" JJ turned and blinked at her.

"You *do* remember," Bird said straight to him, "why I never learned?"

JJ nodded slowly. She slung her jacket over her bare shoulder. As she paced again by the bed, she described how Estella let her bump the Bonneville up and down her dusty side street. How sometimes Estella's thigh would brush her own, or Estella's hand would rest on her knee. Estella would slip her a few more *pesos* on those nights. Kin nodded, releasing slight streams of smoke.

And, Bird went on, Estella helped out when Kin got so sick. She'd paid for Kin's hospital stay. She'd paid for the *dentista* who pulled Bird's bad teeth.

"But last night." Bird faced Kin. "I wasn't trying to pay her back."

"Real*ly*?" Sister Kin asked almost with his old New York edge. Had *he* been feeling little flares of jealousy over Estella?

"Really." Bird looked from Kin and his elegantly suspended barely smoked cigarette to JJ. She wanted them both to understand that it hadn't been for money.

"So." Kin pointed to her with his cigarette as he used to do during their fondue suppers. Their conductor. "What *happened* last night?"

Bird fingered her ring of 8s. "Estella," she told JJ, "knew Kin was my husband. That's all she knew. Last night, I told her that Kin and I would have to leave Mexico soon. Maybe *mañana*. I mean—today."

JJ looked at the floor. Impulsively, Bird stepped toward him, trailing her jacket. "So Estella and I, we went on this long last ride. She let me drive—a celebration, I was driving so fast and easy." Bird draped her jacket onto JJ's lap. His knees supported it like tent poles. He kept his eyes downcast. "For protection." Bird smoothed the leather over his rigid knees. "Case anyone decides to. Sit on you." His eyes flicked up to her, a forbidding gray-blue.

She plucked JJ's sunglasses from his pocket, unfolded them and slipped them on him. "Case we do anything now you don't want to see."

JJ reached up as if to take them off but merely adjusted the curved stems around his ears. His pock-scarred face was flushed, the way hers felt. Half scared and half exhilarated by what she was doing, Bird backed away.

"So you drove," Kin said, easing her into the story again. He ground out his red-stained cigarette in a seashell ashtray, his lips only lightly lipsticked now.

"I drove all the way to Nogales," Bird went on. "With the roof down."

Estella's horse-hair had streamed in wind; Estella had yelled *Ai ya* as they rolled into Nogales, rolled along streets thronged by tourists, by burros painted with zebra stripes, by bouquets of paper flowers huge as bunches of balloons, by street carts of lemons and peeled cukes and sweets with beautiful names. The layered pastry they'd shared was called a *buñuelo*.

Bird hugged herself, remembering the leather and silver-polish smell of the shop where she'd tried on jacket after jacket. "As a going-away present, Estella bought me just what I wanted." She stepped back over to JJ. "Plus coconut oil to protect the leather." She bent and touched the jacket on JJ's lap.

Daring herself, Bird rested her hand on JJ's shoulder as she straightened. Through the cotton, she felt his skin, its surface cool. "Any-how." Her voice shook slightly. "When we got back, I parked her Bonneville behind the dog fence." JJ's body was stiffening under her touch. "No one around but the dogs . . ." Tentatively, Bird pressed his shoulder. "We sat there awhile under these big bright stars, me in my jacket—even in the heat, I wanted it on. And I could've just driven myself home, said good-bye in her car. But I said to myself: what do I want to do?"

Keeping hold of JJ's shoulder, she asked herself again that same question. Then bent closer to him. She felt Kin observe them through his lingering smoke. "So I slid out from under the steering wheel and I climbed into her lap."

Unsteadily, Bird started to ease herself onto JJ's lap. He gripped her bare arm hard. "No, Bird." Half relieved, she pulled away.

"Want me to show *you*?" she asked Kin. He gave a slow-motion nod and sat up, propping his pillows behind him. His legs stretched in a *V* over the sheets.

Abruptly, Bird lifted the jacket from JJ's lap. She held it up like a bullfighter's cape. Kneeling on the bed, she spread it over Kin's legs and crotch.

"I sat in her lap," Bird repeated softly, to Kin. "In my jacket." She eased down in front of Kin as if they were on a bobsled. Careful not to rest her full weight on him, she settled between his outstretched legs. Leather squeaked beneath her. "She helped me unbutton her shirt. Her body was all—round. Watermelon breasts and a big belly and at first, Sister Kin, I felt kinda overwhelmed." Bird settled more heavily against him. "But gradually I kinda. *Sank* into all that flesh. All brown and firm, not soft. Before I knew what was happening, I was—my first time, y'know—sucking her breasts." She leaned fully on Kin as she'd done during a few long afternoons here, once letting him reach around and feel her breasts as if they were his own.

"Sucked so hard I thought my loose tooth'd come out. Then we were kissing, hard too." Bird slowed her words, remembering Estella's wide tongue filling her mouth, filling the holes in her gums. "I took hold of her hand." She groped at her side for Kin's hand. Light, compared to Estella's. Drawing it around her, Bird rested Kin's warm bony hand in her lap. "And I eased her hand under my skirt . . ."

"*Bueno, bueno,*" Kin said, his smoky breath in her hair. Bird shut her eyes, unable to describe how delicately Estella's strong fingers had separated her vaginal lips. Like flesh petals. How Estella's fingertips held traces of the *buñuelo* they'd shared, its oil and flour and powdered sugar.

"Just a touch," Bird whispered only to Kin, her eyes shut. "But she knew—" Bird pressed her hand over Kin's in her lap. "Just where."

She blinked open her eyes. In the growing window sun, she made out JJ's sunglasses, his locked jaw. His lips were tightly sealed. But his face had reddened.

"My first time ever with a woman," she said to JJ. "And the first time in years, first time since you, I've en*joyed* anything like—that."

Lit by the sun, backed by the curtain's red fringe, JJ's hair shimmered with reddish browns. Steadily behind his glasses, he studied Bird and half-hidden Kin.

"I've let men kiss and touch me. All my Would-Be Lovers. But never—" Bird was the one to lower her eyes. "Never like you, Jimmy Joe."

"*Nunca.*" Kin propped his chin on Bird's bare shoulder.

"So." Bird stretched her legs in her jeans. She looked up and leveled her voice, stating a fact. "We can't help it. We keep—thinking about you, Jimmy Joe."

"An' you?" Kin asked, his jaw moving against Bird's shoulder. He was speaking to JJ now, confidentially. Man to man. "You think about us, much?"

JJ leaned forward, re-clasping his hands. "Till this year, I didn't. Much. Didn't let myself. I've gotten good at, I don't know. Control. In some good ways, I think." His Adam's apple bobbed, making Bird want to press his throat with hers.

She only nodded, feeling her hair brush Kin's. "Y'know we never could get very far alone, Sister Kin and me." She kept leaning back. In the dim silken Commonwealth Avenue apartment, she used to lean on Kin, spreading her thighs for JJ.

Boldly now, she let her knees loll open. She breathed the faint rotted-fish smell under Kin's perfume. And she held her breath with longing, though not the old longing. She was worried about leaning on Kin too hard. Her heart knotted up as JJ stared, its ache stronger than the slight moist ache between her legs.

Ceremonially slow, JJ pulled off his sunglasses. He set them down by his *batido*. He gave Kin and Bird his heavy-lidded stare. Gray-green, but no longer chilly. "Bird, I can't." He shook his head, his face more darkly reddened. "My wife back in Phoenix. You know. I can't do that, now. . . ."

Bird cupped her knees. "Yeah, I know," she murmured. Behind her, Kin exhaled as if he'd known too, all along. She eased forward to relieve his tense frail body. Kin's voice startled her, surprisingly steady.

"Jimmy Joe, Jimmy Joe. We aren't trying to—force anything." A cough erupted inside Kin but Bird felt him swallow it back, hard. "Not with everything—all of us—so changed. Especially me. *I* know we can't do like we used to do. . . ."

"But still." Bird drew her knees closed. She pulled herself up as Kin let loose his rumbling cough. Then she stepped over to JJ, who sank low in his butterfly chair. Unmistakably, his face had heated like hers. His lips had taken on their old color. "Still, Jimmy Joe." Bird struggled to keep her own voice calm. "I feel like there—might be something we could do. Not you and me. That's not it now, y'know?" She waited a beat and he raised his eyes. He nodded as if sensing this might've been the point of her Estella story. "But what I said in my letter from Manila," she went on, remembering that letter again herself. "You read it. You knew coming down here I wanted to try . . ."

"Something for Kin." JJ looked past Bird at Kin on the bed. Impassively, Kin met JJ's stare. With his lipstick worn off, his eyes formed the only slashes of color in his face. "In her letter from here," JJ told Kin. "Bird, she said you said. Lately you felt. All your senses overcharged? Like mine were when I was schizo . . . ?"

Kin gave a slow matter-of-fact nod. "Comes and goes in waves," he told JJ. "Like my fear." He switched to his old mock-teacherly voice. "It's an ex-per-ience, boys and girls. And you know I'm a glutton for. Experi-ence." He dropped the voice. "The best part is how sometimes some things—just smoking or playing guitar chords or smelling mint. Feel all at once overwhelming. Like—seeing you two. Together, now." He squinted at them as if they gave off light. His jaw made the chewing motion that Bird knew meant he couldn't speak. He dipped a hand into his ice bag. Shutting his eyes abruptly, he ran an ice chip over his face.

"What *I* fucking need is a cold shower." Kin reverted to his Southern

Belle voice. "'S all too much excitement for my del-i-cate condition . . ." He wiped his face with one slow sweeping motion, then lowered his hand.

JJ bent more sharply forward. "You still have . . . I mean you always have that—" He gestured to Kin's limp slender hand. "Grace."

Kin's bright gaze stayed steady. Bird drew a breath, half hopeful and half afraid that she might see him, for the first time, cry. Even when he found out he'd tested positive, he hadn't cried. But he didn't blink now.

She whispered, "If we could even just lie down together." Her whisper seemed to her disembodied, a voice from the room's shadows. "You don't have to do anything, Jimmy Joe. Except lie there, maybe, between us . . ." His eyes lowered. "It'd be safe, I swear. There's nothing dangerous in, you know, sweat."

JJ blinked, his jaw still tensed. Bird raised one hand to him as if to shake his hand. The knot in her chest tightened. She found herself longing for the old Jimmy Joe, the one with heightened senses and no filters.

"See," she said to him, suddenly inspired, "my jacket, that leather. It'll—protect us." JJ studied her outstretched hand as if unsure what it was. Bird bent down to his ear. She whispered, "You're the only one who ever could join us."

JJ raised his eyes. "I know." He said this flatly, as if it were the one thing in his life he did know.

Slowly, maybe experimentally, he took her hand. She didn't tug. He pulled himself up. She let go of his hand, remembering Jimmy Joe gazing at Kin their first night. She'd seen a flicker of that old fascination when he'd watched Kin smoke minutes before. Now, JJ's gaze seemed lit by something stronger. His eyes shone with a liquid that looked thicker than tears.

"Don't," Kin told JJ from the bed. "Don't do anything you don't want to do, love."

What Sister Kin always told them, Bird thought, turning. She felt sure JJ was remembering that too. The single rule of their old game.

"I won't," JJ answered, low-voiced like a groom taking his vow.

. . .

As she had never done years before, Bird led JJ. They stepped away from the butterfly chair and edged between the bed and wall. JJ stopped behind Bird. She froze, wondering what next. JJ moved first. He sat on the mattress to pull off his black sneakers. Then he stood again. Kin on the bed eased his body sideways.

JJ lowered himself onto his knees, the mattress sinking under him, springs squeaking. Bird touched his shoulder. And he touched Kin's shoulder. One light touch, one nod between JJ and Kin. Hello, they seemed to be saying at last.

Bird breathed JJ's sweat, the welcome smell of healthy flesh. "If we can all just . . . lie down here . . ." Her voice faltered. "In—a row?"

Deliberately, JJ rolled onto his side. Bird touched his rib cage, more padded with flesh than before. But his hipbones still jutted out, his limbs and haunches still lean. A foot of space stretched between JJ's long curved back and Kin, who sat propped against his pillow as if weighted in place by the jacket on his lap.

Bird heard the buzzing flies and the sun outside, its hum as it beat down harder. Time was running short, the limited time they could spend together again. But didn't she already feel a charge in the air among their bodies? Tentatively, Kin shifted his weight, trying to hold the jacket on his lap.

"Let me." Bird edged around the bed, sensing what Kin might want.

She rested her hand on Kin's shirt, his rib cage. Padded by the thinnest skin. Her fingers pressed between his ribs as she helped him roll on his side, facing JJ, the jacket sliding off his lap. Bird took its empty arms. "Wait now . . ."

She held up the unlined jacket. Then remembered Estella's test last night: how droplets of water had sunk into the leather. Because leather is skin, Bird reminded herself. And all skin is porous. She lowered the jacket, wondering what could wholly protect them. She hadn't thought of buying condoms, wasn't even sure Kin would be able to get erect. She blinked over at Kin's ice bag, then stepped quickly around the bed. She lifted the bag, dumped its remaining ice into the trash basket. "Kin calls this the Buddhist brand." Bird read its label out loud, smoothing the airtight plastic to warm it. " 'Clear Pure Ice Chips.' "

"Oh, right," Kin told JJ, his ragged voice calm. "This Buddhist book I read for fun. Tells how to reach the State of Not-Self. A clear state, they say. Clear, pure . . ."

"Right." Bird draped the plastic bag over Kin's crotch. She lifted the jacket again and tied its arms around Kin's waist. The jacket over the plastic covered Kin's crotch and thighs like an apron. A smithy apron, she thought.

"Perfect," she said, stepping back to view her work. The unlined leather was thin enough to let Kin feel the body in front of him. Which was what Kin wanted, Bird felt sure. To feel JJ close to him now. To feel her close, too.

JJ propped himself on one elbow, twisting around to face them. "Guess we had to work a leather jacket in here somehow," Bird said. Kin grinned, curled on his side, his legs bent under the jacket. JJ rested his head again on the bed's second pillow, his back to Kin. His long body poised too.

Bird kicked off her sandals. She had skimmed Kin's Buddhist book. It compared its series of meditations to the process of refining gold from ore. The first stages were bound to be—in the book's curious word— gross. She touched the knot of Kin's jacket apron, making sure it would hold. The early stages were gross, the end result pure.

"The State of Not-Self," Kin repeated, musing over the words. "Such a bad translation." He coughed. As Bird padded barefoot around the bed, Kin's voice took on his familiar gently mocking tone. "I only know one way to reach any such state, Jimmy Joe. Remember? We used to call it going, not coming. All your desires, even your body itself. Just . . . gone."

Bird stopped in front of JJ. She was wedged between the bed and stucco wall.

"I remember," JJ whispered, almost too quietly to be heard.

"'Course it only lasts a moment or so," Kin went on, sounding sleepy.

"But what doesn't?" Bird asked, her voice softened too.

"*Nada*," Kin answered. "Like the book tells us. It all depends on what you mean by. A 'moment.'"

JJ eased closer to Kin to make room for Bird. "Like the summer we were together," she whispered, curling herself on the mattress edge, her back to JJ. "Only a few months, but it's lasted and lasted. Inside Kin and me, anyhow . . ."

"And me," JJ added, his breath hot in her hair.

"We always remembered," she dared to go on. "How the three of us, together, always had this . . ."

"Grace," JJ said.

In answer, Bird moved back close enough so her ass brushed JJ's zippered crotch. Then she heard and felt Kin inch closer to JJ from his side, the mattress springs squealing and the jacket creaking. Under it all, the plastic crackled. Kin, she knew, was pressing his crotch through the leather against JJ's ass.

Bird began to rock a little, hearing the crackle. So many layers of protection needed now to do what used to be simple. Natural. She rocked harder, feeling Kin rock too. The mattress springs sounded strange, new. Always before, they had lain together on a springless futon. Bird breathed JJ's sweat, stronger than the sickly perfumed smell of Kin's body. Not fish, Bird thought now, exhaling. But oysters, rotted oysters. Behind her, JJ's body stiffened. Could he detect Kin's smell? Or was he thinking of his sweet-faced big-eyed wife? His Allie.

"C'mon," Bird murmured, trying not to sound anxious. She rolled onto her other side. Then she giggled into JJ's solemn, intently expectant face, much older than Jimmy Joe's. A computer programmer's face now. Yet the same bones showed and the same nerves were strung inside his pockmarked skin. His same lips sealed as if he were holding his breath. This has to work for Kin, Bird thought. She wanted JJ to understand by her own serious stare. It has to work.

Chastely, she kissed his flat bristled cheek. "Swans," she said, half shutting her eyes. JJ made no answer but tilted back his head, just enough. She rubbed her neck against his neck, feeling his Adam's apple fill the hollow of her throat.

JJ moaned. A sound deep in his throat like the purr in a cat. She pressed her throat harder against his and opened her eyes to meet, sideways over JJ's broad shoulder, Kin's upraised gaze. "Swans," she whispered down to Kin. He shut his eyes prayerfully hard. Bird watched him ease forward a last few creaking inches and rest his forehead between JJ's large beautifully tensed shoulder blades.

JJ gave a low gasp, as if remembering something long forgotten. Then he exhaled, a softly drawn-out vowel of pleasure.

Sighing too, her throat thoroughly warmed, Bird pulled back her head. "Remember our first time, all together?" She ran her hand over JJ's chest, feeling through his shirt his stiff nipples. He breathed in hard again. His half-lidded eyes held, now, a flicker of alarm.

On impulse, Bird covered JJ's eyes with her hand as Kin had done so long ago. "Remember Kin telling you, 'Now look'?" JJ surrendered to her his old full-lipped half smile. Bird felt his lashes brush her palm as his eyes shut. "Kin showing you, showing us how to—" She uncovered JJ's closed eyes. "See with our hands?"

Slowly, so he could stop her if he wanted, she reached down to his waist. "I promise," she whispered as she unsnapped his pants. He tensed his bent legs, but held his body still for her. "We'll stay safe, Jimmy Joe . . ." She inched his zipper down as carefully as Kin had undone her bra that first night, his fingertips barely brushing her skin. She could feel Kin hold his breath at the zipper's last notches. "Just hands," she whispered shakily. "It's safe if it's just hands. . . ."

JJ's eyes stayed shut. His breathing came steadily now as if he were concentrating. He shifted his weight so Bird could tug on his pants and his cotton briefs, pulling them halfway down. She heard Kin's own slow zipper.

"Remember the night I first touched you?" she whispered to JJ, but loud enough for Kin to hear. "Really touched you?" Balancing on one elbow, she reached behind JJ and clasped Kin's hand. "Remember," she continued, easing Kin's arm over JJ's side, "How you, Sister Kin, kinda guided me, my hand?"

"Mmm," Kin answered as she rested his palm on JJ's abdomen. JJ's shirttails half hid his mass of pubic hair, his velvety purplish balls, his shadowed cock—a dusky reddish pink, thick at its base. Bird felt the extra warmth that had made her think, years before—the word had frightened her then—*alive.*

"The only cock I've ever touched," she whispered, to JJ.

He opened his eyes. "God, Bird," he whispered back. "Why?"

She shrugged one shoulder. "There wasn't," she echoed his own words, "ever any other JJ. Never—like I told you—anyone else we both, Kin and I . . ."

JJ was nodding, his eyes closing as if he were basking in her words.

She began to hum. Kin's leather and plastic apron creaked and crackled as he pressed closer to JJ. She eased his hand down, her own curved thumb brushing JJ's cock, its grainy texture deeply familiar. Kin gave the throaty moan Bird hadn't heard for eight years. Under her hand, Kin's hand held JJ's cock. With his own lower-pitched moan, JJ began rocking to Bird's low hum. "It Had to Be You."

She released Kin's hand and embraced JJ, her breasts pressing his chest. Kin began to pump JJ's cock. Still humming, her hum vibrating in her outstretched throat, Bird kissed JJ. His mouth warmed hers, but he kept his plush lips closed.

As she pulled back, she remembered how, when Estella's tongue had filled her mouth, filled all its holes, she'd felt she knew the answer. Why we were here. She took hold of JJ's solid shoulders, feeling Kin's knuckles brush her crotch, imagining Kin's voice. To fill each other's holes, love.

Kin moaned again. Bird's fingers sank into JJ's firm flesh. All skin, Bird thought. Full of pores, holes. Kin's hand was pumping up and down between her and JJ, warming them both. Could Kin reach that moment he most wanted? Bird braced her own body. Moments of purified awareness, Kin's book had defined Buddhism to be. A stream of such moments leading to a Perfect Emptiness. Bird held her breath. Through vibrations in JJ's body, she felt Kin's hips moving. He was breathing hard, like a runner who knows just where he's going. JJ, too, was breathing hard, his eyes shut tighter, rayed with new creases. Kin's hand pumped steadily along with his hips. Bird had stopped humming, but she was still hearing her hum. She shut her eyes, the three of them sharing a smoke-tinged silence. A chapel full of candles, everybody praying.

Please, she was saying inside, gripping JJ's arms. The muscle under the meat. She held JJ steady as Kin pressed him harder from behind. Bird's heartbeat speeded with Kin's rough breaths and the singing springs, the shuddery mattress. *Please, please.* The words beat with thumps of her pulse. *Please let. Kin come.*

Leather creaked, suddenly louder than the springs. "Go," Kin breathed hoarsely from the other side of JJ.

JJ sucked in a breath. Bird gasped too, losing hold of JJ's arms as his big hips jolted forward. His hipbones swallowed hers. His chest flattened her breasts, her nipples prickling. Between her legs, Kin's hand slipped away, replaced by the bare swollen warmth of JJ's cock, its wetness seeping through her denim.

"Oh—" JJ gasped. Suddenly he'd wrapped his arms around Bird, his hands cupping her ass. As JJ held and rocked her, as heat spread inside her own skin, Bird gripped Kin's hands, his arm wedged now under JJ's rocking side. His palm coated with JJ's semen, warm and milky between them.

With strength she didn't think he had, strength he hadn't had minutes before, Kin pulled Bird toward him through JJ. Their arms bent; their bodies strained. Bird felt Kin grind against JJ's haunches, the leather and plastic crackling together. Blacksmith fire, she thought: hot enough to meld solid metal, to separate from gross ore purest gold.

JJ's Adam's apple bobbed; Bird opened her mouth and closed her lips around his throat, his bristly sweaty skin. Sucking so hard her loose tooth ached, she tightened her hold on Kin's miraculously strong bony hands. He squeezed her hands back. He gasped with a sharp inhale like silk torn.

Through JJ, Bird felt Kin's body convulse, her lips fastened to JJ's throat. Her body remembered what she'd felt last night, what she'd felt years before with JJ and Kin, what she felt Kin feel now: veins filled with air, flesh buoyant. Not coming but going, taking off.

A wet *ffwup*, and Bird had pulled back from JJ's reddened throat. Kin squeezed her hands so tightly her fingers mashed together with his. The ring of 8s dug into their interlocked fingerbones.

"Oh—" Kin gasped from behind JJ's shoulder, releasing a breath he seemed to have been holding for months. A sound both relieved and triumphant. Straining her neck, Bird saw Kin open his clenched-shut eyes, clear as black mirrors. Spilling tears Bird wasn't sure she really glimpsed, they mixed so fast with the sweat all over his face. Kin gave such quick panting breaths that she knew he had, as he used to say, gotten there. Between her body and Kin's, breathing hard too, JJ kept his eyes shut as if to give them, Kin and Bird, their privacy. The rich burned smell of JJ's sweat mixed with the sour perfumed smell of Kin's.

"Oh," Bird breathed softly to finish them off. She released Kin's hands, sure as Kin fell back against the mattress that he was breaking out in fresh sweat all over. His whole body crying.

．　．　．

After a brief shared sleep—Mexico asleep around them—Bird woke first. She untied the jacket, eased it from under Kin. She fingertip-lifted the ice bag, still wet with Kin's semen, and carried it to the trash basket. The jacket was unstained, inside. Bird draped it over the butterfly chair like a gracefully exhausted animal.

On the inner legs of Bird's jeans, JJ's semen had left a slight stain, no longer sticky. Bird thumb-rubbed it in. Then she padded into the front room. Sun heated her arms as she arranged papaya and tomatillo slices in a clay bowl painted with dancing skeletons. She heard JJ—she knew it wasn't Kin by the heaviness of the stream—piss in their tiny echoey bathroom. As water ran through the bathroom door, Bird carried the clay bowl to the bedroom doorway. She peered in at Kin's motionless body. The thought only took a second: Is he dead?

She blinked, managing to feel hope in both directions. What she wanted; what Kin might want. What better way to go? he'd say.

The bathroom door thumped; Kin stretched like his mom's long-dead Siamese cats, like his body was savoring what had happened. Bird set the bowl beside Kin. JJ stood in the doorway, his arms folded. His eyes held their ocean colors, each equally strong: green, gray, blue. Slowly, he stepped in the room, moving as if his limbs, like hers, felt warm and loose. Meeting Kin's gaze, he swallowed. Under JJ's languidly bobbing Adam's apple, Bird saw the red mark left by her mouth.

They sat on the bed: Bird cross-legged at the foot and Kin reclining on his pillows and JJ leaning on the headboard, his legs stretched beside Kin's. They talked as they ate, Bird chewing around her bad tooth. She and Kin told JJ about their travels, the best places: Zé's farm in Brazil; the Quingping market in Guangzhou. The 1000-year-old eggs, the twitching bundles of frogs. The Cantonese chefs who could make anything delectable. Like Kin, Bird added, describing to JJ the campfire meals Kin had invented. Tomato and fruit juices dripped down their chins. Their hands grew sticky with wiping. The low ceiling made the room feel like a cave. Bird fetched a six-pack of Tecate and they toasted 8/8/88, their year of marriage. Kin's wrist wobbled but he raised his full can himself.

JJ eyed Carlos's guitar in its corner. He told Kin how he'd played electric guitar with a college band named Box of Anger, eying long-haired boys but going after the girls. How he wound up cleaning up among college girls by playing Unlicensed Therapist, drawing them out. A Sensitive Guy, they called him.

Kin smiled wryly. "We taught you well," he murmured, resting again on his pillows. Bird bent forward to hear him. "—so grat-i-fying to see my former pupils doing so well." He gave a gusty sigh. Bird giggled. "Take Jimmy Joe here," Kin told her, lifting his Tecate. "Sounds like he's had a great past as a—" Kin sipped slowly, as if determining the beer's flavor. "Semi-straight dude with a tantalizing twist." JJ surrendered to them both another full-lipped smile. "And Berta Bird. You've got a great *future* as a—born-again lesbian." Kin sank deeper into his pillows. "Oh Berta. I see you causing epic brawls in butch bars. . . ."

Bird shook her head. "I don't know," she murmured to her lap, the ghostly white stain at her crotch. "I don't wanna think too far ahead. Not today."

She turned to JJ. As she breathed in, she knew that JJ too must be catching Kin's sickly smell under the wilting gardenias. "So tell us about—Allie."

"Alice." He gave a sigh so plainly guilty Bird felt a twinge of guilt too. "Alice Ann. This's the first time I've ever." JJ drained his second can. "Cheated on her."

"Truly?" Kin murmured. Bird handed JJ a third can. She didn't need more than one to feel high now. And Kin, she knew, couldn't handle more than one.

"She was—" JJ's voice softened. Guilty again, tender too. "A virgin when I met her. My first since. You, Bird."

"And you liked that, right?" Kin turned his head on his pillow, facing JJ. Sister Kin, Bird thought. The original Unlicensed Therapist.

"Yeah." JJ lowered his eyes. "I did. I felt like: this one's mine."

"Oh Jimmy Joe." Kin sighed, mockingly affectionate. "You *are* such a boy."

"It even felt, in a way—between Allie and me—almost like with us three. In that we, she and I. We were like two kids . . ."

"Play-ing," Kin mumbled. His favorite verb, Bird thought with a smile.

"Playing." JJ set his beer on Kin's paperback mystery. "The thing about Allie was, is—" His long-fingered hands made a circle, holding an invisible globe. "She's so—amazed by everything. I call her Alice in Wonder."

Bird nodded a little stiffly, remembering the dim bathroom in Ko No's, the soft clean touch of Allie's lips. "She's got those wide eyes . . ."

JJ nodded. "And in bed, even after four years together, she always seems, I don't know—surprised, somehow."

Bird looked at her lap. JJ leaned back as if he couldn't believe all he was finding himself saying. Then he rallied a summarizing tone. "Alice— she's curious about everything but scared of everything too."

"Like you." Sister Kin gave his scratchy cough.

"Like me." JJ swallowed more Tecate. "Right from the start, I felt . . . safe with her. Everything showed on her face. She was so clear. I knew her, what she was, and I—" He made a square with his fingers and connected thumbs. "Love her more *coherently* than I've ever loved anyone."

Bird swallowed warm beer, the sun hot on her back. "But what's she *like*?"

JJ's vividly green eyes gleamed. "She's smart. Always trying to be 'good,' trying to figure out what's the, you know, right thing to do. Not that she always does it. She's got a strong will. She's into control though she doesn't know it, doesn't admit it. And she's—" JJ made this last word defiantly flat. "—sweet."

" 'Sweet'?" Kin echoed with his old audible quotation marks.

JJ ignored him, still answering Bird. "She works with poor kids in New Haven, likes that kind of thing. She used to work with, Jesus, violent mentally retarded people till it got too rough. Worked for a place called Helping Hands."

Kin cracked a thin smile from his pillows.

"Allie's into liberal politics. Big time. She got me started watching the news, which I never used to do. But it's turned out to be fun, a sort of game. Addictive."

Bird stared blankly, trying to remember the last newspaper she'd read.

"It—the news—feels like this porthole we watch on the outside world, with us huddled together inside. . . ."

"Safe." Bird braced her hands on the mattress as if it were starting to rock. "Nice and safe." She looked around the little bedroom. This house was about to disappear out from under them. Carlos's lover was due back in a week. Bird blinked at JJ's unreadable face, older now that the room was brighter.

"'Course," JJ went on. "Hearing that phone message a year ago and going to Ko No's and seeing that photo you sent, that Pan Am pass—you never should've sent those, Bird—and reading your letters with me, then finding out from me I was coming here . . . all that. As they say at Mass. Mental, it's freaked her out."

"I bet." Kin stretched. Avoiding JJ's eyes, Bird began clanking cans into the clay bowl. She'd have to clean up this mess before they left. *If* they left, with JJ.

"And I try to understand how much she's been hurt by this, but." JJ shook his head. "The way she's been acting, re-acting. It's only made *me* feel more . . ."

"Trapped?" Bird filled in. "That's what you wrote us you were feeling."

JJ nodded, adding, "It's not just Allie. It's. Yale too, whether I even want this goddamn degree. Who I'd have to work for, to get it. Who'd own me. That's made me want all the more to break away somehow, run off to—I've kept imagining it—you two. And Allie's been so tense and distracted herself this year, when usually I count on her to be the sensible one, the one who keeps *me*—calm."

"Keeps you on the straight and narrow?" Kin covered his mouth to cough.

Still avoiding JJ's eyes, Bird turned to her jacket and dug a lemon drop from its pocket. "So you had—pneumonia?" JJ asked awkwardly as Kin's cough subsided. Not wanting, Bird noted, to discuss further his straight and narrow wife.

"Oh, please." Kin wiped his mouth. *"Por favor,* Jimmy Joe." He cracked Bird's lemon drop. "Let's talk." Another candy crack. "About *any*thing else."

"Estoy de acuerdo." Bird lifted again the clay bowl of cans. "So what *did* you decide about the Big Y, Jimmy Joe? *Are* you going back there?"

"This September." JJ nodded. "I hadn't wanted to, but then all of a sudden there wasn't any choice. I'm relieved in a way that there wasn't. Isn't. See." JJ turned from Bird to Kin. "Allie and I are going to have a baby."

"What?" Bird backed up, a can clanking from her bowl. "She got *pregnant?"*

JJ blinked at her over Kin. "Not in secret, if that's what you mean."

"But it's—what she wanted?"

"I wanted it too, in a way." JJ gave her a cooler gray-green stare. "I want it."

Kin broke in with an incredulous choked-sounding: "A *baby?"*

Bird lifted the fallen Tecate can and slipped out the doorway. Two steps into the front room, she stopped, straining to hear Kin's confidential murmur.

"—some-times wonder, Jim Joe, if we, if I complicated things. In your life . . ."

She knew from the way his voice trailed that Kin was already worn out by this day. That he'd need lots of rest to recover. But, she thought, where?

". . . think I wanted things complicated," JJ was telling Kin. "Knew they would be, our first night even—"

"So you—" Kin gave a guttural cough. "That first night, you did *want*—?"

Bird heard mattress springs squeak. JJ taking Kin's hand? JJ's voice stayed matter-of-fact. "Listen, Kin. Because I was, you know, curious. And because I found you, both of you, so. God. Attractive, fascinating." JJ's voice slowed. "Because it—what I already felt for you two, that first night—was the first of my life, love." He paused. "Well, sure. Of course. You know I wanted it."

Springs squeaked, someone standing. Someone else rolling over. Bird rinsed the skeleton bowl in the metal kitchen sink. Behind her, she heard JJ's tread. He stomped at something—a cockroach?—and Bird faced him, her hands dripping.

"Kin's asleep." JJ studied her face. She blinked, feeling the prickly half-lashes she'd gotten used to. "God, Bird," JJ mumbled, beer on his breath. "You mentioned your eyes in your letters, but. *What* the hell'd you do to your—?"

"Lashes? Chopped 'em off. Thought they'd never grow back. But they did, but only halfway." She shrugged. "I've kinda figured it out. There's things you can do to yourself that your body just won't forgive. Not all the way."

JJ nodded down at her. She took hold of his wrist. 11:46 by his watch.

"So." She squeezed his watchband, screwing up her courage. "You said before you wanted to help us. And we—we need, for starters, a ride over the border. We're ready. Kin wrote a long letter thanking Carlos. I cleaned house for your visit and we always pack fast. . . ."

JJ's chin moved again: a slower nod. Bird released his wrist.

"This house is way too small for four. Carlos or his lover'd drive us if we waited. But, see, where would they take us? We need, y'know, a place to stay. In the States. Till I can find a job or something. . . ." JJ gave a Tecate-smelling sigh. But Bird pushed on. "You're in—Alice's parents' house now? It *is*, like, a house?"

JJ's hickey darkened along with his face. "It's—complicated. Allie's

mother and grandmother live there. And shouldn't Kin, won't he consider—a hospital?"

"No." Bird shook her head. "No, JJ. In that Ciuad Juarez hospital,
after his bronchoscopy—this tube thrust down his windpipe, sucking
out his lungs—Kin looked . . . he looked like he did after that BU student, the one who paid him and. Forced something metal inside him."
JJ touched her bare shoulder, meeting her gaze. "Kin hates feeling—
invaded. He made me promise no more hospitals. . . ."

JJ pressed her shoulder. His voice came out lower, more confiding.
"Look, it's Allie's parents' house and I can't say what I could do for you
there but—"

"You mean," Bird cut in with a challenging edge. "What Allie'd *let*
you do?"

At this, JJ lowered his hand from her shoulder. He straightened so
his mussed curly hair flattened against the ceiling. He was, as Kin had
said, such a boy.

"Sor-ry," Bird told him, her own voice unsteady. "I know we've already caused lots of trouble between you and her. And we don't mean
to. We know this's hard for you. But it's just—" She shot a glance to the
half-closed bedroom door. "Nothing's hard, really, compared to. Sister
Kin. What Kin's going through."

JJ nodded quickly. "Jesus, I wish I had money of my own. Our credit
cards are all charged up and I should've been working this summer, a
real job—"

"But you weren't," Bird interrupted. He wiped his forehead, his
elbow bumping a wood skeleton on the wire spice rack. Its head vibrated on its springy neck, tapping a brazenly orange jar of chili powder. "So what're you gonna *do*?"

JJ looked from the tiny leering skeleton head to Bird's face. "'Course
I'll drive you over the border," he began, his voice still low as if Kin
shouldn't hear this too.

"And drop us—drop Kin—by the side of the road?" Bird asked more
loudly yet more shakily. Window sun was burning her back, her spotted
shoulders. A panicky flutter was rising in her throat. Couldn't Jimmy
Joe see that pulse?

His eyes scanned the window. Master of the Fast Fade, Bird remembered, tensing her arms as if to block him. He looked down. "Guess
since there's no phone," he muttered to the cracked tile floor. "I can't
call Alice before we—go."

Bird waited till JJ raised his ocean eyes. Then she agreed. "No."

· · ·

Loving Is Living in Sunny Douglas, Arizona. Bird read that sign as the Zephyr rolled by. And she laughed out loud, the border behind them at last. They'd shuffled Kin through Customs, Kin propped between them in his clean loose-fitting traveler clothes. She'd been afraid they wouldn't be let back in. But it had turned out to be simpler than entering other countries. A flash of their battered passports, a mumbled *U.S. citizen.* The bored-looking guard had patted their wooly hastily packed Brazilian bags. Now JJ was driving them through downtown Douglas. They passed the solemn adobe Mission of the Loving Shepherd and its more dilapidated cinder-block neighbor, House of Amedra: Sober Living.

"This's a schizophrenic town," Bird told JJ as they stopped for gas in front of a red and yellow sign: *Sí aceptamos pesos/ Yes, we accept pesos.*

Through the stark outskirts of Douglas, Kin slept in the back. Bird stared out the window as she'd done when they rolled into any new country. Skin here looked bleached—tanned or reddened white faces mixed with the brown faces she'd grown used to—and English letters on signs looked spiky, daunting.

Coronado Motel. An orange three-tiered crown of metal rose from its flat roof. Then open highway surrounded by scrub brush and cacti like Mexican roads. Only here lines were clearly painted and signs held black numbers.

"Look Kin—speed limits!" Bird called out over the hot wind. They'd opened the windows since air conditioning made Kin shiver. JJ flipped on the radio. Blankly, Bird listened to a Mexican version of "Sugar, Sugar" by the Archies, maracas rattling. Kin would've laughed. Young male voices sang the English words carefully, sounding them out. *Ch-Hon-ey hon-ey; Ah, Shoo-guh shoo-guh!*

"Christ." JJ switched to American rock. Bird settled into her traveler's trance in the *Blowing-Dust Area.* The ground looked charred from recent fire. JJ sat beside her as silently as Estella last night, driving her home. An old man had peered from his house as Estella's Bonneville had chugged by. He'd shaken his head as if saying what Bird once overheard a man at the dog track say in Spanish: *Poor Señorita Estella, a woman who has—what could be worse?—no children.*

Bird sighed into the dusty wind. As Estella had rocked the Bonneville to a stop, Bird had leaned over to kiss her good-bye. But Estella nodded toward Carlos's house as if to say Bird's husband might see. Or to say Kin was simply too close for them to kiss. Estella took Bird's hand, though. She stroked with her strong thumb Bird's 8 ring, as if to say she understood—Bird felt now Estella was right, though not quite the way she imagined—that Kin was the one Bird loved.

Bird side-glanced again at JJ, his intent bony profile. *Men always need t'be, after,* she'd heard her mother say once on the phone. *Alone.* Bird yawned. Her mother had reserved her softest voice for her women friends. Bird hugged her arms. Now that she was back in the States, was she going to start thinking of Mother, again? More often than never? Even that prospect seemed unalarming.

She leaned on the vinyl seatback—comfortable, this Zephyr—and shut her eyes. Songs jostled in the wind. "Fast Car" and "Big-Boned Gal" and "What's Love Got to Do with It?" Drifting off, Bird contemplated the elements of her satisfaction. Her body was relaxed from coming with Estella last night; from feeling so vividly Kin come; from feeling JJ's longed-for body pressed to hers, the burned taste of his neck still on her lips. And from—she half smiled as she dozed—being on the move again now, rushing forward into who knew what.

16

This Is a Test

Gringo Imperialism, Allie typed with tense fingers on Dad's ratchety old Royal. In his former study, she stared from the old-fashioned typewriter to the wall clock—4:25—then to the blank screen of JJ's pushed-aside Mac. As the mercilessly sunny afternoon had stretched on without word, she had kept busy. *General Noriega has never truly threatened the Panama Canal*, she typed slowly, her fingers rusty at this. She sipped her milk and smoothed her favorite—no, JJ's favorite—maternity top. Its dusky pink brought out her healthy-looking summer tan, what JJ deemed her peaches-and-blood complexion. She shifted, remembering JJ easing up the loose top to see her white belly beneath.

She squinted at Dad's scrawl: his first letter to the editor composed at Desert View, inspired by the *Arizona Republic* (The Repulsive, Jo called it) urging Bush to invade Panama as Reagan had invaded Grenada. Allie checked the clock yet again. Mom was due back from Desert View by suppertime—six sharp for her, forever—and Allie had been practically praying JJ would get home first.

The United States had sufficient force on hand to protect U.S. citizens in Grenada, Allie typed. *Then-President Reagan made a*—She held Dad's yellow notebook page up in the late sun. A hyphenated word starting with "s." The page shook in her hand. She set it down and looked around at the bookcases Jo and Mom had emptied hours ago, not mentioning that they'd counted on JJ to help. 4:28. Allie picked up the photo cube Mom had placed on the desk like a memorial.

Allie's vision blurred as she studied Dad in his Louisville garden, striking an American Gothic pose with his hoe, delivering his earnest Jimmy Carter stare. The dinner-table dad who expected his daughters' good grades, good behavior. Was that the right thing to do, Alice? Dad had asked in a disappointed voice when she'd skipped gym class, forging notes. *Alice Ann*, Alice had written in Mother's round wavery hand, *is still too weak to tumble*. Sniffling, Allie flipped the cube to the most recent shot, last Christmas. Dad sat propped on the hospital bed in his sick room in this house, his oxygen tank at his side. His smile was wry and weary, his eyebrows raised like Dukakis's brows in the last campaign weeks when Duke took on a what-the-Hell jauntiness. Fighting a lost battle.

Dying, like the Kin man. Allie blinked free her lukewarm tears. On and off all day, she'd cried. She wiped her eyes, wishing she could talk to Dad now, ask his advice, hear his gruff repentant-smoker voice. His carefully considered words, slowed further these days by pills. She glanced up from the photo cube.

4:31 and still plenty of sun left. Home before dark, JJ'd promised. A five-hour drive. What the hell could he—they—be doing out there? For the hundredth time, she told herself that JJ and Kin wouldn't *join, truly join* through sex. That JJ wouldn't put himself at risk. But Bird had claimed there were ways that were "safe." Did she mean Kin watching her and JJ? Alice set down the photo cube, hard. Hating Bird for her long-distance seductions.

Allie blinked, seeing Dad's hyphenated word from a fresh angle. *Self-serving decision,* she typed. Her fingers moved rapidly over Dad's rousing last line: *In the names of the millions of dead in Vietnam, El Salvador, and Grenada, when will we stop "saving" oppressed people by destroying them?*

She unratcheted the letter, her mind skipping ahead. What the Hell could she do next? Anything but watch the—4:36—clock. She was folding Dad's letter into thirds when she heard the distant back-door rattle.

"Grandma?" Allie called out, stiffening up. Central air hummed.

Grandma's raspy voice carried from the kitchen. "Alice—"

"What?" Allie heaved herself up and padded fast down the hall. In her rib cage, a bubble of fear began expanding like the bubble the day of Mom's accident, when Mom had been so strangely late picking her up. That long-ago dentist's waiting room had emptied out till only eleven-year-old Alice was left, pacing by a glass case of plaster molds, patients' jaws. Pairs marked *Before* and *After.*

"A *cah*—" Grandma called. "A cah! Just pulled in the *drive*-way." She turned from the half-open back door, holding her walker, her arms pale as raw chicken meat. She'd changed into her afternoon muumuu.

"OK, OK, I'll go see." Allie brushed by Grandma and stepped into the oven air of the garage. She steadied herself on her and JJ's dusty U-Haul boxes.

Before and *After* Alice had read over and over till Dad showed up in the empty waiting room. Mother, he told her carefully, had a little accident. Allie forced open the garage door. No, she told herself then as now, blinking at the dusty Zephyr in the driveway. Behind windshield glare, two heads were visible.

No. Allie hovered in the doorway. No; couldn't be. From the half dark, she watched JJ climb out of the driver's seat. As if deeply dazed too, he straightened in slow motion, his tall shadow stretching the length of the driveway. He slammed the Zephyr door. As he turned to the garage, one of his Night of the Living Id songs flashed absurdly through Allie's mind. *Where'd you stay last night? Your hair's gone crazy babe, an' your dress don't fit you right.*

"JJ–?" she gasped, half hoping this wild-haired unsteadily moving man wasn't him. And she stepped out, concrete burning her feet. She squinted at the car to see—yes—a white-blond head. Sun spots swam around JJ as he stopped in front of Allie. His sweat carried a taste of something foreign.

He stared down as if he'd staggered out of a flaming airplane and couldn't begin to describe what all had happened. Bending, he took hold of her shoulders, his hands hot and strong. His vividly bloodshot eyes met hers. "I'm sorry; I—I'll explain everything later. But I had to bring them here—"

"Them?" she choked. The Zephyr's passenger door swung open. With the abrupt grace Allie remembered from Ko No's, the Bird woman climbed out in the sunlight: strikingly tanned, skinnier but stronger-looking. Her hair burned white like the bleached-out desert grasses that lined highways here.

"Alice Ann?" Grandma called faintly. The Bird woman bent into the rear seat. Ignoring Grandma, Allie watched JJ's back retreat as he strode to the car.

Sun heated her hair, her part line. She squinted, struck by the way JJ and Bird moved together. They shared, she realized dizzily, that abrupt grace. Bird held the door, her arm brushing JJ as he bent. OK, so they moved like lovers. But—Allie found her own thought ridiculous—at least she's a woman.

"Wore himself out," Bird seemed to be saying to JJ.

From the rear seat, a third head rose. JJ's shoulder blades stood out like wings as he lifted a body. The body, Allie told herself numbly, for it seemed dead, limp limbed. She gripped the garage doorway. JJ held the Kin man like a bride. Kin's black-haired head bobbed and his feet in black slippers dangled.

Allie felt her baby kick. Kin's face gave off a pasty sheen. His hair hung down like Spanish moss, dull even in this sun. His head lolled on JJ's shoulder as JJ stepped forward. Allie lurched back into the garage, onto a sticky patch of oil. JJ carried Kin in, trailing smells of what she imagined to be spicy Mexican dust.

Bird followed the men, a leather jacket—shiny and new—draped on her arm. Allie stared at Bird's shoulder, splotched with brown. Birthmarks? Bird gazed around the garage as if she'd never seen such a building. Then her stare raked Allie's body. Sun had burned the blue out of her eyes. Or maybe her tanned face made her eyes so fiercely pale, lashes spiky white.

Allie hugged her belly, hearing JJ's monotone. "—use that *hospital bed?*"

"Wha—?" Grandma wobbled in the kitchen doorway.

"These're JJ's *friends*." Unsteadily, Allie stepped across the garage floor.

"Friends?" Grandma rasped back, frankly disbelieving.

" 'Scuse us," Allie heard JJ say. As she stopped behind Grandma, she saw JJ's back disappear into the renovated rec room. Dad's sick room. Allie rested a hand on Grandma's dowager's hump. Skinny Bird slipped by, brushing Allie, then disappearing into the sick room too. The door swung half shut behind her.

"Let me help." Grandma's elbows rose. Laboriously, she began maneuvering her walker toward the rec-room door.

"Wait." Allie took hold of Grandma's puckered elbow, folds of crepey skin.

"No, no—" A voice from the sick room called. A nasal man's voice.

"No, it's not *real*," Bird's voice cut in. "Not a real *hospital—*"

Allie steered Grandma by the elbow. "That man's named Kin," she managed as Grandma Hart clanked into the kitchen. "JJ's s-sick friend."

"Make some tea," Grandma muttered, sounding as dazed as everyone else.

"What?" Alice asked. Kin is in Dad's bed, she thought. Needing a doctor?

"He, you." Grandma clanked purposefully toward the stove range. "Ice tea."

Allie splashed sink water on her face, splattering her pink top. Kin in Dad's bed and Mom on her way home. Too exhausted to face that crowded sick room, Allie sank down at the table. She stared out the sunny window at the pool, the lawn chairs. She watched the pool cleaner chug its ceaseless circles.

A sprinkler for Mom's bougainvillea spurted a rhythmic half circle, sparkling the window. As Grandma bustled behind her, Allie remembered Dad's long-ago wild drive from the dentist's. How guiltily glad she'd felt to be alive, especially alive just then, the windshield wipers throbbing as hard as her own pulse. Now, silent behind glass, the sprinkler throbbed with her more fitful pulse. Now too, Allie thought with each beat: What next? What next?

·   ·   ·

"Wha'd she say?" Bird whispered to JJ. Now that they'd settled Kin onto the metal-railed hospital bed—Kin's eyes shut as JJ cranked up the bed, Kin embarrassed that JJ'd seen his confusion—Kin had sunk into another doze. His mouth hung open; his face looked even more than usually stunned.

"What?" JJ touched Bird's bare arm lightly, maybe incredulously. Then he blinked at the air-conditioned wood-paneled room.

Bird hugged herself in the same all-surrounding chill that used to freeze her bones on temp jobs. She stared at her brown feet in her worn Mexican sandals, strangely attached to freshly vacuumed carpet. Then she stared up—far up—to JJ. Her voice felt dwarfed by the refrigerated room.

"Your wife. You told her something when we pulled in. Did you ask her about us—" She swallowed, her throat dry as if from Thorazine. "Staying?"

"No. Jesus." JJ wiped his pinkly tanned face. How could he sweat in this chill? "'Course I didn't, right off. I told you this house isn't mine, Bird. Isn't even Allie's. And you see Allie. You know what a shock this must be for her. All this when she's—" He switched to a harsh whisper. "Six months *pregnant*."

Bird gripped her rib cage harder, wanting to stall the sinking sensation in her chest. She studied the carpet, neat threads of olive green and beige. Of course he hadn't asked, she told herself. 'Course not. Abruptly, Bird turned her back on JJ and sleeping Kin. She lifted her jacket from the rocking chair by the bed and shrugged it on over her chilled skin.

"Hey," JJ called as she strode to the half-open door. But she pushed out, feeling JJ follow hurriedly. To protect his Allie? Bird stepped onto waxed tile. In the door frame, JJ hesitated as if the kitchen held a radioactive force field.

Swiveling her head, Bird followed JJ's gaze to the old lady hunched by the stove, a metal crutch-thing at her side, then to Alice herself, sitting at a table, facing what Bird remembered was called a picture window. In the late sun, Alice's brown hair shone with gold. She turned her head. Bird pushed back her own hair, bleached and unkempt, chopped too bluntly.

"Bird?" Alice asked over her poised shoulder. Her heart-shaped face glowed with a managed tan; her wide dark brown eyes shone with tears or health or both. Bird gave an abrupt delayed nod. "What do you want?"

As Bird drew a breath—what the Hell could she say?—the old lady by the stove cracked a tray of ice. Bird turned gratefully, smelling something familiar.

"Tea?" She stepped toward the hunched-over lady in the loose Mexican-style dress. "Kin—he *lives* on tea—"

Bird fumbled to lift the ice tray from her blue-veined hands. "*Perdóneme.*" Ice popped as she dropped chips into tea the old lady poured. Her grip on the teakettle looked strong. Her glasses glinted like knives. Bird smelled her own sweat under her jacket. She hadn't used deodorant in ages. Lifting another fistful of ice, she glanced over her leather shoulder. JJ now rested his hand on his wife's shoulder. They posed for an old-fashioned portrait, lit from behind by sun. Allie's eyes looked huge. Alice in Wonder, Bird remembered JJ saying.

"Or shall I pour some hot? Hot tea or Sun Tea is bet-tuh in this heat. . . ."

The old lady's New England accent reminded Bird of Boston. She shook her head, groping for English as if it, not Spanish, were her second language.

"I am a nurse, you know." Allie's grandma confided to the teapot.

"You are?" Bird asked. The grandma nodded.

"And what *is* the diag-nosis on your . . . friend . . . ?"

Bird bent to the grandma's ear, its flesh-colored curl of plastic. Was Alice listening too? "Pneumonia about a mouth ago. And the doctor in Mexico thought he might be developing cancer of the esoph-a-gus. Though he—Kin, my husband—wouldn't let them run tests to see for sure. . . ."

How awful, Allie's grandmother said plainly with the click of her tongue.

"Ahr you, you two—" She nodded at Bird's jacket. "Chilly, in here?"

"Think Kin might be. In that cold room, with only his sheet and all."

"Well, I'll fetch a light quilt." The old lady turned to grip her four-legged metal crutch. At the table, as if snapped out of a trance, Alice protested.

"No, no, Grandma, *I* can do that—"

"No," The Grandma rasped back in a voice meant to be obeyed. She clanked her crutch forward. "No, Alice Ann. You—you three—you go *talk.*"

Clank, clank, clank. Bird watched the grandma's hunched back retreat into the carpeted den. Yet another room in this house big enough for three families.

"Ber-ta?" Kin's peevish sleepy voice called from the back room. "Bird?"

Seizing one glass, Bird hurried to the kitchen doorway. JJ and his wife sat frozen in their portrait pose. "Kin won't know where he is—"

Lukewarm tea sloshed Bird's hand as she shouldered open the wood door, heavier than any she'd opened in months. She let more tea slosh the carpet as she walked fast over to Kin, hearing a muffled chair scrape back in the kitchen.

"*Tranquilizarse*." Bird bent beside Kin's cranked-up bed. He had raised his head, his eyes wildly bright. "We're here at—Jimmy Joe's."

"I *know*." Kin's head sank down. He shut his eyes, maybe trying to hide his confusion. "An' when're we leav-ing?" he asked in a drifty half-asleep voice. Bird took a big slurp of tea then set the glass on the empty nightstand.

"I'm hoping we're staying," she whispered, hearing movement outside the door. In answer, Kin opened and rolled his eyes.

"Too bad Carlos's house's so small," he murmured, surprising Bird. Had he always spoken Carlos's name with such tenderness? Did Kin, Bird wondered in a confused rush, want to stay here half as badly as she did? His eyes drifted shut again. "Felt great t'be in that car, Berta Bird." He licked his dry lips, maybe struggling to stay lucid. "I'm sleep-y now but I feel so. Good after this morning, I wanna. Get moving again—" He coughed as the door squeaked open behind them. "We've already said good-bye. T' Jimmy Joe . . ."

JJ's voice interrupted Kin's. "He all right?" Bird stared over her shoulder. Her jacket felt much too warm but she didn't want to take it off. "Is he?" JJ repeated in a new tone, almost fucking fatherly. He led his wife into the room, holding her crooked elbow and guiding the small of her back.

"Sure," Bird answered in flat imitation of JJ. "Kin's hunky-dory."

JJ nodded like he had no memory of David Bowie, the songs they'd made love to. "Hunky Dory" and "Lady Stardust," drums thumping as their bodies contorted.

"Is he asleep?" JJ's wife whispered to JJ, advancing with careful bare-foot steps. But Bird detected her grandmother in the determined set of her jaw.

"Maybe," Bird told her, alarmed to see Kin's eyes sealed shut.

JJ set the cushioned rocking chair a few feet from the bed. Allie sank into it with a tense sigh. JJ rested his hand again on her shoulder. He and Allie faced Bird and Kin. Two against two, Bird thought. Allie's eyes flickered from JJ to them and back. Knitting them together. From the wall, family photos watched.

Allie spoke first, in a clear though wavery voice. "Y'know." Her eyes sought Bird's. "I—I thought that when we—JJ and I—came out here, out west, we were getting away from you two. . . ." JJ's hand tightened on her shoulder.

Bird twisted her ring of 8s. "Well," she answered quietly. "Jimmy Joe, he knew we were out here, in Mexico. . . ."

"I know he knew," this Alice cut in, sure of herself.

"—so we," Bird went on unsteadily. "Kin and me, I guess you think we sorta. Snuck up on you . . ." From behind, she didn't finish. Suddenly, anything she might say seemed crude, taunting. Kin was breathing as if falling asleep. Bird watched Alice glance up at the red mark under JJ's Adam's apple. She had a good angle on her husband's hickey. She narrowed her eyes, her own throat curved. JJ was right; everything showed openly on this woman's face, her body.

"What all *hap*pened down there?" JJ's wife stopped rocking and pointed straight at the hickey. "In Mexico." Her voice sounded older, coldly commanding. "Tell me the truth, JJ; I *mean* it."

He swallowed, his Adam's apple bobbing over his suddenly plain-as-day hickey. Bird tensed her legs. She wanted to back away, but couldn't leave Kin alone with them. JJ's face darkened under his slight suntan. "I—will, Alice. I'll tell you." He lowered his voice. "But not—now. I can't stand here with them here and—it's too." His fingers spread to indicate things too complex for words. When really, Bird thought, it had been so simple, what they'd done.

"*Tell* me," Alice insisted, sharp-eyed and sharp-voiced as her grandma. Then she shot a glance at Kin and Bird as if to freeze them in place, witnesses.

"Look." JJ kept his voice low. "We met in a house in Mexico. Kin was—lying on his bed. And Bird and I, we were . . ."

"Helping Hands," Kin murmured as if in deep sleep. Bird gaped at him.

"Sister Kin—" she gasped, shocked. Hadn't that been a name JJ had mentioned, Allie's old employer? Bird squeezed Kin's bone-thin upper arm, grateful in a way for his what-the-Hell boldness. Or was he confused, half dreaming? These days, when tired, he slipped in and out of semi-sleep. Now, Kin sucked his breath as if waking. Anxiously, Bird watched JJ bend to Allie's ear.

"—nothing at all dangerous," he was assuring her. Alice shifted her stare to Bird's hand on Kin's arm, studying that hand. "Al?" JJ knelt at her side, the rocking chair lurching with his motion. "Allie, you OK?"

Kin gave a throaty cough. Bird reached for his iced tea. "*¿Está bien?*" She propped up Kin's head so he could slurp. He swallowed, darting his eyes at JJ and Allie as if to ask: what are they saying? And what the Hell did *I* say?

"—just talking together at first," JJ was saying behind Bird in a low quick voice. "And," he went on, slowing his words. "We, I mean Bird and I . . ."

"What?" Alice demanded. Bird turned to see JJ shaking his head.

"Look. After Bird and Kin and I talked." He shook his head again, like he couldn't go on. Drawing in her own breath, Bird admired the way Alice didn't blink. "After that, Bird asked me to lie beside Kin on the bed. Just to lie down near him. And then, well--then we were lying there, the three of us and . . ."

"All Hell broke loose?" JJ's wife asked in a harsh but steady voice.

"Hea-ven," Kin mumbled from the bed. Bird felt everyone stare along with her at Kin's sallow face, his eyes closed again. "All heaven. Broke loose."

His cough erupted. Protectively, Bird stepped in front of him. JJ's wife craned to see Kin's contorted face, her own face frozen but not in surprise.

"Stop—" Bird told Alice above Kin's wet coughs. "Stop *watching* him— he's exhausted and. Can't you see?" Cool air hummed. Suddenly Bird hated Alice for this waste of an all-American house that she'd never let Kin stay in, now. Kin coughed harder, his deep phlegmy cough. Bird lifted her hands, feeling her own what-the-Hell boldness. "Can't you see Kin needs—*rest*? A place to rest?"

Turning away from them, JJ's wife fumbled at her side with a box of Kleenex. "God," she said to JJ over Kin's cough. "Should we call a *doctor*—?"

"Let me." JJ reached across Alice, plucking the tissue she'd half torn.

"No." She snatched the tissue from his hand and pulled herself up. The rocker rocked behind her as she stepped slowly toward the bed, Bird backing away. She watched Alice bend as if overbalanced by her belly. Kin, his cough subsiding, looked up at Alice as he took the tissue. Their eyes met and each gave the slightest of nods. Like, Bird thought, opposing generals at a peace talk.

"Thanks," Kin mumbled, wiping his mouth. "Can't help that, these days," he added hoarsely. And Bird wondered if he was referring to his words, too.

Alice nodded again at Kin. JJ stepped up beside her. With the coordination of a longtime couple, she sank sideways and he gathered her against his chest. Her glossy hair hid her face. JJ began steering her from the bedside. Hurriedly, Bird stepped into their place, propping Kin's pillows behind him.

"OK," Alice said, surprisingly loud. Bird and Kin both turned their heads to see Alice pull away from JJ. She tried to steady herself by holding the back of the rocker. As it rocked, Allie wobbled, but caught her own balance. "OK, look," she told JJ, holding up one hand to keep him from taking her arm again. "We've got to talk. Alone." She turned toward the door.

"Call for me if he needs anything," JJ told Bird. And he added, maybe to everyone in the room, "Sorry." He followed his wife to the cold room's doorway. Bird met his eyes—*sorry*, he was really saying now—and felt, too, sharp-eyed Alice take in their exchange of glances. She stepped out of the room first, then JJ. The door thumped, closing Kin and Bird inside. But Bird felt as she watched Allie's jarred rocker rock to a halt that she and Kin were, all at once, outside.

· · ·

"I told Jo," was the first thing Allie said behind the bedroom door. She turned from JJ unsteadily, her feet still sticky with garage oil. Her skin still vibrated with the energy that had charged the air among the four of them. She sank onto the bed, her side, going on before JJ could say again—as he seemed about to—he was sorry. "Told her almost everything. Except that Kin's sick."

JJ nodded. His bony sunburned face looked unfamiliar, raw like Bird's. His large hands hung down empty. Allie clasped her hands below her belly. "Told her, too, that I—read Bird's last letters. Dug them out of your strongbox last night. I'd glimpsed something airmail in there and you left it unlocked—"

"Lost the key in our move," he mumbled, sounding surprised yet resigned. The way she'd felt in the sick room, hearing what had happened in Mexico. "Guess maybe I wanted you to read them. To get some idea, maybe—"

"I did. And I've been *trying* to—understand you three. What's made you feel—Bird's letters say *you* wrote this—trapped. But—God." Allie's voice both faltered and deepened. "I'll n-*never* understand what you did today—"

"Al." JJ knelt by the bed. She jerked away as he touched her shoulder.

"Don't you dare." She swallowed hard, keeping control. "God. Seeing you all together just now, feeling all this—I don't know—intensity between you and them. Knowing, now, you went to *bed* with them today. God, JJ." She raised both hands. "If 'nothing was ever like' what you had—have—with them, then get the Hell *away* from me—" Alice pushed him but he gripped her hands firmly.

"Listen to me, Al. I won't to lie to you. Anymore." She blinked, too struck by his slow, even voice to pull back. "I should've told you all about them years ago. It was too important not to tell. I shouldn't have kept them—the way I guess I liked keeping them—to myself. And I shouldn't have hidden so much these past months—when, yeah, I have been feeling trapped." His face blurred as tears burned her eyes. "But to understand anything about that, anything about today, you've gotta understand. How. Back then, in Boston . . . it was the rest of my life, Allie. My life before them that felt. Unnatural—"

Half wondering if he was, really was, going to leave her for them; half choking on her words, Alice asked, "And after? *After* them?"

She meant after he'd broken off with them, but he went on with his tense monologue. "After I met them, it was like—we *were* kids. But I'd never been one before. You know it was the first time I'd felt connected to anyone. And—completely. Since they were the first people, too, I'd ever talked to. Got to be like there were no barriers between us, our bodies and more than that . . ."

"But today?" Allie managed to ask, clearly. "Today, too?"

JJ squeezed the hands she'd forgotten he held. He gave his slowest nod.

"So today—even with you, with us being married, your connection to them felt all goddamn '*complete*' all o-ver again?"

JJ started a nod. He stumbled like a stuck politician. "Yes and no."

Allie gave a snort, swallowing back the tears she wouldn't let loose.

"No, look." JJ kept firm hold of her hands. "Of course it wasn't exactly like before, Al. I'm not crazy. They're not either. Kin used only his hands, when we were lying there together. *Listen* to me." He pressed her palms together, like he was praying with her hands. "I didn't have any contact with Kin that could put us at risk; I swear."

"Yeah, right," Allie mumbled with another derisive snort. In her head, uncontrollably, a cool part of her was thinking: Make him take that test again. She forced her hands free and heaved herself up. Make him then leave him, she was thinking—hating both thoughts—as she glared down at JJ.

"But what in all Hell—? No matter what, we're having a *baby* and—" She shook her head, at a loss. "God Almighty, JJ: *What* were you thinking?"

He shook his head too. "Jesus, Al. Being here, now, with you. I can't explain. It's just. Something about us, the three of us. Bonds I never expected to feel again but then somehow when I was with them, Kin and Bird. Even though for years that'd all felt like, it'd all been. Another—"

"*Life?*" Her high voice squeaked. "Don't you *dare* feed me that crap again! Another life here, another life there. This is *our* life."

Somehow JJ was both nodding and shaking his head. "I know, I know it should be. I look at you and—I feel I must be some kind of—Stateless Computer." His eyes flickered up to her, gray-green and red. "A file network programmed to have no memory. Breaks down and comes back up like nothing happened. No past, no future. It's wholly inside whatever moment it's in—"

"Oh *please*." Allie cut him short with a chop of her hand. "God, I can't even *listen* to you—I don't even *know* you—" She backed away, her eyes darting around the room she imagined the baby and herself sharing alone.

"Allie, wait." JJ pulled himself up from his knees. As he straightened to his full height, alarmingly tall, she backed closer to the door. "Don't run out on me, Al." He stepped away from the bed fast. "Christ, I'm not saying anything right at all. Look, look, you *know*. How you and I. We, now. *We* fit; you know that." He stepped up to touch her shoulder, demonstrating how perfectly matched they'd always been in size. Cautiously, he touched her other stiff shoulder and pulled her close enough so her belly brushed his crotch. He bent to curve around her stiffened body. "There's just," he mumbled into her hair, strangely helpless-sounding. "So many different ways people can fit. . . ."

Allie tightened her spine, remembering that phrase from Bird's Manila letter. She backed away again, leaving his arms empty, his hands open.

"Y'know." She swallowed, her tears dried up. "It took me a long time just to see this—what you had with Kin and Bird—as a. Love affair. Not some sex experiment or therapy. A—the—big love from your past. And that I could handle, JJ. As long as you weren't still in love with them, long as it stayed in your past. When, I was stupid enough to tell myself, you were so young—"

"And restless," JJ filled in, muttering as if to himself. Then he sealed his sunburned lips, looking shocked that he'd said it out loud.

"You sound like *him*—" Allie stabbed her finger at the door. "Like that *Kin*, like nothing's *ser*ious!" She pushed past JJ, marching back to the bed. "This's *serious* to me." She turned on her heel, wobbling with her weight. "I'm having a *baby*! An' I want those *sick* people outa here!" She swung her fists up and down, beating an invisible drum. "Outta this house! My *parents'* house!"

JJ seized hold of her moving shoulders. "I can't just throw 'em out. We can't." His eyes narrowed as he stared down at her, at—Alice felt sure—the side to her he hated. She panted, feeling suddenly ugly. Through the door, Grandma's walker creaked. Alice heard the linen cabinet squeak. Grandma fetching another quilt, a towel? Kin coughing, spitting up blood? JJ squeezed her arms as the cabinet shut. A thump meant to be heard. "No matter how you feel about me," he went on in a low voice, "you've gotta look at them, at Kin—"

"I am," Allie told him, not shouting now. Grandma's walker was creaking away, slowly and deliberately. "But you've gotta look at—" She pressed one hand on her belly, straining to re-compose her calm. "—me. Me and our baby."

"I am." JJ kept hold of her shoulders. "And. You're strong, Alice. Stronger than you act. You always have been. And you've got—" He lifted one hand and spread his fingers to take in the bedroom: the cream drapes, the pushed-together beds covered by the gold-flowered spread. "You've always had all this—"

"Padding?" She hugged her belly, remembering Bird's stepfather, Bird and Kin huddled in the Boston Youth Hostel. "I know that." She shook her head, "I know I've been dis-gust-ingly lucky all my life and I know Bird hasn't and I know that Kin man is dying out there in our rec room—" Allie glanced again at the closed door. "Don't think I don't see all that, JJ. No, I mean." She sighed, all at once drained. "I've tried not to see it, see them. But I'm starting to now. . . ." She stopped herself, thinking she did hear Kin cough on the far side of the house. A hacking throat-strafing cough, like Dad's.

JJ squeezed her shoulders again. "I know it's—hard for you even to say that." He drew a careful breath. "But listen to us: all our fucking talk. Don't you always say *that*? Talk's unreal unless we're willing to *do* something?"

"Artificial Intelligence, Artificial Compassion," Allie mumbled the way JJ had done on their last New Haven walk. "Saint JJ speaks." She flattened her hands on his chest and shoved as hard as she could, hard as she'd shoved Carter. Tall JJ barely swayed. Alice steadied herself as he, on his own, stepped back to give her room. "You want to talk real?" She turned. With effort, she raised one foot to the bed. Tensing both legs, realizing this was something Bird might do, she climbed onto it. Heaving herself upright; feeling self-conscious, stagey. But she met JJ's shocked bloodshot stare, her bare feet sunk into the mattress.

"Al, God—" JJ rushed forward as she swayed. He gripped her hips; she dug in her heels, feeling garage oil stain the bedspread.

"This here's real." She held her belly with both hands as if presenting it to him. His eyes were level with her swollen breasts, the baby motionless inside her. Alice tried to shove JJ back again. But he stayed planted in place, keeping hold of her hips as her voice rose. Steadier, now. "Jesus

Christ, JJ. You come here telling me you've committed adultery with two—count 'em—two Kins—" She held up two fingers on each hand like peace signs. "And that their troubles are real but our—our baby—your own blood—"

JJ was shaking his head hard. "You know our baby's real to me—"

"I don't." She shook her head as hard as his, remembering Sticks's harsh voice. "*I* don't know nothing. So I might's well leave." She tried to pull back. "I mean *stay*. Me and the baby. We'll stay here with my parents—"

"No." JJ wrapped his arms around her and locked his forearms against the small of her back. His head rested between her breasts, his foreign-smelling sweat dampening her pink shirt. She felt his jaw move. "You know I feel safe with you like I've never felt with anyone. . . ." She tensed again but his hold on her tightened. Safe? she asked herself. Was that all she was, to him?

" . . .with them, Kin and Bird, it's always like—we three're on the verge of—" He raised his bloodshot eyes. Allie took hold of his head, her palms closing over his ears. "Verge of—Wha'd you used to say, Al, with the Severely kids?"

"Going Off." She flattened his ears, hard enough to block his hearing.

"Going Off, yeah." JJ swallowed. She felt the muscles and veins in his skull, moving. "Feels that way even now, even with Bird and me stable like Kin. But with you and me, I always feel we're—" He started to tighten his hold on her body but the baby stirred between them, kicking so strongly they both stiffened. "Here," JJ finished, loosening his hold. "Grounded." Allie let go of JJ's head, his ears reddened by her palms. She breathed his strange yet familiar sweat.

"But what're you going to do?" Her voice came out flat, nearly spent. "Ask my parents to pay Kin's hospital bill—?" Suddenly, a serious question.

JJ blinked, his blue eyes sobered by gray. Red veins in his eye whites stood out brightly. He blinked again, a man who'd been up all night. "Kin doesn't—want a hospital. Wouldn't go, Bird says. And no; no, of course I don't want to ask your parents for anything. Don't want to ask you." He met her stare, his uncertain. "I know this's—Know I can't imagine how hard all this is for you. I know that, Al. And I'm sorry. It's my fault things've gotten to this point. But now, given everything, I have to see if I can't work out a way to. Help."

"But what?" Her voice stayed flat. "Take them to New Haven with us—?"

JJ didn't shake his head no. "They need a place to stay," he told her quietly.

She drew a shuddery breath, actually trying to picture it. "God, JJ—" The knock interrupted her, jarring her since she'd heard no footsteps.

The door opened before she could speak and the Bird woman slipped inside, her half-zipped jacket creaking. She stared at JJ then up at Allie still standing on the bed. She delivered her words straight to Allie. "Your mother's home."

"Oh God, oh shit." Allie bent, steadying herself on JJ's shoulder. He helped her climb down, her feet less sticky now on the carpet. JJ drew a breath he didn't let out. His eyes moved from Allie to Bird like he was at a police lineup.

Bird stood still as a guard, her thumbs hooked in her leather pockets. "Told her I was a friend of JJ's. She hasn't even seen Kin. She's unpacking groceries." Bird nodded sideways. "The door's closed on that—room back there behind the kitchen where your grandma's sitting with Kin."

Allie shook her head hard, as if clearing water from her ears. Then she faced JJ, her belly jutting out. "You go talk to her." She turned to Bird. "And you stay here. With me."

"Alice, come on," JJ began, his mouth sounding dry.

"Go *help* Mom with the groceries," she insisted, her eyes on Bird.

JJ shook his head. He began to edge toward the door, avoiding the charged space between Allie and Bird. He stopped halfway there. "Look, Al, you can't—"

"Just go. Then, JJ—*talk* to Mom." Allie's eyes still locked with Bird's. "But don't tell her anything, OK? Tell her Bird *is* your friend, OK?"

JJ paused again by the door, the room humming with central air. "I don't think you two." He raised his hands like a referree. "I know it's late for me to. Say anything but: I don't want to leave you two alone like this—"

"God," Allie burst out in the voice of a practiced, impatient mother. "Will you do this one thing for me? Just take Mom out to the patio for her *cock*tail, OK? And I'll come *join* you, OK?"

JJ gave a brief resigned nod. He turned, glancing down at Bird. Then he ducked through the doorway, shutting the door with a careful thump.

Alice straightened. Bird stayed slumped, her thumbs still hooked in her pockets. Face-to-face: only a few feet of air between them where there'd once been tens of thousands of miles. JJ's steps retreated. For the first time since Ko No's, Allie studied Bird: the fine bones of her face, her crooked nose and sun-darkened skin and bleached-out hair. Her mouth still slanted like a cat's mouth. Her blue-white eyes met Allie's eyes steadily. Not blind-girl eyes anymore.

Bird unhooked her thumbs. She set her hands on her hips, her leather sleeves creaking again. The jacket was half zipped and it must've been hot. But as in Ko No's, Bird showed no sweat. Allie's stare faltered first.

"What're you worried about?" Bird asked quietly. "He's doing just what you want. . . ."

Through the door, Allie heard faint voices: Mom's rising with a question, JJ's answering evenly. A distant door opened and shut.

"That surprise you?" Allie sank onto the bed, conserving her strength.

But Bird was the one who spoke, quietly again. "All I was trying to say back there was. Kin's sick and you've got a bed."

Alice stared up at this woman JJ loved, the one who must have sucked that mark into his throat hours before. The woman who'd boldly kissed Alice herself. Alice blinked. Had that kiss really happened, a year ago today?

"Kin." Allie looked at her own belly. With JJ, she'd shouted like a child. But now, alone with Bird, she felt she had to act like a—the?—adult. "He oughta be in a hospital. But I guess you haven't got any insurance left, from Kin's job—?"

"No." Bird took a step away from the door, a movement Allie felt rather than saw. "No, and he wouldn't go to any hospital even if he did. Kin decided that. He had coverage, with Pan Am; he coulda used it. He decided not to . . ."

Allie clapped her knees, staring up at Bird's defiantly matter-of-fact face. "But *why*?" she burst out. "How could you *let* him do that—?"

Bird's unnerving gaze wavered. "He—did what he wanted. I—" She leaned forward, wife to wife. "Wasn't going to—make him do what he didn't want to."

Allie sighed in exasperation. "Well good God Almighty. What d'you expect *us* to do now? I mean, God." She managed to keep her voice steady. "Look. Look, if you two really were just old friends to JJ. If you were ex—really ex—lovers, it would be, I would be different. I *want* to be different. But God, you two: you go to *bed* with my husband, and then you come here expecting *help*?"

Bird didn't nod. She took another step. "We don't expect anything from you. We can tell how you feel. But, see." She met Allie's angry stare. "All the things we—I—did to get JJ to visit us, and everything that happened today. It was mostly my idea, my doing. Not Kin's. So if you're gonna blame someone, blame me." She was standing so close Allie smelled her musky sweat. "But now. It's just a—fact. That you've got a bed and he needs one."

Allie made herself hold Bird's gaze. "OK." She shifted uneasily. "I *do* understand that Kin—Kin's in desperate shape. My dad is, too. Real b-bad." She couldn't keep her voice level, thinking of Dad's hawkish nose distorted by tubes. His hacking cough, as harsh as Kin's "And I'm sure you know," Allie went on slowly. "There're plenty of places where Kin could get help. Medical help, all kindsa help if he'd take it. And I—wish we could give you some real money. I mean our credit's all overloaded, but I *can* borrow from my parents. . . ."

Bird's slow unblinking answer was to unzip her jacket. Allie stared at—it was impossible not to—her firmly rounded breasts, bare under her black tank top. Nipples visible. Alice stiffened, feeling again as she'd felt with Kin and Bird and JJ, as she'd felt even alone with JJ, like the outsider.

"We get by, by ourselves." Bird bent as if to whisper a secret. "Matter of fact, I got offered lotsa money—*mucho dinero*—last night. By a—woman. Turned it down 'cause I had *wanted* to do what I did, with Estella. . . ."

Bird touched Allie's stiff shoulder, her fingers light as a child's. She did kiss me, Allie told herself, remembering the name "Estella" from Bird's Mexico letter. Anything might happen now, she felt sure, as Bird bent closer.

In an odd uneven whisper, Bird confided, "See, I don't want you thinking I'm going after JJ anymore, that way . . ."

Then what way? Allie wondered. Bird seemed to study Allie's own tender breasts. And Allie drew a breath of Bird's undisguised sweat, wondering too if this was what JJ'd tried to describe, if she and this Bird woman were floating toward a zone beyond the barriers of courtesy or common sense. *Was* Bird, these days, a lesbian? The room seemed to hum with warmth rather than chill.

Allie blinked hard. Somehow she wished JJ were here to see Bird's eyes swimming over her, Bird's hand resting on her shoulder. As Allie exhaled, she pictured in an unstoppable flash herself and JJ and Bird lying side by side on the pushed-together beds. Allie's own thick nipples stiffened. "But you—you three—" she managed. "What all *did* you do? Today?"

Bird knelt, her breasts bobbing. "You really want to know?"

Bracing both hands, Allie stood with a lurch. Her knee bumped

Bird's shoulder. "Yeah." She shook her head, waking herself from the spell this Bird was conjuring between them. Didn't women with Bird's past traumas, Allie reminded herself, push sexual bounderies? Making what Special Ed teachers called inappropriate advances? Alice tried a firm teacher tone. "Tell me."

Still kneeling, Bird lowered her eyes. "We lay down together, JJ between us. Kin kinda rocked against JJ and JJ rocked too and Kin touched him and. By rocking like that, JJ helped me. Help Kin. To . . . come."

Allie turned away so abruptly the baby stirred inside her. Her loose skirt swayed over her legs. A dying man, she told her baby, pressing her belly as she paced to the door. JJ must love him, she found herself thinking. To have done that. She faced the closed door, hearing no other voices in this house.

"Know what else JJ did today?" Bird's voice sounded hollowed out, as if what she'd just said had exhausted her, too. So it was, Allie sensed, the truth.

"What?" Turning, Allie took two barefoot steps from the door.

"Bought Kin something." Bird drew her jacket closed, still kneeling. "When we were driving into Phoenix, slowly 'cause we were all scared of getting here. And Kin made JJ stop at a little bookstore. Asked JJ to buy a book he wanted. It's out in your car now, Kin's book."

"What?" Alice looked down. Her belly half hid Bird's bowed face. Bird stayed on her knees, her denim jeans loose on her thighs. Allie blinked, struck by the thought—it seemed oddly logical—that Bird was so skinny *because* Allie herself was so heavy. Because she had somehow been eating Bird, eating her up.

"Suicide," Bird mumbled as if making a long-dreaded confession. "A book that tells, like, how to kill yourself. Easily, painlessly." Her eyes flickered up. She gave the scared-animal stare she'd given back in Ko No's.

Allie spoke evenly from above her belly. "So you're saying you're afraid that's what Kin's going to do? Kill himself?"

Bird looked down, biting her lips. Maybe, Allie sensed, Bird felt now the mix of guilt and relief she had felt this morning when she'd betrayed JJ to Jo.

"Think so. Think that's what he might wind up doing." Bird seemed to be trying out her own slow words. "Sometimes feel like maybe. I will too."

"What? You mean after him?"

Bird stared up now like the most violent girl in New Chance Workshop: Connie Botts having her period, facing Allie in blank defiant surprise as Allie gripped her wrists to stop her from beating her own head.

"Don't know." Bird's pulse was visible in her throat. "But I'd. Want to."

"Why?" Allie asked in a shakier version of her Special Ed teacher voice. "You—you wouldn't have to go and—do that. You could, you know—"

"Get therapy?" Bird cut in, mimicking Allie's tone. Abruptly, Bird pulled herself up and Allie stepped back. "Get help, get better?" she asked in a mockingly high-pitched voice. "Make everything OK OK OK OK OK—?"

Allie didn't move, freezing her half-raised hands as she heard its echo: that word she used too often, a childish word.

"Right?" Bird demanded. "Right, right, right?"

Allie shook her head; Bird shook her own harder.

"No," Bird told her. "I'm not like you. Everything's always, I bet, OK for you. OK in the end." She drew a deep breath. "Even if JJ left, you've got your mom and dad and this big house and so, look. Look. Just say what you mean. Don't pretend you're all con-cerned 'bout what I do. Matter of fact, inside, you probably can't help but." Bird slowed her last words. "Want me gone. For good."

"No," Allie told her too loudly. Shaken now, and worried it might show in her face: the shameful rise inside her chest at the thought. Both Kins dead and gone. "No, listen." Her eyes darted to the bedroom door. Still no sound of Mom and JJ, but surely JJ would come looking for her soon. "We're wasting time here. When my mom sees Kin, I know she's going to call a hospital."

Bird blinked, looking almost relieved.

"Maybe my grandma already *has* called one," Allie added. Then Bird started—stiffly, as if against her own will—to shake her head.

"No," she told Allie as if telling herself. "Kin doesn't want that, won't go."

"But wha'do *you* want?" Allie took hold of Bird's upper arms. The leather felt grainy and smoothly cool. She breathed another mouthful of Bird's strong sweat, used to it now. "I mean besides staying here with JJ, with us? Want us to find some kind of free AIDS clinic? Get you some hotel room somewhere? What could we do to make things—Kin's life—easier?"

Bird's blue irises swam. Her lips moved slowly. "Your car."

Allie felt Bird's hard arms tense under the leather. "What?" she breathed, dizzy with Bird so close. Allie watched her lips move as if reading them.

"Give us. Your car."

"Our car," Allie repeated, picturing Kin lying now in Dad's bed.

Remembering Kin's black stare meeting hers, his eyes feverishly bright. "But you're not saying. Surely Kin's too weak to travel now and—?"

"He wants to go. He told me."

Allie pictured Kin lifted by JJ from the car's backseat hours before. She lowered her own voice like Bird's, trying to stay clear headed, focused. "Look. I just. If we, if I gave you that car, are you saying you'd leave? You two?"

With a leather squeak, Bird pulled away. Quickly, she stepped to the door. "If you help me with him, we can do it fast. Like, now? Before—" Bird grinned as if reading Allie's thoughts. "Before your mom even *sees* Kin?"

Alice flushed hotly. Bird widened her knowing grin, displaying gaps in her teeth. A flash of red in one corner of her mouth. Bloody gums? Allie wondered, looking down, trying to hide another foolish hopeful rise in her chest. Ashamed of how much she wanted her mother not to know anything.

"Wait," she mumbled, turning from Bird. "We've got to think this through. We shouldn't do anything right now, we've got to think." Bowing her hot face, she groped with one foot under the bed for her thongs. "What's best, y'know—I know this's what we *ought* to be thinking of—for Kin . . ."

Bird made no answer. No, Allie told herself as she shoved her foot into one thong, parting her toes. No, this is wrong. He's dying; he'll die; it's wrong. She maneuvered her belly into a turn. "Bird, listen. You two shouldn't, can't—"

"*Hurry.*" Bird shoved open the bedroom door.

Hardly believing what she was doing, Allie crossed the floor to her purse. Her numb clumsy hands dug out her car keys on a red-white-and-blue Dukakis key ring. Before Allie could form another protest, Bird slipped into the hall.

Hurry hurry, Allie found herself thinking as Bird broke into a run, her quick cat-burglar steps making no sound on the carpet. The baby stirred. Hang on, Allie told both it and herself as she speeded her steps. I'll take care of you.

She hurried from the hall into the den, deciding almost giddily this *was* for the best. Ahead of her, Bird darted into the kitchen. I'll take care of us, Alice told the baby. You, me, him. Passing the kitchen's picture window, she glanced outside. Mom lay stretched on her usual lounge chair. Her wineglass gleamed beside her, half full. JJ was saying something, soldier-stiff in his own webbed chair. Mom was nodding vaguely, no doubt uneasy about her glimpse of Bird. But—Allie stepped into the open Sick Room—Mom didn't want to know the truth.

"What on Earth?" Grandma Hart was craning her neck, hunched in the rocker beside Kin's bed. Bird was bent over Kin, her back to Grandma.

Kin mumbled as if in sleep, gently instructive. "The bag will not inflate—" He gave a sleep-slowed cough. "But oxygen will be flow-ing . . ."

Bird seemed to be shaking him, lightly. His iced-tea glass sat drained on Dad's nightstand. Had Grandma held it like Bird had done so Kin could drink it? As Allie stepped up behind Bird, she saw a damp washcloth folded on Kin's forehead. A lightweight quilt Grandma D. had sewn rested on Kin's legs.

"We can *go* now, if you still want," Bird was murmuring to Kin. "Have the *car* now, like you said you wanted—Kin?"

Allie turned to Grandma Hart. Her sharp-edged glasses framed her sharply questioning green gaze. Allie felt her own face freeze. The lines of Grandma's face deepened with a frown of confused but unmistakable disapproval.

"Can we use this?" Allie reached for Grandma's metal four-footed walker.

"Wha—?" Grandma rocked forward in the rocker, building momentum to stand up even as Allie, shocked by her own quick movements, lifted the walker out of Grandma's reach. God, Allie thought. What the Hell am I doing?

"Alice Ann!" Grandma sputtered as Bird raised Kin to a sitting position. "This man: he needs a doctor."

"No," Bird answered over her shoulder. "I promised him no."

Her jacket creaking, she eased Kin's legs off the mattress. The quilt slipped to the floor. Kin was moving with Bird now, his eyes downcast. His forehead shone from Grandma's fallen washcloth.

"Use caution," Kin muttered. "When o-pening overhead bins."

Bird glanced up and motioned Allie to bring over the walker.

"Alice Ann!" Grandma half rose then fell back into her rocker.

"Here we go." Bird with her strong arms was easing Kin into a wobbly standing position. Allie—feeling she was back at Helping Hands, co-ordinating to maneuver a patient—set the walker in front of Kin. He gripped the handles.

"Thanks." Bird glanced at Allie. Her eyes gave the grudging flash of admiration with which, after well-handled Incidents, Sticks had rewarded her.

"Contents." Kin licked his dry lips. His breath smelled sour to Allie as she took hold of his elbow. Old-man breath and sweat that carried a deeper sour smell, rotted meat or fish. "Contents may shift," Kin muttered, this time with a slight edge that made Allie wonder if he was really confused. "Dur-ing flight."

He clanked forward with the walker. A determined first step.

"Alice Ann—this man's burning up with *fever*. He's too *weak* to move."

She's right, Allie thought distinctly, averting her eyes from Grandma's.

"*Nunca*," Kin mumbled. His arm tightened under Allie's light touch. "Never too weak. To move." He clanked forward between Allie and Bird.

"They're leaving now," Allie choked out to Grandma Hart, who'd rocked herself to her feet. She stood hunched, her thick-soled orthopedic shoes planted squarely on the carpet. "Sit down, Grandma, please?" Allie's voice cracked. She turned from Grandma's accusatory stare. Hang on, she told her baby again.

"Good," she automatically told Kin—hating her own teacher tone— as he clanked forward. Bird on her side had hold of his other elbow.

"Leaving for a *hospital*?" Grandma Hart rasped. Kin stopped in his tracks, his bone of an arm suddenly rigid in Allie's grasp.

"No," Bird assured him. "No hospital," she whispered plainly. Before clanking forward again, Kin turned his head to nod at Grandma Hart. A salute.

"No hos-pital," he managed. In the polite Southern tone Allie had heard when Kin had taken the tissue from her, he told Grandma, "But thank you. Just th' same."

Gripping the walker, Kin clanked toward the open door. At his side, Alice nodded, stiff-jawed. What he wanted. Not only what she and Bird wanted. Right? Dizzy with an answering surge of guilt, she glanced over her shoulder at her grandmother rooted beside the still-rocking rocker. "Alice Ann, stop this!"

"Sit *down*," Allie begged, her throat thick. "Please? I'll be right back."

She faced front as Kin clanked over the doorway's threshold. His rumpled pants hung loose on his legs; his elbow felt like bare bone to Allie. Can't stop it, she told Grandma silently. Through her hot blur of tears, she saw Kin's grip on the walker stay strong, his knuckles as white and prominent as Grandma's.

"*Alice—*" Grandma began yet again. Blindly, Allie reached back. With the heel of her free hand, she bumped the room door shut.

17

Blood, Love

Alice squinted and Bird did not as severely slanted rays of late sun struck them both full in the face. All three stepped together from the doorway of the dark suffocating garage. Kin leaned on the squeaky walker. Allie and Bird heard it clank the concrete driveway. The cul de sac was deserted, houses hidden behind stucco walls like the one surrounding Allie's parents' house.

Bird held one of Kin's elbows and pressed her hand on his back, feeling his cold sweat through the cotton. Another fever rising. The old lady was right, Bird thought, swallowing down thickness in her own throat. Determined to hold herself together a few more minutes, long enough to get back on the road.

"Good," Allie murmured from the other side of Kin as he clanked the walker into a turn, aiming for the crookedly parked Zephyr. Their elongated three-headed shadow stretched sideways. Beyond the Zephyr, Mom had parked her Buick in the street. Luckily, Allie reminded herself, the house separated the patio from the driveway. JJ and Mom couldn't hear a thing. Could they?

Allie tightened her hold on Kin's knobby elbow. Unlike Bird, she rested no hand on Kin's back. Sweat pasted his shirt between his sharp shoulder blades. And Allie sealed her lips against Kin's faintly rotten smell. Her heart pumped so hard she felt the baby feel each beat. What next, what next.

"Watch him," Bird snapped, feeling Kin slip on Allie's side. So Bird tensed her arm in its leather sleeve. Knobs of Kin's spine indented her palm.

"Sorry." Allie gripped Kin's wrist, his skin wet. She wanted to wipe her hand. But sweat's not dangerous, she reminded herself, keeping hold. She admired how Kin re-gripped the walker and clanked forward, scraping concrete. Sweat's not blood, Allie told herself impatiently. Fed up with her own fears.

"C'mon," she heard the Bird woman murmur from her side of Kin.

Allie saw Bird press his back with her tan, spread-fingered hand. Un-afraid, Allie thought. Bird's jacket—wasn't she dying in that now? Allie wondered—shone in the sun as if wet with its own sweat. "Just a few more steps," Bird urged softly.

"I know," Allie answered, grateful for Bird's sure-sounding voice.

"I'm not talking to you," Bird snapped.

Halting, Kin shot a sideways glance at Bird and shook his head as if to say—Bird heard him loud and clear—Girls, girls; this is no time to fight.

"Sorry," Bird muttered, again to Kin. But Alice Wolfe nodded. A woman, Bird sensed, accustomed to being treated the way JJ treated her. Protectively, respectfully. Even as JJ's wife helped ease Kin into his final clanking steps—the Zephyr loomed before them, one door open like an unfolded wing—Bird's chest tightened with resentment she'd felt for Alice in that cream-colored bedroom. How fiercely Bird had wanted to mess up that room, that smooth double bed.

"We made it," Allie announced, determinedly calm. Their three-headed shadow merged with the car shadow as they came to a more or less coordinated halt. The Kin man gave a satisfied yet exhausted sour-breathed sigh. The black Zephyr shimmered dully in the sun, so dusty Allie knew that it *had* been driven across the desert. That all this was, re-ally was, happening.

She hesitated, sensing the car's bulk and value. Bought used, only a few payments left. As she and Bird eased Kin from the walker, Allie stared past Mom's Buick, up the cul de sac of raked-gravel lawns, walled-in houses.

"Scared what the neighbors'll think?" Allie heard Bird ask. She watched Bird's leather arm stiffen, accepting Kin's full weight as she must often do.

"Look, let's just get going." Allie lifted the walker, her arms straight-ened to make room for her belly. With a final-sounding clank, she set the walker out of their way. Then she shot a glance at the house. *Were* they going to disappear before Mom saw them? And where the Hell *was* JJ? Feeling she was getting away with a crime, she helped Bird lower Kin onto the hot vinyl passenger seat. Bird crouched to ease Kin's legs in-side. Allie remembered that JJ too had watched Bird care for Kin today. What, Allie wondered in a guilty flash, will JJ think when I tell him—she grasped the hot seatbelt—what *I've* done for Kin?

"No, no," Kin protested quietly as Allie, holding her breath against his smell, began stretching the seatbelt over his sunken lap.

"Yes," Bird hissed to Kin, taking the buckle, her sweaty fingers brushing Allie's. "It'll hold you up," she told him as JJ's wife straightened and stepped back. "Let you see out the window." She secured the strap over his chest.

Kin managed a nod, his eyes slit. Bird was sweating now in her leather. A relief after that refrigerated house, she thought, patting Kin's damp shoulder.

"Ready?" From above her pink-draped belly, JJ's wife stared down at them both. Her golden brown hair shimmered in the orange sunset. Her skin looked to Bird especially warm. Wasn't that true of pregnant women, Bird thought as she pulled herself up and faced this Allie. Didn't their flesh hold extra heat?

"What's your hurry?" Bird pushed back her limp hair. Allie's tan face glowed with the healthy odorless sweat Bird found herself wanting to taste.

"Just take these," JJ's wife ordered. Bird held out her hand and—the car felt huge behind her—closed her fingers around the key chain that sported the weird word "Dukakis." The States, Bird reminded herself. We're back in the States. Then, blinking up again at Alice: I know how to drive and I have a car.

"Thanks," the Bird woman murmured. Allie thought she sounded like she meant it. The guilty tightening around Allie's heart eased slightly. Through the hot still air, she heard a rumble of rush-hour traffic on Shea Boulevard.

"Good luck," Allie told this Bird woman awkwardly.

"Oh, *c'mon*," the Kin man mumbled in his low nasal voice.

As Bird started laughing, Allie's heart re-tightened. The Kin man managed a wry wide-mouthed smile. He knows, Allie thought. This dying man knows I'm not letting him stay. Though he, she told herself, wants to go. Right? Dizzily, Allie turned from Kin and laughing Bird to face the house again, the garage. Why the Hell hadn't JJ come looking for her yet? How could he leave her alone out here with them, with this awful decision? Allie made herself turn back to them, feeling sweat gather under her breasts, feeling her knees weaken.

Bird stopped laughing as she saw JJ's wife sway slightly on her feet. "Hey—you're not gonna faint, are you?" She took half a step forward, suddenly scared that pregnant Allie might collapse from all the stress they'd caused her today.

"Me?" Steadying herself, JJ's wife stared down at Kin, who'd shut his eyes.

Bird swallowed hard, tasting blood in her gums. "He just wants to get moving," she said aloud, to Allie and herself. She thought she saw

Kin give an almost imperceptible chin jerk. Yet she kept her feet planted on the concrete. Waiting too, maybe, for JJ to come out. But no, she decided, clutching the car keys. Kin was right. They already *had* said goodbye to Jimmy Joe, in Mexico.

"Listen—" JJ's wife faced Bird again, a fresh glitter of tears in her eyes. "Listen, if Kin does," she told Bird, sounding softly intent. "I mean when he does—die." She drew a shaky breath. "Don't." Bird narrowed her gaze, suspicious of Allie's tears. Yet her eyes locked with those darkest brown eyes that seemed to take in everything, that had taken in JJ. "Don't you—do what he wants to do. After him. . . ." JJ's wife nodded down again at Kin, his face pasty with sweat.

What, Allie was wondering, *would* Bird do without this man she loved so much? This man she'd cared for all year, as a nurse who could stand anything?

"I'll do what I want," the Bird woman answered, but softly too. Then she stepped so close Allie smelled her leather. Bird's white-blond hair burned in the sunset; her blue-white eyes shone fiercely. Don't go and kill yourself, Allie thought. She breathed Bird's musky sweat, delicious after the sickly smell of Kin. You're strong, she wanted to tell this Bird the way JJ had told her.

"Here." Bird broke their shared stare. Shifting the car keys into her left palm, she slipped off her ring of 8s. It had always been loose enough to twist. "You take this." She felt her bared ring finger stick out at JJ's wife like a new fuck-you gesture. "Take it." She shook the soldered-metal ring.

JJ's wife shook her head of shining hair. "Oh no, no. Thank you but—"

"No," Bird insisted, angered by the automatic way Alice said thank you. What she'd been saying all her life as she'd been given and given and given everything she had. "This's *not* a present and it's not for you." Bird raised her voice so Kin might hear. "It's for JJ. To see on your finger. Every day—"

JJ's wife tightened her lips but held out her ringless right hand, her fingers rigid. Anything; she'd do anything to get us gone, Bird thought as she dropped the keys. She took hold of Allie's hand and jammed the ring onto Allie's fourth finger. Surely this woman wouldn't wear it for good. But Bird wanted JJ to see it again, if only briefly: the infinite 8s representing the unbroken connection Bird felt, now more than ever, between her and Kin and him. She looked back up into Allie's easy-to-read sunlit face, keeping hold of her hand. Allie was squinting at the ring as if it had sprouted around her finger. Her eyes darted to the garage—expecting JJ to burst out?—then back to Bird.

"Don't worry," Bird mumbled. "We're going." But instead of reaching for the keys that glittered on the concrete, she held Allie's stiff hand harder. She looked down at Allie's belly, its rose-colored covering close enough to touch.

Alice bowed her head too, half ashamed in front of Bird and Kin. A dying man and his closest friend: his nurse who would stand anything, do anything, for him. "I wish," Allie began, her words slowed by the heat. "Wish I could be. Bigger. About, you know, all this . . ." *Be a bigger doormat, y'mean?* Jo asked in her mind. Allie pushed on, wanting to end as decently as possible. "Wish I *could*—make room for you here. . . ." She looked up to see Bird still gazing down.

"Maybe there's not," Bird told JJ's wife's belly. "Room. Not with . . . this." Baby, she told herself. "JJ's," she added, loud enough for Kin to hear. Feeling she was doing it on his behalf too, Bird raised the hand that wasn't holding Allie's. Slowly enough so JJ's wife could step back if she wanted, Bird reached down. She touched first sun-warmed cloth. Pressing gently, she felt through Allie's warmer flesh a distinctly rounded shape. A tiny body, packed inside her.

"Yeah," Allie murmured, wondering if Bird had begun to see—couldn't she, at least dimly?—her side of this, now. In tentative relief, Alice let her tense stomach muscles relax under Bird's surprisingly gentle touch. "JJ's baby." She finished the phrase Bird had begun. But the Bird woman raised her white-lashed eyes fast, as if Allie's words had been a rebuke, a warning. Bird lifted her hand.

"We *know* this's his baby, and you're his wife," Bird told JJ's wife cooly, annoyed by Alice's softened gaze. As if Alice felt she had everything, everyone, back under control. "But the thing is," Bird added on impulse, wanting to jar this woman's maddening calm. "You'll never really know—what *we* are. To JJ."

What you *were*, Bird expected Alice to correct. But JJ's wife shook her head hard, her dark eyes flashing now. "No, no; from—God, from what I saw today, from your letters, I—think I've got some idea—"

Bird leaned even closer, hoping Kin was watching from the car, hoping he could hear. Performing for Sister Kin, she asked this Alice, "Do you?"

Do you even know what you want? Alice remembered Bird writing to JJ.

And she shook her own head harder. "Look," she admitted to Bird in a rush, "All I *know*—and I wish I didn't—is that it, what's between you two and him, wasn't what I thought, what I assumed, at first. Wasn't something—small . . ."

The Bird woman nodded, giving a full-lipped half smile that reminded Allie of JJ's smile, his lush mouth. Bird lowered her eyes before saying, "It isn't."

And—as if she might mean JJ's baby, too—she touched Allie's belly again. Allie's overheated face flushed. As reddish sunset light hummed around them, she felt through Bird's respectfully light hand how much this woman loved JJ, still. Her first lover, too. Allie wiped her own face, suddenly sick of fighting that. Sick of feeling, as she'd felt all day, left out. JJ's wronged uptight wife.

"Good-bye Mrs. Wolfe." Bird raised her eyes, still half smiling. Inviting Allie inside, somehow? Allie tensed her arms, telling herself to pull back from this Bird. But Bird's mouth made her seem a sister of JJ's, a female version of JJ as she closed in. Expecting to catch Alice off-guard like she'd done at Ko No's?

This time—impulsively hoping JJ might somehow witness the kiss—Allie bent forward too. Inserting herself, at this last minute, into the energies she'd felt humming around her all afternoon. Not an outsider now as she let Bird's lips touch hers, lightly first. Warm salty lips, startlingly softer than JJ's. Allie squeezed her eyes shut, red veins lit up inside her eyelids. Her whole spine electrified as Bird's mouth pressed hers. In her own sun-humming darkness, Allie felt her baby flutter. With, she sensed, shared pleasure.

Alive! Bird thought, incredulous. Through skin and cloth, JJ's baby was moving under her touch. Alive inside this Alice whose smooth heated lips were—incredibly, too—opening under Bird's the way JJ's had refused all day to open. She cupped Allie's hot glossy head with her free hand. Tasting milk, Bird widened her mouth. Her tongue swelled, joining Allie's.

Blood. Alice tasted the meaty tinge of it. In a head-clearing flash, she pictured that glimpse of red in Bird's grin. Through leather, she gripped Bird's skinny strong arms then pulled back so fast their lips made a *suck* sound, forced apart. A string of saliva popped soundlessly in air. The Bird woman blinked. Allie gaped, her own mouth still open, her lips wet like Bird's. How could she have kissed this woman? Fearless Bird: who might be sick too, infected too?

"No," Allie gasped. Tightening her grip on Bird, she lunged forward with her full pregnant weight. Harder than she'd pushed Carter or JJ or anyone else in her life, she gave Bird a mighty shove.

"Whoa—" The Bird woman staggered backward, her body shockingly light. God I'm crazy too, Allie thought as Bird fell. She landed on her ass, her head bobbing like her neck was rubber and her jacket slipping halfway off one arm.

"No," Allie gasped again before she even knew what she was seeing—clearly—on Bird's bared shoulder. Dark brown splotches. Alice shook her head in numb disbelief. How could she have forgotten her glimpse of those spots in the garage? How could she not have remembered then—as she did, blindingly, now—that dark lesions were the most famous symptom of AIDS? "Oh, God." Allie sucked back so hard the roof of her mouth strained. She spat a bubbly wad of her spit mixed with Bird's spit. Tinged pink? "God, God—" Her heart pounded and her baby kicked like both wanted out. The Bird woman was staring at her from the ground. In a feverish blur, Allie saw the Kin man reaching for the open car door. To pull himself up, protect his Bird?

"Get *outa* here," Allie told both of them. She lurched sideways, stepping over her spit wad already drying on the concrete.

"Watch it—" Bird choked as JJ's pregnant wife swayed dangerously above her. Still sitting on her sore tailbone, her jacket hanging off one shoulder, Bird held up her hand—sure that Allie was going to fall on her, on her own baby. Freaked out over a kiss? A kiss she'd seemed to want? Bird jolted onto her knees, reaching for Allie's hip, half to protect herself and half to steady Allie.

"Stay away from me!" Lurching sideways again, Allie bumped Grandma's walker. She gripped one rubber handle, dizzy in the heat. Her mind teemed with half-formed pictures: herself sick; the baby born sick, born dying. Still on her knees, the Bird woman reached for the nearest walker leg, starting to pull herself up. And Allie felt adrenaline electrify her arms.

"Stay *away*—" Gripping both handles, Allie hoisted the walker, not much heavier than a patio chair. She tilted it like a lion-tamer's chair. The rubber-tipped walker feet framed Bird's startled, plainly affronted face.

"Leave her a-*lone*," Allie heard the Kin man protest hoarsely from the car as Bird reached again for the walker's leg. Trying to wrest that walker away?

"You leave *me* alone!" Allie raised the walker higher, its hollow metal legs gleaming. Her eyes took in the shadow of Bird on her knees reaching toward Allie's own huge-bellied shadow wielding this square four-pronged weapon. Allie's arms trembled. The weight of the walker itself swung it down. A joint popped in her elbow as Allie bent her arms instinctively, aiming.

The *crack* split air: metal rod against melon, hard against soft. Allie's body vibrated, then doubled over as the walker clanked back down. *Upside tha head*: Kentucky high school words filled Allie's mind in the stunned seconds after she hit Bird's head. With no moan, Bird staggered on her knees then fell onto her bare shoulder, her jacket creaking and her head lolling on the concrete.

"*Ber*-ta," the Kin man cried out from the Zephyr.

The stricken pitch of his voice made Allie freeze, still doubled over the walker that lay between her feet and Bird's limp bent legs. Allie's heartbeat had halted but her baby kicked. What, Allie asked the baby numbly, did I do?

"Ber-ta, Ber-ta," the Kin man called. Shakily, Allie straightened to see Kin yank at the shoulder strap that bound him to his seat. One of his skinny legs poked out the car door as he strained toward Bird's body.

"*Berta—*" Bird heard Kin shout through the ringing of her head. Stiffening her spine, she lifted her head, her elbow poking concrete through her bunched-up leather sleeve. Her face throbbed without yet hurting. The walker leg had smacked her cheekbone and jawbone. Why had JJ's wife hauled off and hit her? *Hadn't* Allie wanted the kiss, leaned forward for it? Bird turned her stiffened neck, twisting on the sun-warmed concrete to see Kin reach toward her. He halfway fell out of the Zephyr's front seat, held in by his stretched shoulder strap. His black slippered foot touched the driveway.

No, Bird opened her mouth to tell him but something on her tongue stopped her. Bending, she spit it out: her last loose tooth. It glinted, tipped with red.

Blood, Alice thought, raising the walker again to defend herself. But from what? She stared at Kin, struggling weakly with his seatbelt buckle, then back at Bird on the ground. Both of them staring up at her as if at a maniac. Feeling suddenly ridiculous, hysterical, Alice lowered the walker with a muted clank.

Bird rose on her knees to grip the open car door's handle. Letting go of the walker, Allie watched Bird pull herself up on shaky legs. She shrugged back on her jacket. Then she faced Allie, showing a shockingly reddened cheek.

"You—O-K?" Alice whispered, hoarse now like Kin. Bird half nodded and stepped forward, wobbly as a colt. I hit her, Allie told herself plainly, stepping back fast. Hit this woman who kissed me. Intending what? Allie wondered—about Bird's kiss, about her own hit. She drew a whole-body breath, Bird and the driveway and the bloody wraparound sky all blurring.

"Then can't you just *go*?" Allie shouted. "Now—go *now*? Can't you just leave us *alone*?"

A door banged. In a blur, Allie saw JJ step from the garage. He headed toward her, his hands raised as if to catch or grab her. Behind him, Allie saw her mom in her beige sundress and high-heeled sandals hurry to follow, sloshing a glass of wine. "What, what?" Mom seemed to be saying, all sounds blurred too. Allie turned to face the nightmarish sight of Bird struggling to push Kin back into his seat, Kin's leg still hanging out the door.

Allie focused on the red branding-iron mark that ran from Bird's cheek to her jaw. Then Allie broke into horrified sobs. How could she have hit this woman? Hit anyone? Kin's foot disappeared. At the car door's slam, JJ took hold of Allie's elbow. He let her collapse against him, her belly overbalancing her at last. She pressed her face to JJ's solid chest, her elbow ache sharpening.

"*¿Está bien?*" Kin whispered hoarsely behind Bird.

Light-headed but steady now on her legs, Bird turned from JJ and his weeping wife. She nodded down at Kin. Bending, she grabbed the red-white-and-blue key chain. Squeezed the hot keys. Her cheekbone and jawbone had started to hurt: a dull throb. Shit, Bird thought clearly, directing her thought toward Kin. Shit, I been hit harder than that.

Armed with her keys, Bird faced Jimmy Joe bathed in orange light, his hair crackling with all its colors. His wife was choking back her sobs and hugging her own belly, the warmly dense belly Bird had just touched. "Sorry," Bird heard Allie telling JJ. Beside them, the walker stood crooked on three straight legs and one bent. "Sorry, but they—they *want* to leave—"

Bird turned back to the Zephyr, the left half of her face aching. But nothing broken, she sensed. No bones. "Yeah, let's go," she muttered to Kin through the open car window, her mouth bloody. Kin's chin jerked, an emphatic nod. *Blood, love,* Bird remembered Kin telling her one year ago as she swallowed her own, now. *Blood, love, blood.* She blinked with her first step, her vision vividly blurred. Allie's huge ranch house shimmered, a mirage.

"What—who—?"

Bird glanced over her leather shoulder to see Alice's mother gesture toward Kin. "—call 9-1-1?" this mother was asking silent JJ. Alice still leaned on his shoulder, anchoring him though his whole body tensed as if ready to move.

Beyond JJ, inside the doorway to the garage, Bird saw Allie's grandmother wobble in her Mexican dress, holding the doorway edge with white clawlike hands. Her glasses flared in the fading light. Her stare alone met Bird's.

"Wait," she shouted in her rasp: "I already *called* an *aum*bulance!" The grandma drew a determined breath, hunching lower. "It's *coming!*"

"Thanks," Bird shouted back, raspy now too. "But we're *going!*"

She took a shaky step. Leaving behind JJ and his bewildering wife. A woman unhinged by a single spontaneous—on both sides, Bird felt sure—kiss. Or maybe, Bird told herself, steadying herself on the Zephyr's hot hood, Alice had simply been getting back at her for what happened with JJ today. Bird stepped around the car. Maybe Alice *did* have everyone under control again, everyone doing what she wanted.

"Stop," her mother was calling out. Bird craned her neck to stare over the Zephyr's roof at the people staring back: JJ and Alice standing side by side; Alice's hunched-over grandma steady now in the garage doorway; Alice's plump wide-eyed mom tottering forward on her heels, her glass slanted in her hand.

"Stop them," she called out uncertainly, staring at the Zephyr, at Kin in the passenger seat maybe staring back.

Bird stood on tiptoe to see Allie's mom's wineglass fall with a deli-cate crack. Allie's mom turned to JJ as if he'd knocked the glass from her hand. Her voice wavered. "Isn't she *stealing* your car, that woman, your—*'friend'*—?"

Still balanced on ballet-lesson tiptoe, Bird shouted over the car roof, aiming her correction straight at Allie's mom. "*Lover*," she called out plainly, the word cutting through the buzz inside her own head. Her face was throbbing harder now. Why the Hell was JJ staring so blankly, as if he didn't know them?

"All *three* of us." Her sleeve creaking, Bird pointed at herself, then into the car at Kin, then over the car roof at Jimmy Joe, maddeningly dead-faced to the end. Bird moved her eyes fast from the frozen green of JJ's stare to the frozen brown of Allie's. Allie's mom sidestepped in front of Allie to shield her daughter. But Bird felt her own unstoppable voice rise, filling the whole desert driveway, her whole body upright on her toes.

"We *three*—" the Bird woman pointed again through the window to Kin, whose black eyes glittered straight at Allie. "We were lovers *together!*"

Allie stood at attention. Bird's words echoed over Mom's curly head, Mom's hair solidly gray from the back. Beyond Mom, beyond the Zephyr and Mom's Buick, Allie saw across the street a middle-aged red-haired woman in a bikini staring over her own raked-gravel yard. Mrs. Van-something.

"What *happened* with—these two?" Mom turned to JJ as if, Alice thought, he'd been caught playing dirty games. Alice alone felt the serious tension in JJ's body, poised now to run toward them, his Kins.

Bird wiped her mouth, smearing the sticky blood. Wanting to shout that they'd loved each other; that's what had happened. But Allie's face looked so scared and JJ's so sad that Bird aimed her last words at him alone. At Jimmy Joe. Speaking loudly but no longer shouting over the roof of his car. "*You* know."

He nodded. Relieved by this sign of life from him, Bird gave her own brusque nod back. Only you, she added silently as she ducked her head, catching through the car window a fresh whiff of Kin's sour sweat. Soon, she knew as she heaved open the door, only she and JJ would know what they'd had with Kin.

Alice blinked. As the car door slammed, she took hold of JJ's hand. It tensed in her grasp. Bird bent over the wheel, maybe searching for the ignition. Around Allie, Mom and Grandma and JJ stood paralyzed as the Zephyr rumbled to life. Across the street, bikini-clad Mrs. Van-something advanced on her gravel yard with mincing barefoot steps.

"*Ai ya!*" the Bird woman shouted above the engine. The Zephyr jerked so suddenly the Kin man's head bounced, Bird's head too. Through the windshield, Allie saw Bird clench her jaw, no doubt struggling with the gears.

"Hey—" JJ shouted, pulling away from Allie. "*Can* you drive?" He sprang forward. Allie gripped Grandma Hart's walker again. "Bird— *wait*—"

JJ stretched his arms to grab the Zephyr's front bumper. With a lurch, Bird, who apparently *could* drive, sent the car shooting backward down the driveway. Mrs. Van-something shrieked as if it would knock her flat. But Bird swung into a sharp reverse turn. The Zephyr backed fast onto the street, aiming up the open-ended throat of the cul de sac.

"Bird—he'll *die*—" JJ ran down the driveway, reaching again for his car. As he seized the driver's door handle, Bird jerked the car into gear, hunched low over the wheel like a jockey on a horse. All four tires screeched. The Zephyr shot past Mom's Buick, the Kin man's head bouncing violently and JJ knocked off-balance. He swayed like a basketball player bumped under the hoop, his arms still half raised. Dust from the yard clouded the Zephyr as it roared down the walled-in street: up the cul de sac's curve toward busy four-lane Shea. Fresh tire treads showed on the road.

Allie clutched the bent-legged walker, feeling her mother step toward her. JJ turned too with his hands hanging down empty. As he stepped forward, he still seemed knocked off-balance. The fading remains of his sunset shadow zigzagged over the driveway.

"Al?" he called in a drained voice. He stood where the Zephyr had stood.

Mrs. Van-something in her bikini backed up with the high-kneed steps of a barefoot woman suddenly aware she was standing on gravel.

"Oh Alice." Mom reached Allie first.

"Is she awl-right?" Grandma Hart hobbled up to Allie's other side.

From both sides, Allie felt her mother and grandmother face JJ as if he were indeed the wild-haired intruder he'd always appeared to be in family photos. He studied Alice as if she looked strange to him too. Far behind him, the front door of the red-haired woman—Mrs. VanDam, Allie remembered—slammed.

"Come now." Mother took hold of Allie's elbow; Allie winced at the pain. The elbow that popped, she told herself. Popped when I hit Bird upside the head.

She blinked, her lashes damp. I kissed her; I hit her. Hit her hard. Allie's throat felt raw from all her shouting and crying. A big baby, she told herself. Remembering as if from long ago how in the bedroom with Bird she'd smugly imagined herself to be a—the—adult. How a year before, just as smugly, she'd imagined her own life to be so unshakable. Alice stood rooted now in the concrete. JJ looked as if he too felt too heavy to move. Behind him, around them all, the orange desert sky was marbled with peachy red. Through the muffled rumble of distant traffic, Allie thought she heard a siren.

"Come." Mom tugged Allie's arm, her wine-scented breath lukewarm in Allie's ear. "We've got to get you back inside."

18

Both at Once

The ambulance, when it came, wound up carrying Alice. Mom and Grandma insisted. So Allie was hoisted onto her first stretcher (a relief, her new weight hefted by professionals) then driven to the hospital with lights spinning but siren off. The ambulance was followed down darkening Shea Boulevard by the Buick, JJ driving with hysterical Mom and stony calm Grandma in the back.

Now, at 7:30 P.M., Allie sat between JJ and Jo, propped in a hospital bed. Mom had convinced Allie to stay overnight to monitor the baby, make sure nothing was wrong. Aside from her sprained elbow, braced now by an Ace bandage, the doctor found Alice healthy. Though agitated, he'd said. Weak from heat.

Mom had been sedated when she'd kept insisting that Allie had collapsed, that something may be *seriously wrong*. In her own more muted Emergency-Room hysteria, Allie had insisted blood be taken from herself and JJ for HIV tests. Now, she lay limply doped up on something resembling Xanax but, the doctor had said with a Republican chuckle, kinder and gentler. Allie gazed from JJ to Jo with a groggy guilty sense that the hospital had the wrong patient. She kept picturing Kin falling out of the car and Bird with the smear of blood on her lips that no one had mentioned, just as no one had seemed to notice the dented leg on Grandma's walker. Allie fingered her lightweight blanket.

"No *coverage*?" Jo was saying to JJ. They were seated in molded-plastic chairs on opposite sides of Allie's metal-railed bed. "No car insurance at all?"

"Only minimal," JJ mumbled, his eyes on Allie's fingers toying with the blanket, the ring of 8s dully glinting. In this harsh light, his suntanned face looked bony and older. His pockmarks seemed unnaturally pink, like the unnaturally brown spots on Bird's arms. "So it's not worth reporting."

"Not worth reporting your *car* stolen?" Jo leaned forward, her short blondish brown hair mussed. The scar between her knit-together brows made her blue stare look like a glare. No, Allie thought; she *was* glaring at JJ.

"It wasn't stolen," JJ repeated for what seemed to Allie the hundredth time.

"But if you *tell* the police it *was*, then you can collect—"

"No. I don't want any police anywhere looking for that car."

Allie nodded so slightly neither JJ nor Jo noticed. Their eyes had locked over her body. Allie turned from Jo to JJ, his clouded-blue eyes tired yet bright as if he felt like she felt. Drained yet overfull of, he'd say, things to process.

"How'll you get back to Connecticut?" Jo demanded, folding her arms. Trying to fill the role of mother while their real mother sat in the visitor's lounge in a tranquilized daze, watched over by hawk-eyed Grandma Hart.

"Rent a real U-Haul. A truck." JJ dared a glance at Allie.

"Maybe JJ oughta go see how Mom's doing," Jo told Allie. You wanna talk? Jo's eyes asked. Wanna hear me agree what an incredible shit he's been?

Allie shook her head wearily. "No, Jo. Why don't you just . . . take Mom and Grandma home in your car. I'm too tired to see anyone else. . . ."

"Yeah," JJ cut in. "You go on ahead, Jo, and I'll follow later in the Buick."

Jo shot Allie a look: Is it OK to leave you alone with him? She had been grilling JJ about his day, obviously frustrated by his monotonic replies, but not asking Allie as if Allie were too fragile to talk. Allie nodded. The motion of her head felt separate from the numbed floaty feeling of her body. "Please, Jo."

With a sigh—half exasperation, half relief—Jo stood, her body sturdy in her ASU T-shirt and her nurse's-aide pants. She smoothed Allie's hair.

"See ya tomorrow." Jo rallied a bossy tone. "10 A.M., checkout. And don't worry about Mom. Grandma and I'll take care of her." Jo turned, her hips broad in those white pants. At the door, she turned again, staring over Allie at JJ.

"Ever heard of the straight and narrow?" Jo asked in her loud stagey voice. JJ nodded as dazedly as Allie had been nodding. "Get on it." Jo took hold of the door's long handle. "Stay on it." The door wheezed open, thumped shut.

Allie sighed, sinking into her pillows. JJ shot her a sideways look as if he wanted to say, the way he used to after a long day: Let's just lie here and twitch.

But he kept his full sunburned lips sealed, maybe not wanting to speak first.

Who *is* he? she thought with possibly drug-induced clarity. She half wanted to shout for Jo to come back. Instead, she rested her hands on her belly, her baby motionless, her Ace bandage a slight weight on her right arm.

"How d'you feel?" JJ asked, awkwardly as any stranger.

"Bad." She breathed the dried smell of JJ's sweat.

"Allie. Look at me." She kept her eyes on her belly. From the hall, an elevator tone sounded. "All right, just talk to me. Tell me. What happened."

She shook her head, feeling JJ watch. Feeling, nevertheless, she was speaking to herself. "Bird asked for the car, y'know. Told me she knew I didn't want them here. Said what they really wanted was to keep moving. Then on the driveway, everything went—wild." She kept shaking her head. "I wound up—God, I can't believe this was me—hitting her. With Grandma's walker."

"Hitting Bird?" JJ leaned back in his seat, away from Allie. He began shaking his head too. Deciding that the side to her he hated had taken over?

"See," she went on with effort. "I accidentally got some of her blood in my mouth out there. And what if she's been infected too? That's what I was thinking, I think, when I swung that God-awful thing." She'd begun twisting her hands together though her voice stayed steady. "So hard I knocked Bird down—Could've really hurt her. But her blood—I tasted it—in my *mouth*—"

"She couldn't have it." JJ avoided Allie's eyes but he pressed his hands over her hands. "Bird and Kin never have sex together. I'm sure of that. . . ."

Allie's hands stiffened under his. "What about the spots on her shoulder?"

"No." JJ addressed their clasped hands. "No, no—those aren't lesions like what you're thinking. Those are from *sun*, she told me. She's been flying all over the world with no, you know, skin protection—"

Allie managed a nod, wanting to believe it, thinking that it did sound like something Bird would do. The Bird she now felt she knew, partway.

"She couldn't, I'm sure she couldn't." JJ squeezed Allie's hands tightly. He shifted his downcast eyes to her belly, maybe imagining their baby at risk. Improbable yet, Allie felt as she pressed her own hands together, possible. Anything, she thought with her new odd clarity. Anything can happen to anyone. She watched JJ shut his eyes, deep creases raying out around them. "Jesus," he muttered, then blinked. They released each other's hands, their awkwardly shared prayer complete. Allie faced JJ with what she supposed must still be calm induced by the pseudo-Xanax. Her hands hurt from his grip.

"I knew something must've happened on the driveway," he mumbled.

"How? Did you and Mom *hear* the whole thing, from the patio . . . ?"

"Not till you shouted." JJ shifted so he could dig into his pants pocket. "But when they were loading you into the ambulance, I picked up this."

His hand opened. Allie blinked at Bird's tooth, its nubby tip veined by dry blood. "Don't touch that—" she burst out. At last JJ's eyes met hers. Cold green.

"Al, for Chrissakes." He closed his fist around the tooth, jiggling it like a pill he was about to pop in his mouth. "You've gotta stop—" He cut himself short as he so often did, tossing the tooth onto her metal nightstand like a dice.

"Don't *you* lecture me," she told him, hating her own sharp voice. He sighed as if bracing himself for years of such comments. She blinked again at Bird's tooth, small as a child's. "You want," she made herself ask, "to keep it?"

"What? No." He sounded surprised. Allie raised her eyes, wondering if he was only saying what he thought she wanted. "Throw it away," he told her. Then he pointed to the ring of 8s on her right finger. "Guess you'd want me to throw that away, too." His fingertip touched the ring. She clenched her hand.

"No." Her nails dug into the heel of her hand, waking her. Alice remembered the jolt of the metal rod smacking Bird, her head bobbing as she fell. And Kin's head bouncing helplessly as Bird speeded him away. "No," Allie repeated in a loud tense voice. "I'm keeping this, keeping it *on*. I told Bird I'd keep it on so you'd see it every day. And I will." She shook her head, remembering as JJ stared Bird's intent blue-white stare. "I know that Kin could die sooner because of me. I feel like I owe them this or something. . . ."

JJ nodded, respectfully silent. Allie relaxed her fist. She sighed with exhaustion. "And I *can't* stop feeling so scared." She shut her eyes against JJ, trying to pretend again she was speaking to herself. "Not only of AIDS—I can't even think of that now, though you're probably right about Bird and I know *my* mouth wasn't bleeding. But also. I'm scared that we aren't, won't be. Good enough."

"To?" JJ prompted from behind her closed eyelids.

"Be parents," she found herself saying in a small voice. Disgusted with herself, with JJ. She blinked up at the blank oversized TV bolted to the wall. "When you think what we've done these past months, this past year. You lying to me—for years, really—and keeping Bird's letters from me and going to bed with the two of them today. I mean no matter why you did it or what exactly you did do—and how the Hell will I ever know?—you were in bed with them. . . ."

JJ's eyes fixed on the TV too, like they were watching the same show, intently. One thing about JJ. When he listened, he listened intently.

"Then me too. Me hiding Bird's letter and lying in my own ways and letting all my mean fears take over. And today. Sending Kin and Bird away—"

"We both did that," JJ cut in, a self-contemptuous edge to his voice.

"No," she told him sharply. Sick of being treated like a child. "You know and I know I did. Though Bird wanted to go, I believe that. She and Kin both. But even if they hadn't wanted to, I think I somehow would've made them. Though I knew it wasn't right. Knew it when I watched them today: Bird so careful with Kin, him so weak. But I felt I had to send them off. Felt it was—self-defense. Defense of me and the baby and—us." She pushed back her hair, roughly. "But I *didn't* have to hit Bird. God, I've never *hit* anyone, and so hard. It scares me. See, I've always been scared I'll turn out to be too—small. Inside." Allie sank deeper into her starched pillow. JJ turned from the TV, his eyes gray-green like its screen, only not blank. The opposite, always, of blank.

"God, JJ, don't you see? We have to get—bigger. Some way." Allie pressed her left hand again on her belly. "It—the baby'll—*force* us to, won't it?"

"Get bigger?" JJ asked, as if the phrase meant something different to him.

"Or—smaller," she added, sensing he was thinking there were parts of himself she'd want him to shut down. If such a thing were possible. Muffled steps sounded. "Listen, JJ. I *do* know that you—part of you. Wants them, still."

JJ didn't nod or shake his head. He looked at his rumpled sweat-stained clothes. He inhaled, maybe thinking—as she was thinking, looking at his clothes too—that he'd been to a foreign country today and back.

"Look," he began in a quiet tired voice. He kept his eyes low. "They, Kin and Bird, they're just—in me. You know. They—without them back in Boston breaking my, my ice or whatever you'd call it." He hesitated, then pushed on in a flatly unembarrassed tone. "I don't think I could've

loved you, loved anyone. I think that they—I can't expect you to understand this, but—saved me."

Allie made no move. Her voice came out carefully flattened too. "I
know. Reading Bird's last letters, seeing you with them. I know you love
them, JJ. But I want you to tell me something different. *Do* you want
them now, still?"

JJ raised his teeming green eyes. "You know everyone *wants*. Lots of
things. Some of which aren't even possible. . . ." She nodded, her neck
stiffening as she remembered JJ in their bedroom saying there were so
many different ways people could connect. "But I want. Right now." JJ
rested his hand on the white-covered mound of her belly. "I want this,
our life."

She swallowed, her throat dry. She looked at his hand, wanting to
believe him. Not wanting that want to show. "Know how I got her blood
in my mouth?"

"I thought—" JJ lifted his hand. "You two struggled somehow before
you hit Bird—?"

"No. I kissed her. On the mouth."

JJ blinked, gray in his eyes clouding the green. "You kissed her," he
repeated, as if this were a sentence he couldn't parse. "You kissed. Her?"

"I—part of me." She felt herself try a joking tone. "I got parts too,
y'know—wanted to. In the driveway and also back in Ko No's. She kissed
me then too. She's into women, too, y'know." A mechanical bell
sounded. Visiting Hours nearly over. "But only on the driveway did we
use our tongues."

JJ stared at her with his clouded green eyes the way she might've
stared at him at midnight. At least, she realized, that's how she hoped
he was staring: as if he wondered if he knew her. He swallowed, his
Adam's apple bobbing wildly.

"Shit." Allie pressed her hands over her ears. "I sound like her, JJ. *Try-*
ing to shock you." She lowered her melodramatically raised hands, determined not to play this like a soap scene. "I don't know. I'd been feeling so left out all day. And I did feel, just then—attracted to Bird.
Which's maybe—part of what made me hit her. My own shock at my
own—attraction." She sighed, exhuasted all over again. "I don't know
why I'm saying this, except that I'm trying to tell the truth. For a
change. I want to—no, I mean," She corrected. "I don't want to, but feel
like I have to. See things the way they are."

JJ nodded again. "Me too," was all he said, but clearly.

What did that mean to him? she wondered, narrowing her gaze. Did
it mean acknowledging desires for men? Or one lifelong desire for Kin

and Bird? Would she ever know what he wanted, her own husband? She glanced down at Bird's tooth on the nightstand. *Nothing,* she imagined JJ saying, *is your own.*

"I don't know," he mumbled as if she'd spoken her worries. "I told you I'd thought, wanted to think. What I'd felt eight years ago with them was part of another life. But today so much came rushing back like. It'd never—left me."

"And what *about* now?" Allie repeated levelly. "Now that they're—?"

"Gone. The three of us. Without Kin, that'll be gone." He gave his harsh-sounding sigh. His own eyes flickered to Bird's tooth, then away. "I. Don't know. I don't seem to have as much, you know. Control. As I thought I had over what I—want." He shook his head then added—because he knew she needed to hear it?—"But that doesn't mean I can't control what I. Do."

Allie fixed her eyes on JJ's throat. The reddened hickey showed, though faintly. "So you're telling me, actually wanting me to believe—" She drew a big breath, re-gathering her strength. "That what you decided to do with them today you *won't* decide to do with any other man or woman or man-and-woman you might in the future find yourself oh-so-uncontrollably '*wanting*'?"

He let her words echo around them. Then, cautiously, nodded.

"God." Allie released her breath. "God, JJ, I *do* want to believe that. 'S probably pathetic how much. But God, y'know, this tranquilizer's starting to wear off." She squinted, picturing him in bed between Kin and Bird. "When it wears all the way off, I think I'm gonna. Hate you. I don't know how long."

He nodded yet again, maybe wanting to say, *I will too.* An old joke between them, that phrase. His square-cut Adam's apple bobbed with another swallow.

"And I bet," Allie pushed on, raising her voice above the muffled surge of steps in the hall. "You'll hate me too. Part of you will. For my whole reaction to them. For sending them away." Again JJ didn't say yes and didn't say no. The hallway outside the rectangular window was going still, most visitors no doubt gone. "I *knew* that was wrong," Allie finished. Picturing Bird now, Bird struggling to ease Kin back into the car. "But I felt like, feel like. I had to do it."

"Me too." JJ met her stare fully with his clearer, less gray-green eyes. "I told you, that's exactly how I feel too. About what I did, today."

She didn't nod or shake her head. JJ went on slowly. "But look, if you do, I." He lowered his stare yet again to her belly. "Hope you don't hate me for good."

Allie looked at her own clasped hands. The twin gleams, dull and bright, of her two rings. One smooth, one twisted. "Might leave that to my mom and my sister," she muttered. But she stared up before a trace of JJ's half smile could form. She added tersely, "I do think part of me will. 'Hate' is not the word, but—"

He nodded. Bending close like they were teenagers hiding from teachers stalking the hall, he told her, "There ought to be some word in some language that means love and hate. Two opposite feelings. Both strong enough to tear you in half. Both alive—existing together—inside one person, at one time. . . ."

Allie nodded uneasily, annoyed that he was trying to talk to her this way so soon. To wax philosophical. "Didn't Bird write something like that in her letter from Mexico?" she asked, maintaining her cool tone. Sensing with resignation this wouldn't be the last time Kin and Bird would speak through him.

JJ looked down. "We need sleep," he murmured, standing up. Cutting himself short, as always. He straightened to his always startling height. His sunburned face showed its deeply shadowed bones. Allie reached up with her unsprained arm, not sure what she wanted. The Band-Aid from her HIV blood test strained the skin of her inner elbow. Foolish, she realized now, to have taken those tests today, before anything contracted today could show. We'll have to be tested again, Allie told herself. As JJ reached down, her eyes flickered to his own flesh-colored blood-test Band-Aid. He took her hand, squeezing it so hard her wedding ring dug into her finger bones. What he gave her was a slow firm handshake. Partners? she wondered as he released her hand. Still? The door rattled, opening.

"Go sleep," JJ told Allie from far above. His downcast eyes were blue now, always blue for the best or the worst moments. She shook her head, meaning as JJ seemed with his last brief nod to know: No. I want to lie here and twitch.

" 'Scuse me, Mrs. Wolfe?" A big-bosomed Hispanic nurse shouldered through the door, holding a tray. "Little late supper here for Mrs. Wolfe, and you know, sir, it's past eight—" The nurse bustled over to the bed, trailing steam.

JJ took the tray, setting it on the nightstand's edge as the nurse wheeled Allie's bed table into place. Then before Allie knew he'd stepped from her bedside, JJ was standing in the doorway. The nurse was lifting the tray. JJ glanced back at Allie and ducked as if under the weight of his hair. This doorway, like all doorways, too low for him. His shoulders tensed as he stepped away, his big shoulder blades standing out under his shirt like, Allie thought as she'd thought many times, aborted wings. The door wheezed and he was gone. It thumped, sealing the room like the recording booth at the Library for the Blind.

Trapped, Allie remembered JJ admitting he'd felt. Trapped in many ways. He better be, Grandma would add. After the nurse had arranged the tray and eased the bed table closer to Allie—Allie's belly brushed its underside—and after Allie had nodded at whatever the nurse had asked, the door thumped again.

Alice faced her food alone. Meaty TV-dinner steam made her eyes but not her mouth water. Still sitting propped by her pillows, she shut her eyes. Go sleep, JJ'd said. And she remembered how back in New Haven he'd reported the talk they'd shared in her sleep: him telling her to *Go sleep*, her answering *I will* and then her adding in a wholly different voice: *I will too.*

She blinked now. It might've been the pseudo-Xanax, but something in that memory made sense. Eat for two, the brisk Hispanic nurse had said. Eat for at least two, Allie thought. She peeled back the plate's crinkly foil. A gray brown square of meat, an ice-cream-scoop mound of mashed potatoes.

A gurney clanked. Someone groaned. Even this expensive single room Mom had insisted on wasn't soundproof. It rose through the wall: a plaintive old-man groan. Allie flipped on the TV remote control. A picture without sound. As air bags bloomed into the faces of dummy drivers, their car hitting a brick wall, she listened to the hidden man. She made herself picture the Kin man in JJ's arms, his wasted body and pasty face, his wide slack mouth open wider in pain. In pleasure. The groan faded, a nurse's firm soft-toned voice overriding it. Allie tried to picture Kin as she'd seen him back in Ko No's: his striking high-cheek-boned face, the bright black slashes of his eyes. She pressed the remote's channel dial, picturing too a young long-haired JJ and young long-haired Bird; picturing young JJ and Kin embracing. JJ's mouth opening with moans she knew so well. She zapped past Princess Di and *Wheel of Fortune* and a teenage boy holding a gun to his own head and the Earth seen from outer space.

The planet hung frozen before vanishing, sucked into a star that vanished too. TV off. Allie turned to the window. Even through drawn drapes, it was clear the sky was black. With her right thumb tip, she touched the ring of 8s she felt so strangely determined to keep on. She blinked, still seeing the planet Earth. Bird and Kin had flown around the world and now were driving still farther. Allie pressed the sharp-edged 8s. Bird wouldn't let some spineless white girl's whack on her head stop her motion. They were on the run, those two. Allie uncurled her hand, deciding wearily that she herself had been on the run.

Scared all year of hearing what, in a way, she had just heard JJ say. That his attraction to them, his love for them was still alive. Allie stared at the beige drapes as if pictures were flashing there, switching second-by-second. So many lives being lived at once, so many lives one person could live. So many ways people could fit with each other, live with each other, live off each other.

Her empty stomach gave a queasy stir. Her baby; no doubt hungry now. Gray meat, jewel-bright Jell-O. Have to, she thought, lifting her spoon. Eat.

She cut a curved, quivering slice. Holding the Jell-O on her tongue, she pictured Kin in the mirror at Ko No's holding an oyster in his mouth.

Allie swallowed, picturing JJ's cock in the Kin man's mouth. JJ's head thrown back, his neck sharply arching with his moan. Jell-O slid down her throat like Mom's grape jelly, a bitter motion-sickness pill crushed on top. There, Allie thought, thumbing open her milk carton. She'd taken the first bite. She sipped from the carton, the milk sweet and cool. Then she cut a square of meat. Its smell made her want to gag, reminding her of the rotted-meat smell of Kin's flesh. She forced her lips open. The meat's anemically bloody juices mixed with her saliva. Her jaw chewed. See? she told herself, swallowing.

Any natural act seemed disgusting if you thought about it. She force-fed herself another slice. Eating, drinking, anything that uses your mouth, your body. She unwrapped her straw with her clumsy left hand. She sucked her milk. Flipping the remote control back on, she found news to chew by. A newscaster's voice boomed in her empty room. A plane crash in Africa had killed black Congressman Micky Leland as the long-time Democrat was flying home from a risky mission of mercy. Congressmen extolled Leland's courage, his selflessness. Allie muted the sound. Even a Republican congressman seemed to ask with his squinty eyes: why him? Why is he dead and I'm here?

She lifted her milk again. Thank dumb luck, Dad always said as his supper blessing. Always reminding his girls that good luck didn't mean they themselves were good. Not, Allie thought now, that she'd really believed it. She hadn't needed to believe it until her luck, this past year, began to change.

Whiteness filled her straw. *She was as good as she was lucky*. As Allie swallowed, she saw herself shoving Carter, shoving Bird, swinging Grandma's walker. As her fork clanked, she heard the *crack* against

Bird's flesh-and-bone head. Alice sliced more meat, half the patty gone. Beneath, her plate gleamed.

I can see myself! She remembered a housewife exclaiming in an old dishwashing liquid commercial. Allie squinted at her distorted reflection, her features lit by the still-flickering TV. Two eyes and one mouth munged together into a liquid blob, a fleshy face without bones. A murderess's blurred face, led past cameras. I could have killed Bird, she told herself. Any injury to the head, she'd read somewhere, was potentially fatal. Chewing, she wondered with a calm she was beginning to think might not be drug induced if this was simply the next stage in growing up. After you stopped wanting to know *what next*, but found you had to know anyway; after you stopped wanting to see the truth about yourself but started seeing it anyway; after all that, it seemed only natural you'd want to start over again. A whole new life, new generation.

Milk re-whitened her straw. Swallowing, Allie looked at the TV-lit curve of her belly, cut short by her tray, half hidden. A boy or a girl? Only in the last few weeks had she really begun wondering. Before—she almost smiled, her mouth stiff—she'd pictured the fetus floating in a serenely sexless state.

Mom's doctor had looked bemused when Alice had described what JJ'd once told her: how he'd read in Freud that fetuses have no sex at first. Then one emerges and the other sex characteristics fall back, though traces remain. No, Mom's doctor had told Allie. Freud was wrong. So when *does* a baby have its gender? Allie asked. Always, the doctor had answered. It just takes awhile to show.

She stabbed a last bite of meat. As she sipped more milk, she remembered looking down at Bird, feeling that she'd somehow been eating her, that Bird was so thin because she herself was so heavy. Her straw made its vacuum sputter.

Of course, Allie found herself thinking now, Bird must have grown so thin in her months of caring for Kin. How had Bird been able to stand that, alone? To stand, as Grandma Hart had said all nurses must, anything. Across the wall, the old man's groan rose again, inconsolable.

Maybe, though, Bird wouldn't be able to stand Kin killing himself. Allie lifted her empty milk. *Would* he kill himself? She set the carton on her plate, denting the untouched mound of mashed potatoes. Yes, she thought with calm that definitely wasn't coming from a drug. Would Bird? As the groan rose, Alice gripped her bedrails the way she'd gripped the walker. *Did* she want Bird dead?

No, Allie told herself, gripping so hard her bandaged elbow ached.

No: she admired Bird, now. Felt Bird deserved a better life. But she wanted Bird gone from JJ's life. Gone for good, if truth be told. And she was trying to tell the truth, if only to herself. So, yes: she wanted Bird dead, in a way. Not, Allie told herself in exasperation, that anyone could be dead only "in a way." So: yes, she wanted Bird dead. Hated wanting it, but wanted it. Which meant she wanted JJ too, still. Allie released the rails. What, she thought, an ugly measure of love.

As the groan died down, she studied her milk carton set on the dried-up half-eaten meat. *Did* JJ want her the most now? After this last year, after seeing the side to her he hated? Or was it more, now: he wanted to want her the most? Because it was easier, because of the baby. Or: maybe he loved her enough to want to change his other desires? No; not, he'd said, change his desires, but his actions. Look what he did in the end, Allie reminded herself. Letting Bird and Kin go; staying with her. But would he have done that if she weren't going to have a baby? If Kin weren't going to die? The groan rose yet again, as if the old man was tired of groaning but couldn't stop.

A gurney clanked past Allie's door window, white figures rushing. She cupped her hand back over her baby; her knuckles grazed the underside of the bed table. She pressed hard, remembering JJ's hand on her belly minutes before. And she watched the shut door, feeling temporarily safe in this room.

"Stat one, Room 312," an intercom voice announced. Live voices called out farther down the hall. It hadn't been the old man they'd run for, this time.

Allie blinked at the door as if it had spoken. Her baby felt so large under her hand it was impossible to imagine it coming out. But it would have to. One way or another. Her left hand, already used to doing all the work, pushed back the wheeled table. On the exposed blanket, a hair curled. Allie fingered its distinctively coarse texture. JJ's. She let the hair drop, picturing JJ's nine-year-old hair coiled in its braid inside one of their taped boxes in her parents' garage.

She would unpack it next fall, she felt sure. Yes: she saw herself kneeling before a torn U-Haul box on the floor of the new apartment where they would live. Not in the old way, in some new way. But together, she told herself. Right?

She glanced at her nightstand. A paper napkin from her tray was lying on it, askew. Allie lifted the napkin, expecting to find Bird's tooth still there. But it wasn't. Allie scanned the floor around the bed, clean and empty. She sighed so hard the napkin she held fluttered. Maybe the nurse had swept the tooth away as trash. Or maybe JJ, in the bustle before he left, had taken the tooth, pocketed it. Keeping it—the way he'd said he'd liked keeping Kin and Bird—to himself.

Allie crumpled the napkin, sensing that even if JJ hadn't taken Bird's tooth, he'd wanted to. A part of him. Sighing again, feeling resigned all over again, she settled back on her pillow. And she remembered opening her mouth in that warm dizzy moment when everything between Bird and herself had felt so charged. Bird, the tough girl in her jacket; Bird, the nurse who could stand anything. One moment, humming with sun. A part of her had loved Bird, then. I got parts too, Alice told herself as she'd told JJ, half joking. Here now, alone, the words felt different. I got parts too.

Lightly, Allie dropped the crumpled napkin into the hospital trash basket that held nothing but a plastic bag. She breathed the chilled disinfected hospital air, picturing the tubes that weighed down her father. Maybe Kin had been right to refuse a hospital. Go in like him or Dad and you never come out.

Twisting around, she flipped off the harsh light. It died with a meek buzz. Alice sat still, feeling as she often did enclosed by the sides of her bed. A new bed, tonight. But all beds, she told herself slowly—as if she were JJ's computer, learning the world—have four sides. All marriage beds. Two for each body. She let black sooth her eyeballs. Groggily glad her baby too was afloat in darkness.

In her room's air-conditioned dark, Allie fiddled with her hospital ID bracelet. She thought of buzzing a nurse for paper. But her head sank into her starchy pillow. No address, and what would she say to Bird? That—yes—she had wanted the kiss. That she knew Bird might have accidentally or purposefully killed her with a taste of blood. That she knew this was wildly improbable, yet—wildly, in its own way—possible. Her eyes drifted halfway shut. The old man's groan stayed gone. Allie's heart stayed steady. Beating for at least two. Maybe she wanted to say that she knew even if Bird died too, Bird and Kin wouldn't be gone. Not in JJ. And—this was the main thing, she believed, her eyes fluttering open—she wanted to say that she would keep the damn ring on.

Yes, Allie told Bird without moving her lips, the way she always talked to her baby. Sending her signal, now, into the desert night sky outside. *You don't believe I will but I will. So JJ will see it every day.* She shut her eyes, her thumb tip pressing the ring of 8s. Sleepily sure that Bird would pick up the message, Alice slowed its last words, her last conscious words. *And I will too.*

Last

Hello Alice.

We want to send this last one straight to you. Or straight as we can make it. Meaning I'll mail it east from here, addressed to you Care of JJ Wolfe at the Big Y University. One thing we know is, you're still—maybe always—in JJ's care. Kin and I want our good-bye to JJ to remain what happened between us that last time, in Mexico. Actions speak loudest. But we want to send word to someone of what we are about to do. And, as we used to say, Alice: it had to be you.

(We realize that means both of you. And we intend that, for a change, JJ will decide whether to keep a letter for you from you or—like I bet he will, after the baby is born—let you see it, see us. Not that you want to.)

But here we are. We write to you from a motel bed on a scrub-brush highway somewhere near (no joke) Truth or Consequences, New Mexico. Kin lies at my side, curled up on my spread-out leather jacket. We've turned off the room's air-conditioning and opened its window. Under his sweat, Kin smells of what his Juarez doctor called *decaimiento*.

I'm used to it, his rotted-oyster smell. Rising as if ripening. Kin says he can't smell it anymore, but he feels it. His body beginning to decay from inside. Under our room's light, I sit close to Kin in my stained white linen shirt and pants, my knees up. I grip my pen so it won't lurch off the page. I'm bearing down hard on the Hemlock Society book. As our room darkens, Kin is watching my pen move. I'm stopping to read him lines as I go along. He wants me to write what I want. But he wants my letter to be from both of us.

Understand this, first. Our minds and bodies feel clear. All afternoon, I beat on Kin's back while he coughed up phlegm, clearing his lungs. On the nightstand, a bottle of wine sits, still full, and beside it a jade and ivory jar that belonged to Kin's mother. Full too, of pills. Enough for what the Hemlock Society calls Self-Deliverance. But first, slowly, the way we've learned to do so much this past year, we are composing this last letter to—a big first—you, Alice.

(Last? you may be wondering, maybe trying to stop a rise in your heart.)

See, we know what you want us to do. Disappear. No details, please. I understand. You don't want to read what I didn't want to read. Those pages Kin had marked in this Hemlock Society book JJ bought for him. Weeks ago now, how many I'm not sure. I know we are in New Mexico; I think we are still in August.

We've traveled slowly too, stopping often, sleeping in the car. Kin barely left the car. Up from Phoenix along the Verde River to—like the *turistas* we no longer fear resembling—the Grand Canyon. Too grand to be seen whole from any one point. Down the Painted Desert along the Little Colorado River then, following the Zuni River, into New Mexico. Land of Enchantment, the signs say.

The black Zephyr has suited us. Windows open, radio on full blast, engine rumbling away. A miracle on wheels. Desert moonscape has suited us too: dry and multiply brown and, for all the heat, cool. The perfect setting, Kin once mumbled, for a born-again Buddhist. Always, Kin half-mocks the Buddhist book he has me read out loud. Surrounded by desert sky, he meditates on Emptiness, on the Not-Self. On the 8-Fold—yes, 8-Fold—path to Clear Pure Nature of Mind.

An hour or so left to us now before dark. Down the Continental Divide we've wound our way, my Estella money beginning to run dry as we rolled through Magdalena and San Marcial to stop for a week in (how could we resist?) Truth or Consequences. This morning, outside Truth or Consequences, I pulled over at a Swap Meet. I woke Kin so he could see the hand-painted sign. USED CLOTHES, FURNITURE, LAWN MOWERS, JESUS IS RISEN. The folding table displayed Bowling Balls for five dollars each and unworn baby clothes for You Name It. I tried on worn brown cowboy boots. Lying in the back seat, Kin motioned me over to the Zephyr. The boots made me stride. I posed for Kin: my hands on my hips and my square boot heels planted in sandy grit. My hot hair felt shiny white. Kin paid for my boots with his best remaining clothes. He told me I'd need boots for my future—he keeps saying I've got it if I want it—as a born-again lesbian. And besides, he added through a fit of dusty coughs: he wanted to spend the rest of today in something soft. Something old. The loose white shirt and pants he wears now. And, soft too, his mom's black silk scarf, which rests on the side of our motel bathtub beside the emptied ice bag.

With the last of my Estella money, see, we can afford tonight what Kin calls a halfway decent room. Yellow drapes opened by a plastic wand; clean sheets and, most important, clean bathroom. Perfect, Kin managed to say, leaning his weight on my arm. He's always told me that when he grew too weak to keep moving, he'd stop. And so. This afternoon, after we arrived, Kin had me dress him in his year-old wedding outfit. Like, he told me hoarsely, a good wife. You or me? I wanted to ask back. But I only smiled. Already my throat was tightening to contain my pulse. I only nodded when he made me write, for this motel's morning maid, a note warning her not to open the bathroom. My wrist aches now along with my fingers but I keep my pen clenched. Keep my eyes on the page and not on Kin's jar of pills. Seconal, *de Mexico*.

En Mexico, see, in the Juarez hospital, Kin bought two bottles with a secret stash of Pan Am money. He wants to do this—a favorite word of yours—right. To that end, along with the wine, I bought at a Convenience Mart today the brand of ice chips I used to buy in Mexico. Not for the chips themselves—which I've dumped in our bathtub to melt— but for what they came packed in. The 2-foot-long plastic bag, airtight. Blue letters dripping ink icicles. *Clear Pure Ice Chips.*

And me? You can't help but wonder. Will I, like I told you, follow Kin? When I said that back in your bedroom, I saw the hopeful flash in your dark giveaway eyes. Though you made yourself tell me: No, don't.

Thing is, Alice: just then, just after seeing JJ in Mexico, I felt more ready than ever to follow Kin. I mean that in the best of ways. In Mexico, see, I felt we said and did what we needed to, with Jimmy Joe. Are you still wearing his—our—ring of 8s? You want to throw our ring away, but I sense you haven't. And I sense you weren't trying to kill me when you hit me with that crutch, not hard enough to crack one bone. I wasn't trying to kill you—only after did I realize that may be what you thought—when we kissed. I am—Kin made me take an HIV test at the health clinic in Truth or Consequences—negative.

Patiently now, still curled beside me, Kin breathes through his mouth the way he does lately even when he's not sleeping. White sores make his mouth hard to shut. His long dried-out hair has been brushed smooth by me. It's thinning like the fine black hair of his mom or the finer black hair of balding old Asian ladies I used to hang above on Boston subway cars. Our room is more than half dark. Kin is coughing on and off, watching me write you. Write and write, scared to stop. Speaking for two, Kin's throat too raw lately. Not that I can talk at all just now, not even to read Kin more lines from what I'm writing. But he muttered to me to keep going, to finish our letter. My pulse throbbed in my throat and I wanted to answer—selfishly—that I don't want to finish.

No, I kept telling Kin in the Zephyr when he first told me about his secret Seconal. No and no. But I need to stop saying that to him, now.

That word. No, I tried to tell Stepdad #2 but it wasn't a word, just a sound in my throat and he said No right back, only he spoke in actions. No, you won't move; No, you won't tell anyone what I did. And I didn't, till Kin, tell. No, Jimmy Joe told Kin and me after we three got too close, did too much of what no one wanted us to do. No, he was leaving for good, he claimed. And No, JJ told us years later at your house, where we wanted him to let us stay. No, you said first; No, JJ seconded not in words but in action, lack of action. Letting us go.

I set down my pen just now to shake out my hand. Then I picked it up again fast, before Kin could notice. In fifteen minutes or so, when stingy small American stars begin to dot the sky, Kin wants me to run a lukewarm bath, to prop him up while he swallows his Seconal. As quickly as possible, the Hemlock Society advises. So many pills swallowed so fast may hurt his sore throat and mouth. But wine will help. I will help. In the bathroom, Kin wants me to lower him into the water, then stand back. Make sure he can do the rest, himself.

The plastic bag over his head, the scarf around his throat. The Hemlock Society points out that there's no need to resort to giant rubber bands. The tie you use can be soft, as long as it's tight. When the scarf is in place, I'll bend over the tub. I'll check the knot. Then, through the plastic—at the last possible moment; for the first time ever, on the lips—I'll kiss him.

¿Comprendés? ¿Entiendes? Understand?

No, Nao, No.

See? We can say that too. We don't feel, like you might imagine, weak. Kin's body, yes. But bodies are not our all. So the Buddhist book tells us. One thing I do know. Something more than our bodies—bodies only entangle for hours—got mixed up with something more than your husband's body, for good. ("Soul Love" was one of our songs; ask JJ if he doesn't still feel its beat.) Like a circle of 8s soldered from metal. Inches long, yet it never ends.

Right? Sometimes all that feels real; sometimes it feels like something I only want to be real. Either way, says Kin, he knows what he wants to do. Already, his breaths sound slow inside his open mouth. His eyes are open too. He's here beside me but I feel he's already somewhere else. Alone. Waiting only for me to finish what I want to tell you, from both of us.

Don't, you'd want to tell us. Let Kin die of what would be called natural causes. A suicide sends a message you don't want to receive. You don't want to think that if you'd opened your home to us, you might've saved his life. (Which of course only means—ever—prolonged it, in his case none too long.) But still.

I know what you want. For some bad and some good reasons, you want Kin to die tied down by tubes. I plan to leave this letter unsigned, but right now I'll call myself B. Here's what else I know: A. wants B. dead too so A. can stop thinking about B., stop feeling B. out there. Somewhere.

Kin is coughing harshly, wetly, telling me without words that he's ready. And—the one thing he always is; I want JJ to know this—curious. Like, he told me when we pulled into this motel, It'll be a whole new kind of trip.

My bent neck aches now with my wrist but I'll keep this pen moving for one page more, every tremor of mine knotted up inside my ribs and what do you think, Alice? Am I strong enough, after all our travels, to lift him then ease him down? A few unmelted ice chips afloat. Kin's body, all bodies, weightless in water. The plastic bag, like the water, shining in the light. Clear, pure.

I won't see beyond that point. Kin wants me to leave him in the tub, still breathing under his tightly fastened bag. He wants me to shut off the light, shut the bathroom door. Change into my lean jeans and leather jacket and cowboy boots. Kin says he wants to picture me changing.

As I change, he'll have a chance to call out. If by the time I've changed, he hasn't called out—and he's sure he won't—I will step into the cool New Mexican night. Step hard on my boot heels so grit crunches good and loud. Stride across the motel parking lot under desert sky almost as high as sky in Brazil. Climb inside the Zephyr and slam the driver's door, good and hard. And, Kin told me right before I began this letter. Just go.

I will, I managed to say like a real wife. I am his wife. And I'll do what he wants me to do. What I want to do, now. What, deep down, you don't want me to do, Alice. Live, that is. Living is an action. My answer to your unspoken wishes.

See. With each action we're about to take, Alice, we'll be saying, in our different ways, No. I'll say it when I fold this letter into the pocket of the jacket that Kin is lying on and that I'll soon be wearing; when I walk to the bathroom and draw Kin's tub of water. Kin will say it when he swallows his Seconal, two by two; when he reaches up with arms as bone thin as any girl's, letting me take hold of him, my arms thin too but strong as any boy's. We'll say it together as I ease Kin up from the leather jacket on our bed, as I lower Kin into his soaplessly pure bathwater. As we kiss through clear crackling plastic. See us? Hear us?

No.

ELIZABETH SEARLE is the author of *My Body to You,* a story collection that won the 1992 Iowa Short Fiction Prize. Over twenty of her stories have been published, both in periodicals and in anthologies. She graduated from Oberlin College and received an M.A. from Brown University. A former Special Education teacher, she now teaches in the graduate writing program at Emerson College.

A Four-Sided Bed was set in ITC Legacy, designed by Ron Arnholm. Legacy reinterprets Renaissance typographic masterpieces for digital composition. The roman is based on type cut in Venice by Nicolas Jenson (1469). The model for the italic was cut in Paris by Claude Garamond (1539).

A Four-Sided Bed was designed by Will Powers, set in type by Stanton Publication Services, Inc., and manufactured by Edwards Brothers, Ann Arbor, MI, on acid-free paper.